WHAT LIES BEYOND THE VEIL

OF FLESH & BONE BOOK ONE

HARPER L. WOODS

ADELAIDE FORREST

Cover Design by Adelaide Forrest

Editing by Light Hand Editing

Chapter Headings & Scene Break Art by Etheric Designs

Map by Abigail M Hair

Created with Vellum

For the ones who find freedom in the dark.

ABOUT WHAT LIES BEYOND THE VEIL

Once, we'd worshipped them as Gods.

For nearly 400 years, the Veil has protected us from the Fae of Alfheimr. In their absence, our lives have shifted from decadence and sin to survival and virtue under the guidance of the New Gods. I've spent my entire life tending to the gardens next to the boundary between our worlds, drawn to the shimmering magic like a moth to the flame.

Then, we died on their swords.

All of that changes the day the Veil shatters, unleashing the fae upon our world once again. The magic of faerie marks those of us they mean to take, but the Mist Guard protecting Nothrek will kill us all before they let the fae have us. There's no choice but to flee everything I've ever known, not if I want to live to see my twenty-first birthday as a free woman.

Now, they'll claim what's theirs.

But before they capture me, Caelum saves me from the Wild Hunt. Fae-marked and on the run, he is able to fight back in ways I only dream of. From tentative alliance to all-consuming passion, our bond strengthens as the fae close in and evil lurks ever nearer. With my life on the line, he is everything I shouldn't dare to want and a distraction I can't afford. I can't seem to stay away, not even with something greater on the line.

My heart.

TRIGGER/CONTENT WARNINGS

What Lies Beyond the Veil is set in a medieval style world where human women are subservient to their male counterparts. The world is a dark, dangerous place for women, particularly those who do not conform to societal standards and the purity culture that determines how they live. As such, some elements may be triggering to certain readers.

- Religious purity culture
- Verbal and physical abuse (NOT the male lead)
- References to grooming behavior & assault of a minor by an authority figure (NOT the male lead)
- Ritualistic Sacrifice
- Suicidal thoughts & ideation
- Graphic violence
- Graphic sexual content

NOTHREK
THE MISTY ISLANDS
MISTFELL
ISLE OF RUIN
CALFALL
DARK ISLE
BLACKWATER
ISLE OF DESPAIR
INEBURN CITY
DESERT ISLE
MOUNTAINS OF ROCHPAR

TARTARUS
SHADOW COURT
WINTER COURT
CATANCIA
NSEELIE COURT
AUTUMN COURT
SUMMER COURT
VALLANIA
SEELIE COURT
SPRING COURT
RIODURA
ALFHEIMR
HE VEIL

GLOSSARY OF TERMS

Alfheimr: The Fae realm.

Calfalls: The Ruined City that was once a tribute to the God of the Dead before he destroyed it in the war between the Fae and humans.

High Priest/Priestess: The top Priest and Priestess who profess to commune with The Father and The Mother and pass along their messages.

Ineburn City: The capitol of the human realm, a gleaming city of gold.

Mistfell: The village at the edge of the Veil, where it is closest to Alfheimr. Serves as the access point between realms when the Veil does not block passage.

Mist Guard: A separate army with the sole purpose of protecting the Veil from harm and fighting the Fae should it ever fall.

New Gods: The Father and The Mother. Worshiped by humans after they discovered the truth that the Old Gods were truly Fae. The Father and The Mother make the choice of whether a soul goes to Valhalla, Folkvangr, or Helheim after the true death at the end of the thirteen-life cycle.

Nothrek: The human realm.

Old Gods: The Old Gods are the most powerful of the Fae race known as the Sidhe. Most commonly, these are the offspring of the Primordials.

Priest/Priestess: The men and women who lead the Temple in service of the New Gods and their wishes (The Father and The Mother).

Primordials: The first beings in all of creation. They do not have a human form by nature, though they can choose to take one for various reasons) and are simply the personification of what they represent.

Resistance, The: A secret society living in the tunnels of the Hollow Mountains (as well as elsewhere in Nothrek) that resist the rules of the Kingdom and live their lives as they please. They also resist the Fae and offer protection to the Fae Marked and other refugees from fleeing the Royal or Mist Guard.

Royal Guard: The army that works on behalf of the King of Nothrek, ensuring that the Kingdom remains peaceful and compliant with his wishes.

Sidhe: The human-like Fae who are *not* of the first generations and are less powerful than the Old Gods. Their magic exists, but is far more limited than their older counterparts.

Veil: The magical boundary that separates the human realm of Nothrek from the Fae realm of Alfheimr.

Viniculum: The physical symbol of the Fae Marked. Swirling ink in the color of the Fae's home court extending from the hand to the shoulder/chest.

Wild Hunt: The group of ghost-like Fae from the Shadow Court that are tasked with tracking down the Fae Marked to return them to their mates in Alfheimr, as well as hunting any who may be deemed enemies to the Fae.

Witches: Immortal beings with powers relating to the elements and celestial bodies; i.e. the Shadow Witches, Lunar Witches, Natural Witches, Water Witches, etc.

HIERARCHY OF THE GODS & FAE

PRIMORDIALS

Khaos: The Primordial of the Void that existed before all creation.
Ilta: The Primordial of the Night
Edrus: The Primordial of Darkness
Zain: Primordial of the Sky
Diell: Primordial of the Day
Ubel: Primordial responsible for the prison of Tartarus
Bryn: Primordial of Nature
Oshun: Primordial of the Sea
Gerwyn: Primordial of Love
Aerwyna: Primordial of the Sea Creatures
Tempest: Primordial of Storms
Peri: Primordial of the Mountains
Sauda: Primordial of Poisons
Anke: Primordial of Compulsion
Marat: Primordial of Light
Eylam: Primordial of Time
The Fates: Primordial of Destiny
Ahimoth: Primordial of Impending Doom

Old Gods of Note:

Aderyn: Goddess of the Harvest & Queen of the Autumn Court.
Alastor: King of the Winter Court and husband to Twyla before his death.
Caldris: God of the Dead.
Jonab: God of Changing Seasons. Killed during the First Fae War.
Kahlo: God of Beasts & King of the Autumn Court.
Mab: Queen of the Shadow Court. Known mainly as the Queen of Air & Darkness. Sister to Rheaghan (King of the Summer Court).
Rheaghan: God of the Sun & King of the Summer Court. Rightful King of the Seelie.
Sephtis: God of the Underworld & King of the Shadow Court.
Shena: Goddess of Plant Life & Queen of the Spring Court.
Tiam: God of Youth & King of the Spring Court.
Twyla: Goddess of the Moon & Queen of the Winter Court. Rightful Queen of the Unseelie.

The Wild Hunt

Sidhe

1

The icy wind of the North whipped through the gardens at the edge of the boundary, blowing toward the shimmering Veil marking where the world ended. Curving and rippling in the breeze, the thin, white barrier extended as far as the eye could see, until it faded into the sparkling sun of autumn.

Blood slid over my skin as I brushed a stray hair away from my face with frozen, aching fingers, and tried to ignore the slick, viscous feeling where it coated the skin at my temple. My hand trembled as I reached back into the twilight berry bush once more, grasping the round, periwinkle berry and carefully maneuvering it through the thorny branches to place it in the basket that hung from my other forearm. Shifting my body to relieve my aching back from the same hunched-over position, day in and day out for weeks, I looked through the branches for the distinctive coloring of the berries that were large enough for a single one to fill my palm.

"Faster, Barlowe," one of the members of the Royal Guard snapped at me, making his rounds as he supervised the harvest. One could never be too careful with the food that grew in the King's Gardens, which Lord Byron would send to the capitol, Ineburn City, to feed the Court through the harsh winter season. Meanwhile, those of us who remained in Mistfell year-round were left to suffer and starve, with only our meager personal gardens to sustain us.

I jolted, expecting the crack of his whip to follow as I shoved my hand into the bush with a wince. The thorns caught the edges of my palm, tearing the skin on the pads of my fingers until the moment when I finally wrapped them around the soft flesh of the berry.

I pulled it back, depositing it gently into the basket and grimacing at the way the ruby of my blood stained the light purple fruit. Lord Byron would make me wash them myself before he sat me on his lap and fed them to me, as if I should be thankful for the gift of his attention and the food that was otherwise forbidden to me.

The thin white scars that covered my hand shone like the web of the arachne when it caught the sunlight, too pale against my skin that was bronzed from working under the sun year after year. I had spent far too many harvests tending to the twilight berries when I displeased Lord Byron. Too many summers harvesting the crops that were considered a delicacy because of the pain the plant wrought on those who sought to pluck them. The last day of the year-end harvest was always the most difficult, and yet it was also the most important to secure the prosperity of the Court, and it drew us to the edge of the Veil like moths to the flame.

Driven there by the Royal Guard, which supervised the garden and worked in tandem with the league of elite Mist Guard who guarded the Veil, people like my brother and I had no other choice. We worked mostly in silence for the long, arduous hours every day, not daring to risk the wrath of the Royal Guard who wanted to return to court before the first frost.

No one could blame them for their urgency to escape the village of Mistfell; to get away from the magical boundary that separated us from *them*.

The Fae of Alfheimr.

Everyone who had any sense hated being so close to the Veil and what it represented. Crafted from the magic of the ancient witches who'd made the ultimate sacrifice to protect us from the nightmares beyond, it was like the thinnest of fabrics blowing in the wind, shimmering with the light of a thousand stars trapped within it. Somehow transparent, and yet not, the mist of the waters beyond provided us with the illusion of being alone in this world.

Even when we were very much not. Even when we'd never been alone.

Despite our fear of the Veil and the Fae beyond it, there was a part of the land of Faerie that drew us back here, the magic of the Primordial of Nature stretching through the soil itself. It compelled some of us to live in this hellhole of a village, where it snowed for over half the year and winter plunged the world into a darkness that seemed never-ending to those who craved the sunlight.

The gardens of Mistfell closest to the Veil yielded the lushest, most bountiful crops every year, with berries as big as my palm and vegetables massive enough to feed an entire family. This was the reason we braved the proximity to the Veil and the cursed magic of Faerie.

It was the richest soil in the land. The life of Alfheimr itself coursed through the earth beneath the Veil and bled into ours in such a way that the crops of the human realm could never compare. The Primordial of Nature was the one being from Alfheimr that we were thankful for, because she had taken soil and water and made the first humans, breathing life into the resulting clay form. She'd been our champion against the Fae, but even she was rumored to have treated us as errant pets, in the end.

The Veil shuddered and grumbled, thunder and lightning streaking through it, as so often happened with no explanation, as if the magic itself was made from storms. Yet it was not made of the sky, but of pure, unpredictable, wild magic. The shards of light that illuminated from within were quite possibly the most beautiful things I'd ever seen, causing the barrier to glimmer like spun moonlight.

The people who were forced to work in the King's Garden were the poorest of Mistfell and the neighboring villages; the ones who were the most expendable to Lord Byron. He needed our labor to supply the King with his favorite crops for winter, but that didn't mean he couldn't play favorites in the jobs he assigned to each of us.

This was how my brother and I had been assigned to harvest the twilight berries at the rear of the gardens. The bushes were furthest from the Veil and the magic anchored there, as well as closer to Mistfell Manor, for the Lord of the village to watch over me from the balcony of his library when he so desired. We were among the poorest families, people who should have been working against the Veil, suffering from the pervasive magic that tried to reach across the barrier. Our mother should have been at our sides, doing the backbreaking labor that she was unable to accomplish. No matter that she was disabled after her difficult pregnancy and delivery with me, and that the work itself would likely kill her.

Duty was duty, even in death.

Instead, she worked inside the manor, helping to preserve the produce that wouldn't be used before it could expire. But that kindness came at a price, and I swallowed when I thought of paying it later that night, when Lord Byron's soft, manicured hands would feed me twilight berries and other delicacies as the hard length of him pressed against me.

He couldn't take from me, not with our laws and the Gods' demand for purity until marriage. Not without condemning us both to eternal suffering.

But that didn't mean he couldn't touch. It didn't mean he couldn't hurt.

As I fought the shudder in my limbs at the thought, the Mist Guard moved on, tormenting another harvester as he finally turned his attention away from me. I heaved a sigh of relief, drawing a small measure of comfort in the fact that I hadn't been whipped for moving too slowly. On the last day of the harvest, all of us were bone-tired and exhausted, ready to drop and sleep for a week. The end of the day couldn't come soon enough.

"Brann," I hissed at my brother under my breath as he shoved two of the twilight berries into his pocket. He was lucky they hadn't torn yet with all the times he'd stolen the fruits from the King's Garden, risking his hand for a few bites of the luxury he would have never tasted otherwise. "They'll catch you one of these days."

"Relax, baby sister," he said with a hushed laugh, seeming entirely unconcerned about the watchful eyes of the Mist Guard as they walked through the paths in the garden. "No one will notice two missing berries in the rush to complete the harvest."

"And yet that will not stop them from taking your hand if they catch you stealing," I snapped, irritated with his recklessness. He judged me for my propensity for going on midnight walks in the woods, yet he risked everything for a few bites of fruit. Not only would he lose his hand, but he would lose all the favor I'd curried for him over the years with Lord Byron. Favor that had come at a great expense to me personally.

Horrifyingly enough, no matter what the price might be, or how unimaginable it seemed in the nights when my body slicked with sweat and I couldn't sleep, for fear of what memories would haunt my dreams, working at the edge of the Veil was a far more terrifying prospect. I'd heard rumors of the plants that grew just before the shimmering curtain itself—that they were nearly as likely to eat you as you were them. If you survived those, there was the magic-induced sickness that stole the youth from a person's flesh and reduced them to little more than skin-covered bones.

"Fine. Then I guess I won't need to share with you later, will I?" he asked with a smug grin, knowing very well the twilight berries had once been my favorite as a girl. I'd adored the hint of luxury during those first days after my father's death, when Lord Byron summoned me to his library to have the Priestess tutor me privately. Had it not been for the way the Lord of Mistfell had ruined their sweetness, turning it sour with his bad intentions, they would have still been my favorite. Brann's eyes darkened as my skin went cold, watching as I reached into the bush and wrapped my hand around another berry. A thorn caught in the skin on the back of my hand, pulling free from the branch and embedding itself in me when I jolted back and hissed.

I pulled my hand out of the bush slowly, careful not to drop the berry clutched in my fingers as I shoved away the memory of whispered promises against my skin about the life I could have if only I was patient. If only I could overlook the details that made a relationship between us both impossible and disgusting.

Like his wife, his age being twice mine, and the fact that he'd forced me to watch as the High Priest slit my father's throat and sacrificed his life to the Veil.

Those little details.

I winced as I caught sight of my hand, depositing the berry into the basket and setting the entire thing on the ground as gently as I could. The thorn buried in my skin went deeper than I'd hoped, the flesh moving around it as I spread my fingers. More blood welled from around the edges of the thorn, staining my skin as I touched a tentative finger to the wound.

"You really must be more careful, Lady Estrella," a male voice said from behind me. My body stilled as dread sank inside my heart, and I watched from the corner of my eye as Brann turned his attention back to the twilight berries with renewed energy.

I turned slowly, dropping my gaze to the ground respectfully as my knees dipped into a curtsy, my dirty, bloodstained hands clutched at the edges of my worn pea-green dress. "With all respect, my Lord, we both know that I am no Lady," I said, rising to full height but keeping my eyes averted in an attempt to show him the respect he believed he deserved.

"Patience," he murmured, taking a few steps closer to me and taking my hand in his. He pinched the thorn between his thumb and forefinger, pulling it free slowly as my lips twisted in a pained grimace.

He watched the hole it left fill with blood, transfixed, enjoying the sight of my suffering and knowing it would give him a reason to tend to my injuries in the privacy of his library later tonight. "Will you allow me to clean this for you later?" he asked, raising his brow.

He might have phrased it like a question, but it was really nothing less than a demand for my company that night. "I apologize, my Lord, but I must admit I am exhausted after the harvest," I said. He studied my face, undoubtedly reading the truth in the circles under my eyes.

"Very well. Tomorrow then," he said, smiling lightly as he bent forward to touch his mouth to the wound on the back of my hand. His lips were stained with my blood by the time he pulled away, sliding his tongue out to lick them clean.

"Tomorrow," I agreed, hating the words the moment they left my mouth. I wanted nothing more than to tell him to tend to his wife's health instead of spending his time with me, but I kept my mouth shut and turned back to the twilight berry bushes.

Because duty came first.

2

The luminescence of the Veil came with the setting of the sun and with it my inability to sleep. Gleaming in the moonlight, it drew me toward the window of my small, cramped bedroom until my breath fogged the glass. My father's last words rang in my head as they always did, calling me to the freedom of the night and the temptation of what might wait for me outside this miserable village.

Fly free, Little Bird.

I curled my threadbare quilt tighter around my shoulders, attempting to chase away the chill as the late autumn air filtered through the gaps at the edges of the window. After my father had died, I'd stuffed scraps of old cloth from outgrown dresses into the holes many winters ago in a pathetic attempt to keep the coldest of winter nights from entering my protection from the elements.

In the fall, I could almost convince myself that it was enough. But once winter well and truly arrived, I would join my brother on the floor in front of the fire while my mother slept nearby in the wheeled chair Lord Byron had fashioned for her after my father's sacrifice.

My bedroom was mostly empty, my meager belongings taking up precious little space in the room that was barely more than a closet. My bed had been carved by my father's hand; the wood of my floor patched repeatedly by my brother every time it rotted out beneath my feet.

I touched my fingers to the cool, cracked glass, drifting over the circle I'd rubbed clean with my sleeve more times than I cared to count over the years. When those trembling fingers finally touched the latch in the middle, I only glanced over my shoulder once to make sure my brother hadn't appeared in my doorway to catch me sneaking out yet again.

Then I tugged them open, the wind nearly blowing them wide as it entered the ramshackle cottage so suddenly the shock of cool air stole the breath from my lungs. I caught them, but only barely, saving myself from the humiliation of waking the house. The tendrils of dark hair that had fallen free from my braid blew away from my face. I lifted myself onto the windowsill and swung my legs out—my skin prickling as moonlight kissed my bare hands.

I couldn't suffer through another moment of my nighttime imprisonment, of being trapped inside the structure that was too broken down to truly be a home. Not when the night sky called my name and the fresh scent of pine in autumn flooded my senses from the other side of that windowsill.

There was something deeply therapeutic about my rebellious little walks in the woods. Something appealing in the way they went against the strictures placed on me by a corrupt society that was so often determined to keep women pure and virtuous for the husbands who hadn't even been chosen yet. Good men were few and far between in Mistfell, a rarity rather than the norm. I didn't dare to hope for a marriage like my parents had shared, a life filled with happiness and affection.

Dropping the blanket to the floor of my room behind me, I lowered myself down to the grass and fumbled around in the dark while my eyes adjusted, searching for my stick. I dug my fingers into the dirt below me, dusting myself in the neglected soil that never seemed to flourish. Dry and sandy grains slipped through my fingers as I rose to my feet and tugged the window panes closed. I slipped the twig into the gap in the windowsill beneath them and turned it until the branch caught on the other side, holding it closed until I could return to sneak back inside before my brother discovered I was missing.

The mix of wooden planks and wattle and daub that made up the outer walls had warped and cracked over years of neglect, the thatched roof was in need of repair in the spots where rain water had leaked in over time. There were only two glass windows in the structure, cracked and broken things my father and brother had been given as a gift after they'd helped one of the wealthier families replace them.

Leaving the house behind me, I walked toward the copse of trees that hovered just beyond the outskirts of my village. In the distance, something howled at the moon, calling me into the darkness where creatures roamed beneath the stars and the people of the village of Mistfell feared for their lives. But instead of the dread that should have pulsed through my body, there was only the sensation of what I could never find during waking hours when people roamed the streets.

Freedom.

It was a temporary illusion in my world, a deception I granted myself to ease the stinging reality; the privilege of making my own choices was not mine to have. For the time being, my life was determined by the Lord of Mistfell and the elite force of Mist Guards who had strayed from their original purpose and grown into a twisted army that did whatever he demanded. My brother's opinion came only after theirs, his choices dictating my life in the absence of the father Lord Byron and the High Priest had sacrificed to the Veil.

One day, sooner than I cared to acknowledge, my fate and my activities would be decided by my husband, and that was when the true horrors of my life would begin.

I dragged a hand over the bark of the first tree as I came to the edge of the woods, not bothering to glance behind me as I drifted around it and into the tree line. Darkness quickly swallowed me whole, wrapping me in a steady embrace that beckoned me forward and called to the part of me that was different from those who feared the night that I craved.

Even the sounds of small creatures slithering through the underbrush at my feet couldn't force me to flee the forest. Even the chill air on my skin that brought a pink stain to my cheeks couldn't force me to turn back.

All that mattered to me was the darkness surrounding me, the privacy afforded in the dead of night when I didn't have to tolerate the prying eyes of Lord Byron's men watching me for signs I might be acting out once again.

I slipped further into the woods, navigating as far from the village as I dared to go. The rock trolls didn't often stray too far from their homes, instead choosing the prey that willingly walked right into their habitat to shelter from the elements, but that didn't mean I wanted to tempt fate and wander too close.

My moment of freedom would mean nothing if I spent it trapped within the jowls of a beast three times my size, my flesh torn to ribbons while what remained of me bled out on the ground.

I stayed away from the paths that the Mist Guard would undoubtedly patrol, dragging my fingers over the trees as if I could memorize each and every one to find my way back home. I'd come this way before, navigated with only the moon and stars to light my way, more times than I could count.

A scattering of lights twinkled in the distance, moving through the trees in a circular pattern that drew my attention straight to it. I paused, halting as I glanced back over my shoulder for any sign that I might have been followed, or that Lord Byron and his Mist Guard might have waited to trap me like a curious housecat wandering where she didn't belong.

There was nothing behind me but the woods I'd already traveled, and after a single moment considering turning back, I ducked low and crept forward to approach the strange glints.

They reminded me of the faerie lights my parents had told stories of when I'd been a girl, of the twinkling wisps that tempted human children away to be replaced by changelings in the time before the Veil. In those centuries, the Fae had run rampant in the human realm, taking what they wanted and leaving the rest to rot and suffer the consequences of their thefts.

I couldn't turn away from the faint lights that moved through the clearing up ahead. When I got close enough, my breath caught in my chest at the sight of the people dressed all in white.

A single candle rested atop the gleaming, beige bone of a skull at the center of the clearing, with figures walking around that centerpiece as they spoke in secretive murmurs to avoid being heard. I crouched low at the base of an evergreen tree, pressing my cheek against the rough bark as I watched them moving rhythmically. Curiosity warred with fear within me, sending my heart pounding until I felt certain they would hear it.

They walked in a circle, chanting softly as they moved within the boundary they'd drawn with twigs lined up end-to-end. With the skull at the center like a bullseye, the outer boundary was perhaps a dozen steps out from it.

Every so often, one of them would turn their face my way, the white of their teeth glimmering in the flickering light as they raised and lowered the candles held tightly in front of them. My eyes couldn't seem to stop wandering to that skull on the ground and the way everything centered around it; I wondered what person could be so unfortunate to have their bones used in some sort of ritual.

I had no idea what I was witnessing, but there was no doubt it was anything but the worship of The Father and The Mother that had been sanctioned by the Crown. Centuries had passed since King Bellham the First had liberated us from the Old Gods, who'd kept us entrenched in lives of sin and depravity, then led us toward the virtue we found with the New Gods.

One of the robed figures stopped walking, body twisting to the side to reveal the curves of a woman. Her head turned toward me, her gaze landing on me so pointedly that she left me with no doubt I'd been spotted. Where I might have expected animosity and fear, for the worship of the Old Gods was strictly forbidden by the Crown, she gifted me a kind smile and sighed as she tipped her head to the side, her dark braid falling over one shoulder.

She broke from their pattern, stepping over the circle they'd drawn around their fellowship with sticks and branches. Everyone within the circle paused as she made her way toward me, while my legs seemed unwilling to move, even though it would have been the smart thing to do. My own curiosity would get me killed if these people decided leaving me alive came with too great a risk; my ability to report them to the Mist Guard could see them burned at the stake for heresy.

My breath shuddered in my lungs, the faint fog it caused floating in front of my face before dispersing into the night air. She approached, that smile never leaving her face as she moved slowly, treating me like a frightened animal. As she came closer, I knew without a doubt she was not from Mistfell, and glancing around, her companions matched her, their clothes in good repair and skin and hair clean. Wherever they'd come from, they didn't belong to the grimy village I called home.

"You are safe here," she said finally, her voice a murmur hanging in the air between us. She shifted her candle into one hand, stretching out with the other to entice me forward. "The Gods welcome all who wish to know about them and their customs."

"The Father and The Mother would never condone this," I said, shaking my head as I stared at that hand. Something in the gesture called to me, pulling me forward until I felt the brush of her fingertips against mine and realized it wasn't her who'd moved.

My cheek stung where the cold air touched the skin that had scraped against the tree bark; while my left hand dragged over the rough branches as I moved further from the illusion of safety they provided. "I do not speak of the Gods they worship indoors, begging for clemency on their knees before an entity that promises salvation only to those who do as they are told." Something in her voice sounded wistful and sad, as if it pained her that I didn't know about the alternatives to the faith that had been shoved down my throat for as long as I could remember.

"Worship of the Old Gods is against the law. If they catch you..." I trailed off when her knowing gaze held mine without fear.

"We know the consequences of discovery, and still we choose to worship. Some faiths are greater than life," she said, sliding her hand against mine until she could grasp me more firmly. She pulled gently, tugging me away from the tree—my safe haven—and drawing me toward the circle at the center of the clearing.

"At least leave Mistfell. The guards aren't far from here," I said, grimacing at the smile she gave in return.

"And yet here you are, risking punishment by being out this time of night. I think you understand better than most why we must take the chance. There is beauty in knowing who you are, and in embracing that in spite of the potential consequences. We come here to be closer to the Gods, to feel the energy coming from the Veil itself," she told me, nodding her head toward the boundary that separated Nothrek from Alfheimr. It twisted, dancing through the air as we watched through the gaps in the trees, the shimmering light continually beckoning me toward it, despite the dangers.

Rumor had it that those who touched the magic of the Veil itself relinquished their life to it, fed the power that kept it strong. It was forbidden, tampering with the single entity that kept us safe from the Fae of Alfheimr, considered the worst of all our trespasses against humanity. But in the interest of preserving the Veil and feeding the energy that sustained it, the High Priest chose one person to give to it every year, one person to sacrifice at the border of the Veil, spilling their blood upon the soil on the last day of the fall harvest in thanks for another year of safety.

Just as they had done to my father.

"This is wrong," I said, pausing at the circle of sticks they'd laid upon the ground. I couldn't seem to convince myself to walk away, but stepping into the inner circle where they worshiped felt wrong. It felt like a betrayal of everything I'd had beaten into me, of the virtues that were supposed to matter to me but had never appealed.

It wouldn't just be the act of a curious girl observing something she'd stumbled upon. I knew if I stepped over that line, I would be an active participant in a ritual I didn't understand. "You should not judge something that you've never experienced," the woman said, stepping over the boundary while she watched me. She still entwined her fingers with mine, our clasped hands hovering over the sticks while she waited. "And no matter what you believe now, there is no harm in experiencing a faith other than your own. You can explore other beliefs without converting. If you still think of us as heathens by morning, tell the Mist Guard what you've seen and absolve yourself from sin."

Sucking in a deep lungful of air, I lifted my foot and stepped into the circle, unable to ignore the pull any longer. Like diving underwater, everything from outside the clearing seemed to fade away. She grabbed a candle off the ground, lighting it with hers and handing it to me as the dozen people still waiting within the circle made room for me to join them. "Who was he?" I asked, glancing down at the skull at the center.

"Jonab," she said, regarding the skull on the ground. "During his lifetime, he was the God of Changing Seasons. Killed during the First Fae War between the Seelie and Unseelie Courts, when Mab fought against her brother Rheaghan."

"How did you come to have his skull?" I couldn't even begin to wrap my head around how long ago the First Fae War must have occurred.

"The same way we have these traditions. Passed down quietly through generations and protected," she said, finally turning her back on me and beginning to walk forward. With only a step or two between each of us, the circle of human figures walked around the skull, just inside the stick-drawn barrier. The others followed, sweeping me up onto the path around the skull that mimicked the circle drawn by sticks.

I swallowed, raising and lowering the candle in my hands as the others did, copying the motions that I had no clue the purpose of but couldn't help but mimic. If I was going to earn an eternity of suffering for participating in a forbidden ritual, I might as well commit. I knew I didn't agree with the beliefs of the New Gods, and found something lacking in their promises for me.

Minutes passed, fading into hazy hours of walking in that circle. My legs tired long before we stopped, the soft chants falling from my lips in unison with theirs as I fell into a dreamlike state. With only the changing of the night sky above to demonstrate just how much time had passed, the words felt written on my soul, like they'd become a part of me in a way I didn't understand.

From death to birth.

From Winter to Spring.

Life renews in time,

from ashes and dust.

When the footfalls eventually stopped, the woman in front of me turned back, bending down and pulling a stone from the pocket of her robe. She placed it on the ground as the others followed suit, forming another circle. Setting her candle atop the stone, she reached into her other pocket and handed me a stone to do the same.

"If a candle falls in the night, it is a warning that the person will not survive the winter," she said, making me pause and take care to center my candle on the stone perfectly. I didn't know that I believed in fortune or prophecy or the Old Gods, but I would do everything I could not to tempt fate.

She chuckled under her breath, watching me fuss over my candle as I stood straight and followed the group when they stepped over the sticks forming the outer circle. They gathered at the edge of the clearing, sitting on the ground with smiles on their faces.

"Is this something you do regularly?" I asked, taking my place next to the ageless woman who had invited me to join them.

"Once a year," she said, lowering herself gracefully. "Only on Samhain. The day we welcome the long Winter."

"The end of the harvest celebration isn't for two more days yet," I said, staring at the sky in the distance. In just two days, we'd be forced to watch the High Priest slit the throat of whatever sacrifice he chose. In just two days, I'd be out of a job for the cold season and need to find random work around the village just to help feed my family.

"According to the Lord of Mistfell," one of the men said, "the worshipers of the New Gods hate anything to do with the Fae, and delayed the celebration out of spite centuries ago. But they all know as well as any, the harvest should have been celebrated today."

"How could you not hate the Fae? After everything they've done throughout history?" I was skeptical.

"One should always remember that history is written by the victor. We may not have won the war, but our lands have been free of the Fae for centuries with no one left but the people who fought against them to pass down stories. What do you think the Fae would say about us and the part we played in the war? If they could share their perspective, I doubt it would be so black and white," another woman said.

She rummaged through her pack, pulling out a bundle of cloth that she unwound on the ground. The parcel was filled with a dense cake, and she cut it into slices.

"I think Adelphia should explain the cake before you eat it. Having seen you mess with that candle for an eternity, I think you may want to pass on this," she said, glancing toward the woman who'd drawn me into the circle in the first place. Adelphia.

"There are objects baked into the cake," Adelphia explained with a chuckle. "According to tradition, if you choose a piece and find one of those objects, it symbolizes what will happen to you before the next Samhain."

One of the men nearest the cake leaned forward, snatching a piece off the fabric. He lifted a chunk to his mouth, chewing thoughtfully before he spit a hand-carved tiny baby into his open palm. "Fuck's sake. Just what I need. Another mouth to feed."

"Keep your dick in your pants then," another man said, slapping him on the back.

I jolted, my body going rigid at the crude words. It wasn't often men spoke so freely in front of women, who were supposed to be pious and virtuous. I knew what a dick was, had even seen one and experienced one in the dead of night while watchful eyes were closed with sleep.

Aside from Byron and his conquests in the privacy of the library, nobody had ever spoken of one in front of me, outside private lessons with my tutor so I knew what to expect come my wedding night. She'd been entirely unaware of how uselessly late that lesson had been for me.

Adelphia took the next piece, and the others followed suit. Without conscious thought, I leaned forward and snatched a piece of cake off the cloth before logic could stop me. Adelphia chuckled at my side, her piece free of omens for the future as she wiped her hands on the grass to rid them of any crumbs.

I lifted the first bite of cake to my mouth, flavors of vanilla and cinnamon on my tongue as I chewed. There was nothing hidden within it, just the sweetness of the cake itself as I watched the others around me chew theirs.

I was through my second bite before something struck my tooth and I raised a hand to my mouth to pull it out. The ring glimmered in bronze against my palm, a sign of the shackle I'd spent my entire life knowing was coming.

Death or prostitution were the only escapes from marriage in the Kingdom of Nothrek. Still, the clear symbol in my palm felt like a noose around my neck, like a death all its own.

"Congratulations are in order; I see?" Adelphia said, her voice tentative. There was no joy on my face at the prospect of my pending nuptials. It didn't matter that I had no knowledge of who my husband might be.

Men were almost all the same, in the end. Looking for a warm place to stick their cock and a trophy to sow their seed.

"It would seem so," I said, smiling and trying to shrug off the dread coursing through my veins. I'd never believed in the fortune tellers who worked at the market every week, predicting which of the thirteen lives a person found themselves on in the cycle of reincarnation before the true death. I'd never put any stock in the magical items a person could purchase if they spoke the right words at the right stands.

I wouldn't start believing in prophecy just because it predicted something I'd always known was coming anyway.

There was a soft thump behind us, the group going still as they looked over my shoulder at the circle. I turned slowly, following their gazes to where a single candle had fallen off its stone and extinguished the moment it touched the grass, as if by an unseen force.

I swallowed, working out the placement for a moment before I turned back to the group with a shaky breath. The silence between them as they watched me rise to my feet spoke volumes about their belief in their Samhain traditions and the clairvoyance they brought.

"I should get home," I said, looking at the sun just cresting the horizon through the trees.

Adelphia nodded, not even bothering to argue with me. There was nothing left to say.

The only candle that had fallen was mine.

3

“You’re awfully quiet this morning,” my brother quietly observed, nudging me with his shoulder as we walked along the path toward the village center later that morning. Evergreens and oak trees lined the way, stretching to either side of the road. I couldn’t force myself to walk past the gallows and see what remained of the last body they’d hung for crimes against Lord Byron, so we had to take the long route, unlike the other villagers who didn’t seem bothered by the macabre of it all. “Did your walk in the woods not settle you last night?”

I glanced Brann’s way, smiling despite my better instincts when I saw the exasperated smile on his face. His blond hair was cut short, his skin golden from all his time spent working under the hot sun of the harvest season. His brown eyes, which were normally filled with mischief, felt heavy on my face, as though he wanted nothing more than to punish me for continuing to risk my reputation.

He’d long since given up trying to discipline me, knowing that if my lessons with Lord Byron and the Priestess hadn’t successfully made me an obedient woman, he stood little chance of making a difference when *he* wasn’t willing to hurt me.

It was a miracle he hadn’t nailed my window shut at this point, for all the times he'd caught me sneaking out or back in. He'd been in my room waiting for me when I'd returned home this morning and hauled myself up and into my window in a daze as the sun rose behind me.

"It was an interesting night," I said, evading telling him about the circle I'd stumbled across. While I didn't think he would condemn others for practicing a faith different from ours, I couldn't see him being supportive of my risking the gallows for mere curiosity's sake. Especially not when the ritual the night before had predicted my death before the next Samhain.

"You really must stop sneaking out in the dead of night, Estrella," my mother said, her voice scolding as she twisted to look at me over her shoulder. Brann pushed her wheeled chair in front of him, his fingers gripping the wooden handles tightly. "What will the men of the village think if they find you? No man wants to marry a woman if he has any reason to believe she is not virtuous."

"That's hardly a motivation to stay inside. We both know Estrella doesn't care much for the idea of marriage," Brann said with a laugh, earning a scoff and chuckle from our mother. She wasn't exactly supportive of my hatred for marriage and the way women were treated as if we were nothing more than broodmares, but she didn't condemn me for it in the same way I suspected most would, either.

I loved her all the more for it. Her tolerance for letting me be who I was in the privacy of our home was something that had enabled me to survive the past two years. Since my coming of age, I'd been being poked and prodded at Temple, my face repeatedly turned from side to side and studied, my manners dictated by the Priestesses of the Mother who sought to train me to be a dutiful, obedient wife one day.

The weekly rite of Temple was something I dreaded with every fiber of my being; it threatened to consume me in the hours of night, leaving me sleepless in my bed. Those nights were when I wandered the most, giving myself deep circles beneath my eyes for the Priestesses to disapprove of.

The large stone building loomed as we approached the western side of the village, the sight of it drawing my nerves tighter. The tower jutted upward, the sole room at the top the temple where the High

Priest went to convene with The Father, but though the otherwise square building was well-built, there was nothing spectacular about it. It served a purpose, and that purpose wasn't a life of excess, but of restraint.

If the ritual the night before had felt wholesome, everything about walking into the home of the Priests and Priestesses felt obscene.

We stepped into the line of villagers making their way into the temple, murmuring happily amongst themselves like they were truly oblivious to the reasons I hated it.

"Mrs. Barlowe," Lord Byron greeted, stopping to greet my mother as we wheeled her up to the doors. My mother smiled back at the man who'd paid for her wheeled chair out of his own pocket and given her working accommodations that we would never have hoped for.

There'd been many days when I'd gone to Temple and my prayers were filled with pleas for her to never discover the price I'd paid for it in the privacy of his library; I prayed she'd never learn the true cost of his kindness.

"My Lord," my mother said, accepting the hand he offered and touching her lips to his ring dutifully.

My brother bowed his head respectfully when Lord Byron turned his attention his way while glancing at me out the side of his eye as I dropped into my well-practiced curtsy. I could still feel the impact of my teacher's cane against my skin when I hadn't held my posture properly. Could still recall the way Lord Byron had watched my face twist with pain as the blow struck, even years after I'd long since memorized the motions.

Dipping my chin toward the ground at his feet, I waited for the moment his hand would appear in front of me, knowing he'd never miss an opportunity to force me to kiss his ring and remind me of the power he exerted over everyone and everything.

I grasped his hand in mine gently, leaning forward to touch my lips to his ring as I counted.

One.

I want to gut you while you sleep.

Two.

You are the worst of humanity.

Three.

From the corner of my eye, I watched a stately Lady Jaclen glare at me as she saw the exchange for what it was: her husband's version of flirting. One of these days, she'd kill me herself.

I released his hand smoothly, letting it drop to his side while I waited for his command, so that I could end the torment of prostrating myself before him. Villagers passed us by as I held my position, while Lord Byron forced me to show just how long I could maintain the stance that was never meant to last more than a few moments of respect.

My body didn't twitch even as my muscles strained. To twitch was to disappoint my Lord and to disappoint him was to suffer.

"Estrella," he greeted finally, freeing me from the pain consuming my body. I rose slowly, keeping my face a blank mask in an attempt not to show him how much it had cost me.

"My Lord," I murmured. Peering at him through my lashes with my head angled down the way he liked, I sank my teeth into the inside of my cheek to suppress the words I wanted to scream.

Words I wanted to throw in his face to wound him as much as he had wounded me.

"Lady Jaclen," I said, greeting the frail woman who stood at his side.

She glared at me in return, her scowl heavy on the side of my face. She didn't offer me her hand in the way our customs demanded, deeming me so far beneath her, she didn't want to taint herself with the press of my skin against hers.

The message was clear to anyone who observed the interaction as they passed. I may have been how her husband chose to occupy his evenings more and more often, forgoing her bed altogether as her health declined, but I had less worth than the dirt beneath her jewel-studded silk slippers. "Still no husband, I see?" she asked, humming thoughtfully as she looked over my shoulder for the man she knew did not exist.

"No, my Lady," I agreed, shaking my head subtly. Every month that passed without a formal declaration for my hand came as another blow to my family's already low status.

What good was a daughter you couldn't successfully marry off?

"Perhaps one day soon," Lord Byron said, offering his flagging wife his arm. She leaned into him, allowing him to absorb her weight as she struggled to stay on her feet. With every day that passed, she grew sicker. With every day that passed, villagers whispered of what illness might have consumed her for so many years, and of who might follow to replace her after she finally passed.

Byron was a Lord without an heir, and the women of Mistfell postured and hoped for the death of his wife for the very same reason many of them barely tolerated me.

I had his favor, even if I didn't want it.

Lord and Lady Jaclen moved into the Temple, leaving me to shove my dread down into the deepest part of me where no one could see. He'd said as much in vague words repeatedly over the years, but until the day his wife died, there was nothing he could do.

He was permitted mistresses, so long as they were not deemed virginal, and thus appropriate for marriage to other suitors. My most recent virginity test should have condemned me to a life as a mistress or Lady of the Night, but the doctor had deemed me pure. I knew it was a lie, and I suspected he did as well.

I just didn't know why he'd hidden my secret, why he'd protected me from the harsh consequences for the things I did in the night, when my body seemed to come alive and hum with energy that I couldn't restrain. Perhaps he'd protected the son of his friend, the only boy I'd trusted enough to be intimate with, even though Lord Byron would have benefited from the loss of my virginity.

Perhaps the doctor had acted out of nefarious purposes. I hoped I'd never learn the truth either way.

My brother and I leaned down, grasping my mother's chair by the wheels and lifting it up over the step into the Temple. Moving inside, I took over steering my mother toward the right of the cavernous space and the rows of women who knelt on the cold, stone floor with their heads bowed as the Priests and Priestesses waited at the front of the sanctuary.

Stopping her chair in the aisle next to the space on the floor the other women had left for her, I moved around to her front. Taking each of her hands in mine, I guided her up and out of the chair as her legs trembled under her weight. Hugging her tightly to my chest, I used my entire body to shift her around her chair, shuffling her nearly limp legs over as I slowly lowered her to her knees.

I'd learned long ago that, even though she couldn't feel the impact when she fell, I felt the stain of those bruises on my heart if I failed to move carefully enough. When her knees touched the floor beneath her, I lowered her until she sat on her heels and she lifted her palms to rest atop her thighs. Leaving her there, I took her chair to the back of the sanctuary where it wouldn't be in the way of the Priests and Priestesses as they made their way around the room.

At the front of the room, one of the servants helped Lady Jaclen to her knees as well. Everyone knelt for Temple—gave themselves to The Father and The Mother—even the Lady of Mistfell.

I returned to my mother, lowering to my knees beside her. Everything in her body trembled, the difficulty of maintaining her position evident in the strained lines on her face. My palms rested on my thighs, facing up and opened to The Mother as my head tipped down to look at the floor in front of me.

Across the room, the men knelt on embroidered cushions the Priestesses had stitched for them by hand, as the Priest spoke to them in low tones that faded into the space between us. I stared at a spot on the stone floor that was lighter than the area surrounding it, fixating on it as the Priestesses moved between the rows of women. They touched a few as they passed, correcting posture with firm hands.

"Hmm," Bernice, the severe High Priestess who'd once been my tutor, murmured as she passed by us. She didn't touch me, knowing she had long since beaten my slacking shoulders and lazy elbows out of existence, but just the thoughtful sound of her voice in the air sent my heart pounding. It took everything in me not to flinch away from the blow to my shoulders that she'd conditioned me to expect.

"Look upon The Mother," the tall, spare woman said, walking to the front of the room and taking her place next to the stone statue of a woman, which sat beside the statue of The Father. The Mother's head was bowed as she knelt at The Father's feet, her palms opened to the sky to accept the gifts he bestowed upon her for her obedience and dutifulness as his wife.

His love. His protection. His seed that she would take and use to create children.

"The harvest season ends tomorrow," Bernice said, a smile on her face as she glanced around the group of women gathered. "The Father has communicated his wishes to the High Priest, and one of our own will give their life for the continued protection of the Veil. It is our turn, after the sacrifice of Mr. Daugherty last year."

"Yes, Priestess," I murmured, the sound of my voice echoed by those around me with the well-practiced words. "It would be our honor." The words burned down my throat like acid, stinging with the noise of my betrayal.

That honor had left me without a father and my mother without a husband, alone with two children. It was no honor at all, but a twisted promise of obedience that proved we would walk willingly to our deaths if so demanded by those who claimed to speak for the New Gods.

"We are women. Our duty is to our homes and our husbands, to our sons and daughters so that the next generation may be even stronger. Now we bow our heads and pray for forgiveness for our wicked thoughts, for our sinful desires, which tempt us away from the absolution only The Mother can provide."

I bowed my head once again, studying that same spot on the stone floor as the men across the space rose to their feet. Bernice spoke to the High Priest and Lord Byron as they joined her on the women's side, while my gaze refused to leave that light speck in the limestone.

"The married may depart," the High Priest said from the front of the room. At my side, Brann helped my mother to her feet as another of the men brought her chair. They lifted her into it as I waited for the part of Temple that I had even less tolerance for than kneeling for a Goddess I was losing my faith in.

This life couldn't be all there was. It couldn't be the point.

When the married men and women had vacated the space, the sounds of footsteps sounded throughout the room as the unattached men walked between our rows. "Will Miss Ead have a bigger dowry this year after her father's deal with the Lord of Copstage?" one asked.

"Yes, her dowry has doubled since last year," the Priest announced happily. I sat still, hoping to avoid notice. The dirt and grime on my old, stained clothes turned away most men, and I could only hope they would continue to do so. Only a peasant would be interested in marrying another peasant, and with the coming winter, none could afford another mouth to feed.

"And what of Miss Barlowe?" another man asked, stepping up beside me and dropping his hand to my shoulder. His fingers toyed with the end of my tangled braid, pulling the tie free and working my hair loose until it hung about my shoulders. I froze solid, my bottom lip twitching as I fought for the composure to remain still.

This was what I was supposed to want.

"She continues to have no dowry to offer," the Priest said, something in his voice sounding tight and reserved. "That is unlikely to change given her situation," he added, referencing the fact that I was fatherless, and that we'd long since spent the meager compensation they'd provided when they'd killed him in the name of Mistfell's security.

"I inquired after her hand last year, though nothing ever came of it. The dowry matters little to me, but she kneels so prettily, I think I should like to see her do it elsewhere," the man at my side said with a chuckle. I sank my teeth into my cheek so deeply the coppery tang of blood covered my tongue.

"I'm afraid The Father has plans for Miss Barlowe now," the High Priest said, halting my breath in my lungs. I glanced up at the High Priest at the front of the room, and the look of confusion written onto Lord Byron's face as he snapped his attention to the robed man beside him.

The cane cracked against the back of my neck, toppling me forward from the force of it. I barely had time to catch myself, my cheek just glancing off the stone floor rather than cracking against it with all my weight. My back throbbed, the pain radiating down my neck as I stayed bowed in submission. I squeezed my eyes closed, waiting for the next strike, which never came.

"Enough, Bernice. I think Miss Barlowe has remembered her manners, haven't you, my dear?" Lord Byron asked, the slime of his voice sliding between us.

"Yes, my Lord," I murmured, my cheek rubbing against the stone as I turned my head to the side and nodded. Bernice's glare met mine, her hatred of who she believed was an ungrateful swine, undeserving of Lord Byron's kindness, glimmering in her eyes.

She claimed I hadn't deserved his wandering hands or ministrations after her canings. Hadn't deserved his attention or the lessons he gave me out of pity for the loss of my father and for my disabled mother who couldn't care for me properly.

I'd have given it all up in a heartbeat to never have known what his hands felt like as they pressed into the welts she'd left on my skin, so perhaps it was true I was ungrateful.

I would remain that way until I returned every moment of suffering they'd caused me.

Lord Byron stepped forward, moving through the rows of women that remained. The men who browsed their potential wives moved out of the way as he closed the distance between us and drew a ragged gasp from my lungs when he stopped in front of me. His shoes filled my vision, the brown leather of them far too clean and shiny when I considered how worn and filthy mine were.

My eyes shifted to Brann where he stood with the women, his hands clenched into fists and his jaw tight. There was nothing he could do to save me from the coming storm, from the wrath I'd incur from Bernice if I so much as twitched a muscle.

I held perfectly still as I shifted my eyes up to meet Lord Byron's where he stood over me, and watched as something passed over his face. He lifted his hand from his side, holding it palm-up and turning his focus to Bernice. She smirked as she glowered at me, setting the wood of the cane in his open palm.

"I need a few moments with Miss Barlowe," he said, curling his fingers around the instrument of my pain.

"But my Lord, Temple is still—" the Priestess interjected as the people around us paused, waiting with bated breath to see who would be the victor in the power struggle that might follow. The High Priest was an extension of The Father himself.

"In honor of the coming celebration, The Father releases you all from Temple early so that you may have more time to enjoy the weekly market," the High Priest said, a chill spreading through my body with the words.

My fingers scrabbled for purchase along the stone as I turned my face to it, the cool press of the surface under my forehead grounding me against the dread rising within me. Against my slowing heartbeat as I drew in deep breaths to prevent the trembling in my limbs.

I didn't watch as the women around me rose to their feet, fleeing the uncomfortable scene without so much as a moment's hesitation. They left me alone to the married man who shouldn't have even known my name; such was the way of a lowly harvester who was so far beneath the Lord of Mistfell.

I braced against the coming pain—against the blow that I expected to land across my back or the tops of my thighs at any moment. My throat closed, saliva filling my mouth when I couldn't swallow.

He made me wait, his torment of me well-rehearsed. Lord Byron understood the pain itself was only one of the tools he wielded against me, and the dread of what was yet to come was an even greater torment.

"Kneel," he ordered, his voice sliding over my skin; an insidious menace, tangible and grimy as I rose slowly to my knees. Keeping my head bowed in submission, I fought back the burning in my nose and the threat of tears at the back of my eyes. Time seemed to slow as I waited for the next instruction, narrowing to the rhythmic sound of his breathing.

The cane touched the front of my throat, pressing firmly as I bit the inside of my cheek to quell the urge to flinch. He slid it over my delicate skin, hooking it under my chin and lifting until I raised my eyes to his finally. "You didn't come to the Manor last night, and yet you look as though you haven't slept a wink. Do I need to worry that you've found companionship elsewhere?" he asked, quirking his brow as I swallowed.

Everything in me felt heavy, the bone-weary exhaustion of the harvest and the coming struggles of winter weighing me down. "Of course not, my Lord." I didn't tell him I'd found that months prior, sneaking around on the occasions when Byron didn't demand my company.

His knowledge of that would be disastrous for me. My purity was all that protected me from him taking everything. There were many ways to touch a woman, many ways for him to torment me that didn't rob me of my alleged virginity, but his belief meant that one part of me remained mine.

That one part of me was safe.

"Do you think I did not know about the Mist Guard? What was his name—Loris?" Lord Byron asked, arcing the cane through the air with precision.

It didn't touch me, but it was enough to make me feel like my eternal soul would jump out of my skin at any moment. Combined with his words and the confession of what he knew, it was enough to make my body go slack and slump as dizziness consumed me.

His cane cracked against my ribs just below my breasts, a hot trail of fire bringing my body back to life as I forced myself to sit up straight. The mark he left burned with the sensation of a thousand needles stabbing me. I barely resisted the urge to cover myself, to cower away from the pain.

Only the knowledge that retreat would cause more punishment kept me still.

I fumbled for words, unable to find the right ones to say. I'd been so certain that he'd have progressed our relationship if he'd known the truth—that he wouldn't have hesitated to make me into another one of his conquests. "I don't—I don't understand," I said finally, stumbling over my words. Instinct drove me to apologize, as if he had some Gods-given right to my body and it wasn't truly my own.

I shoved that down, focusing on my lack of understanding. Focusing on the *why*.

Lord Byron dropped the cane to the ground beside me, tilting his head to the side as if it hadn't occurred to him I might not have realized he knew the truth. He took my chin between two fingers, the intimacy of the touch sending my nerves racing.

Surely he couldn't mean to *touch* me in the Temple?

"You have no secrets from me, Estrella," he said, releasing my chin slowly. That hand came down on the side of my neck as he bent at the waist, leaning forward until his forehead touched mine. "But remember what happens to men who take what is not theirs. It would be a shame if the Mist Guard learned what he's done."

"No, please. You can't—"

Lord Byron pulled back, glaring at me as if to remind me of who he was. He could, and would, for there was no one to stop him, condemn a man to death just because he'd stuck his cock where it didn't belong.

I hesitated, sinking my teeth into my bottom lip. "I just wanted something that was mine. A choice I-I could make for once," I explained. Confessing my sin in the Temple felt like the greatest crime, an apology for something I couldn't force myself to regret; not when it meant that whatever husband they chose for me would be sorely disappointed in the wife he ended up with.

"I know exactly what you wanted. You are rebellious, reckless, and most often foolish. If you were so determined to ruin yourself for marriage and make yourself into a common whore, the least you could have done was allow me to be the one to do it," he snapped, the words striking against my skin like a physical thing.

"You would know, my Lord," I said, my voice curling into a high-pitched mockery. It resembled the well-practiced moans of the women I'd watched him with, who he'd tried to throw in my face over the past two years, when he'd needed to fuck because of the frustration he said I built in him.

Because I'd been off limits—but I hadn't, and he'd known it all along.

The back of his hand cracked against my cheek, the sound echoing through the empty space. My head snapped to the side with the force of it, my cheekbone throbbing from where his ring struck. "You will remember your place," he said, grabbing me by my face. His thumb pressed into my cheek on one side, his fingers on the other as he leaned over me with his lips twisted in fury.

"Yes, my Lord," I mumbled, my voice restricted by his cruel grip.

"You will come to the library tonight. There are things we need to discuss, and I need to calm down from your insolence or I will cane you until you bleed. Thank me for my kindness, Estrella."

"Thank you, my Lord," I said, wincing as he released my face suddenly.

"Tonight. Do not disappoint me again," he reminded me harshly. He straightened his clothing, donning the persona he wanted everyone else to see, his lips tipped up into an appeasing and kind half-smile. Only I seemed to see the truth of who he really was. He made his way toward the doors, the sound of their creaking echoing through the sanctuary as he shoved them open.

Left to pick my beaten body up off the cold stone floor for what seemed like the millionth time in two years, I knew whatever was coming that night would be far worse.

4

I didn't sneak out through my window that night, instead walking straight out the front door as I so often did on the evenings when I was summoned to Lord Byron's private library at Mistfell Manor. There was nothing to hide from my brother—not when I'd been commanded to behave inappropriately on these nights. With my heart in my throat, I tried to sink into the comfort the night usually provided and take solace in the familiarity, before everything changed.

Lord Byron had mentioned we needed to speak. He hadn't said he intended to take my body in the way he hadn't before, and he wouldn't have hidden those intentions from me if he'd had them. He would've wanted to torment me through the day, to drive my heart into my stomach and fill me with dread.

I pushed branches away from my face as I moved through them, keeping to the trail. Eventually it would lead me toward the barracks and the manor close to the village center. Even though my walk in the night would be sanctioned if the Mist Guard brought me to the manor, I didn't particularly want to deal with the likely brutal escort I would receive.

I looked toward the trees and the glimpses of the moon shining through the canopy overhead. The shock of amber eyes studying me from the branches made my slow steps falter, freezing me in place to stare back into the too-intelligent eyes of the blight watching me.

Similar to the crows that were common during the daylight hours, the blight were nocturnal birds said to be crafted from the magic of the Court of Shadows itself. Born from the darkness, they were spies for the beings who could no longer cross over the Veil.

I swallowed as it cocked its head to the side while it watched me, shifting so its talons got a better grip on the branch before it blinked with a nearly-translucent eyelid, which added a misty quality to the eye that never left me. Launching into the sky, it flew back toward the Veil at the edge of the Mist, lending evidence to the rumor of its purpose.

Even though the Veil was believed to be impenetrable by any form of life, chills broke out over my skin and goosebumps raised at the very thought of a spy reporting about me to the monsters on the other side. There was no reason to believe the Fae cared in the slightest about my existence, but nothing could stop the ominous feeling from spreading through me.

Shaking my head, I continued my walk down the path even though a part of me wanted to return home. Knowing that, while I might be able to prolong the inevitable visit with Lord Byron, I couldn't escape it altogether. It had been such a small encounter, a bird watching me in the night, but some legends were better left as whispers meant to scare children.

In my father's words, some secrets were better left in the dark.

Through the trees to my right, the gardens next to the barrier between realms were illuminated by the shimmering Veil as it swayed in the breeze. The Mist on the other side disguised whatever lay beyond, casting shadows on the space between our lands.

I turned to the left, against the pull I felt toward the Veil, determined not to tempt fate by wandering too closely when my life seemed dominated by upheaval and change as of late. I'd hardly taken a few steps forward when an arm wrapped around my chest from behind.

It pulled me back into the hard, unforgiving body of a man that I could not see. My blood raced with the sudden shock of adrenaline in my veins. My neck stung with the cold press of a blade to my skin. Another pulse of fear coursed through me.

Any number of Lord Byron's men would have been angry to discover me gallivanting through the night once again, at least, until they discovered he'd summoned me.

"Now what have you been told about sneaking about in the night? I'm likely to mistake you for a Fae lover," the man said, ducking his head lower to softly murmur the words in my ear. I relaxed, my body sagging in relief the moment I recognized the familiar voice and the fact that he wouldn't report me.

With my initial fear of being caught gone, I sprung as quickly as he'd taught me, reaching up with both hands to grasp his wrist at the same moment I dropped my weight to the ground and spun. He grunted when his arm twisted with me, extending out behind him as I hooked a foot behind his knees and forced them to collapse beneath him.

"What was I thinking when I taught you that?" he asked, narrowing his warm brown eyes on my face as he looked up at me. His stare focused on the light bruise on my cheek, the spot of skin that was just a bit too dark after Byron's strike earlier, but he clenched his jaw and ignored it as his duty demanded.

I smiled, releasing his arm and letting him shake out the pain before he sheathed his dagger. Loris's leather chest piece was secured at his side with clasps that clinked together as he moved, rising to his feet until he once again towered over me. He grinned, thin lips tipping up and taking away some of the harshness that was such an inherent part of his features.

As a Mist Guard, kindness had been trained and beaten out of him. He was a minion of his purpose, driven by the need to protect the Veil and keep the Fae on the other side of it at all costs. Nothing could matter so much as that duty.

It came first, even when that meant taking part in the sacrifice of innocent people.

"Perhaps you like being the only one to—"

Loris interrupted my response, leaning forward to crush his lips to mine urgently. His brown eyes drifted closed the moment he touched me, as if some part of him settled when I didn't speak any words to demean what we'd become to one another.

It wasn't love, but it was as close as the two of us would ever come; a rebellion against the life chosen for us where his duty demanded he never marry and mine condemned me to it.

Gentle hands raised to touch my waist, tugging me closer as I returned his kiss and leaned into his warmth. I knew it would be our last, that after I confessed Lord Byron knew about our tryst, he wouldn't want anything to do with me again.

He kissed me sweetly, making me believe for just a moment I might be worth something to a man in our world. I might be something special, if even only to one person. When he pulled away, he looked down at me with heavy eyes and a condescending twist of his lips. "You know you shouldn't be in the woods at night," he mumbled, tucking a runaway strand of my dark, wavy hair behind my ear and holding my green eyes captive with his.

"I like it out here at night," I returned, tugging back and raising my chin in defiance. Every moment I spent delaying my confession felt like a lie by omission.

"Only the Ladies of the Night are out at this hour. Even if a cave beast doesn't find you and make a snack out of you, do you want one of the travelers visiting Mistfell for the celebration to mistake you for one of them?" Loris asked, pulling me back into his chest and teasing the corner of my mouth with his. The temptation to give in rolled over me, but I shoved it away with two hands at his chest.

"Then I suppose it would be a terrible idea for them to see me wrapped in your arms, wouldn't it?" I asked with a saccharine smile, turning on my heel and continuing toward the manor.

Until the day I had an official master, I wouldn't be owned in the night.

"Estrella, wait!" Loris called, hurrying up behind me and grasping my wrist. He tugged, pulling me back into his chest as that confident smile consumed his face. "You know I just worry about you." He kissed me again, this one deeper and holding the heat of a single moment of passion that he knew I couldn't say no to.

"I'm not yours to worry over anymore," I said with a sigh, murmuring the harsh reminder of what we both knew was coming. He just didn't know it had likely already arrived. "Lord Byron knows about us."

Loris pulled back, his brow furrowing as he stared down at me. "What?"

"Apparently he's known for some time," I admitted, shrugging my shoulders and feigning a casualness about the situation that I didn't feel. Something inside me recoiled, just thinking about the potential fallout with Lord Byron for what I'd done.

"But your lack of purity would make you ineligible for marriage. Why hasn't he put you to work with the Ladies, or told the Commander what I've done, for that matter? That makes no sense whatsoever, for him to keep our secret when we violated The Mother's doctrine," he said, raising a hand to scrub down his face in confusion.

"He does nothing without a purpose. I'm on my way to find out what it is," I admitted, hanging my head and touching my forehead to his chest briefly. "He requested my presence in his library, so I'll know more soon. But no matter what he has to say, we can't meet anymore. It's too dangerous for you."

"He didn't seem to object to it, if he allowed it to go on for this long. He could've had me hanged months ago for ruining you in the eyes of The Mother," Loris said, scoffing as he took a step back. Even if his words were an argument that Lord Byron seemed willing to allow another man to touch me, Loris had already put the necessary distance between us, recognizing the danger in continuing to have a relationship with me when the secret had been discovered.

"I don't think he would have told me he knew unless he wanted it to stop. Whatever his reasons, I don't think they apply anymore." I didn't speak of the words the High Priest had said at Temple earlier in the day, nor did I mention the hint that The Father had plans for me, and what that might mean with the coming sacrifice. It seemed like the odds of Lord Byron's plan for me carrying weight for very long were slim.

Loris let me go as I backed away and turned toward the manor, because to go against the wishes, even unspoken, of Lord Byron, would violate the vows he'd taken to serve Mistfell and the Veil.

And his duty came first.

He disappeared in the opposite direction on the path as I turned my back on him as well; both going our separate ways as we'd always known we'd need to one day. I hadn't expected it to sting as much as it did, stripping me of any illusions I'd allowed myself for those few moments wrapped in his arms.

He'd been my safety for a few hours during each week, when we managed to find time together in secret while he was off-duty. He'd made me feel like I mattered—I was more than a broodmare and might be worth risking the consequences to be with—but Loris still turned his back on me without much regret. He'd still walked into the woods to do what was expected of him, in the end.

I continued on my original path through the woods, blinking back the sting of tears I hadn't expected at the loss of something that had never been mine. Hurrying into the shadows of the trees to avoid further incident, I stuck close to the path but let them cover me as I approached the barracks that housed the Mist Guard.

The Manor lay behind them, protected from the Veil by the imposing building that was practically a fortress. It was said to rival the palace in the capital of Ineburn City in terms of fortitude. I'd never been permitted inside the barracks themselves. No one who wasn't a member of the Mist Guard had. Loris was quiet about the details of the life he lived within those walls, to keep me from really feeling the differences between us. The other guards, however, weren't nearly as aware of the poverty that ran rampant within Mistfell and the way most of us suffered while they lived in luxury.

The Mist Guard were deemed a class all their own. In an ideal world, not tainted by Lord Byron's corruption, they weren't supposed to report to anyone or anything other than their own doctrines and hierarchy. Not the Lord of Mistfell; not even the King of Nothrek. They were intended to be a separate entity from the crown.

As such, it was only natural that they were treated like royalty as well. This was the reward for choosing a life of service protecting the Kingdom from the creatures on the other side of the impenetrable Veil.

The stone walls surrounding the fortress had been stained brown by time. I skirted around the edge, keeping distance between myself and the patrols that I expected to jump out at any moment. I wistfully eyed the horses that poked their heads out of the barn stalls. It hardly seemed fair that they had the finest horses in the village, while the farmers often had to cope with aging nags that weren't made for hard labor.

The barracks acted as a barrier, separating the Veil from the village, so that no matter what corner of Mistfell one found themselves in, the Mist Guard waited as a silent sentry to the Veil itself. The Guard would be the first thing the Fae encountered, aside from the gardens, if they ever came to Nothrek. If they ever crossed the Veil, it would be to claim the humans they thought belonged to them, after centuries of forced separation kept them away from their mortal counterparts.

Stepping through the edge of the woods, I approached the shimmering white Veil where it swayed on the other side of the trees. The branches reached toward it, as if they couldn't get close enough to the pervasive magic of Faerie, which promised a better life and more fertile soil.

I followed suit against my best intentions, making my way to the edge of the boundary, where the land disappeared into the shimmering magic and the mist that lay beyond. With the gardens to my right, the barracks through the trees behind me, and the Manor gleaming in the distance as it rose above the trees, I swayed like a sapling toward the Veil. It fluttered like the lightest of fabrics when caught in the ocean breeze, the clouded mist on the other side making it impossible to see through to the land of Faerie. Sometimes, in the night, I looked into that mist and swore I saw the shining beacon of dazzling blue eyes staring back at me.

But that was impossible, and sometimes I wondered if that was as much a blessing as everyone insisted. My own idle curiosity and a boring life drove me to the Veil at night to see the stars twinkling in the mist and the lightning storms that rippled through the boundary, like the Old Gods themselves were angry for what had been taken from them.

Considering the Old Gods we'd once worshiped had eventually been revealed as the most powerful of the Fae, I thought it was likely they were angry. After their real identities had been exposed, the resulting war had torn Nothrek in two. Entire cities had been laid to waste at the hands of those Old Gods in their fury at the prospect of no longer being worshiped.

A sense of nothingness settled over me when I raised a hand as close as I dared and stared into the Mist beyond the Veil, the twinkle of stars resonating with something inside of me. If the quiet of darkness was a welcome reprieve from the chaos inside my mind, then my morbid curiosity of what might exist just on the other side of the Veil was my defect.

"I see that our last lesson in propriety was ineffective as usual, Miss Barlowe," Lord Byron said from somewhere behind me. I flinched, dropping my hand from where I'd reached up to feel close to the magic that called to my curiosity.

Spinning, I turned to face the owner of the smooth voice that haunted my nightmares. "Lord Byron, I can explain—"

"My Lord," he corrected, sauntering through the copse of trees that I'd thought would provide me cover. A legion of Mist Guard followed at his heels, having none of the natural grace he did and moving only with brute force as they'd been trained. They were a reminder of everything I didn't want to consider, of the ticking clock he held over my head now.

"My Lord," I said, tilting my head down until my eyes landed on the yellowing grass at his feet. I preferred that to the false kindness in his blue eyes and the attractive features that undoubtedly fooled many girls into aiming for his bed.

To be a consort to the Lord of Mistfell was no small feat—even if he did have a wife.

"I am fairly certain that this is not my library, Estrella," he said when he stopped in front of me, sliding two smooth fingers under my chin and tipping my face until he captured my stare with his.

“It isn't the library,” I confirmed, the urge to spit in his face sneaking through me.

“Mumbling is beneath a woman of your grace.” He slid his fingers down the column of my throat, pressing them to my collarbone and pushing me back until I stood straight, noble, as if my dress wasn’t stained and torn, and my boots didn’t have holes in them from too many harvests.

He looked at me and saw something to polish and own, when all I wanted was to be free.

“It won’t happen again, my Lord,” I said, resisting the urge to mumble all over again.

"Be certain it doesn't," he said, removing his hand from my body and taking a step back. "I meant it when I told you there are things we need to discuss."

"We're both here now," I said, glancing over his shoulder. Even if the presence of the Mist Guard was a false comfort, it helped when I didn't feel alone with him. The worst of his punishments came where there were no prying eyes.

He studied me, stepping back and grasping his chin in the same fingers that had touched me. "Loris, would you be so kind as to help Miss Barlowe find her way to the library? We wouldn't want her to get lost again." Lord Byron turned to Loris with a stare, where he’d tried to hide behind other Mist Guard soldiers. Loris's throat worked as he swallowed, meeting Lord Byron's eyes and knowing the older man knew what he'd done, and he stepped forward with a brisk nod of his head.

"Yes, my Lord," he said, his voice carrying through the otherwise quiet space as his fellow guards, some of them friends, watched. He moved toward me, his face blank of all apology or care as he took my elbow in a tight grip and tugged me toward the manor.

I attempted to yank it away. "I can walk myself," I snapped, glaring at him. He didn't bother to turn his attention toward me or release me, instead setting a steady pace as he practically dragged me toward the manor in the distance.

"Perhaps this will serve as the reminder you needed that I am in charge, Estrella. Whatever happens in Mistfell is because I allow it. Because I own this village and everyone in it," Lord Byron said, taking up pace behind Loris and I as he left the meaning of his words to hang between us. I turned to look at him over my shoulder, watching him straighten his cloak and brush the rich red velvet over his shoulder as he met my gaze. "Just as I own you."

The light stone of Mistfell Manor gleamed in the moonlight as Loris led me along the path until we approached the servants' entrance at the side. The same entrance I used every time Lord Byron requested my presence in his library and I had to sneak into the house without alerting one of the High Priest's spies. The Ladies of the Night entered through the front door, their presence anything but hidden, while he snuck me in through the side as if I was the dirty secret no one could ever know about.

One of the manor guards hurried to open the door for us as Loris guided me inside, taking me through the halls quickly until he placed a hand on the gilded handle of one of the enormous library doors and shoved it open for us to enter.

As soon as we'd stepped over the threshold onto the polished stone, veined with gold, Loris released me and turned his face downward toward the floor as I stumbled to catch my footing. I lifted my hand to rub at my elbow, the skin blooming with a bruise. Loris watched from the corner of his eye, his face pinching as he witnessed the show of vulnerability for a moment.

The betrayal lingered between us, even knowing what he would choose if forced to decide between his affection for me and his duty to Mistfell. I'd only deceived myself when I tried to convince myself I didn't care. The hurt made my throat tight, leaving me to swallow against it as I tore my eyes from his and looked around the room I was too familiar with.

"Leave us," Lord Byron barked as he stepped into the room, dismissing the Mist Guard from our presence for what came next. For the punishment that had to follow.

“What do you propose I should do with you for your continued disobedience, Miss Barlowe?” he asked the moment the doors to the library closed behind the retreating guards, sealing me into the room that I'd come to dread more than anything. I'd come to hate this place for the association it bore with my own pain and the depravity of Lord Byron's actions within those four walls.

Books lined the ornate, wooden shelves. Stacked to the ceiling with generations worth of knowledge that required ladders to access. Knowledge that Lord Byron himself could very rarely be bothered to read; his focus on the present and growing his own power within the Kingdom demanded too much of his time.

His desk sat at the back edge of the room, parchment laid out on top next to his bottle of ink and quill. I'd spent far too many nights bent over the surface, my nails gripping the edge of the smooth, polished wood as I listened to the whistle of his switch cutting through the air, waited for the fire of his strike.

How many nights had I spent reading the texts he assigned to me, filling my head with the chastity of The Mother and the consequences for sin, while he wrote letters to the King in Ineburn City? I'd lost count long ago, and something like desolation made my chest throb.

He moved to the decanter on his desk, calmly pouring himself a glass of red wine. With his back to me, he reached up and unclasped his cloak, draping it over the chair beside his desk. "I would never assume myself worthy of determining my own punishment, my Lord," I said, biting my tongue to keep from worsening whatever might be coming.

He poured another glass of wine, turning and holding it out to me. "Drink," he instructed. I stepped forward, confusion furrowing my brow as I closed the distance between us. In all my nights spent in the library with him, he'd never offered me wine. "It will help you relax, and for tonight, I think that is needed."

It would dull my senses too much, according to him, and vertigo made the room spin as I closed the distance between us and accepted the glass from his hand. What kind of torment did he have planned where this was necessary in his mind?

"I'm sure you must have questions," he said, leaning back until he rested against his desk with his arms crossed over his chest. I took my first sip of wine, the bitter notes making my face pinch.

I nodded, not lending voice to any of them. I knew better than to assume this was an invitation to question his motives, as if I had any understanding of the games he played.

"Always so curious. Sit," he said, gesturing to the chair directly in front of him. I obeyed, lowering myself into it as he refilled his glass and took out yet another one to fill. "You get one question, Estrella. That is the extent of my kindness after your behavior today."

I swallowed, taking another sip of my wine as I met his harsh stare. "Why did you not send me to be trained with the Ladies of the Night? Why didn't the physician report me as impure?" I asked, catching myself before I could continue on. The urgent thoughts running through my head demanded attention, and perhaps the smartest question to ask would have been about the High Priest's plans for me in the name of The Father.

But I couldn't think about that, about the possibility of dying in the same way my father had years ago. Not if I wanted to keep breathing, to keep functioning until the moment of my death arrived.

"That was two questions," Lord Byron said, raising an eyebrow as he scoffed. "But the answer is the same for them both." I heaved a sigh of relief, hoping this would mean he wouldn't penalize me for my impudence. He pulled a small vial out of his pocket, staring at it for a moment in thought before he twisted the cork out of the top and placed it on the desk. "You were always a pretty girl." He tipped the vial over, pouring the amber liquid into the third glass of wine. The bittersweet aroma of belladonna filled the air as he emptied the vial into the glass, lightening the color of the wine a fraction.

"My Lord," I murmured, my voice hushed as my body went still. A dose of belladonna like that would be lethal, would make certain I never saw the morning come. He lifted it from the desk, stepping around me and moving toward the library doors. He knocked on them, waiting until a servant pushed them open and accepted the wine from him without a word. She left the library, closing the doors behind her as Byron turned back toward me and stood beside my chair.

"She was meant to die slowly, gradually, over the years so that no one would suspect anything, but it appears we have run out of time," he said, running the backs of his knuckles over the side of my cheek as I tried to process what he was saying.

I kept my mouth shut, not asking the question that didn't concern me. Whoever he'd sent that poison to, I couldn't let my curiosity prevent me from having the answers to what actually mattered to my life.

He waited, smirking down at me when I bit my tongue. "I prevented the physician from reporting you and didn't send you to train as a Lady of the Night because that would have interfered with a plan that I've been working toward for a very long time." He reached over, capping the vial of poison and depositing it into the waste bin beside his desk. "You would have ruined everything had I not intervened."

"Lady Jaclen—" I said, snapping my mouth shut before the question could come. My tongue burned with the force of my bite, my hands trembling where I clasped them on my lap.

"Will be dead before morning," her husband said, leaning back onto his desk once more. He stretched his hand out and caught my chin, leaning forward until his face was only a breath away from mine. "Do you understand now, Estrella?"

I nodded, squeezing my eyes closed as the horror of his intentions took root inside of me. I'd always thought myself safe from that kind of attention, so long as he never discovered I was not a virgin. Another man would take me in that way, but I'd thought myself safe from him, at the very least.

I'd never truly been safe at all.

"Why did you allow it to continue?" I asked, risking the next question.

He grinned, something evil lurking in his eyes, and I knew that whatever came next would horrify me. "Your virginity never mattered to me, though taking it would have been enjoyable. That is the High Priest's prerogative alone. If anything, your Mist Guard saved me the trouble of listening to you cry during your first time. Now I needn't worry about any of that nonsense, because he already broke you in. I might have arranged for it to happen myself, in time."

"But the High Priest said The Father has plans for me. I hardly think any of that matters now," I argued, trying to push away the image of what might have come. For once, the idea of being sacrificed to the Veil wasn't the worst horror I could imagine. "You can't make me your mistress if I'm dead."

"I wouldn't need to kill Jaclen for you to become my mistress," he said, grabbing a cloth off his desk. A bowl of water sat beside it, and he dipped it into the liquid as he lifted one of my shaking hands off my lap. "I need her to die so that you can become my wife."

I flinched, the agony of those words striking me like a physical blow. I couldn't be the Lady of Mistfell. I wouldn't long survive a life with Byron as my husband—my days and nights dominated by his demands and his company.

"I've shocked you. Why did you think I brought you here and taught you to read? Why did you think I taught you the decorum of a lady at great expense to myself? My whore would not need to have such abilities," he said, pressing the cloth into one of the wounds the twilight berries had left me with the day before.

"I never considered this," I admitted. It hadn't even been a possibility in my mind. Killing his wife, who was a distant relation to the King, was something unthinkable even for him.

"Mistfell needs an heir. Before the sacrifice tomorrow, I will announce Jaclen's death and inform the villagers that I have chosen another wife to give them the heir they deserve. They'll learn that The Father himself made his will for our union known to me as I sat beside Jaclen's death bed. The High Priest will not dare to take you from that divine purpose, and he will need to choose another to sacrifice. We'll be married within the week—"

"No." The word hovered between us, filling the library with the muted sound of my voice and the quiet defiance that I hadn't even meant to say aloud. My ears rang, while nausea swirled in my gut.

"What did you just say?" he asked, his body stilling as his gaze hardened into a glare. All traces of gentleness he'd deigned to show me as part of his act disappeared, the truth of him showing in his anger.

"No," I repeated, my voice coming through with more strength. My heart was in my chest, my skin slick with a cold sweat as I drew my line in the sand. Some fates were worse than death.

This was one of them.

"You do realize the alternative is having your throat slit, just like your father?" he asked, the incredulous laugh that fell from his lips only serving to make me more determined to escape him. To make the choice that he wouldn't approve of.

"I do" I lifted my chin and straightened my shoulders, projecting the posture of the woman he'd tried to mold me to become.

"Don't be ridiculous," he scoffed dismissively, but behind his gaze, disbelief turned into knowing. He knew as well as I did that I'd meant the word. That I fully intended to say no to him.

"I was six when you held me still and forced me to watch them slice my father's neck open. When they'd wrung all the blood they could from him, they burned him on a pyre and celebrated around his ashes. I hadn't even turned seven yet when you first invited me to this library and allowed the Priestess to beat me until I curtsied properly, until I stood straight enough, and I knelt as long as ordered without complaint. I have spent a lifetime tolerating your touch and your attention. No more," I said, the burn of tears stinging my throat and my nose and I held them back, refusing to give him that last part of me.

"And if I decide I do not need your permission? You think I have done all of this just to bow to your wishes?"

"Then I'll tell the High Priest what you've done. You cannot keep me alive and keep me silent, as well, my Lord. Whether it is tomorrow or in a year, I will tell anyone who'll listen that you've murdered your wife. What do you think the King would do with that information about his relative, when you and I both know you strive for far greater things than Mistfell?" I asked, sinking my teeth into my bottom lip. It wasn't a hollow threat; it was a promise I would spend every day of the rest of my life attempting to fulfill.

I just didn't know if the King or the High Priest would care, or if

Jaclen had any power at all, but his original plan to poison her slowly over the course of years made me think that maybe, just maybe, he would be condemned for his crime.

That damage was already done, the fatal dose of poison given to her before he spoke to me. He'd been so confident I would do as I was told and be who he wanted, he'd never stopped to consider that I would reject him.

"It would be such a waste of what could be a luxurious life. Think of what you would be able to give your family with me as your husband. They would be cared for beyond your wildest imaginings."

"They would," I agreed, nodding my head. Once upon a time, that had been everything I'd wanted, the promise I'd never thought to actually obtain. I was just so tired, so exhausted from the games I'd played to keep us alive for years. Brann would be more capable of providing for himself and my mother without me to consider.

They'd be okay.

"Take the night to think about it, and know that if you tell anyone what I've done, it will not be only you to suffer the consequences in the morning. I'm sure you'll change your mind by the ceremony tomorrow afternoon. It is easy to be brave when you think I'll back down, but I promise you, Estrella, if you don't come to me in the morning, you will die for your insolence."

"I would sooner die than allow you to shove that flaccid flesh between your legs inside me," I snapped, baring my teeth at him and allowing all the hatred I felt to show for once. So long, I'd been forced to play submissive to the man who dictated my life.

But he couldn't dictate what no longer existed.

The back of his hand cracked against my cheekbone, his signet ring cutting my cheek open on the spot that he'd already bruised earlier in the day. Darkness hovered at the edges of my vision as I sprawled to the floor.

"Get out of my fucking sight," he said, leaving me to pick myself up and move toward the library doors. "You will pay for that tomorrow night, Estrella. We both know you'll change your mind."

I put my hands on the doors, ignoring the throbbing in my cheek as

I shoved them open. Servants moved through the halls, panic on their faces as they paced. One shoved past me to enter the library, informing Lord Byron of his wife's passing.

Death called my name next.

I would step willingly into his embrace.

5

My last night in my bed was spent staring at the ceiling. Even the bone-weary exhaustion that had claimed each and every one of my muscles couldn't force me to sleep.

Rest eluded me, knowing that I'd be in the Void between lives in a matter of hours, and I had a brother and a mother sleeping down the hall with no idea how precious little time we had left together. The sun rose outside, the village sleeping a little bit later than usual with the harvest behind us. The festivities usually ran late into the night, with villagers surrounding the bonfires that they lit only one time during the year.

Celebration was frivolous and unnecessary, but it distracted people from the horrors of what they'd done. From the burning corpse on the pyre as a soul waited for reincarnation.

My bedroom door swung open and Brann stepped into the room as I slowly eased myself to a sitting position. "You've been out again," he said, his voice full of accusation as he approached my bed.

Under normal circumstances, this would have been the moment when I denied sneaking out, because Brann hadn't known about my meeting with Lord Byron. Without knowing exactly what would come of the conversation with the lord, I hadn't wanted to worry my brother needlessly.

Now I was grateful I hadn't said anything, wanting one last day with him and my mother that wasn't tainted by what was coming. It was better if they didn't know for as long as I could keep it from them, better if we didn't spend our morning grieving the loss that hadn't happened yet, the way we'd done with my father.

My lumpy mattress creaked as he sat down on the edge of it, his brow furrowing as his gaze fell to the fresh cut on my cheek that hadn't been there the day before. "What's this?" he asked, his nostrils flaring as he raised the backs of his knuckles to touch it gently.

"It's nothing," I said, shrugging off the touch with a smile that pulled at the tight skin.

"This is not nothing, Estrella. Did someone hit you? Were you caught out?" he asked, his logic automatically leading him to the punishment the Mist Guard would deliver to those who were found too close to the Veil in the night.

I might not have been delivered to the gallows immediately, but the end result of my wandering would be all the same. I shifted on the bed as it groaned again, imagining for just a moment how soft and plush the bed that waited for me in the manor must be.

As tempting as that thought may be, the prospect of who would occupy it with me was enough to pebble my flesh with goosebumps. All I'd ever wanted was to be free, and in the end, the pretty cage he offered was still just another prison.

"It doesn't matter. I promise; everything will be just fine," I said, swinging my legs over the side of the bed and standing with a dramatic stretch. The wood planks bowed beneath my weight, threatening to snap with the rot infecting our ramshackle home.

I could give them better, if I only spread my legs.

I winced. "Estrella," Brann scolded, reaching across the distance between us to grasp my forearm gently. "What's happened?" His inquisitive stare was too attentive for my liking, leaving me with little doubt that he wouldn't be able to let the issue rest until I gave him *something*.

"Lady Jaclen is dead," I said, my lips twisting as I admitted the words. My brother could know everything but the sacrifice. He could know what Byron had asked of me, because that was something he would have no choice but to resign himself to, and perhaps even see the benefit, too.

So long as Byron didn't poison me the same way he had Jaclen.

"She—what?" he asked, dropping his hand from my forearm. "You were at the manor last night? That's where you ran off to?"

"Lord Byron requested my presence in the library again," I admitted, sinking my teeth into the inside of my cheek. He didn't know the details of what happened within those luxurious walls lined with books, only that I never wanted to speak of the bruises and stripes covering my back and thighs sometimes.

He'd press. I'd refuse to answer, but we both knew it didn't take a genius to put the pieces together. We'd all seen the way Bernice favored her cane at Temple.

"I assume there's to be a funeral today?" Brann asked, his head nodding as he considered the information. He didn't question Jaclen's cause of death, as I suspected most wouldn't. She'd been sick for years, Byron's deception of her failing health serving its purpose in making her death seem natural.

"I assume. Lord Byron has declared his intentions to marry me after the rites," I admitted, making him squeeze his eyes closed.

"I had a feeling he would," he said finally. "There have been a couple of suitors who inquired about your hand in marriage over the years. We submitted the details to Lord Byron for approval, but he denied each one without explanation. I know it isn't the kind of life you'd hoped for," Brann said gently, reaching across the space between us to place his hand on top of my shoulder. "But that kind of title is something none of us could have ever dreamed of for you. He'll take care of you, keep you fed and rested. Particularly if he intends to have children quickly." His face pinched as he stepped away from me, beginning to pace as if he knew exactly what battle was ahead of him.

To some, the life that Lord Byron offered me seemed like a dream. All I had to do was spread my legs when he desired, and I'd live in the nicest building in the village. I'd be warm, with servants to take care of my every need as I raised my children without any of the fear of going hungry that most of the villagers faced.

"I don't want to be taken care of. I want to come and go as I please, and live," I argued. To be forced to submit to a man I didn't want for the bare necessities in life wasn't living.

It was just not dying.

"That is not the way our world works, Estrella. For now, this is your place," he said, but the gentleness in his eyes communicated that he didn't like the status quo any more than I did. He wanted freedom for me; he was just as powerless as I was to achieve it.

"And what happens to me if Lord Byron is in fact the one who is incapable of producing an heir, and I do not give him a son, Brann? Does that mean there will be a slow death by belladonna waiting for me as well?" I asked, scoffing at the shocked expression on his face.

"He poisoned her?" Brann asked, his throat working as he swallowed against the tightness there.

I turned my back on Brann's shocked expression, unable to tolerate his ignorance for another moment. Arguing about my place in Lord Byron's life was not how I wanted to spend my last day with my family, not when I'd already made my decision. Every moment I spent hating him in the aftermath of what he'd done only served to solidify that choice.

I'd walk to my death with my head held high rather than spend the rest of a long life on my knees.

My mother waited in the kitchen, her chair already pulled up to the table where she struggled to slice through the stale loaf of bread resting on top. "Let me," I said, taking the knife from her hand and slicing through the bread quickly. I spread her favorite homemade jam on top of it, handing it to her and turning away to allow her to have a private moment of feeling embarrassed.

She'd never adjusted to being taken care of by her children after her husband died, and with every year that passed the weakness in her body worsened, spreading from her legs to her upper limbs. Her hands shook as she raised the bread to her mouth and took a bite, chewing slowly.

"You're happy here, aren't you?" I asked, dropping the knife into the bucket of dishes I would need to take out to wash in the basin outside before we left for the celebration. The last thing I wanted to do was leave them with work to worry over while they were grieving.

She smiled wistfully, saying, "Of course I am, sweetheart. This is the only place that reminds me of your father." I bit back the flame inside at the reminder, seeing the phantom of his memory all over the kitchen and realizing that, soon enough, my ghost would join his. My mother would only have her recollections of our moments together to remember me by. "Besides, Lord Byron has been so accommodating with my condition. I couldn't expect to be treated better anywhere else. Why do you ask?"

"No reason," I said, forcing myself to shrug and smile back at her as tears stung my eyes. "Finish your toast. I'm going to wash these dishes. It's the last thing we'll want to deal with when we roll into bed after the celebration tonight."

"Aren't you going to eat something?" she asked, her brow furrowing in concern. If there was one thing I was known for, it was my love of food. There was never enough, and as such, I could never pass up the chance to eat. But I'd be gone in a few hours, anyway. They needed the food more than I did.

"I'm not very hungry today," I said, giving Brann a meaningful look when he finally stepped out of the hallway into the kitchen. My mother would have been pleased with Lord Byron's offer, knowing it would mean a better life for all of us. Like my brother, she didn't know all of the details of my relationship with him.

Unlike my brother, she had no idea why I'd wept every time she'd sent me to the manor with my Mist Guard escort when I'd been too young to walk alone. Brann and I had worked hard to protect her from my injuries, hiding me away for the worst of the healing.

I stepped out of the kitchen and went to wash the dishes as I'd said I would, leaving Brann to make excuses for my poor appetite. The yearly sacrifice made my stomach churn every year, seeing my father's face in each and every person they bled.

What would I see when it was my throat the knife came for?

6

The celebration was already in full swing by the time Brann pushed Mother's chair along the path at the center of the village. The Veil loomed in the distance, sparkling like a gateway to the afterlife.

For me, it would be.

My blood would stain the ground, my body left there to rot until the villagers brought me to the funeral pyre. I smiled at my brother for a moment as we walked, everything in me and our day spent together feeling like a deception. We'd entertained ourselves with a card game, the three of us sitting around the kitchen table in a way that was so rare when Brann and I always had to hustle to make sure our family survived.

The streets of the village were wide, the paths lined with dirt between the many houses and shops as we neared the central square. There was a well at the center where most of us drew our water, and the buildings surrounded it, curving around the edges of the dirt roads that were packed down from the foot traffic of villagers going about their day. There were dozens of buildings, all pressed neatly in rows beside one another to save space and protect from the elements once winter arrived. As the roads led farther from the main part of the village, the houses became more sporadic and in ill repair.

Lord Byron waited in the center of the village square as people offered him condolences on the loss of his wife. His eyes were heavy on my face as he waited for the conversation that we both knew we needed to have. He needed to understand that I wouldn't back down, and the speech he was prepared to give would not end the way he wanted. "I'll be right back," I said, touching Brann's arm with a smile before I took a deep breath.

My skin tingled, goosebumps rising to the surface beneath the fabric of my dress. It wasn't the autumn air that brought the chill to my skin, but the triumphant look on Byron's face as I crossed the distance between us.

"Estrella," he said, his lips tipping into the arrogant expression of a man who was so certain he'd caught his prey in his trap. "Walk with me."

"Yes, my Lord," I said, accepting the arm he proffered. A hush fell over the square, because the Lord of Mistfell shouldn't have offered his arm to a peasant woman. He shouldn't have bothered with me at all.

"I knew you'd change your mind," he said, guiding me down the path toward the gardens. Soon enough, everyone else would follow to witness the yearly sacrifice before the evening's celebration could begin in earnest.

"I have a question before I make my final decision," I said, not lifting my gaze to meet his eyes. His arm twitched with surprise, and I realized he truly believed, from something as simple as walking to his side, I had accepted his place in my life.

"Then ask it so we can be done with this nonsense. I need to make my announcement before the High Priest makes his," Lord Byron said, his voice filled with all his impatience. The fact that he'd even bothered to give me the illusion of a choice meant he truly feared what the King would do if news of his crime reached Ineburn City. He'd thought me so far beneath him that I couldn't hurt him the way he had hurt me.

Men always underestimated the women they saw as insignificant.

"Why did you choose me?" I asked, finally turning my gaze up to his. I kept my chin tipped down, peeking up at him through my lashes to offer the image he preferred to see. "We both know there are far more beautiful women you could have given favor to, so why?"

His jaw clenched, his eyes narrowing for a brief moment as he considered my question. "I didn't know you even existed until the day your father died. Most of the children remain silent if their parent is chosen, but not you, Estrella. You wept, sobbing so loudly I'm certain they heard you in the Hollow Mountains."

"You chose me because I cried for my dying father?" I asked, swallowing around the nausea rising up my throat.

"You must try to imagine what it's like being raised as the only son of a Lord. If you think I've been harsh with you, you know nothing of what it was like to be me as a child," he returned, his eyes looking into the distance as we strolled along the empty path. "I didn't grieve for my father when he died. Seeing you suffer so openly—the way you cried at Temple every week for months after his passing and couldn't even stand to look at the High Priest—that was what initially drew me to you. I didn't understand it for what it was at the time. I invited you to my library because I wanted to see that sadness in your eyes, but as the years passed and I remained without a child, I realized you could teach your children to love so fully, as well."

"You chose me because I loved my father, and you wanted me to teach our children to love you that way?" I asked, simplifying his response and taking out the horseshit that was designed to make me pity him.

I wouldn't, because he'd stopped being a victim a long time ago and chosen to abuse me, even knowing how much it hurt. My steps faltered as I considered whether he'd done it to others in secret, or worse, when he didn't have the prospect of marriage to restrain him from causing permanent damage.

"Yes. I chose you because you love with all your heart and do not care what people think of you for it. What more could a father want for his children?" he asked, turning to stare down at me in a moment of vulnerability. "They'll be lucky to have you."

He raised a hand to cup my face, the soft fingers of a life of luxury touching my swollen cheek. I wanted nothing more than to grab that hand and shove it away, but I let it stay as the first people started to trickle onto the path beside the gardens.

They passed us in silence, stepping onto overturned dirt from the gardens, which we'd pulled every plant out of during the harvest. They made their way toward the front in groups, approaching the place where the sacrifice happened every year with solemn expressions.

They'd be sad as they watched the horror unfold, but then they would celebrate as if I'd never existed.

"They won't," I said, murmuring the words quietly. My voice caught —the reality of what was to come staring me in the face. I couldn't look toward the gathering assembly without seeing my father unwillingly dragged to the front, the echo of my screams and the burn in my throat assaulting me through my memory.

"Estrella," he scolded, utter disbelief filling his expression as I took a step back.

"Your children were never going to love you the way I loved my father. Do you know why, *my Lord*?" I asked, letting the hatred I felt for him show in a rare moment of honesty. I couldn't do much to hurt him, not with the pyre calling me, but I could strip away the motivation for everything he'd spent over a decade working toward.

"Why?" he asked, his throat moving with his swallow.

He glanced over his shoulder at the figure lurking at my back. I didn't need to look to know who waited for me if I only turned, instead blasting Byron with the full force of my glare. "Because you will never be worthy of that kind of love."

"I won't intervene once you make this choice. You understand that?" he asked.

"I do," I said simply, lifting my chin higher as I stared back at him. I didn't expect him to, didn't even want him to; not when survival was tied to his bed and his sadistic pleasures.

Lord Byron's nostrils flared as he glared down at me, nodding briskly to the man behind me. I turned to the High Priest, finding his soft gaze on mine as he said, "You've been informed?"

"Can I say goodbye first?" I looked over his shoulder to where my mother and Brann approached the Veil. He heaved her wheeled chair over the raised rows of dirt in the enormous garden bed, pushing her forward as her body jostled.

"Of course," the High Priest answered, his words solemn as I stepped away from him and walked over to my family. I helped Brann, turning my back to the Veil and grabbing my mother's chair by the wheels and hauling it toward the shimmering white boundary.

Toward the place where she would have to sit and watch me die.

My one regret.

I smiled. The people around us faded into a haze until there was only my mother's eyes on mine, her sad expression filling her face as she undoubtedly remembered the times we'd made this journey in the past. She remembered my father pulling her to watch his sacrifice, Brann and I trailing behind them with tear-streaked faces.

We finally stopped moving, settling into a space that was as good as any. It was toward the back of the crowd, and I had to hope that would shield them from the worst of the details.

I lowered myself to a squat in front of her, taking her trembling hands in mine and pressing a kiss to the top of them. "I love you," I said softly, smiling through the burn in my throat. I shoved back the tears that threatened, memorizing her features for one last time.

Her brow furrowed as she gazed back at me, removing her hand from my grip to touch my cheek softly. "I love you too, my girl. It will all be over soon," she said, assuming the sadness in my eyes was due to the torment I felt on this day every year.

I pushed to my feet, stepping around the edge of her chair to draw Brann into a hug. I squeezed him too tightly, savoring the moment his arms wrapped around me. "Estrella, what's going on?" he asked, pulling back to look down into my face.

"Take care of each other," I said, staring at him meaningfully.

The High Priest's voice interrupted whatever he might have said next, arrowing through the garden like the crack of a whip as everyone fell silent. "Would the chosen please step forward?"

I pulled out of Brann's embrace, turning slowly and drawing a deep breath. Facing the Veil ahead of me, my eyes landed on where the High

Priest waited with the ceremonial dagger clutched in his grip. It was the same blade that had parted the flesh of my father's throat fourteen years prior.

I chanced a glance over to where Lord Byron waited at the High Priest's side, his face closed off and expression reserved. There was nothing to be seen of his frustration on his stoic face—only the hands clenched at his side.

Another breath, and I took my first step forward toward my death.

"Estrella," Brann said, his voice oddly calm as he began to understand my movements. Another step, and the eyes of the villagers focused on me as whispers broke out. It was unheard of for two generations of one family line to be chosen by The Father. "Estrella!" my brother repeated as I took the third step.

I moved through the people gathered, allowing them to part and reveal a direct path for me to approach the Veil. No one wanted to get in the way of the sacrifice. No one wanted to risk drawing attention to themselves.

"No! Not my baby girl!" my mother cried out behind me. Her voice trembled, her words shaking just like her hands as I squeezed my eyes closed and kept walking forward. This was never the fate any of us had seen in store for me, but as I moved through the foggy details of the crowd surrounding, my father's last words to me rang in my ears.

Fly free, Little Bird.

I never had. I'd never escaped the life that he'd hated with every part of his being, but something in me felt freedom waiting just beyond.

I stepped in front of the High Priest, bowing my head forward in submission as my mother sobbed behind me. Her wails echoed through the gardens, each one striking against my heart.

"Kneel," the High Priest said, the order a murmur between the two of us as he guided me forward. The Veil swayed just in front of me, close enough to touch, and for just one moment I pictured reaching out to touch it.

I wondered what would happen if I did, then watched my fingers stretching forward as if compelled. The magic pulsing off of it touched my skin, sliding over my fingers as the curtain swayed toward me in perfect unison. The High Priest pressed his hand to the top of my shoulder, guiding me to my knees. The movement pulled my hand away from the magic that covered my skin before I could touch the Veil itself, tearing away the warmth I'd almost known.

In a world filled with nothing but cold, bitter half-truths, the Veil beckoned like a warm embrace, welcoming me into a place where I would be protected at all costs.

My hands dropped to my thighs as my knees hit the sandy soil beneath me, my palms facing the sky as I tipped my head up to stare into the eyes of the High Priest. He stood just to the side of me, his body close enough that he could stop me from falling into the Veil itself when I died, but out of the way so that my blood would stain the soil and not him.

"We thank you for your sacrifice, Estrella Barlowe of Mistfell. May you find peace in your next existence, wrapped in the arms of The Mother." He sank his hand into the hair at the back of my head, gripping the strands tightly to pull me to the angle he needed. The tip of that dagger pressed into the side of my throat, digging into the flesh as the warmth of blood trickled down my skin. "Close your eyes now, child."

His eyes bore into mine, willing me to do as commanded. I understood at that moment that he didn't want to watch the life fade from my eyes as he slit my throat—that he took no pleasure in doing the will of The Father.

I did, letting them drift closed. Ringing filled my ears, drowning out my mother's hoarse cries and the sound of Brann trying to console her. My body filled with warmth despite the cool ocean breeze against my face, like the press of a warm hearth on a cold winter's night, the stars shimmering outside the window as I cuddled up with a book.

It was the first moment of contentment I'd felt, the first moment when there wasn't any pain. I didn't want to hurt anymore. I didn't want to be afraid of what was to come.

I drew in a breath, feeling the High Priest dig his knife deeper into my skin and begin to drag it to the side. Sudden awareness burst through my contentment, the impression of someone banging on the other side of a doorway, though there was none to be found.

The world shook as an animalistic roar came from the other side of the Veil in front of me, raising the hair on my arms, and making the back of my neck tingle.

My eyes sprang open to watch a streak of black surge through the fabric of the Veil. "Did you see that?" Lord Byron asked, stepping forward and closing the distance between us. I turned my attention back to him, following his line of sight to where a ripple of bright light followed the black surge.

Behind me, everyone froze as a collective unit as we stared in awe-filled horror at the Veil. The Mist Guards approached the boundary, their hands on the hilts of their swords as they prepared for the worst.

"What do we do?" Lord Byron asked, staring at the curtain of magic as it pulsed and throbbed as if it was being battered against from the other side. Sounds of tearing and wordless anger crossed through the barrier, while silence reigned on our side.

Another shock of inky darkness spread through it, throbbing in time with the beating of my heart in my chest. I couldn't breathe, didn't dare to close my eyes as I rose to my feet. "We need to strengthen the Veil," the High Priest said, turning to me once again.

He touched my shoulder, shoving me to my knees in a way that was far less graceful than I'd managed the first time. I sprawled forward, landing on my hands and knees with my face only a breath from the shimmering and pulsing magic. Blood dripped from my throat and landed upon the soil, trickling over the grains as if in slow motion.

The ground convulsed as if the world itself was angry, quaking beneath me as another wave of black rippled through the wavering white at the edge of the boundary. The High Priest moved toward me, his knife coming straight for my throat in a way that I knew would kill me without delay.

I reached out with one hand, touching a single finger to the magic that called to me. A shock of electricity spread up my arm, drawing a pained gasp from my lips as the sky rumbled in response, the sound reverberating through the open field of gardens.

The High Priest froze as he stared at the way darkness bled through the Veil, bathing the world in shadow and drowning out the sun. It spread forward, oozing across the sky until it covered the clouds above, eclipsing all the light from our world. "What have you done?" His eyes were wide with terror, having heard the myths we'd all been taught. The legends of what lies beyond the Veil shaped us all, a warning of what could come if we made the mistake of poking at things that were better off left alone.

Of the monsters who would come to steal us from our beds in the night, never to be seen again. Of the humans unfortunate enough to be marked by the Fae, chosen for a life that amounted to being nothing more than a wretched pet.

The ground shook so violently that the High Priest and Lord Byron fell to their knees beside me. The people closest to the boundary behind us screamed, turning and racing through the gardens that stood between them and safety as cracks fissured through the Veil and the mist that separated our worlds filtered through.

Black streaks penetrated the mist, creeping like spider veins over the horizon. The Veil stopped blowing in the wind, suddenly, as if frozen to glass.

"Run," Lord Byron whispered, getting to his feet clumsily. There was nothing but panic in his expression, the terror of what would come should the magic fail after centuries of protecting us.

And then the Veil shattered.

Broken shards rained down across the crops closest to the boundary. The wave of pure, undiluted power broke across the field. In the place where the Veil had once shimmered, only the wall of mist between realms remained, open to any who dared to traverse the land and sea between realms, to cross from here over to Alfheimr or enter the realm of humans.

Time slowed, and what felt like an eternity passed while I turned my head and locked eyes with Lord Byron. He fell first, knocked backward before I felt the blast of inky power against my skin. Like nothing I'd ever felt before, it seeped into the cracks in my skin and made itself at home within this body, which had once been mine, but now felt like something else entirely.

The power sank inside me before it shoved me backward, lifting me off my hands and knees and twisting my body in the air with the force of the explosion that rippled through the gardens. I only stopped when my spine hit the soil and my eyes stared up at the slowly blackening sky, as those tendrils of darkness wound their way around the sun.

Night fell in truth, and when the blades of grass tickled my skin where it peeked out of my dress and light cloak, for a brief moment, I wondered if the sun would ever rise again.

And then I felt nothing but blinding pain.

7

My entire body throbbed as I fought my way to my knees, gasping through the pain that erupted inside me, as if my very soul was being burned alive and ripped in two, tearing through my skin until it was open for all to see.

My determination to check on my family was enough motivation to push through. I sank one hand into the dirt beneath me, clawing at the grains until they wedged under my nails. The other went to the searing pain on my neck, covering the skin that felt hot to the touch. I tore my hand away before the burn could scald it, my neck sizzling like a fresh brand on a horse's hide.

I spun as I stood, glancing over to where Brann knelt over our mother, her chair knocked backwards by the force of the shattering Veil. His gaze met mine, his wide eyes filled with terror as I closed the distance between us. The High Priest and Lord Byron hadn't yet managed to get to their feet, lying on the ground as I moved past them in confusion.

Why wasn't anyone else moving?

Brann shoved our mother's chair upright as I knelt in front of her, grasping my cloak and bunching it up around my neck. My skin burned anew when his fingers brushed against me, and I barely resisted the urge to scream out in pain, to vent my agony into the darkened sky, but something written in the lines of his face warned me to stay quiet.

I drew in deep lungfuls of air instead as my eyes watered, my throat closing around the need to free the icy fire spreading through my body. "It hurts," I whispered as my mother snagged my gaze, her eyes filling with tears while she stared at me and then slowly nodded to Brann with some meaning that I didn't understand.

"Shh. You have to be quiet," Brann murmured, taking my elbow and helping me back to my feet. The Mist Guards around the gardens had finally shoved their way to their feet, as well, gripping their blades tightly as they moved through the people who remained lying on the ground.

My mother grabbed my hands, squeezing them and leaning forward to place a lingering kiss on the back of each one. "Take her and go," she said to my brother, her voice dropping low, in command despite the tremble of her bottom lip.

"What? Why would we—" I fell silent when Brann nudged me with his elbow, taking my hands from our mother's. He lifted the hood on my cloak up to cover my neck fully, pulling the braid out of my hair with frenzied fingers that tugged at the strands until they fell around my shoulders and hung around my face. "Brann," I murmured, lost in the urgency of his expression.

What was wrong with him?

He caught my hand in his, starting to inch us back toward the woods at the edge of the gardens. We watched to see if anyone would notice as we slipped away while Mother nodded in encouragement. My gaze went back and forth between them, not understanding what was happening.

Where were we going?

Brann paused, wincing as his eyes caught on something in the front row of twilight berries. A Mist Guard stood over Rook, one of the swordsmiths from our village, and glared down at the spot where he clutched his neck. Pain had transformed his face into a picture of torment, and I lifted a hand to touch the same spot on my body—the very same place that had burned with cold heat when Brann's hand brushed against it.

"Please, don't!" Rook yelled. The guard ignored him, shoving his blade through the smith's chest and pinning him to the ground before he withdrew it. The villager's eyes relaxed almost instantly, his chest shuddering with his final breath as I lifted a hand to cover my mouth and keep silent.

He'd been a well-loved member of the community. He'd supplied the Mist Guard with the very swords he'd used to run him through. There'd been no moment when I ever thought they would be capable of executing him so coldly.

But with the Fae able to walk among us once again, anything was possible.

"He was Marked," my brother said pointedly, his eyes dropping to the cape that concealed my burning flesh, which seemed to worsen with every moment that passed. As if something cut through me, bit by bit, tearing the skin from my body to reveal that which should have always been there.

The Mist Guard kicked Rook's hand away from his neck, giving me my first view of the swirling patterns on his skin. They glowed the color of freshly grown grass in spring, the Mark of the Fae whose magic claimed him as her consort. An otherworldly scream filled with anguish made the ground tremble all over again, and it took me far too long to realize it hadn't been one of the beasts from the caves in the woods.

The sound came from a female on the other side of the Mist, feeling the loss of a treasure she'd only just found.

Something like her would come for me.

I reached up, sliding my hand inside my cloak to touch that cold fire on my skin as understanding crashed over me in sudden awareness.

Oh Gods.

I turned back to my mother, her words lost to the wind that howled toward us over the open water where the Veil had once been, but her lips moved clearly, making sure I could understand even with the distance between us. "Go. Quickly," my mother mouthed, turning to watch Lord Byron as Brann pulled me toward the trees. The woods were dark and menacing without the sun shining down between the branches, and fear lodged deep in my chest. Even I didn't dare to wander in the woods in this kind of darkness, without the moon and stars to illuminate the dangers waiting for us.

I didn't want to leave her, to abandon her to the village and the danger that was coming.

"Brann, the woods—"

"At least you'll stand a chance this way," he said, picking up his pace as we ducked beneath the low-hanging branches at the edge of the forest. Even having seen what had come of Rook, even understanding what that Mark on his neck had meant in the vaguest sense, the reality of what that meant for me lingered just out of reach.

All that mattered in the moment was survival, and that the people I'd worked alongside, who'd been a part of my life for as long as I could remember, would now want me dead.

The very same man who'd only moments ago been determined to stall my execution, so he could get me into his bed, would now be the one to order it, as if I'd never existed in the first place, wiped from memory and record. I'd been willing to die, but not like this.

"Find her!" Lord Byron shouted behind us, and Brann and I exchanged a quick glance before we picked up our pace.

I could barely make out his features as he ran by my side, barely see my hand in front of my face with the darkness spreading across the sky. My cloak slipped as I hurried, dropping away from my neck, and the sudden burst of white light that filled the trees drew a startled gasp from me as I stumbled.

Any doubt I might've had whether the magic of Faerie had claimed me was gone in that moment.

The rest of my left arm burned, a line trailing down from my neck until even my fingers felt like they'd been lit on fire. I watched as black and luminous white swirls appeared on my wrist, giving way to a black moon that covered the top of my hand as I came to a complete halt in the middle of the clearing.

My legs stopped moving. They stopped listening to my brain

entirely as I pulled my unmarked hand away from Brann and met his eyes with fear. "Estrella, what are you doing?!"

"They won't stop," I said, a ragged breath leaving me with the realization. They would hunt me down until they found me, kill anyone who helped me, and burn entire cities to keep me from being taken by the Fae who would make me his consort.

From the Fae who would become stronger with his mate at his side.

"We'll deal with that later. Please," he said, reaching out to take my hand once again. I knew without a doubt that all I would achieve by running with him was to put him in danger, and I couldn't risk his life for this.

Even if we managed to get away. Even if the Fae didn't cross the Mist, what kind of life could he have on the run with me? What kind of life could our mother have without either of us to take care of her?

"I love you," I whispered. Taking his hand in mine, I squeezed one last time and then pushed him so hard he stumbled back into the brush on the edge of the narrow path and disappeared beneath the massive fern leaves.

The footsteps that sounded behind me seemed to loosen my feet, letting me turn slowly to face the guards who had watched me grow up. Who had known me when I'd been nothing more than a child, and would still put a blade through my heart without hesitation, ensuring that I would never reincarnate. There would be no more lives for me, not with my soul destroyed along with my heart.

The Fae could never be allowed to have their human consorts, in this life or the next. Of all the myths that had been lost over the centuries, all the legends, and the reasons and the whys, that one truth remained.

When a Fae took his human consort, the consequences were devastating.

"Gods," Loris murmured as he stared at me, and I felt the glowing marks on my skin pulse in response to his words, as if they'd awakened something within me. "Is that..." he trailed off, and my heart dropped into my stomach when he seemed like he didn't dare to speak of that which had marked my skin.

Of the monster who sought to own me.

I didn't know enough of the legends, because only the guards needed to know the specifics of what they might face when the Fae finally broke through the Veil. The rest of us knew only what they deemed necessary.

When the Fae crossed the Veil once more, all would be lost.

"Kill her. Quickly," one of the oldest guards said as he came up behind the younger two. The one at Loris's side was his friend, someone I'd seen him with often during his hours on duty. "Don't let her suffer," the older man said, and tears stained my cheeks as I turned back to Loris and our eyes connected.

"Loris," I said, swallowing past the lump in my throat. I didn't have many friends, particularly not within the Mist Guard, since they were considered above and beyond the trivialities of man. But he'd been one of the few I trusted—enough to let him have my body, and to know about the nighttime walks in the woods, and to share those moments when I shed the roles I was expected to fill and just became me.

The betrayal threatened to cleave my heart in two, even knowing that he was right in his purpose. There was no point in escaping, because the alternative was a fate worse than death.

Being found by the Fae.

"I can't," he said, shaking his head and turning back to face his superior, staring into the face of the man who had trained him and been all but a father to him over the years.

"You will," he ordered. "She's not the girl you knew anymore. Now she's nothing more than some Fae bastard's whore."

I winced, feeling those words resonate somewhere deep within me. My Mark revolted, writhing and twisting inside me as if it had a rage all its own, and I shoved it down. That was my future, if I lived. Death would be a blessing.

Loris stepped forward, his face twisting into a pained grimace when I made no move to run from the fate that was coming for me. The ferns at the edge of the path rustled as Brann moved, vaulting to his feet when he realized Loris intended to follow through. I pinned my brother with a look, trying to communicate the inevitability of what was coming.

"I'm sorry," Loris said, and the pain in his voice left me with no doubt that his words were sincere. But duty came first.

"Me too," I said, wishing it could have been anyone else. I had no relationship with any of the other Mist Guards and generally thought they were terrifying and cold.

But he'd been different.

He swallowed, lunging forward with his sword and looking to the side, as if he couldn't bear to watch as he fulfilled his duty. I lifted my hands instinctively, flinching back from the impending blow with a shudder.

But the pain never came.

I opened my eyes to watch as Loris tried to pull his sword free from the ball of swirling light held between my hands. Tendrils of it climbed up over the hilt, twining around his wrist and up his arm while I watched on like a spectator. The icy fury in my hands was so cold it burned as a flame spread through my chest and the white fingers of light seared through Loris's leathers to get to his skin beneath.

His eyes widened in a moment of shock, and then his mouth dropped open in a silent scream. "Estrella," he gasped, and I released a loud sob as Brann took a step toward me.

"Don't," I warned him. There was no controlling the power that came from within me, nothing to stop the instinctive protection that acted without my permission. "Stop," I begged the magic, whimpering as those vines of white crept up over Loris's neck and touched his face. His brown eyes filled with white, the skin on his face cracking, and he seemed to age before my eyes. And all I could do was watch in shock as I drained every hint of life from his body.

As the *thing* that had claimed my body used me as a weapon.

My old friend's head twisted to the side suddenly, the snap of his neck echoing through the silent woods, and his body crumpled to the forest floor. By the time he touched the brittle leaves of autumn, he was nothing but a pile of snow on the ground.

The older guard stared down in surprise at what had been one of his men, his brow furrowing as his mind tried to make sense of what he'd seen. Of what I'd done, that even I couldn't understand.

"I don't want to hurt you," I said, shaking my head from side to side. The magic in me didn't care about what I wanted, only about keeping me alive, and preserving my safety until the male who commanded it could find me.

When the guard struck, I threw my weight back to the forest floor to try to spare his life, but the vines of white took what they wanted anyway, wrapping around his throat and squeezing. He dropped his sword to clutch at them, desperate with the need to breathe past the suffocating embrace of the magic. He soon joined the pile of snow by my feet as I let out a strangled sob. The single remaining Mist Guard retreated, hurrying back to Mistfell and safety from the power taking control of me.

It had all happened so quickly. They were there one moment, ready to kill me to save me from what would come, and then they were just...gone.

"We have to move," Brann said, but he kept his distance and didn't take my hand.

"I-I—" I tried to find words to communicate the emptiness that filled my chest. What I'd done could never be forgiven.

"Move!" he ordered, the sharp sound of his voice through the woods snapping me out of my moment.

Others would follow when they realized Loris and the other guard hadn't returned.

I didn't want to kill them, too.

8

Everything ached. My body throbbed with each and every step that took us farther from the village that had been our entire world. Leaving my mother behind without anyone to care for her wasn't something that I understood how to accept, looking at Brann where he walked by my side.

He belonged with her. I was supposed to be dead anyway.

As the hours passed, wandering through the night that had come in the middle of the day, I grew more and more resolved to make Brann return home. There would be no one to protect our mother when the Fae crossed the mist and came to Nothrek once again. No one to stop them from cutting her down along with the rest of Mistfell in their hunt for the Fae Marked.

I'd need to do whatever it took to send him back to take care of her while I continued forward on my own, running until there was nowhere left to go.

"You have to go back," I gasped. My lungs burned with the cold, heaving with exertion as we ran through the woods. Brann raced at my side, his longer legs keeping pace easier than mine, and I had to put everything I had into the deadly sprint to keep up with him. Pain tore through my side, the muscles cramping as everything inside me seized.

I hadn't had a moment to rest or recover from the magic that had changed me as the Veil fell, not in the hours since we'd started running. There wasn't time for such luxuries when my life was on the line.

Branches tore at my face when the path faded into nothing but the haunting shadows of darkness, and I couldn't tell if the rustling leaves were the ones beneath my feet or if something else was in the woods with us.

All manner of animals lived in them, from the rabbits that had no doubt made a dash for their warrens, to the rock trolls that lurked in the caves during the day. Their heavy footfalls that shook the ground would have felt different from a rustle, but the arachne and snakes could have kept pace alongside us in the dark without ever being seen.

"I can't," Brann said, and even though I couldn't see him, I could swear I felt him shake his head in denial. "Listen to me, Estrella. No matter what happens, you cannot let the Fae catch you. Do you understand?"

"I know that," I wheezed, panting through the effort to keep up with him. How he wasn't even the slightest bit winded, I would never understand. Brann had always been the fastest boy in our village. One of the strongest fighters, even though he had no interest in joining the Mist Guard.

Pain exploded across my forehead suddenly as something struck me, a flare of white spreading across my vision. I stumbled to the side and raised my arm to touch the thick branch that had knocked my head back. Falling to my knees, I touched the bleeding wound at my hairline and wiped the moisture on the cloak I couldn't even see in the pitch black.

"Estrella!" Brann hissed in a whisper, and his booted foot touched my knee as he felt around for me. "Get up."

He didn't bother to check to see if I'd recover or ask what happened; only his urgency to put distance between us and the monsters that would follow drove him forward. "I can't," I said as my vision swam in a swirl of darkness and shadows.

A howl came through the trees on a blast of frosty wind, and everything inside me cramped with terror. "The Wild Hunt is coming," I said, voice hollow.

The pounding of hoof beats echoed through the sky like thunder. My heart lurched, and, glancing into the darkness behind me, I couldn't even see the trees we'd only just passed through. The darkness surrounding me only added to my rising fear, leaving me certain that something was watching us.

Something I couldn't see.

"Get up," Brann repeated. He fumbled for my arm, grasping my elbow and hauling me to my feet.

"You should leave me," I warned, tugging at my elbow as he helped me through the woods. He slowed his pace, giving me time to catch my breath before quickening his steps when the heavens flashed with a plethora of colors that tore through the onyx sky.

"I will never leave you," he said, even as he faltered, turning his face up to watch the black of night stained with watercolor pastels, which twirled and slithered through the clouds.

My mouth dropped open as I watched the colors writhe and twine, consumed by the unearthly beauty, which didn't belong in the human realm. In the silence that followed as we stared at the sky in wonder, the burning of my lungs seemed to settle with a begrudging acceptance.

I would never be able to hide from beings who were strong enough to paint the sky. I'd never tasted true freedom, so consumed by the life laid out for me in Mistfell that I'd never thought to wonder what might be waiting for me further inland.

Now I never would.

Drawing a deep breath of frigid air into my lungs, I turned to stare at my brother's face. Illuminated under the watercolor sky, his amber eyes reflected the light until the moment when he turned his face down to stare at me. He swallowed, the breath catching in his lungs when a flock of birds whipped over our heads and navigated through the trees, as if the risk of flying into a tree was far less than the danger that followed at their tails.

Another pair of amber eyes stared back at me: the only bird that didn't flee in terror. The eerie eyes of the blight gleamed in the darkness before it took off into the sky and was lost to the night.

"We have to keep moving," Brann said, pressing forward and dragging me along with him. My steps were slower, and dread settled over me for the day when I would need to say goodbye. Because the emotion I'd seen in his eyes only confirmed what I had already known in my heart.

We both knew parting would be inevitable.

His golden hair gleamed with the colors in the sky every time we came to an opening in the trees, and I tried to focus on him. On his strength beside me, pushing and pulling me to keep trying.

A scream pierced the air far behind us, drawing a shudder from him.

"We'll never outrun them," I said, knowing it would be pointless in the end. Even without knowing what kind of magic they had that would enable them to travel across the human lands, we were on foot. We were tired, and we were not used to walking long distances, let alone running. The arduous pace we'd set at the start of our journey hours ago wasn't sustainable.

But even if it had been, it wouldn't have been enough.

Brann nodded, seeming to accept the truth as I spoke it. We kept walking through the woods, staying as quiet as we could, as we both understood that any noise could be our downfall.

After what felt like an eternity of walking in silence, the colors in the sky disappeared in a slow wave of black that seemed to swallow the rest of the light from the world. My stomach clenched inside me, tightening as the black swirls on my arm felt as if they writhed in response to that eerie darkness.

"He's here," I whispered, turning to look for the brother I couldn't see, as the woods were plunged into darkness once again.

"Who?" he asked, his voice so quiet that I knew instantly he already knew the answer.

I didn't know his name—this faceless Fae who thought to claim me through magic.

But I felt him, pulsing inside me like an infection in my blood. It was different from the knowledge that the Wild Hunt were hunting through the Kingdom, the howl of their hounds and stomp of horse's hooves echoing through the air.

I'd felt the moment his feet touched the human realm, treading upon the soil of Nothrek. I felt him inside my skin, my Mark writhing as if it could reach out and call to him.

"*Him*," I said, and Brann's presence at my side disappeared as he stumbled. Just like that, he was gone, lost to the night in a way I didn't have a hope of finding him by sight. "Are you okay?" I asked, lowering myself to a crouch and feeling around the ground. The dirt beneath the layer of leaves on the forest floor was damp, the soil rich and hearty as my fingers dragged through it to feel for my brother.

Something slithered over the back of my hand, all smooth and scaled as it went past me without stopping. I squealed, lifting a dirt-covered hand to my face to cover my mouth and muffle the sound. "Brann!" I whispered, spinning around in my crouch and trying desperately to find him. Panic coated my skin, waiting for his answer, and then finally he groaned.

"I'm here, and I think I fell into our hiding place." Something touched my ankle, reaching under the hem of my dress and grasping it. "It's me," Brann said, holding me steady when I tried to shake off his grip.

"You scared the—"

"Give me your hand. I'll help you down," he said, and I did as he bid. He helped me step down off the ledge I was standing on, the moist decay of a tree root touching my free hand when I lowered myself into the hole.

Sitting beside him and leaning my back into the dirt and roots behind me, I couldn't stop the hysterical giggle that bubbled up in my throat or the feeling of Brann's incredulous eyes trying to glare at me. "How are we supposed to know if we're hidden, when we cannot see?" I asked when I could finally breathe past my laughter.

He snorted, dropping his head to rest on my shoulder as he shook it from side to side. I curled my legs into my body, hugging them tightly as he wrapped his arms around my shoulders to keep warm. With the frigid night air surrounding us, the lack of movement made freezing to death a very real possibility. We needed a fire, but nothing would attract all manner of predators from the woods like a flame in the night.

Would the sun rise in the morning? Or had the Fae plunged us into an eternal darkness that we would never escape?

My eyes drifted closed as the exhaustion became too much for me to bear. Longing for the feeling of the sun on my skin, I drifted into the realm of dreams, where monsters didn't threaten to take me to a world of mystery and enchantment, and the most dangerous being in my life was the lecherous Lord who wanted to make me his wife.

And I slept.

My eyes flew open. The press of a hand at my mouth jolted me awake and tore me from my nightmare. A shrill scream burned its way up my throat, clawing to get free. "Shh," Brann whispered in my ear, his voice trembling as I nodded frantically against his hand, which was covered in dirt and smelled of rotting leaves and decay.

He pulled his hand away from my mouth finally, and I lifted my own to cover it. I didn't know what had made Brann wake me so fearfully, but I did my best to muffle my breathing. My own skin bore the metallic scent of blood along with the dirt that caked my skin, while the crumble of fallen leaves dusted my wounds.

The sky was still dark, and I had no sense of time or whether it was truly night now. I could have slept for minutes or hours, but all I knew was, it hadn't been enough. I waited, tempted to ask him why he'd scared the life out of me as the silence spread and nothing happened. I was about to do just that when I heard it finally.

The thudding of hooves striking against the earth, muffled by the foliage covering the ground and the lack of a hard surface for the horses' shoes to tap against as they moved. Whoever rode kept their pace slow and steady, and I spun to look up through the tree roots above our heads.

There was only darkness, only the stillness of the night in front of my face. I watched, pressing my hand tighter against my mouth as I squinted, pressing my body into the dirt in front of me, making myself smaller and for once being grateful for my stained, lackluster dress as it blended in with the rotting woods.

For once, being poor and not able to afford a new dress seemed to work to my advantage.

I stopped breathing the moment the first hoof stepped into view, gleaming silver as if it created its own light and sparkled in the pitch black. Where there would have been hair on any normal horse, the smooth surface of bone was glossy and polished as it lifted and fell in its next step. The entire body was made of bones, a skeleton of an animal that was no longer alive.

And yet it moved through the night, step by step, and more followed in its wake once it had passed. I lifted my gaze to the spectral form of the man who rode it. He seemed to glow, a twisting mass of white and black shadows. Dark hair fell just past his shoulders, floating off them as if it could defy gravity. It faded into the inky, dark air, bleeding outward and becoming part of the shadows themselves.

His eyes shone with a shock of white, all traces of color missing from them as a magical haze enveloped him. His shoulders were broad, encased in a fur cloak that would have made the wealthiest of men in Mistfell jealous. Feathers were braided into the dark locks of his hair, shaking with every one of the skeletal horse's heavy footfalls.

The only color in the swirling tendrils of shadows, which seemed to compose his entire being, was the shock of icy blue tattoo on his face. It stretched down the center of his forehead, severing his face in half and arching over the bridge of his nose before the glowing ink separated and curved across each of his cheekbones.

Even though there was nothing solid to his appearance, he was devastating. A translucent being that felt Other in a way I'd never dreamed of seeing.

He moved past us, a line of other horsemen following at his back on their own skeletal steeds. They each varied in appearance—different hairstyles, a different blend of shadows and light that very nearly resembled a person—but each bore that glowing blue mark on their face.

I knew without a doubt who they were: the force that our legends told would be the first to hunt down those marked by the Fae.

The Wild Hunt.

I turned to look forward, watching in horror as the man at the front of the line pulled on the reins and halted his steed. He spun quickly, his head and shoulders twisting, to stare at the back of the line. That shock of white eyes aimed toward me, feeling for just a moment as if he not only saw me, but saw straight through me to the core of everything I'd become. The burning on my neck intensified, throbbing with the cold heat of a warning.

Spinning to lean my back into the earth once more, I pulled my cloak tightly around my head and neck and hoped to suppress the feeling that lit me aflame from the inside.

The thump of a man dismounting carried through the woods, the sound echoing off the trees around us. I pressed my hand tighter against my mouth and fought back the panicked breaths that filled my lungs, while my heart felt like it drummed against my chest.

I was so certain he could hear it, positive that the creature who trudged through the underbrush at his feet sensed the pounding blood in my veins.

I waited, counting the breaths between each footstep. There were too many, too long a pause between each scuff of his foot against the ground. Either he meant to torment his prey, or he genuinely wasn't certain where we might be hiding. I didn't dare to hope for the latter.

Already prepared to offer my cooperation for Brann's life, I reached over to grasp his hand in mine. Desperate to feel the warmth of my brother's hand against mine for one more moment before all else was lost, I hated the chill that had swept over his skin.

Another step came, bringing the spectral being closer, until I wasn't certain he wasn't a ghost sent from the underworld to punish me for attempting to flee.

The last step came directly above our heads, and the ground shifted with his weight. Clumps of dirt rained down, falling between the tree roots that concealed us until my cloak and hair filled with them.

We held perfectly still, waiting with bated breath for the moment he reached through the roots and tore us free from our hiding place.

I sucked in a breath of air, panic seizing my lungs as the image filled my head. Brann spun to stare at me, a silent reprimand for the too-loud noise, but the howl of a hound in the distance had covered the gasp I'd stolen at the worst possible moment.

The wind carried the sound of the hounds who'd found their prey, and guilt immediately claimed my body in a trembling embrace.

As the leader of the Wild Hunt mounted his horse and the entire group of them rode off into the distance, all I could feel was gratitude that it hadn't been me the hounds scented out. That I would live to hide another day, even when it meant that someone else hadn't been so fortunate.

9

I opened my eyes to light. Despite all my questions of whether or not our world had been plunged into eternal darkness, the sun rose in the morning. Illuminating the forest with sparkling light, it made the evergreen needles of the canopy around us glimmer.

I resisted the urge to rub the sleep out of my eyes, thanks to the dirt caking my hands. I felt far too tired after the long and arduous effort of falling back asleep after the near encounter with The Hunt.

Moving to my hands and knees, I kept my body low as I crept out of our hiding place beneath the tree roots. Careful not to disturb Brann while he slept, I pushed to my feet in the small clearing and looked around the woods. I hadn't been able to see a thing the night before, but I'd crawled around in the very dirt beneath my feet. I'd plunged my hands beneath the leaves when looking for Brann and found nothing but decaying foliage and wood rot.

I climbed out of the alcove that had offered us refuge, looking around cautiously as I moved. My steps led me to the center of the meadow, spinning slowly as I looked at the fresh bloom of wildflowers growing from the trunk of the fallen tree we'd taken shelter under.

They couldn't have existed the night before, with the chilly nights and frost on the horizon, and yet somehow here they were. A verdant trail dotted with marigold and lavender followed the path the Wild Hunt had walked, the new blooms opening for the first time and turning to face the sun while I watched. I tipped my face up to feel the heat on my skin, smiling bitterly at the realization that the Fae had somehow chased away the threat of winter with the rising sun. The frost that had felt so near in the days leading up to the end of the year harvest was gone, giving me hope that I'd be able to find some kind of shelter and warmer clothes before the snow came.

I turned slowly, taking in the beauty of the woods briefly before I turned my gaze back to Brann's sleeping form. His chest rose and fell evenly, rhythmic and without a care in the world as he momentarily slept away his worries. I knew the instant he woke, he'd remember all that had happened and all that he'd given up for me.

My bottom lip trembled as I watched him for a beat, my breath shaking as it escaped my lungs, and I turned in the direction I thought we'd been running the night before.

When he woke up, he would hate me for what I'd done, but at least he would be alive.

I put one foot in front of the other, focusing on the only thing I could do when the future seemed impossible. When living was so far away from running and hiding in the woods until the day I died. That one, next step was the only thought in my head, even as the fall of tears wet the front of my cloak.

"You won't last a day on your own," he said behind me, making me spin in place to see him sitting up and alert, watching me with a disgruntled scowl as if I'd failed a test he'd presented me with. "For one, you're going back the way we came. Second, you're about as quiet as a rock troll."

"Oh, shut it," I said, my lungs wheezing with laughter as he pushed to his feet and approached.

He stopped in front of me, wrapping trembling arms around me and pulling me into his chest. I loosed a sigh, sinking into the comforting touch and sniffling back my tears. This felt like goodbye, like he understood there was little choice but to let me continue on my own.

When everything was stacked against me, and my odds of surviving and remaining free were practically nonexistent, the knowledge that maybe Brann and my mother could find a new semblance of normal with the Veil down gave me comfort. The Fae had no interest in them, and they wouldn't join the ranks of fighters who would get in the Hunt's way.

"I'm scared," I admitted, lifting my hands to wrap around his upper arms.

He pulled back enough to nod at me in confirmation. Only a fool wouldn't be terrified of death or the unknown, and everything we'd been familiar with up until yesterday was gone. Even the humans who hadn't been marked would never be the same.

Not with the threat of the Fae walking among us.

"I'm afraid, too," he admitted, giving me a bittersweet smile. "But whatever happens, we'll face it together."

"Brann," I objected, shaking my head from side to side. His willingness to follow me was foolish at best, deadly at worst.

"I will not leave you to die alone. Don't you dare ask that of me." His face was stern, the intent clear in the lines of his oval face. He shook his head in a final warning, his shaggy hair swaying from side to side.

"Maybe I should have just let them find me," I said, heaving out a sigh. Even saying the words, there was no doubt that Brann would refuse them. They were also true, the right thing to do. "At least then you would be home with Mom."

"Listen to me, Estrella. I meant what I said last night. No matter what happens, you must never allow the Fae to take you to Alfheimr. Promise me," he said, his voice dropping low in something like a plea.

The vehemence in his voice made me pause, staring at him in confusion. Of all the people in Mistfell who cursed the Fae and all that they stood for, Brann had never uttered a word about them. He wasn't drawn to the Veil in the same way as me, and he now insisted upon keeping a healthy distance from all things related to the monsters beyond the Veil. "What are you—"

"Nothing is ever easy, and nothing is as it seems. If it looks like you're going to lose the fight, you end it," he said, pulling a small dagger from his boot. He tore off a strip of cloth from his cloak, shoving the sleeve of my dress up my arm until he could secure the sheath against the inside of my forearm with the torn fabric. "You do not risk losing this using it on anyone else. This is for you."

"For me?" My brow furrowing as he pulled the fabric of my dress back down to cover the weapon I couldn't wrap my head around.

Why did my brother have a knife in his boot?

"If I'm gone and I cannot take the burden for you, you have to be the one to do it," he said, leaning forward to touch his forehead to mine.

"Where is this coming from?" I asked, staring up at him with blurry eyes. The emotion clogging his throat matched mine, his gaze going wet as he touched his lips to my forehead in a brotherly kiss and his hand wrapped around the back of my head. The knowledge that my brother intended to kill me before he allowed the Fae to take me filled me with a conflicting sense of dread and warmth.

I'd been willing to die before I let Lord Byron have me; the same could be said for the Fae, but he wouldn't have made that choice when the male coming for me was human.

"I love you more than anything. Surely you must know that." He pulled back far enough to watch my face for a reaction, saying, "Trust that I would not ask this of you if it weren't important. There will be no light for you in the realm of the Fae. Only darkness and torment, the likes of which you couldn't even begin to imagine."

I stared up at him, my mind dancing with so many questions, I thought I would drown in them. But for the moment, I chose to trust my brother, who had only ever wanted to protect me. I nodded, fighting back the tears that stung my throat. He had to know that I would voice the questions that hung between us, but I wasn't certain I was ready for the answers waiting in his eyes. Still, I asked, even knowing from the steely expression on his face that it would be pointless. "What are you hiding?"

"One day, I will answer all of your questions, but today is not that day." He shook his head when I opened my mouth to protest, his forehead dropping to mine again as he closed his eyes. "Sometimes ignorance is bliss, little sister. Enjoy it while it lasts."

He took my hand, guiding me with him as we continued on. We walked together, all the while knowing that the stalemate between us would have to end at some point. When the time came, I would do whatever I could to make sure it was only me staring down the edge of a blade, and Brann would be free from the consequences of what I had become.

When the opportunity presented itself, I would set him free.

He helped me up and out of the hollow of the meadow, the two of us then continuing on through the woods. We set a brisk but sustainable pace, knowing the inevitable reality was that running day in and day out would never last.

Brann paused, swinging his arm to the side to stop in front of me. It struck me in the chest, halting me immediately as he tilted his head to the side. "Did you hear that?" he asked, spinning to look back from where we'd come.

I froze, a chill sweeping over me as I followed his gaze to the edge of the trees on the other side of the clearing. The gleaming silver of armor shone through them as a horse came into view, the protective metal covering his face and legs like a beacon with the sun on it. The rider atop him bore no expression, no measure of guilt for the terror he'd caused or the violence he would commit if he caught us. He kicked his steed forward, its full height revealed as they stepped onto the path where the Wild Hunt had walked only hours before.

Brann turned to me, his expression filled with fear as he spoke. His words were lost to the sound of the horse's hooves beating against the ground as it charged toward us, but I read the message loud and clear all the same, and I turned to obey.

"Run."

10

My boots pounded against the foliage-covered forest floor, my breath heaving out of my lungs as I tried to keep up with Brann's steady pace. "Hurry!" Brann encouraged, reaching behind him to grab my hand and tug me faster. My feet slipped in the leaves, making me stumble as I looked over my shoulder.

The Mist Guard on our trail was nowhere to be seen, but I wasn't naive enough to believe that he'd given up the chase when we'd run.

Brann pulled me forward, yanking me through the trees as I fought to get my footing once again. My chest throbbed with the force of my beating heart, my mind focused only on keeping up with Brann so he could get to safety. The Mist Guard wouldn't hesitate to cut him down for helping me.

I suddenly slammed into Brann—my heart dropping into my stomach, my body feeling weightless as I knocked him over. He sprawled on his belly at the feet of a massive chestnut horse, the rider atop it glaring down at us as I scrambled off of Brann's back and to my feet.

I spared one last look for my brother as he rose to his knees, hurrying to stand upright as the rider slowly dismounted his horse. The sound of his sword leaving its scabbard rang through the air as he pulled it free, holding it at his side as he took that first step toward me.

I felt his boot strike against the ground in the echo of my racing heart, the sound carrying through the silent forest as Brann pushed to his feet to face the Mist Guard. He was unarmed, his hands clenched at his sides as if he stood a chance against the gleaming iron sword of the other man.

My throat ached with the desire to beg for Brann's life, something I knew would fall on deaf ears. I stood taller, staring down the Mist Guard in an attempt to divert his attention off my innocent brother. "Some Mist Guard you make," I snapped, forcing a sneer to my face when all I felt was terror; for myself and for Brann. "Can't even properly kill one Fae whore in the woods."

My lips twisted as I held my stance, watching as the Guard's head turned away from Brann and toward me. I shoved my hair away from my neck, letting the Fae Mark glow in the softly lit woods where the sun shone through the canopy of pine trees above us. There was something robotic in his motions, all semblance of humanity gone from him as he raised dark eyes to sweep over the Mark on my neck.

His iron helmet covered the top of his head and curved around to lie against his cheekbones, leaving only the space from his eyes to his mouth visible. His dark eyes were sunken into his face, his skin unnaturally pale, as if he'd never seen the light of day. His crooked nose and tense mouth gave no illusion of kindness, while his nostrils flared slightly as he fixated on me. I'd thought I knew all the Mist Guard, thought they'd lived among us and walked Mistfell freely, but this man with no trace of emotion was a stranger to me.

But it would seem I was no stranger to him.

"Estrella Barlowe. The girl who turned two men to snow," he said, shifting his hold on his sword as he spun away from Brann. He stepped toward me, the heavy falls of his feet where his armor encased him clattering with a metallic ring. "I've been looking for you."

I backed away, pulling him further from Brann's side and demanding all of his attention. I gave Brann the chance to escape, drawing the Mist Guard soldier to follow me further into the woods. "What makes you think that number won't become three, soon enough?" I asked.

When I was certain he'd come far enough that pursuing me was more likely than turning back for my brother, I turned and bolted through the trees.

He chuckled behind me, the sound filling the air with menace. Metal clanked as he followed, running as quickly as he could manage with all that weight on his body. "Have you ever heard the rumors of what happens to the Fae when you cut them with an iron blade?" he called to me as I hurried away from him, the words slithering over my skin. I ducked behind a tree, zigzagging to try to throw him off my tail.

I didn't answer; didn't give him any sound in response that might have given away my location. My spine pressed into the oak tree behind me, my breath heaving as I waited and listened for where he might have gone. I carefully turned to peek around the tree, finding no sign of the Mist Guard who meant to cut me down.

Turning forward once again, I scanned the trees for any sign of him and found none, as if he'd vanished into thin air, a figment of my imagination.

A whistle came as his sword cut through the air in an attempt to sever my head from my body. I ducked low, dropping to my ass on the ground and scrambling to the side as the thunk of his blade cutting into the tree reverberated through me. "They *die*. So what do you think my iron blade will do to you?"

I scrambled to my feet, jumping back as he swung once again. Magic surged along my skin, consuming my Mark with every strike he committed against me. I shook as I tried to hold it back, undecided on whether I should live or die.

Even now, staring my death in the face, I couldn't commit to going into the Void that awaited, after the end. I couldn't surrender to the resounding peace I'd felt the day before, in the moments when I'd thought it was all over.

Something had awakened within me, and it was only when staring down the edge of a blade that it felt hungry to live for the first time.

My fingers burned with the cold as I dodged his blows that were intended to cut me down. Minutes passed, the building power within me coming far slower than it had when we'd first fled. Then finally the freezing ice of winter consumed them, turning my fingertips white as I jerked to the side to avoid his stab for my waist. I reached up with those white fingers, gently touching the tips to the bare flesh at his neck.

White specks like snowflakes danced across his skin, the patterns swirling and writhing like the lightest of snow upon a field when the wind caught it. I watched them, mesmerized for a moment as they danced up his neck and toward his eyes.

Something heavy pressed against the front of my throat and the cut left by the priest, snapping closed around the back as my body felt weighed down. The white swirls on his skin stopped dancing, fading from view entirely as he sucked in a relieved breath. I wheezed, my lungs tightening with the need to breathe. There was no energy left in my body, nothing left to keep me upright as my knees buckled and I fought to stay on my feet. "You're a clever little bitch," he said, pressing the hand that gripped the front of my throat tighter into my skin and helping to hold my weak body up. The metal there burned me, lighting my skin on fire as I fought for breath. "But not clever enough to fight with my iron dampening your magic."

He gripped my neck cruelly as he raised his sword and touched the tip to my dress. He cut the top button away, parting the fabric so he could see the skin above my heart. "It's almost a shame to end it so soon," he murmured, leaning forward until his dark eyes stared into mine. "I like a woman with some fight."

"Then take off the collar and fight me like a man," I hissed, trying to think past the press of his blade sinking into my flesh, against the burning that consumed me just from that minor cut.

He tilted his head to the side, studying the burning skin that began to char around his blade. "What are—"

He gurgled around his own blood, choking on it as I looked to his throat, and to the dagger I hadn't known Brann still possessed. He pulled it free, sending a shock of red arcing through the sky. The Mist Guard crumpled to his knees in front of me, staring up at me as he fought for breath.

Brann wiped his dagger on the man's coat, studying me quickly and stepping forward. He fought with the clasp at the back of the collar, yanking it free from under the curtain of my hair. I heaved a sigh of relief as soon as it was gone, drawing my first full breath since my shackling.

"It's almost a shame," I said, quirking my brow at the dying Mist Guard as something dark and hateful consumed me. That darkness within me made me bitter, taking joy in the sight of the man who would have killed me drowning in his own blood. "I do so like a man who can fight."

11

There was blood on me, yet again. I was quickly becoming far too accustomed to the red stains on my skin, and the monster in me wasn't as horrified by it as I would have thought. I'd felt guilty when I'd killed Loris, wanting nothing more than to stop the magic that took control and ended his life. I'd even felt bad for killing the commander.

But with this Mist Guard in the woods, I felt only pride in my brother for ending him before he could end me. He'd shackled me with the iron collar like a dog, and, according to his own words, rendered me unable to defend myself.

I trudged through the woods as the sun began to disappear over the horizon, the natural night coming without magical interference. It was less all-encompassing than the false night we'd spent stumbling around in the dark, the hint of stars in the sky now lighting our way.

My feet throbbed as the blisters on my heels where my boots dug into the flesh bled into the wool socks that made my feet soak with sweat. I'd been dressed for winter, but the weather couldn't seem to decide what to do with the Fae magic. The air had the fresh scent of spring; the plants revived with vibrancy all around us, despite the frost we'd feared would come too quickly only a day before.

Hunger and thirst cramped my belly, making it impossible to think about continuing on for another day without food or water. The berries we'd snuck off the bushes in the woods as we passed them could only last so long, and I touched a hand to my grumbling torso as if the pressure of the contact could will it away.

"Look," Brann said, pointing to a light up ahead. Through the gaps between the trees, I could just make out the glow of torch lights.

The brief rays of hope were quickly extinguished by the reality that being around people would likely be impossible for me. We had no money to purchase food or drink, and nothing of value we could sell.

Anyone who got a good look at me would try to dispose of me, and there was a brief, blinking wonder inside me at the thought. Would I hear the male who'd claimed me roar his rage before I died? Or would that only come when I was already gone from this world and wouldn't be able to hear it anyway?

"We need food," Brann said, taking my hand and tugging me to the edge of the woods. We watched as torch lights dimmed and then winked out, people settling into their homes for the night. I couldn't blame them. I didn't want to be outside either, when the Wild Hunt rode in the darkness.

"Wait here," he said, giving me a pointed look as he moved into the small village. Nobody noticed him with the streets empty, at least not that I saw until he ducked out of sight. A few long moments passed with me waiting, considering continuing on into the woods and leaving him behind. He would be far better off for it, and I'd already endangered his life more than once.

But he was right; we needed food and water, and the unfortunate reality was, if anyone saw my neck, I'd be doomed. I couldn't move through villages the way he could without drawing attention to myself.

He touched a finger to his lips when he stepped back into view, waving a hand for me to follow. I hauled my filthy cloak up over my head, keeping the Mark that I had yet to see hidden, and stepped into the clearing in the woods.

Hurrying quickly, in spite of the pain climbing up my legs with every step, we made our way around the edge of the village. Brann led me to an empty barn tucked away at the back of the clearing, hauling the door open a crack that was just wide enough for us to slip through.

A single horse stood in a stall to the left, chewing his hay loudly, but the rest seemed to be empty. "We passed a little pub a few buildings down. I'll see if I can get us food in exchange for doing some work in the morning."

"We can't be here in the morning," I protested. "If they see me—"

"Nobody will need to see you. You'll be tucked inside the woods by the time the sun rises." He nodded at me one last time and slipped back out the door without another word.

I spun in the space, twiddling my fingers as I looked around and tried to decide what to do. It felt wrong not to be moving, as if my body knew if it wanted to keep breathing, it needed to keep walking.

Ignoring what my body knew, I sank down on a pile of straw at the side of the barn aisle, easing the weight off my feet with a groan of satisfaction. They throbbed, swollen inside my boots, but I didn't dare take them off, in case I needed to make a quick getaway.

Dropping my head back, I stared up at the rafters supporting the ceiling. The straw beneath me was warm, almost too warm, given the cloak wrapped around my shoulders. But it was all that concealed the Fae Mark.

"I'm really trying very hard not to frighten you," a deep, amused voice said, and I froze solid in fear. "You've made that quite difficult staring at the ceiling."

I sat up slowly, holding the cloak cinched tight at my neck as my fear spiked. Only the knowledge that quick, hasty movements could make me more likely to be discovered by others kept me from running.

The rugged, dirty hands held out in front of the man who'd spoken seemed massive, cracked with callouses and worn in the way that only hard work could achieve.

Suppressing a shudder as my heart lurched into my throat, I set a hand down in the straw and pushed myself to my feet, ignoring the prickle of each stalk as it sank into my already wounded hands—courtesy of the twilight berry bushes. He gazed at me with dark eyes, peering out from a breathtakingly handsome face surrounded by short ash-blond hair. His bottom lip was thick and lush as he curled his mouth into an appeasing smile, and his frame was tall, shoulders broad enough that I knew I didn't want him getting anywhere near me.

My breath caught.

His tall body was packed with the kind of muscle I wouldn't stand a chance of escaping once he caught me. "I don't want any trouble," I said, swallowing past the icy dread working its way through my body.

"No trouble," he agreed, nodding his head. I raked my eyes over his face, feeling small even on the other side of the barn, as he seemed to be nearly a foot taller than me. I pursed my lips as I glanced toward the door where we'd come in. It was the sole exit, and the stranger followed the path of my gaze with dark eyes that seemed to track everything.

"There's no need for that, Little One," he said, the deep chuckle of his voice resonating through the air. It struck me in the chest, drawing my eyes back to his and that intense too-dark stare. "I promise I have no interest in hurting you."

He reached into the pocket of his cloak, and I did the only logical thing, when presented with a man who radiated a predatory grace that would mean the end of me.

I spun, sprinting for the door at the side of the barn.

"Fuck," the man grunted, abandoning whatever he'd been reaching for in his cloak to chase me. His long legs ate up the distance between us quickly, closing in before I ever got close to the barn door. I couldn't scream for help, not when doing so would mean people discovering me, and the potential fallout could mean taking a sword to the heart or unintentionally slaughtering an entire village full of innocent people.

A strong arm wrapped around my waist, yanking me back into a very male body as the other hand covered my mouth. His skin against my face smelled of the first frost of the season, as if he'd been clearing ice away from the flora in a garden to preserve the plants just a bit longer. "Shh," he murmured softly, the spearmint of his breath caressing my cheek.

I thrashed in his grip as he lifted me off my feet easily, twisting my body from side to side and kicking my legs frantically. His hand slipped while he carried me further into the barn as if I weighed nothing, and the tips of his fingers pressed against the seam of my lips.

I bit down with all the strength in my jaw, not relenting when the coppery-sweet taste of blood filled my mouth. When any normal person would have shouted, or at least tried to get me to release his appendage from the vice-like grip of my teeth, he only chuckled in my ear and dragged me back to the pile of straw where I'd thought to relax.

"Careful, love. I just might like that."

I mumbled against his skin, wincing when he tore his finger free without care for the way my bite tore his flesh open further. My teeth clamped together, the vibration of the impact radiating through my jaw. "Put me down!" I said furiously, my voice carrying through the otherwise empty barn.

He didn't relent, giving me no choice but to fight against the threat I didn't understand. He didn't want me dead, not yet at least, but he also wasn't letting me go free. In the world I lived in, especially with the Fae on the loose, the unknown was something to be feared.

I slammed my head back, aiming straight to take out his nose. He moved with lightning-quick reflexes, narrowly avoiding the strike that would have broken his pretty face. In doing so, his grip on me finally loosened enough for me to slip through.

I spun, moving with all the adrenaline coursing through my veins and snatching the dagger from the sheath on his belt. Twisting it in my hands the way Loris had taught me and ignoring the pang of guilt I felt over my lover's death, I leaned into the thrust that pressed the sharp edge of his blade at his neck.

He blinked down at me in surprise, his features darkening, but he made no move to step away from the threat. He held my gaze, his body still and his breathing steady while I panted for breath and tried to fight my rising panic.

Why wasn't he afraid?

He stepped closer, pushing the edge of the blade into his skin until little red droplets ran down his throat. He smirked as I bled him, that arrogant look broadening into a full-fledged grin when I didn't back down and held my stance. "You're a vicious one, aren't you?" he asked, running his tongue over the top of his perfect bottom teeth.

"Only when it comes to pushy men who seem to think they have the right to touch me," I snapped, leaning further into the knife against his throat.

"Fair enough," he murmured thoughtfully, moving so quickly I didn't have time to track what happened. His hand raised, shoving my elbow until the dagger slid across his throat, leaving a thin slash. Once it was clear of his throat, he disarmed me with the speed and grace of a professional, twisting the blade out of my hand and into his, until he threw it into the wood floor at our feet.

He shifted, drawing me into his arms, and lifted me off my feet. He tossed me gently, just far enough that my back hit the straw pile once again. Straw billowed up on impact, filling my face and hair with the itchy needle-like stalks that seemed to get *everywhere*.

His eyes dropped to my neck, and I swallowed back the unrelenting panic I felt when I could sense his gaze on that burning part of me that had been revealed in our skirmish by the shifting of my cloak. His square jaw tightened, teeth clenching down as he stared at the Mark, and something primal filled his gaze. "You're safe with me," he said, reaching up to grasp the collar of his hood. He tugged it to the side, revealing a swirling mix of black and white color on his golden skin.

"You're Fae Marked," I said, unable to take my eyes off the design as I brushed straw out of my hair and face and sat up. He reached into the pocket of his cloak once more, pulling out a waxed cloth canteen and holding it out to me.

"You need to drink. I suspect those lips are much prettier when they're hydrated." He stepped closer, holding out the canteen pointedly. Cautiously, I took it from him, staring into the small opening warily and sniffing the contents. Finally, lifting it to my lips, I poured the first drops of water into my mouth and groaned at the fresh taste.

The crisp water felt cool despite having been tucked into his pocket. I swallowed greedily and forced myself to stop before I was ready, in the interest of not taking all of his water. "All of it," he ordered, touching the bottom of the canteen and tipping it up so that I had no choice but to swallow the entirety of it.

When I was done, he moved to the edge of the barn and the water pump I hadn't seen tucked behind a saddle rack, refilling the container immediately and tucking it back in his pocket for safekeeping. "Thank you," I murmured, my eyes dropping to the spot where I'd sunk my teeth into his finger. I grimaced, wiping the sleeve of my dress against the corner of my mouth. The pea green fabric smeared with blood and grime hinted at how much of a mess I must look.

The night in the woods hadn't done any wonders for my appearance, if the filth was any sign.

He closed the distance between us, taking a seat beside me and drawing my hands into his grip. I shifted, watching him with wary eyes as I tried to make sense of what he wanted.

Up close, the ruthless beauty of his features was overwhelming. He was nothing like the boys and men of Mistfell, and, as he unfastened his cloak and tossed it to the side, the first glimpse of just how broad his shoulders were made the breath catch in my throat. His tunic strained at the seams to accommodate his body, his trousers tight through the thighs as he turned on the straw to face me.

He poured water into his hand, raising it to my neck and cleaning what remained of the wound from the High Priest. When he'd finished with that, he held one of my hands out to the side and shoved the cloak out of the way and the sleeve of my dress up my arm. Taking out his canteen once more, he slowly poured water over my hand until I started to feel a little more human as the blood and dirt washed away, revealing my skin beneath the layers of filth that had accumulated since we'd left Mistfell.

When he was satisfied with how clean my hand was, he turned it over and inspected the thin cuts and the white scars that covered it intently. "What happened?" he asked, lifting the limb to look at the wounds closer. Soft, plush lips touched the back, the strong cupid's bow of his mouth emphasized as it curved up into the barest hint of a smile.

"Twilight berries," I said, swallowing as the feeling of his lips spread through me with an odd, tingling numbness. He took my other hand in his, repeating the process slowly and working his thumbs over the injuries as he inspected them to make sure they were clean enough to prevent infection.

"You're a harvester," he said, nodding as he splashed some of the water on his own hand. His enormous palm came toward my face slowly, waiting for me to panic and back away from the touch. The moment his skin touched mine, I leaned into it, even though I didn't understand the urge.

The skin surrounding his callouses was surprisingly soft. His thumb dragged over my cheekbone, drawing a ragged gasp from me as his palm cupped my cheek. He set to cleaning my face with his wet hands, moving slowly and with a gentleness that I wouldn't have thought him capable. I couldn't help but stare, wondering what had possessed me to allow him to touch me, and to care for me like I mattered when he was nothing but a stranger to me

"Much better," he said after he'd finished, clearing his throat and drawing his hand away slowly.

"I'm sorry for biting you," I said, conceding that I'd perhaps misinterpreted the situation.

"I'm certain that's not something you say every day," he said, pursing his lips in thought.

I cracked a smile, chuckling at the ridiculousness of it all. "No, I can't say that it is."

"Well, the least you can do after wounding me is tell me your name. I must have something to tell people when they ask who bested me, and I am sad to say claiming a harvester I call 'Little One' doesn't make me sound intimidating. I have a reputation to uphold, after all," he teased, resting his hand on top of my knee.

It was a move that Lord Byron had done on more than one occasion after feeding me twilight berries, but whereas his touch had felt lecherous, this stranger simply rested his hand there. It wasn't a pathetic attempt to touch me, but rather just a convenient place for it.

"What makes you think my name will be any better to that end?" I asked, leaning back on the pile of straw until I laid sprawled out beside him. I wasn't sure when the shift had come, but at some point in the brief interaction, I'd realized that he truly didn't mean to harm me.

At least not immediately.

"A woman who can bite so powerfully and cut me with my own dagger must have a terrifying name to accompany it," he said, shrugging his shoulders and lying back beside me. His hand rested only inches from mine, the awareness of his body like a living thing inside me. His fingers shifted until his pinky brushed against mine, and I wondered briefly if he felt the same current of tension.

Perhaps it was because we were both marked by the Fae, and the magic within us called to like. But whatever the reason, he seemed to be in no hurry to break the small contact between our bodies as he turned his head toward mine.

I followed suit, staring back at him and studying the way his dark eyes seemed to glimmer like onyx, with the faintest sheen of frost within his iris. My breath caught when his eyes dropped to my lips, and I wondered briefly if he might kiss me.

"Your name, Little One," he repeated instead, making my cheeks flush in embarrassment as I studied him.

"Estrella," I said, shrugging off the awkwardness I felt when his lips tipped into a smile.

"Estrella," he repeated in a murmur, making the name sound filthy in all the best ways. "A star is much more intimidating than a harvester."

"I suppose it is," I agreed, wishing I had the strength of even just a single star that burned in the sky. Instead, I was the coward who ran and hid, who endangered my brother by taking him with me. "Now you know who I am. What am I to call the man who likes to sneak up on innocent, resting women and terrify them?"

"Caelum, Little One. My name is Caelum."

12

"I suppose it's nice to meet you, Caelum the Marked," I said as that pinky finger of his brushed against my hand once more. He didn't seem the type to fidget, his body unnaturally still next to mine except for the single place where we touched.

The brush of his skin against mine soothed something inside me, a place where I'd wondered if I'd ever find somewhere I truly belonged. Caelum may have been a stranger. We might have been two passing ships in the night, who would never see one another again. But he was Fae Marked like me, a sign that maybe, just maybe, there were others like us out there somewhere. Preparing for a life in hiding.

I studied the contours of his face, noting that, despite the calluses that covered that pinky finger he used to touch me so delicately, his skin didn't seem weathered by the sun. He didn't bear the wrinkles that came from a life of outdoor labor and exposure to the elements. His skin gleamed with a natural golden bronze, but the freckles and sun spots I'd come to expect were nowhere to be found.

A swordsmith, maybe? The hilts of the swords peeking over his shoulders would certainly lend credence to that notion: weapons only the extremely wealthy or skillful could afford outside of the Mist Guard or Royal Guard. His clothing was well-made and mostly clean, lacking the signs of wear that mine showed.

"The pleasure is all mine, Estrella the Star," he said, his lips tipping up into the hint of a playful smile. The way he practically purred the word "pleasure" coated my skin, hinting at all manner of indecent things I had no right to be thinking of at that moment.

Even if he was easily the most beautiful man I'd ever seen.

The barn door cracked open, and I instinctively sat up, ripping my hand away from Caelum in guilt for the direction my thoughts had wandered. Caelum chuckled as my cheeks pinked, sitting up beside me as Brann's face poked in the cracked door.

His body followed as his brow furrowed, his lips pursing as he tried to hide his obvious concern. "It's okay," I said, standing and stepping away from Caelum and crossing toward my brother. He left the barn door slightly ajar, making for an easy escape in the event that he decided my judgment wasn't accurate.

I could hardly blame him. A man like Caelum made it hard to think rationally, quickly disarming all my thoughts of escape with his charm.

"Explain to me what exactly is okay?" Brann pointed toward my neck, which was visible with my cloak pushed to the side. It seemed to pulse as I lifted the fabric to cover it once again, as if it had a mind of its own and hated being concealed once again.

"Caelum is like me," I said, turning back to look at Caelum. His dark eyes that had previously glittered playfully were like hardened stone as he glared at Brann, and the air around him felt tense, as if the power lurking inside him saw my brother as a threat.

I swallowed, pushing forward to find a way to keep the peace. They didn't need to be the best of friends for us to be civil, and I wasn't ready to say goodbye to the first living person like me we'd seen. "This is my brother, Brann."

Caelum swallowed, his jaw clenching as he reached up to his heavy cloak and pulled it to the side until it shifted and revealed the mark. The two of them exchanged a look of confusion, and I watched from the sidelines as I waited for them to work their way through whatever male moment they were having.

"Her brother?" Caelum asked, glancing over at me. He paused, studying my face intently before finally shifting his attention back to Brann and giving an appeasing smile. "How unusual that you would flee with her."

"I wasn't about to leave her to the mercy of the Fae and the Mist Guard on her own," Brann snapped back. His focus finally fell to the Mark on Caelum's neck, studying it intently with his gaze narrowing on the entwined black and white before raising his eyes back to Caelum's. Brann glared openly.

I just wanted to eat and go to sleep in the relative safety of the barn and with the warmth of straw at my back.

"We're leaving," Brann announced, reaching forward and taking my hand in his.

"It's dark out," I protested. "We won't find shelter anywhere else so late, and Gods only know if we'll be fortunate enough to find another place to hide. We should wait until morning."

Caelum cleared his throat, and I turned to find his body holding perfectly still. His gaze wasn't on me or Brann, but on the spot where my brother clutched my hand tightly. "I really think it would be wise that we stick together." The words came through gritted teeth, as if he'd clenched his jaws so hard they'd melded into one.

"Why is that? So you can use me to go into the places you can't be seen?" Brann asked, narrowing his eyes on the other man.

"Yes," Caelum agreed, not even bothering to deny how useful Brann would be. "We can help one another. Unless I am mistaken, I don't see weapons on either of you. It would be unwise to continue without any form of protection."

"What good will a sword do us if the Fae come to steal her away?" Brann asked. "I'm assuming you haven't had to defend yourself just yet, because if you had, you'd know that Mark on your neck is more than capable of doing it for you," Brann argued, pausing to smirk in a moment of pride. "Or at least hers is."

Caelum's attention shifted to me, his eyes narrowing on my face as he studied my reaction to Brann's words. Shame heated my cheeks, the reminder of what the Mark had done making me turn my eyes to the floor. "Someone tried to kill you?" he asked, his lips thinning with anger.

I nodded. "Two of the Mist Guard from my village when we fled. I didn't mean to kill them," I mumbled, scuffing the dirt on the floor of the barn.

"Of course you didn't," Caelum said, surprising me. His eyes were sympathetic and soft when he cleared his throat. "The *Vinculum* only acts as a last resort to preserve life."

"The *Vinculum?*" I asked, watching as he approached. He closed the distance between us with slow strides that somehow seemed to take forever and happen too quickly, all at once. Brann's hand tightened on mine when the strange man stopped in front of me, lifting a hand to the Mark on my neck.

It awakened, blazing with the swirling light that glowed through the gaps in his fingers where he rested his palm against my skin. "The Fae Mark," he explained, his dark eyes lit by the white radiating from my body. Whereas the Mark had burned when Brann touched it, it came to life at the touch of another like me.

"How is it that you know so much about this mark?" Brann asked, tugging at my hand until he pulled me away from Caelum, whose hand dropped away. The shock of fresh air against my skin felt too warm, as if I would overheat and burst into flames in the wake of his skin on mine.

"My father was a fan of our histories. He spent a great deal of time studying the forbidden texts he kept hidden in his library," Caelum answered, and I nodded even as Brann kept pulling me back toward that door. If his father had truly risked owning the forbidden books, his knowledge of such things made sense, no matter what my overprotective brother seemed to think. "Don't be foolish, Little One. We are far safer together."

I paused, holding his gaze as Brann tugged at me. "Let's go, Estrella," he warned, his voice dropping to the deep command he'd used when we'd been children and I was caught in a place I shouldn't be.

It wouldn't have been the first time I'd gotten myself in trouble, or even the tenth. Not when my need to wander around in the woods had seen me punished in Lord Byron's library far too many times.

"I'm sorry," I whispered, sinking my teeth into my bottom lip and turning to follow Brann.

"Estrella," Caelum warned, and then his voice was cut off as the door closed behind me. Brann led me into the woods, and I let him take me to safety despite the hollow feeling that I'd done exactly what Caelum had warned me not to, and that going out into the night would prove to be very foolish indeed.

I ignored the pit in my stomach, following the brother who'd risked everything for me.

Family came first.

"I cannot believe how foolish you were. What were you thinking, showing him your mark?" Brann asked a few minutes later as we trudged through the woods. Our pace was slow, the stars above only doing so much to illuminate our path with the tree canopy so dense overhead. The leaves hadn't completed their change of colors, sticking to the branches in their last efforts to survive the weather, which had changed once again toward the cool, crispness of an approaching winter.

Once they fell, we'd have more light in the night, but we'd also have less cover to conceal us from the things chasing us.

I'd wanted to go back the moment we left. The shelter of the barn, the warmth of the straw, and the presence of another person like me all pulled me back toward the village we'd left behind. "Foolish was leaving. What harm could it have done to allow him to travel with us? He would've been one more person to keep watch and help in a fight," I argued. We'd been fortunate enough this far to only encounter limited numbers at once, but if a group of Mist Guard found us and they had one of the iron collars with them that seemed to take every bit of my energy from, we wouldn't stand a chance.

"He would have also been one more mouth to feed," Brann snapped, shocking me with his lack of concern over another human life. All traces of the caring and gentle brother I'd known were gone in that moment, his features appearing sharper in his ire.

"Brann," I mumbled, shaking my head. I didn't want to live in a world where everyone was my enemy. Where everyone was a threat or a sacrifice I needed to make to save myself. "We should go back," I said, turning to stare at the way we'd come. I wouldn't have been able to find my way to the barn on my own without Brann's help, and the knowledge kept me from trying, even when my legs twitched to change direction.

"You don't know him. What do you think he'd do if it came down to it and he needed to escape? He would sacrifice us to save his life, Estrella. You cannot trust anyone but me, do you understand?" Brann asked, gripping my hand in his and staring down at me. "There are things you don't know. Things you were never meant to know..." he trailed off, his head raising as he looked into the distance in the night.

"What is it, Brann?" I asked, following his line of sight. I couldn't see anything, couldn't hear anything other than the sound of him telling me to be quiet. We stood in silence for a moment, watching the darkness through the trees until finally I heard what had made him freeze in place.

Hoof beats.

The howls of the hounds on the wind.

They battered against my heart as they came on the wind, driving me forward after one more exchanged look with Brann. We'd stumbled around in the dark for too long, looking for a new hiding place, thanks to his ridiculous idea to wander out at night.

Anything was better than this.

Sweat trickled down my back as I ran, and dripped all the way to the hands that pumped at my sides. My cloak got caught on a branch, tearing my head back with the force of it. I fought to pull it free, struggling against the grip on my throat. "Leave it!" Brann ordered, and I reached up with trembling fingers to unknot the tie at my throat.

My body ached. Everything hurt, and I was so damn tired I thought about standing still and letting them take me. I was under no illusion that the magic coursing through my body would protect me from the Wild Hunt itself—not when it came from a Fae.

Three breaths passed as I fumbled. In and out in rapid succession, the sound drowning out everything else as I coughed with the exertion threatening to break my body, but once freed I turned back toward Brann and ran at his side. Leaping over a large tree root and nearly falling on my face, my breath coming in short, desperate pants, I growled, "We should have stayed in the fucking barn!" When I turned to him with a glare, his apologetic stare met mine, and he nodded as he pushed his body to the limit.

All we'd consumed was a loaf of bread shared between us immediately after leaving the barn, and the lack of fluid in his body made his body sag. He hadn't been fortunate enough to drink the water from Caelum's canteen. I kept pace at his side, when he would have needed to drag me along under any other circumstances.

"Brann!" I gasped, reaching out to grab his arm and jerk him to a stop. What I saw through the trees was a surer death than what chased us. He skidded to a stop beside me, his foot only a few steps from the edge of a cliff. The channel far below was so deep it looked black, even with the moon gleaming overhead in the sky. The fall was impossible to survive. It would turn a body into a mangled mess of limbs and blood.

Three more breaths wheezed out of my chest.

I turned a terrified glance to Brann, spinning to look behind me. The hoof beats grew louder, echoing through the forest at our backs until I knew with absolute certainty they were gaining on us.

My brother pulled his arm free from mine, blinking rapidly as a shaky breath left him. His fingers brushed against mine as he shifted our hands to lace our fingers together. He turned toward me as if in slow motion, his eyes sad and gleaming in the moonlight. "Together," he murmured softly.

My skull throbbed with how hard I shook my head. "No. Run."

Refusing to acknowledge what he'd offered as a solution, I tilted my head to the left and the opening I knew he would have if I offered myself up as a distraction.

He could go home. He could take care of our mother instead of dying pointlessly.

Brann gripped my hand tighter, smiling softly as he shook his head. "She *cannot* have you. *Together,"* he repeated, leaning down to rest his chin on top of my head. In the background, the Wild Hunt drew closer. I could practically feel the skeletal horses' harsh breaths on my neck. "One."

I squeezed my eyes closed, the word jagged as it bubbled up my throat. "Two," I said, holding back the sob that clenched my heart in my chest. Fear consumed me. Fear of the unknown.

Fear of the pain that might come before the moment of death finally brought peace.

"*Three*," Brann and I said together, darting the last few paces to the edge of the cliff. My legs shook with each step and my heart stalled in my chest as my foot pushed off the ledge. Cold air rushed up the skirts of my dress, dancing around my legs in a moment of suspension. For those brief few seconds, everything was weightless around me, hanging in limbo as I waited for the blackness of death to rush in and swallow me whole.

Still, Brann's hand clenched mine as we flew.

And then we fell.

A scream tore free from my throat, pulled from the depths of my soul as my terror reached an apex. I didn't want to die, but better death than an eternity in a prison. I'd already made that choice once.

Something slithered over my stomach, pulling my focus in those endless moments of suspension. Brann's gaze was harsh on whatever he saw on my stomach, and when he met my eyes one last time, all I saw was a guilty apology and resignation.

He knew as well as I did in that moment that he was going to leave me alone, after all.

"No!" I screamed at the top of my lungs, the sound shrill and somehow *other.* My body snapped to a sudden halt as the shadows around my waist solidified. Something cracked within my body, and sharp pain radiated through my torso as I hung limply for a moment.

Brann continued to fall, and my shoulder popped, echoing above the sound of waves crashing against the shore below when Brann continued to fall. Grasping his hand with my other one, I held on more tightly and refused to drop him as my shoulder throbbed with the aching pain of dislocation and hung limply at my side.

His fingers slipped through mine, slickened with sweat by our escape attempt, and he hung below me, his eyes on mine and pleading. "Let go, Estrella," he whispered, releasing my hand. I shook my head through the pain, clinging to him even though, in the back of my head, I already suspected it was pointless.

The solid shadows at my waist retracted, pulling me back up toward the top of the cliff as I squirmed in my pathetic bid for freedom. We should have both been dead.

A strong hand gripped the back of my dress as I crested the top, hauling me up the final distance until he could lay me out on the forest floor. Brann's body landed atop mine, sprawling across me as I tried to force air back into my lungs. The inky shadows at my waist retracted, slithering over the fabric of my dress. Wheezing breaths wracked me as my entire body throbbed with pain. My right arm hung limply at my side; even just the thought of moving it making it ache with warning.

Brann moved slowly, slipping his hand beneath the sleeve of my dress and taking the dagger he'd strapped there. A spectral ghost of a man stood over me, glaring down at the way I grimaced beneath Brann's body and unaware of his slow, cautious movements to arm himself.

The Fae Mark was still, none of the pulsing magic I'd expected to protect me making itself known. Whether it was a continued consequence of the iron collar or whether the magic that flowed through the Mark didn't work against the Fae, I suspected I may never know.

The being who'd pulled me back from the cliff grabbed Brann by the back of the cloak, lifting his frame off of me so he could get a good look at me and my injuries. His body was corporeal, despite appearing transparent, taking little effort to grasp my brother. The silver dagger gleamed in the night, shining as the member of the Wild Hunt released Brann suddenly and reached for his sword.

Brann caught himself when he fell, placing a hand next to my head as he leaned over me. His eyes were wet as he stared down at me, time seeming to suspend as his lips turned down. "I'm sorry," he whispered, raising his arm quickly.

The dagger sparkled as it carved through the air, descending toward my chest. I blinked up at my brother in shock, the realization of what he intended to do hitting me too late to react. All I could do was stare up into his agonized face as the dagger fell.

It was only a breath from my chest when he froze in place, his body jerking forward as the tip of a silver sword protruded from his stomach.

He gasped, looking down to stare at the blade as the member of the Wild Hunt pulled it free, tearing Brann's body off of mine with the motion. I scrambled to my knees, fighting to get to my brother where he lay, blood trickling from his lips. He mumbled something, the sound trailing off into a gurgle as the Fae grabbed him by the front of his cloak and dragged him to the edge of the cliff.

He thrashed once as I tried to crawl after him on my dislocated shoulder, a scream tearing free as the member of the Wild Hunt lifted him off the ground and hurled him over the edge. *"No!"* I shrieked, rushing forward to follow. After a moment, there was a splash below, the sound piercing through me as I peered over the edge.

I couldn't see his body, couldn't see anything but the dark depths of the salt water below. There was no second splash to signify Brann breaking back through the surface, clinging to life.

The Fae stood over me, wrapping an arm around the front of my chest and hauling me backwards. He pulled me as far away from the cliff face as he could without bumping my broken body into any of the trees. "She's injured," he said, turning his eerie white eyes to the figure that waited atop his horse. This was the same male I'd seen that night in the woods, the ink on his face glowing blue as he regarded me with a bored look.

The male at my side reached down, touching my chin and turning my head to the side so that he could get a good look at my

Fae Mark. A crowd of other members of the Wild Hunt broke through the trees, following behind a handful of creatures that snapped at the air.

The growls filled my ears, the menace in them sending my heart racing. Black oozed from their mouths, the viscous fluid dripping from fangs as thick as my wrist. It faded into the shadows before it could touch the ground, vanishing into thin air as if it sizzled out of existence. They were what might have been dogs, had the skin stayed on their bones and not melted into rotten ribbons. Their skeletons showed through the gaps in the oozing, red flesh, a mangled mess of life and death. Their claws sank into the dirt, too large for their paws and curling over the front. Glowing white eyes matched their more humanoid masters', their stances ready to attack at the leader's command.

My Fae Mark warmed as the eyes of the Wild Hunt fell upon it, as if it recognized the immortal beings nearby, calling out to them and glowing in the darkness like a beacon. It wasn't the same feeling as when it was about to kill, but a deep contentment that tried to settle itself within me. As if it had a mind of its own and wanted to soothe me, to tell me all would be right now. Somewhere in the group of hunters who'd joined us at the cliff face, someone laughed in disbelief. "Well, I'll be damned," the leader said from atop his horse, leading the steed closer to get a better look at me.

The other Fae male released my chin and placed his hands on my shoulder. He shoved it back into the socket suddenly and without warning, the sharp pain radiating through my body while I screamed out in surprise. Numbness settled into me in the wake of it, my body heavy with the weight of my shock.

My brother was gone, and I lived on in a world filled with decaying monsters and murderous, spectral men.

All that mattered was my brother. All that mattered was vengeance and finding whatever remained of him.

The male shoved his long, gray hair back from his face, moving to lift me off the ground with steady hands at my waist. I screamed, kicking my legs out until I caught him in the groin, grinning in satisfaction when I discovered that the ghosts of the Wild Hunt were just as weakened by a well-aimed kick as human men were.

Glaring at me as the other Huntsman staggered with a grunt, the leader tried to get a better grip so he could lift me onto the front of his horse. He jumped down from his mount, his heavy boots thumping against the ground as he landed in front of me. “Fine then. If you can’t play nice, you’ll ride with me, Beasty,” he said, reaching out to grab me from his companion. I sank down, making myself as heavy as possible until my ass hit the dirt beneath me. Grabbing a fistful of it, I cursed the magic of my Fae Mark for remaining silent while I truly needed it to protect me.

I threw the dirt in the leader’s face, grinning in satisfaction when his eyes closed suddenly as the grains struck him. He reached up to brush them off and I scrambled to get my good arm beneath my body. My ribs ached as I got my feet beneath me once more, pushing backwards and trying desperately to stand as the other male tried to get a grip on me.

“That,” the leader said, pausing as his white eyes gleamed and he wiped the last of the dirt from his face. “Wasn’t very nice.”

“I’m all out of fucking nice today,” I spat, hauling myself backward and trying to angle my body toward the cliff face. He stepped between me and my goal, shaking his head in silent reprimand. I fumbled around on the forest floor in the darkness, looking for anything I could use as a weapon.

Looking for the dagger Brann might have dropped after he tried to kill me. My heart hurt with just the thought of it, but there was no sign of the gleaming silver.

The best I did manage to find was a tree branch that even I would be able to snap in half with my bare hands, but I lifted it in silent threat anyway. A warning formed on my lips; I was ready to go down with a fight and give everything I had left. I didn’t care that it was a battle I was destined to lose.

I’d make them feel my pain.

A male body vaulted between us, the scraping sound of metal on leather bursting through the night as he unsheathed a sword. A single slash with the heavy weapon and the leader of the Wild Hunt stumbled back in surprise. My sudden protector took the opportunity to turn back and stare at where I lay sprawled on the ground in shock.

Familiar black eyes stared down at me, gleaming and furious, even as he held out a hand to help me up. Caelum growled, his lips curling back to reveal his white teeth. "I told you not to do something fucking foolish."

13

I scrambled to my feet with a glare, my cheeks tear-stained as I wiped them furiously and raised my tree branch higher. "You couldn't have come to the rescue sooner?" I asked, the bitterness I felt weighing my voice lower.

Caelum tilted his head to the side, his eyes narrowing on the way my body hunched over my aching ribs. "Apologies, *Estrella*. I'll try to stalk you faster the next time you walk away from me." Caelum shook his head at me as if I was amusing, turning back to where the leader of the Hunt stared at him like he'd been consumed by hysteria.

I had to imagine the Fae Marked didn't usually run toward the danger of a life of captivity, but instead, as far away as they could manage. The Huntsman who'd wrapped his inky magic around my waist and prevented me from falling to my death stepped closer, tipping his upper body toward me as if that might protect his balls from my wrath.

I swung with my branch, following through on the swing even though he ducked back to avoid it. He chuckled, shaking his head from side to side as he stepped closer and evaded my second swing too. The branch was just too heavy for me to move with any speed, in spite of the adrenaline surging through my body as I fought for my freedom.

To my right, the sound of swords clashing together rang through the night. I glanced over, daring that moment of eye contact away from my opponent to watch Caelum move as if he was one with his blades. Wherever he'd trained, whatever his life had been, he avoided the leader of the Wild Hunt with a grace I'd never seen. His swords carved through the air gracefully, almost like he was dancing despite the bulk of his body and breadth of his shoulders.

He should have moved like a slug with all that muscle mass—more brawn than skill. Instead, he was as if carved from nightmares and crafted in sin. He was dangerous and beautiful and all the things a woman had no right to want for herself.

He was my only chance at freedom and a distraction I didn't need, all at once.

The branch tore out of my hands when my opponent used my moment of gawking at Caelum to his advantage. The wood splintered under my skin, drawing a gasp from me that distracted Caelum from his fight. He turned to me, his face concerned as one sword paused in the air. "I'm fine!" I shouted, ducking down to avoid the Huntsman's arms closing in to grab me.

Lunging forward, I pulled the knife from the sheath strapped to his thigh and quickly stabbed him in the side three times. The Huntsman groaned, dropping to his knees in front of me as I spun on mine and darted to my feet.

"*Gods,*" Caelum breathed at my side, his eyes narrowing on my face for a brief moment as I drove my aching body away from the fallen Fae. There was no guilt. No self-reprimand within me for sinking a blade into his flesh. Not when he hadn't hesitated for a single moment before running my brother through with his sword.

With the second Huntsman immobilized, I spun and raced for the cliff face with only regret for leaving Caelum to fight on his own.

He'd interfered on my behalf, rescued me from capture, only for me to abandon him in turn. The Huntsmen lurking at the edge of the woods kicked their skeletal horses forward as I turned my back on them, their hounds snapping their teeth as they exploded into movement. They kicked up the dirt as they raced toward me, their mouths dripping with the thick saliva that melted into shadows as their claws sank into the ground.

"*Estrella!*" Caelum yelled, raising a booted foot to kick the leader of the Wild Hunt away from him with a sudden burst of force that sent the other man sprawling onto his back. His voice echoed through the air, raising the hair on my arms as a chill swept over my skin.

The hounds snapped at my heels as I ran for the edge of the cliff, those enormous teeth clicking together as I reached it and threw myself off while shifting the dagger into my injured arm.

I fell, spinning as my body went weightless and I had to fight to suppress the scream that tried to claw its way up my throat. I faced the hounds who growled at the missed opportunity for a taste of my blood before they returned me to their master.

Caelum's dark eyes landed on mine, his face twisting with shock as he stumbled back from his fight with the Huntsman and ran toward me —heedless of the hounds waiting for him at the edge. I dropped below the cliff, flailing my arms and legs.

I grabbed onto one of the tree roots sticking out from the dirt and clay of the cliff face, and my shoulder jerked from the sudden stop, the bones throbbing as I clung to the root in desperation. Unlike the weak and nearly useless one, my shoulder held as my body swung. The skin on my hand tore open, the bark of the root scraping it off.

"Estrella!" Caelum roared again, his voice echoing through the void where the land dropped away to ocean. I ignored the plea in it, pushing past the overwhelming urge to tell him I was safe.

Reaching with a pained grunt, I dropped the dagger, listening for the sound of it splashing into the water. I grabbed a lower tree root, searching for a place to put my feet as I prepared to lower myself down the wall. Brann had to be there. There had to be some sign of him and what had happened after he fell. I needed to see him, needed the closure that would come from laying eyes on his body.

The clay supported the very tips of my shoes, allowing me to move myself down the cliff with painful slowness while the sound of fighting rang out through the air above me, reassuring me that, at least for the moment, Caelum was okay.

He hadn't yet been captured, but it was only a matter of time.

My arms ached as I continued to lower myself, my toes grappling for purchase to take some of the pressure off my limbs that were nowhere near strong enough to support my entire weight for long. I couldn't believe I'd survived the fall at all, that I'd been capable of the strength to catch myself in the first place.

It had definitely been one of those moments where I'd acted first, with no thought for how exactly I would get back up to the top after I found what remained of my brother.

I shoved down a strange surge of guilt for choosing to look for Brann instead of helping Caelum fight. My brother would always come before a stranger, even one who called to the part of me that wanted to belong somewhere. It was my fault I was plunging down a cliff to try to find my brother's body.

He couldn't be dead, but I couldn't move on until I knew. And I wouldn't be responsible for the same happening to Caelum, if he did manage to escape the Wild Hunt and leave me behind. He was far better off without me to put him in danger.

I lowered myself down the cliff, dropping to a rocky ledge, my urgency making me careless about whether it would hold or crumble beneath the sudden impact of my weight. My legs buckled beneath me as I rocked forward to prevent them from breaking, then scrambled to my feet and stumbled down the sand and dirt to the receding tide below.

At the edge, I walked farther until the icy seawater rushed into my worn boots and filled the soles with needles of ice, until the water claimed me as I stumbled to my knees and the waves crashed over my head.

I rose, emerging from the salt water and flinging my hair back as I scrubbed my hand over my face. *"Brann!"* I screamed, searching left and right. The night was too dark to see far, the water a well of black at my feet as I felt around for where he might have landed, but I couldn't rest until I saw him for myself. Until I laid eyes on his body and knew beyond a shadow of a doubt that my brother was gone, I wouldn't be able to stop.

I turned to look back at the steep slope behind me, searching for a body on the shore with my eyes as I searched under the surface with my feet. If he'd managed to swim to land, the cold could have rendered him unable to move any farther. There was no sign of him, so I spun forward and prepared to dive back into the water.

I'd been meant to die with him anyway, so I'd search for him until I did.

Unforgiving hands wrapped around my waist and sent a shock of pain through my torso, lifting me off my feet as their owner walked us back toward the shore. "No!" I screamed, kicking my legs through the black water at our feet. "Let me go! I have to find him!"

"He's gone, Little One," Caelum murmured in my ear as he dragged me back. "You should be, too. What the fuck were you thinking with that stunt?"

A strangled sob climbed up my throat as I clawed at his arms in a last bid to get free. I'd barely managed to climb down on my own, stumbling over my own feet as I hurried down the last of the hill at the bottom of the cliff, but somehow Caelum navigated up with one arm wrapped around me, dragging me with him.

"Let go!" I screamed, the sound bouncing off his neck where he wrapped me in his embrace to haul me up the last of the hill.

"You have to be quiet," he snapped, looking up at the top of the cliff where the Wild Hunt probably still waited for us. "Your brother is gone. He will not answer you from the Void, no matter how loudly you call to him. Nothing human could have survived that."

"I did," I argued, glancing back toward the water.

"And you are no longer human," he said pointedly, touching a freezing hand to the Mark on my neck as we crested the hill, above the high tide line, and he settled us down flat against the dirt as he watched the cliff for any sign of movement. He laid his body atop mine, pressing me into the ground at my back with his weight as he spoke the words. They resonated with the part of me that had clung to my hope. Brann had always been stronger, more agile than I was, but even he wouldn't have been skilled enough to climb down, especially not after being stabbed in the stomach. My body went lax beneath Caelum's; all the fight draining out of me as reality settled over me.

My brother was gone. He'd never annoy me with his overprotectiveness again. He'd never smile at me when he thought I was being foolish but he loved me anyway.

He'd never *live*.

My bottom lip trembled as I shook my head, staring up into Caelum's dark eyes as he dropped his forehead to mine. "I'm sorry, Little One," he whispered, watching as I let my eyes drift closed. The urge to follow Brann into death like I'd promised plucked at the edges of my consciousness as the cold settled into my bones. "I need to get you warm."

Caelum lifted himself off me, hauling me into his grip until my legs draped over one arm and he wrapped the other around my back. He carried me over the ledge at the base of the cliff, poking it with his toe every step he took.

My teeth chattered as I glanced down at the pea-green fabric of my dress, wincing when I realized how it clung to my skin. Caelum didn't allow himself to be distracted by it, searching along the ground for something until he breathed a sigh of relief.

A cave just large enough for the two of us and high enough that we should be safe from the rising tide stared back at me when I turned my head to look at what he'd seen. He stepped inside it quickly, glancing up at the top of the cliff as he did, to make sure we weren't spotted.

Once we were tucked as far back as the cave would allow, he gently lowered me to the ground and stripped off his cloak. Draping it around my shoulders and drawing the hood up to cover my wet hair, he didn't so much as shiver as he gathered what wood and moss he could find from the cave entrance.

He pulled flint from his pocket, striking his dagger against it until sparks lit up the cave. He got a fire going with efficiency I'd never seen, stepping away as it touched the wood and started to emit heat. He came back to me, arranging himself behind me and pulling me against his chest.

I stared at the flames, watching them dance over the dirt walls of the cave that had offered us shelter. Caelum laid us down, curling his body into the back of mine. Indifferently, outside the numbness in my body and the numbness in my heart, I realized I'd never been held this way.

I'd never lain down with a man and just...been. In another time, another world, it might have been nice to fit together with someone so perfectly—to feel complete in another person's arms—but in this one, it felt like a betrayal of everything Brann had warned me about.

I wept, watching the fire dance until my eyes drifted closed to the rhythmic sound of Caelum's breath behind me, his heart beating in tandem with mine.

14

The smell of food cooking tickled my senses, pulling me from the depths of a dream clouded in nothing but darkness all around me. The threat of the Fae, the loss of my brother: all of it had led me to the darkest place I could ever imagine being.

My eyes fluttered open, landing on where Caelum squatted between me and the fire. He clutched a stick in each hand, a fish speared onto the end of it and roasting over the flames. I covered my mouth as I yawned, wincing at the metallic taste and wishing for a way to brush my teeth.

I shifted, lifting my head off the arm I'd used as a pillow and wiggling my stiff body to test the soreness in my limbs. Caelum turned, sensing my movement and giving me a cursory glance before he turned back to the fire and inspected the fish.

"It will be ready in just a few more minutes," he said, his voice louder than the rumbling in my stomach.

I sat up, my brow furrowing when my body didn't hurt. There was a distinct tightness to it, a reminder of all the places I'd been injured in my attempted escape from the Wild Hunt, but my shoulder no longer throbbed with pain. My ribs didn't feel like they would crush my guts at any moment. The fabric of my dress was still damp from digging through the water for Brann's body, lending a distinctive chill to my skin that even the fire couldn't seem to chase away.

"How are you feeling?" Caelum asked, maneuvering himself back away from the fire. He took a seat next to me, his legs touching mine as his body heat spread through my thighs.

"Cold, but okay otherwise," I said, evading the hidden question. We both knew the physical trauma of the night before would never compare to the loss of my brother and the scars I'd wear for the rest of my life, knowing I'd been the cause of his death.

Caelum nodded, allowing me privacy for the moment. I swallowed past the tears burning my throat, watching as Caelum set the fish down on an enormous leaf he must have gathered while I slept. Using a freshly cleaned dagger that showed no signs of the fight the night before, he removed the head and tail and then cut from the backbone to the cavity so that he could peel off a filet. He moved with sure hands, with a muscle memory that spoke to his experience with fish. "Is it safe?" I asked, watching as he picked up a chunk of the flaked meat between two fingers and held it out near my mouth.

"Why wouldn't it be safe?" he asked, the words grumbled like he couldn't quite believe the question.

"We weren't allowed to eat fish in Mistfell," I explained. "The Mist Guard said there was too great a risk the magic of Faerie would touch us if we consumed it."

Caelum smiled, touching the fish to my lips. His smile shifted into something darker the moment my stomach rumbled in response. "I hardly think it matters now," he said, his eyes dropping to the Mark that seemed to pulse in response to the attention of another like me. "Eat, Estrella," he growled, the command clenching something low in my belly.

I opened my mouth, letting him set the chunk of fish on my tongue, and his fingers brushed against it before he withdrew them, letting me chew while he gathered another bite for me. I wrinkled my nose as the unusual flavor touched my tongue. "It probably takes some getting used to," Caelum said with a chuckle.

I paused my chewing when he lifted another bite to my mouth, swallowing the fish down and holding up a hand. "You need to eat too."

"I will after I feed you. The faster you eat, the sooner I will," he said, smiling as he stared down at my mouth. Choosing the path of least resistance, I opened again, even though I wasn't sure I liked it, having trained my entire life for eating meals however they came. In the back of my mind, part of me wanted to protest that I could feed myself, but a quick glance down at the mud and filth covering my hands compared to his sparkling clean ones made that impossible.

Beneath the mud was the clear tinge of red staining my skin, blood from the Huntsman I'd stabbed. Caelum's gaze followed mine, landing on the gore with an amused smirk. "I suspect not many humans can claim they've stabbed a member of the Wild Hunt, Little One," he said, feeding more bites of the fish until the last of mine was gone. It was the only food I'd had aside from the bread Brann had brought the night before and a handful of berries we'd picked as we walked.

I'd never fished, and hunting was forbidden for a woman. I had absolutely no skills that would keep food in my belly. Nothing that could help with my survival. What value did my skills as a harvester have when I had no crops to tend to? The wild plants through the kingdom were vastly different from the those grown in the gardens at Mistfell, and every step further from my home meant exposure to plants I didn't know.

But at least I could stab a Fae male without feeling a hint of remorse.

That would do.

"I imagine not," I agreed, watching as he prepped the second fish and held up another bite for me. Shaking my head, I touched my content belly and told him to eat it.

He did, eating quickly and neatly until all that remained were the carcasses left behind. My guilt scratched at the back of my mind, a tingling reminder that I should be dead with my brother, not eating fish with the very man he'd warned me to stay far away from. But in the wake of my loss, with the grief threatening to consume me, I wasn't strong enough to stand on my own, and I wasn't sure I ever would be.

The thought of navigating the kingdom I'd never seen and evading both humans and Fae alike was something that now terrified me. It seemed easier with someone at my side, for better or worse.

"There's a tide pool just below the cave," Caelum said, pushing to his feet with fluid grace. He held out a hand, staring down at me where I sat huddled on the floor. "Let's get you cleaned up."

There was no concern for the dirt and grime as he held that hand out to me, waiting for me to reach up and take it, with something dancing behind his eyes. The challenge in them made me want to shove to my feet on my own, ignore the help he offered, and prove I could do this alone.

Instead, I placed my hand in his, accepting the help even though it pained the proudest part of me to admit I needed it. The unfortunate fact was, I no longer thought I could continue on my own. Without someone to push me, I felt like I might lie down in the cave and wait for death to come.

Caelum reached out with his other hand to adjust his cloak, which was draped over my shoulders. He pulled the hood up to cover my still-damp hair, fastening the clasp at the front. The earthy green of the fabric blended into the natural landscape above the cliff.

His trousers were black, his shirt a dark gray that would serve him well in the night if his ash-blond hair didn't shine like a beacon. "You'll be cold," I said, protesting the cloak settled around my shoulders even as it provided heat I desperately needed.

"I quite like the cold, actually. We'll see if we can find you a warm change of clothes at the next village," he said, tightening his grip on my hand as he led me from the cave. The dim light of early morning shone in through the entrance, lighting the way as he guided me down toward the tide pool at the base of the bluff below the little ledge where the cave protected us.

Caelum stepped down first, releasing my hand to traverse the slippery rocks. I gathered my dress up in my hands to follow, lifting it so that I could see where my feet fell.

Once Caelum had navigated down, he reached up his long arms to place his hands at my waist. Lifting me up off the ground, he lowered me to where he stood, so that my body slid down the front of his. I felt every hard ridge of muscle as he maneuvered me, until the moment when my feet touched the ground in front of him.

I stared up at him for a moment, lost in the deep glint of his eyes as he looked down at me. The tide lapping against the rocky base of the incline finally drew my attention away, and I automatically scanned the shore for any trace of my brother.

There was none to be found, and Caelum seemed oblivious to my search as he took my hand and guided me to the tide pool. I lifted my dress as I squatted down, tucking it between my legs to keep the fabric from getting even more stained by the mix of mud and sand at my feet.

Plunging my hands into the freezing water, I felt a moment of shock as I realized my entire body had been submerged in it the night before. In my desperation to find Brann, I hadn't felt the truth of how cold I was, or realized how close to freezing to death I'd come.

"Don't even think about it, Little One," Caelum ordered, snapping my attention back to him. I realized I'd been staring at the surface of the channel and the way the mist touched it. "It's too dangerous. We've already spent too much time in one place. We need to move if we want to avoid another run-in with the Wild Hunt."

I scrubbed the blood from my hands, and as soon as I finished, Caelum grabbed my hand and led me up the small incline to the cliff face. "How did you manage to get down, anyway?" he asked, heading straight for the cliff face. He eyed it, undoubtedly scanning the steep wall for the best way to climb back up.

"I jumped," I answered, meeting his stunned expression when he stared down at me. It felt like stating the obvious when he'd watched me go over the edge and begin to fall; I'd seen the shock in his expression as I disappeared from view.

"You jumped? Are you out of your fucking mind? I thought you'd found some way down that I didn't see when I came after you."

"I scaled the wall. I didn't just plummet to my death, though that was the initial plan," I said, shrugging my shoulders when he clenched his jaw.

"So you are out of your fucking mind," he said, rolling his eyes skyward as if the Gods would save him from having to deal with a reckless woman as his traveling companion.

"It's highly probable, yes," I snapped, shrugging off his touch when he reached over and grabbed me. Tugging me toward him, he pressed his chest into my spine, sliding his hands over the sleeve of my dress until he covered the bare skin of mine with his palms.

He guided them to a spot where there was a notch in the stone, curling my fingers around it as I stretched up onto my toes. "Alright then, Little One. Let's see if you can manage to get yourself back up or if I'm going to have to carry you." I turned to glare at him over my shoulder, finding his mouth twisted in a smirk.

A pounding in my ears nearly distracted me from the task at hand, leaving me twitchy with the need to smack the arrogant look off his face. "Fine," I huffed, releasing the spot where he'd placed my hand. I bent down, gathering the fabric of my dress in my hands and twisting it up around my knees.

Cold air touched my legs, dancing over the bare skin, and I shivered in spite of myself. I twisted the worn, mangled fabric into a knot, letting it hang at my thighs so that I'd have full range of motion.

"Look up my dress, and you may find you wake up without any eyeballs one morning," I said, narrowing my eyes at him as I raised my hand up to that notch he'd shown me before. I reached with my other hand, searching for a spot to place it as I put all the energy I had into pulling myself up.

My feet fought for purchase, looking for a place to take some of my weight. Coming down had been easier; I'd been so filled with adrenaline and desperation that *nothing* could have kept me away.

My fingers trembled as I gripped the rock, taking it one reach at a time, one step at a time. Caelum waited until I was halfway up the cliff and turned to look down at him, my vision swimming with nausea as I stared down at the sheer drop.

In the middle of the night, it had been so easy to underestimate just how far that fall was. So easy to convince myself Brann might have survived. But in the light of day, I knew the fall into the sand or water below would have broken every bone in his body.

Even if he hadn't been stabbed first.

Caelum scaled the wall at my side, moving much quicker than I could, with an agility that seemed impossible. His arms and legs were so much longer than mine, letting him cover more ground with every precious movement.

He paused at my side, staring at the way that I fought for my grip. I tilted my face forward, letting the cold of the stone touch my forehead as I drew in a deep breath. "I can still carry you."

"Fuck you," I snapped, turning to pierce him with a glare. The thought of anyone carrying me up this steep embankment was ridiculous, but there was no doubt on his face as he moved up with ease at my side. He stayed with me, offering guidance when I needed it but otherwise leaving me untouched, when I needed to prove I wasn't a complete waste of breath—even if only to myself.

My lungs heaved with the effort of shoving my body up the cliff I'd jumped over in a moment of impulse, which had turned out to be pointless. By the time we reached the top, I was half-tempted to throw myself to the ground and kiss it.

I grabbed the ground at the top, trying to pull myself up as my arms shook with exertion. Caelum scaled it at my side, pulling himself over the ledge and holding out a hand for me to take. I grunted as I placed mine in his, hating the moment of weakness but accepting the help anyway. At that moment, I was too tired to care beyond a fleeting thought, even knowing it would nag at me the next time I tried to fall asleep.

I sprawled out on the ground, trying to catch my breath as Caelum spun in the clearing at the top of the cliff, with his hand on his sword. There was no sign of the Wild Hunt that had sent Brann and I over the ledge the night before; they were gone without a trace as they sought out more of the Fae Marked.

"How did you escape the Wild Hunt, anyway?" I asked. The signs of the scuffle of the night before could be seen in the boot marks in the dirt, in the torn grass and disturbed foliage at the edge of the woods and the hoof prints all over the clearing.

In the spots of blood staining the ground.

Caelum paused, turning to look at me with his brow raised in question. "They were far more interested in getting to you than they were winning the fight against me. After you went over the edge, they mounted their horses and tried to find another way down the cliff," he said, his stare intensifying as he gave me a cursory look-over. "So tell me, Little One. What's so special about you?"

My thoughts froze as I blinked up at him, turning his words over in his head. The Wild Hunt *had* seemed interested in my Mark, as had the Mist Guard back in Mistfell. "I don't know," I mumbled, my mouth feeling filled with sand with the dryness in my throat.

Being hunted was bad enough, believing I was just one of the masses the Wild Hunt needed to collect. The idea of being singled out was inconceivable.

I shook my head slightly, waiting for him to push the questions, but he only nodded as if he understood that I couldn't give him answers. I knew nothing about why they had chosen to go after me while abandoning him. What I did know was that I would never be able to fight them off on my own. I hadn't fared well the first time, but Caelum had held his own. He'd have lost eventually, if they hadn't given up, but I'd need someone at my side to help me fight if and when the time came again.

I needed him far more than he needed me. The pang of guilt within me was an echo of the knowledge that I'd probably get him killed, just as I had Brann. "What do we do now?" I asked, feeling awkward in the face of the attitude I'd given him at the bottom of the cliff. I should have been more appreciative of the fact that he'd come to save me, but something about him just brought out my impulsiveness.

"We stick together. Head inland toward The Hollows. We'll follow those as far as we can, and eventually we should make our way to the Mountains at Rochpar," he explained.

"That's on the other side of the Kingdom," I protested, trying not to think about how many weeks a journey like that would take on foot.

"That's the point. The more distance we put between us and the Fae, the better it will be for both of us," he said, his voice dejected as he said the words. "But first, we both need a change of dry clothes."

"Okay," I said, fighting back the nagging voice in my head that I shouldn't leave this cliff alive. Brann's words rang in my memory, his urgency that the Fae never take me. He'd been so desperate that he'd tried to kill me himself, nearly plunging a dagger into my heart.

I wished we'd had more time, more chances for him to open up about what he knew about what waited for me beyond the Veil.

"Promise me, Estrella," Caelum said, stepping closer to me. Those dark, glittering eyes stared down at me intently, his body tilting forward over me until his forehead touched mine and he sighed contentedly.

"Promise you what?" I asked, swallowing back the nerves I felt around him. Something about him put me on edge, as if he could hear my thoughts and knew just when I was doubting I was making the right choice by going with him.

"Promise me we'll stay together. Everything will be okay, and we'll find a safe place to settle. But we have to do it together; do you understand?" he asked, that same compulsion in his voice that I'd felt with Brann's.

I nodded, sealing my fate with three little words, while utterly failing to understand their impact. "I swear it."

15

I trailed behind Caelum as he led the way through the woods, walking with the calm assurance of a man who knew how to navigate in a place where everything looked the same. I suspected we might be heading in the direction we'd come the night before, back toward the village with the barn that had changed everything and sent us spiraling down a path that I regretted with every breath.

Every so often, Caelum tried to interject and start a conversation up, but I think he grew tired of receiving one word answers from me. He studied me with the wariness of a man who thought I might just lie down in the middle of the forest and sleep for an eternity, and in my weaker moments that was exactly what I felt like doing.

"He wouldn't want you to give up," he said finally, acknowledging what we both knew kept me quiet. My grief consumed me, the knowledge that I'd been responsible for Brann's death sitting heavy on my shoulders.

"You know nothing of my brother," I snapped, my vision filling with the memory of Brann's remorse as he raised the dagger high and prepared to sink it into my heart. I didn't know what Caelum had seen on the cliff before he'd intervened, didn't know if Brann's attempt on my life was shared knowledge between us, but even I understood that my brother had been keeping secrets from me.

"I know that if I were fortunate enough to have a sister, I would protect her with *everything* I had to give. Even if that meant losing my life so that she could continue on. You can't quit now, not when he gave his life for you," Caelum said, his voice gentle despite the harsh words. It was as if he knew he needed to temper them with something soft, that my breaking point loomed just out of reach.

"And what am I supposed to do if what he wanted was for me to die?" I asked before I could think better of it. I regretted the words as soon as they'd left my mouth, squeezing my eyes shut as I berated myself for my stupidity.

If I needed Caelum, adding more to the possibility of there being something fundamentally wrong with me was probably the stupidest choice I could make.

"What?" Caelum asked, his voice nearly silent as his steps stopped altogether. His hands clenched and unclenched at his sides, his jaw tightening as those dark eyes glared down at me. "What do you mean he wanted you to die?"

I sank my teeth into my bottom lip, turning away from him and his blinding intensity as I continued in the direction we'd been walking only a moment before. "Death was preferable to being taken. That's all I meant." I brushed off my near admission, hoping he wouldn't read further into something that really could be so simple.

"Do not lie to me, Estrella," he said, grasping my forearm and spinning me around to face him once again. He invaded my space, his stomach so close to my chest that a deep breath would force us to touch. The moment would have felt intimate if it hadn't been for the hatred blazing in his eyes. "That is the one thing I will not tolerate from you. If you want to keep your secrets, then fine. Keep them, but at least give me the respect of not looking me in the eye and tainting that pretty mouth with ugly lies."

"Fine," I grumbled, snapping my mouth closed as soon as I'd clipped out that one word. If he didn't want me to lie, then I wouldn't lie. I'd just keep my Gods-damned secrets to myself.

Caelum chuckled, the rage fading off his face with an odd sort of rumble from his chest. "Oh, Little One. I am going to enjoy unraveling every part of you slowly," he murmured, lifting one of his calloused hands to brush a lock of hair back from my face. His skin touched mine gently as his finger curved over my cheek and down the line of my jaw, stopping to grip my chin for a moment before he released me.

"You just said I could keep my secrets," I said, my voice cracking as his smile washed over me. His voice was the greatest sin, wrapping around the words as if they were a sensual promise.

"You're welcome to try," he said, releasing my forearm where he'd grabbed me, in favor of tracing a single finger over the sleeve of my dress. It was the same spot where my dagger had rested before, pressed against my skin and waiting for me to use it to kill myself.

Brann had saved me the trouble, pulling it free and trying to take my burden from me himself.

"But I think we both know it's only a matter of time before you let me inside your head. If we're both being entirely honest," he murmured, his gaze burning into mine. "I'm already there."

"That's a bold presumption to make toward someone you've just met," I said, jerking my arm away from his grip and continuing on my way. His hands came down on my shoulders, pointedly turning my body to the proper direction so I didn't walk off our course. He came up beside me, strolling as if he didn't have a care in the world and hadn't insisted he would invade my privacy bit by bit.

"Perhaps, or maybe it's just the truth. If it's any consolation, you're already in mine, too, Little One. Every time I close my eyes I see you holding a blade to my throat with your eyes burning as if you were born in blood and violence," he said, immediately drawing from the horrific stories I'd heard from my father when he spoke of my birth.

Of the way my mother had nearly died trying to deliver me.

Caelum took my hand in his, the coolness of his skin drawing a shiver from me as he guided me to the side and into the space where the trees were closer and provided better cover. The village Brann and I had abandoned the night before loomed ahead, the structure of the barn both a taunt and a reminder of all that I'd lost since then.

"Let's find you something warmer," he said, ducking low and pulling me to follow him as he skirted around the edge of the village. People meandered down the road that went between the houses, unaware that we were sneaking around nearby. We passed the pub where Brann had gone to search for food in exchange for helping out the next morning, my heart leaping into my throat when a man his age hurried around inside the dirty windows. "Stay here."

I did as he said, watching as he bent forward and made his body smaller. He crouched as low as he could, approaching one of the houses on the outskirts of the village and the clothesline where a woolen dress hung. He pulled it off quickly, hurrying back into the tree line unnoticed as I sighed in relief. The last thing either of us needed was to attract attention for stealing, and I suspected we would have a lot of it in our future, since we couldn't be seen with our Fae Marks.

He returned to my side, draping the dress over his arm as we continued to circle around the outskirts of the village. "I haven't seen any cloaks."

"Most people have just started wearing them. I doubt they're all that dirty yet," I said, shrugging even though it pained me to think of not being able to find one. I couldn't wear Caelum's forever, and a winter without even a cloak to cover me wouldn't be survivable.

When we emerged back to the place where we'd first come upon the village, the barn once again tormenting me, Caelum heaved a sigh of resignation. "We'll look in the next village," he conceded.

I yearned for even the thin cloak I'd lost, and I'd hoped we would stumble across it as we made our way back to the village. Part of me was even certain we'd passed the very same copse of trees where I'd lost it, but there was nothing to be found.

As if it had floated away like ashes in the wind.

He carried the dress as we passed the village and headed in the opposite direction of the cliffs. We walked in near silence for a few minutes, his cloak feeling heavy around my shoulders. I still felt chilled to the bone, my dress cold and slightly damp, and the knowledge that I would need to give it back soon didn't help matters.

"Go ahead and change," he said, stopping when we were far enough away from the village that our risk of being stumbled upon had diminished. I swallowed, staring into his dark eyes as he watched me reach up trembling fingers to unclasp his cloak.

I turned to the side, draping it over a fallen log in the woods so it wouldn't touch the ground. "Do you mind?" I asked, finding him still watching me as I unlaced the top of my dress.

"Not particularly," he said, smirking as he watched my fingers cease to move. I bit the inside of my cheek, shoving down the sharp retort I wanted to give.

"I'm not taking my clothes off in front of you," I said, trying to ignore his infuriating, arrogant expression.

"I promise you, I have seen a naked woman before, Little One. I'm capable of controlling myself," he said, raising a brow at me. I snatched the dress from his hands, turning and walking into the thicker parts of the trees with a huff.

"I promise you I don't care!" I called over my shoulder, ducking behind the biggest tree trunk I could find.

His aggravating laughter echoed through the woods, wrapping around me as I dropped my pea green dress to the ground and slid the new, dark brown one over my head.

Dick.

Once I'd changed and successfully hidden my body from Caelum's prying eyes, we continued trudging through the seemingly endless woods. The hours passed by in a monotonous blur, and all I could think was that it was far too similar to my days spent staring into twilight berry bushes.

I regretted my boredom the moment night fell over the forest, bathing me in darkness that made me startle at every sound. I'd always loved it, always found comfort in the inky shadows as they wrapped around me. Something about it, after being pursued in the eclipse when the Fae took over our world, while running for my life with my brother at my side, just didn't feel like home anymore.

It was just one more thing the Fae had taken from me, and I hated them even more for it. If I didn't belong to the night, then where exactly did I belong at all?

"We should stop for the night," Caelum said, looking at the sky above us.

"Where though?" I asked, looking around for any place to hide and take shelter. There wasn't a clear spot that would hide us from the Wild Hunt or the Mist Guard; nothing that could provide any semblance of cover whatsoever.

"We won't always have a barn or a cave to sleep in, Little One. Tonight we'll have to sleep beneath the stars and take turns on watch," he said, moving to a place where the trees were thicker and provided just a little bit more shelter from hunting eyes.

"How do I know I can trust you to watch over me while I sleep?" I asked, crossing my arms over my chest as he dropped to the ground gracefully, his massive body seeming fluid as it melted down to the forest floor.

"If I wanted to hurt you, I wouldn't have to wait until you're asleep to do it, my star, and I most definitely wouldn't have bothered saving you from the Wild Hunt," he said, his lips curving into a grin. I grimaced at the words and the reminder of my own weakness. It shamed me to admit that I liked when he called me Little One, against my best intentions, though I would never tell him that. "My star," on the other hand, sent a wave of something that felt a lot like affection through me, warming my cheeks.

I shoved it down in my irritation.

"You're so pretty until you speak," I said, smiling at him sweetly. "Do try not to ruin it."

He chuckled as I took a seat next to him, my cheeks flushing at the smirk that claimed his lips. He sank his white teeth into his bottom lip as he studied me intently, like a predator stalking his prey.

"Why is it that you blush when you compliment me? Shouldn't it be my face that turns pink?" he asked, grasping my hand in my crossed arms and tugging as if he wanted me to sit closer to him. I resisted.

"Only you would take it as a compliment when someone tells you that you're prettier when you're silent," I returned with a scoff, refusing to answer his question. Caelum didn't need to know that I found him far more than pretty, that something I didn't understand compelled me toward him. He seemed larger than life. He terrified me, but he also appealed to me, turning my insides liquid and me into someone he could play with and mold into whatever he wanted.

"I've heard worse," he said, shrugging his shoulders and quirking a brow at me. "I wonder how much you'll blush when I tell you that you're the most beautiful woman I've ever seen." Everything in me stilled, and I turned my face away from his to hide the deep red stain to my cheeks. Even knowing it was a lie or an exaggeration, or both, I couldn't stop the flush that lit my face on fire. "Like that then."

It should be criminal to be so handsome that he threatened to make me lose my senses while his mouth tormented me so easily. I recovered as quickly as I could, clearing my throat. "Perhaps it is you who should be worried, Caelum the Marked," I said, twisting my lips into a saccharine smile as he watched me. I fought back a shiver as the cold from the ground seeped into me, even with my dress as a barrier.

I knew without asking that there could be no fire to keep us warm tonight, not without a hiding place to shield the light from all manner of predators or the beings hunting us. I shuddered just thinking of what might find us, uncertain if I preferred death by fang to death by freezing or blade.

"Are you planning to gut me while I sleep, my star?" he asked, as he laid himself out on the ground. Even with his cloak still wrapped around my shoulders, he didn't seem bothered by the cold dirt beneath him. Stretching his arms over his head and cocking a knee so the bottom of his boot pressed into the ground, he bent his elbows and used his forearms as a pillow. "Perhaps burn me with the fire that smolders inside of you, waiting to ignite?"

"I need you alive for now, but that doesn't mean I need you to have *all* of your appendages functioning. I've kind of always wondered how a man would scream if I cut off his prized flesh between his legs," I said, wrinkling my nose. My only hesitation in doing it to Lord Byron, aside from the obvious death sentence it would bring, had been that I would need to touch it in order for that to happen.

I would pass on that any chance I got.

"There's my girl," he said, pursing his lips in a move that only drew attention to them. All I wanted was to lean forward and sink my teeth into the plump, tempting flesh, to draw blood in a way that felt so unlike me. I'd enjoyed being able to protect myself in the past, but I'd never thought of myself as being particularly violent.

Not until the Fae Mark took everything I thought I knew about myself and changed me, twisting me into the bitter, rage-filled woman I felt myself growing into more and more, every hour that passed. The darkness lurking inside of me seemed overwhelming in the moments when I overreacted to Caelum's ridiculous commentary and his desire to irritate me.

He pushed me, challenged me, but there was nothing that he'd done to deserve my ire. He'd even saved my life. So what was it about the stupidly handsome man that kept me in a constant state of vacillating between wanting to fight with him and wanting to kiss him?

"I'm not your anything," I said, laying myself on the ground next to him. I kept my distance, ensuring that no parts of our bodies touched. I wouldn't allow myself to show how cold I was, gritting my teeth as I fought back the chattering that wanted to overtake my jaw.

"We'll see how long that lasts," Caelum retorted with a chuckle, turning his body toward mine. He scooted forward, inching across the grass, dirt, and dead, dried leaves beneath us. They crackled, the sound grating on me as I stared up at the last, bare hint of light in the sky above us. Shortly enough, there would only be the moon and stars shining in the dark sky.

Something slid over my wrist, and I squeaked as quietly as I could and shoved it off. The flesh of a male arm against my hand drew a relieved sigh from me, the lack of scales or slime reassuring against the initial instinct that I'd attracted something far more menacing.

Though some nights in Lord Byron's library had made me question if there was anything more menacing than a man when he didn't get what he wanted.

"What are you doing?" I asked, flinching back as he wrapped that arm around me more tightly and pulled me into his chest. He was somehow warm, his body heat radiating into me as I pressed my freezing hands against his stomach.

"You're going to freeze," he said, acting as if it was obvious. The shadows hid the expression on his face, masking it from my view except for the faintest trace of his bone structure. He grabbed hold of his cloak where it was wrapped around me, unclasping it from around my throat and shifting it to cover us both as he slid his other arm underneath my neck and offered it to me as a pillow. "Get some sleep, Little One. I'll take first watch."

I nodded, and I would have sworn that my mind wouldn't allow itself to fall asleep with a stranger so near. I'd never just been held in my life, never lain with a man at my side. For all that I'd experienced in terms of physical affection, between the abuse of Lord Byron's hands on my skin and the hurried moments of passion I'd had with Loris, had I ever really known anything of true intimacy?

I could think of nothing more intimate than the feeling of Caelum's breath rustling my hair, and his rhythmic heartbeat thumping against my face softly as I curled closer into him.

For warmth, I assured myself as he shifted his body, and I felt his gaze on my face as my eyes drifted closed. The softness of his lips brushed against my forehead, sending a tingle through the back of my neck in response as my exhaustion claimed me.

Most definitely for warmth.

16

We were on our way once again after Caelum caught a quick breakfast of wild hare. He'd managed to trap it while I was still sleeping. He'd never woke me in the night to take watch, and I didn't know if it was because he had fallen asleep, as well, or because he'd been afraid I might in fact take his balls off while he slumbered.

I'd slept straight through the night, waking long after he had, at any rate, and we'd continued our trek toward the Hollow Mountains, much to my dismay.

The dress Caelum had snagged off the clothesline was a size too small, the fabric clinging to me more tightly than felt tolerable, but the alternative had been to continue to wear my thinner, damp, and muddy dress that had more holes than I cared to count.

Caelum had continued to be largely silent most of the day, letting me stew in my grief as we traveled. Being with him stung with betrayal when Brann had wanted me to stay away and go our own way, but I wasn't capable of making the long trip to the safety the Mountains at Rochpar might offer on my own.

I didn't know the way. Didn't know how to navigate the same way

Caelum seemed to, only pulling an engraved compass from his trouser pocket every now and then.

My legs throbbed with endless movement, the walking and uneven terrain something that I was far from used to. My midnight strolls to the Veil could never compare to the steady and relentless pace Caelum set.

We came to another dip in the valley, a drop of uneven terrain that would have hurt, had we dared to continue our path in the darkness last night. Caelum jumped down, landing smoothly on steady feet as he bent his knees to absorb the impact.

He stood, turning back to face me as I approached the ledge and prepared to follow suit, hiking my dress up my calves. He gripped me around the waist, lifting me off my feet and pulling me into the front of his body, lowering me down as he'd done countless times. I stared up at him and resisted the urge to argue. There was something in Caelum that needed to care for someone, a gentleman who couldn't let me prove to be capable of taking care of myself.

I'd been fending for myself for so long, part of me liked being taken care of for once, even if I would never admit it. I'd jumped off the edge of a cliff and managed to get myself to the bottom without dying; I could handle a dip in the path, and he Gods damned knew it.

The moment my feet touched the ground at the bottom, he lifted a single hand from where the fabric of my dress hugged my waist. His cloak still hung off my shoulders, wrapping me in a warm embrace. His tunic couldn't possibly be warm enough, but just like with the drops in the valley floor, he somehow insisted on my comfort over his. Despite how strangely he made me feel, I couldn't help thinking that there weren't enough men like him left in my world. Too many were far too consumed with the need to own people and possessions, to the point that they forgot what it meant to care for others.

He tucked the hair behind my ear, those cool fingers lingering on my skin as he stared at the point of contact. My heart fluttered in my chest, the nerves I always seemed to feel around him bubbling to the surface.

When he was quiet, it was easy to forget just how strong his attention was. When he was quiet, it was easy to miss the intensity that blazed in his eyes and the way nothing existed around us the moment his gaze touched mine.

My Fae Mark buzzed with warmth, heating me beneath the cloak and giving me a moment of guilt when I realized just how cold his fingers felt. He had to be freezing, had to be suffering so that I could stay warm.

His Fae Mark glowed a soft white in response, the color of it transfixing me as I raised my hand between us and clutched the clasp on his cloak. His other hand lifted to grasp mine, shaking his head softly to prevent me from giving it back. "You need it more than I do," he said, leaning in and touching his lips to my forehead softly.

It reminded me of that same brush of lips I'd felt from him before I fell asleep the night before. Something in the touch felt protective, which I couldn't even begin to contemplate—not when our lives hung in the balance and uncertainty surrounded us.

Tomorrow wasn't promised, and while that might have made some people want to live life to the fullest, it only reminded me that Caelum could be taken at any moment. He could be killed or we could be separated, and I'd be left alone all over again. That pain would be even worse if he somehow betrayed me or chose to abandon me.

I wouldn't allow myself the heartbreak of losing someone else I cared about, so I wouldn't go there with him, no matter how tempting it might be. Because the one and only man I'd ever allowed to touch me had turned into a pile of snow when he tried to kill me. It was safe to say, my vagina was unfortunately off limits.

"We should reach the mountains by the end of the day," he said, taking his hand away from my cheek where it lingered and lowering the one from his cloak when I didn't push to return the garment to him. "We'll stay close to their bases as we travel, and there'll be caves we can hide out in at night. Fires will help us stay warm as the weather gets cooler," he explained, taking my hand in his and turning back to continue the way we'd been traveling.

His long legs had to move considerably slower than seemed natural for him so I could keep up, but he didn't seem to mind as he kept my hand clutched in his and swung it between us casually. As if we were a married couple out for a stroll in the pre-dusk hours, and not two Fae Marked humans on the run for our lives.

"Okay, but what will we do when the snow comes?" I asked, glancing down at the dress I wore and his thin trousers and tunic. Even if we'd both had cloaks, they would do nothing when we were trudging through waist-deep snow in freezing temperatures with the wind howling through the trees. We needed protection from the elements and layers of blankets and a fire if we were going to survive.

"Before the snow comes, we'll find a safe place to wait out the worst of the season. We won't have a choice. Our tracks in the snow will just lead the Mist Guard right to us," he said. "We probably have a week before we have to worry about the snow if the weather holds. We can put some decent distance between us and the boundary before then."

The words he didn't speak hung between us, a harsh reminder of the one undeniable truth. A lot could happen in a few weeks, and we'd need to survive them before we had to worry about where we would be for the winter.

Even if the thought of hiding out in a cave with him for an entire season, with nothing to do, did make my stomach flutter. No interruptions and no worry of someone stumbling across us. No awkward fumbling to get dressed if we heard people on the trail.

Just the two of us.

I shook my head, blushing when I noted Caelum's attention fixated on me as he walked. He smirked, as if he could sense the direction my thoughts had gone, then he took pity on me, clearing his throat with a chuckle and turning his attention back toward the path we walked through the woods. "Tell me about your family. Was it just you and your brother?" he asked, his face solemn and sympathetic as he glanced at me out of the corner of his eye.

"My mother too," I said. "But we had to leave her behind. My birth was difficult, and her legs just can't support her anymore, so she told us to run after I was Marked." I sighed, wishing I could turn back and make sure she was safe, but my presence would only put her in danger all over again if I dared, because the Mist Guard wouldn't hesitate to use family against me if it meant ridding the Kingdom of one more of the Fae Marked.

I shuffled my feet as I walked, dragging them through the leaves in a small protest that my steps continued to take me farther and farther from her and the life I'd known. "Your father?" Caelum asked, his brow furrowed.

With no mention of him in my first response, he had to know there was no happy ending where he was concerned. "Dead. Sacrificed to the Veil when I was a girl," I answered, my hand unconsciously rising to feel the spot on my throat where the High Priest's blade had touched me. The wound was gone, and I swallowed past the reminder that I wasn't entirely human any longer.

"Sacrificed to the Veil," he said slowly, as if he were turning the idea over in his mouth and trying to decide what to make of it. He tightened his grip on my hand momentarily, apparently brushing off whatever thought had consumed him. "I'm sorry, Little One."

"It was a long time ago," I responded, ignoring the flash of pain in my chest, as if time could ease the loss of someone so monumental in my life. My ghosts followed me wherever I went, my grief for them hanging over my head as a constant reminder of how fleeting life could be.

Even so, I didn't open up and mention that I'd been about to suffer the same fate, or that I'd touched the magical fabric of the Veil in the moments before it fell.

It couldn't have been my fault. Even so, no one could know what I'd done; I'd touched it in the moments just prior to it shattering. Not if I wanted to live without the blame people would place upon my shoulders.

"The memory of the people who matter to us never leave, no matter how many years pass," he said, pausing until I met his gaze from the corner of my eye. Something dangerous shifted behind his stare, a dark reminder of how little I actually knew about the man who'd become my travel companion. "Never hesitate to own your love for them, and to make it known that you miss them every day."

I smiled despite myself, curving my lips up at the corners as he watched the subtle movement. "Who is it that you miss every day? A girlfriend?" I asked, wishing I could mentally stab myself in the mouth.

That was not the kind of question I'd intended to ask to get to know him better, completely inappropriate considering I had no intentions of trying to fill that void if there was one.

Gods. Just kill me.

"I wouldn't call her a girlfriend, so much. The relationship we had was complicated at best, distant if I'm honest. But things have changed. I don't miss her anymore," he admitted. "Relationships are like that. Constantly evolving and changing. Not like family."

"No. Not like family," I said, thinking of Loris. While I wouldn't call him anything more than a friend, in spite of our sexual relations, I'd cared for him in my own way.

"Did you have someone back home?" he asked, his fingers tightening on my hand almost imperceptibly. I only caught it because of my fixation on his body, the way I seemed to be so in tune to the way he moved and the nuances of it.

Everything had a purpose.

"It's complicated," I said, huffing a laugh when I realized how similar our answers were. "I had a friend, who was something a little more, but it never could have gone anywhere."

His jaw clenched, annoyance crossing his face as he turned back toward the path and gave me his profile. I took pleasure in the stern set to his jaw, and the way his anger was practically palpable in the air. Even if I wouldn't dare to venture there with him, it was nice to know I wasn't the only one who felt the strange draw between us. "Why not?" he asked, the words coming out forced through gritted teeth.

"The Lord of Mistfell took an interest in me," I said, glancing toward the sun in the sky as it slowly made its way across the horizon. Night would fall soon enough, and I hoped Caelum was right and we would reach the base of the mountains by then. I didn't want to spend another night out in the open if I could avoid it. "He poisoned his wife and determined we would be married instead."

Caelum twitched, his arm going taut. He kept walking as if he hadn't flinched from my words. "You said he determined this? Did you agree to it?" The judgment in his tone disappointed me and stung; the men in Mistfell were never judged for their affairs.

Only the women they had them with.

"Of course not, but it isn't like I would've had a choice," I snapped. "He is a Lord, and I'm nothing more than a peasant who can't afford a new pair of boots. He made it quite clear I didn't have much choice if I wanted to live." I yanked my hand out of his grip.

With the intimacy of our stolen moment gone, I wanted no contact with him and the reminder of what all men did. They judged and they took and they left women to deal with the consequences.

I wanted no part of that.

"I didn't mean for it to sound as if you had any responsibility for it," Caelum said, pausing his steps. I continued forward, storming past him in my aggravation with myself, unable to believe that, even for a fleeting moment, I'd allowed myself to believe he could be anything other than what all men were. He took a few quick steps, placing himself at my side as he caught my wrist in his grip and turned me back to face him. "I'm sorry, Little One."

"I have a name," I said, the words coming out more sternly than I'd intended.

"I'm aware. It is a beautiful name," he said, the corner of his mouth tipping up in amusement. It filled me with the urge to punch him in the throat, knowing that he didn't take my anger seriously.

Moving to do just that, I curled the tips of my fingers in and jabbed my knuckles at his voice box. He caught that wrist with his free hand, staring down at me with a raised eyebrow. "That would have hurt."

"Fuck you. It was meant to," I snarled, tearing my arm back from his unrelenting grip. He didn't release me, holding it firm and using it to tug me closer to himself.

My breasts pressed against his stomach, his face leaning over mine as he grinned down at me. His eyes twinkled as those full lips parted to reveal his perfect, white teeth. "Are you ready for that, *Estrella*?" he murmured my name in that smooth, deep voice of his sounding like a purr of satisfaction. "I was under the impression you were still pretending that wasn't *exactly* what you wanted."

I flushed, shoving two hands against his chest as I attempted to step back. His knowing smile and the gleam in his eyes as he stared down at my pink cheeks meant that I needed distance.

Needed not to feel the ridges of his muscles against my heaving chest.

"That is not going to happen," I said with a glare, lifting my free hand to pry at where his fingers gripped me. He somehow didn't hurt me, but there was no releasing his grip until he willed it.

"Whatever you tell yourself to help you sleep at night, Little One. I sleep quite peacefully with my head filled with thoughts of you, and your breathy voice moaning my name while I devour you," he said, relaxing his grip on my wrist. I stumbled back, finally gaining that desperately needed space between us.

"Don't be disgusting," I snapped, straightening his cloak around my shoulders and pulling it closed tight over where my nipples hardened in response to the way he stared at me. My chest heaved, my arousal and humiliation feeling tangible, stealing the very air from my lungs.

"For you, I can be downright fucking filthy, Estrella, and you will love every Gods damned second of it," he said, taking a few steps toward me and closing the distance between us once again. He raised a hand, toying with a lock of dark hair where it rested against the fabric of his cloak hanging around my shoulders. I swatted his hand away, gritting my teeth and watching his face light with mirth. "The next time a man like the Lord of Mistfell tries to put his hands on you without your permission, you stab him in the fucking throat," he said, touching soft fingers to the bottom of my chin and tipping my face up to meet his stare.

Something in those words resonated with me, awakening the part inside that had rebelled against the need to be subservient, for my family. The part of me that had wanted something more.

"Does that include you?" I asked, yanking my head back from his touch.

"If I had any intention of mistreating you, it would. I have no need to violate you like that, Little One. You'll come to me willingly soon enough," he said, the arrogance in his voice only driving my aggravation higher. He dropped his hand between us, my body immediately feeling the absence of his touch as he strolled past me and continued down the path.

"We should hurry if we want to reach the mountains by nightfall," he said casually, as if the tension of the last few moments between us had never happened. I gaped after him for a few seconds, unwillingly staring at the way his muscles seemed to ripple with every movement. He'd be the death of me.

If I didn't kill him first.

17

The Hollow Mountains were larger than I'd ever dreamed they could be, the rolling peaks towering over us as we traveled along the base. All the texts I'd read in Lord Byron's library talked of how small they were compared to the Mountains at Rochpar, and even smaller compared to the legendary mountains of Faerie that existed on the other side of the boundary.

Caelum followed my gaze as it tracked up the face for the hundredth time. True to his word, we'd reached the range before dark, but now the sun retreated behind the peaks, bathing the forest at their feet in an eerie golden glow. This far from the boundary with Faerie, the leaves had already turned yellow and orange with the frost and begun falling to the ground. The magic of Faerie was too far to sustain the signs of life through the cold autumn nights.

He'd only spoken to me in passing since the claim that I would come to him, that I'd give him my body willingly one day soon. He couldn't possibly understand that, while I had no notion of a happily ever after with a man who would be my husband one day, I needed something more than the promise of one night of pleasure.

No matter how I might want to keep my heart my own, I suspected a man like Caelum would slither his way inside and take it for himself, if I let him. With no promise of a tomorrow, or a future at all, such an attachment could only end in heartbreak for me, whether we lived or died. I wasn't naive enough to think that a man like him would stay interested for long after his initial conquest, if we ever found others like us, anyway.

Such was the way of his intensity—of his power—as it rolled over my skin when he turned his gaze on me. It wasn't the same as the power I'd felt from the Wild Hunt or the magic of Faerie when the Veil had shattered, but still a force that came from within him.

It wasn't magical in nature at all, I suspected, but something he'd possessed long before the Mark. It was just Caelum, and that made him all the more dangerous.

"We should find a place to camp for the night," I murmured finally, hating the way my voice shook with the slightest tremor at the thought of another night exposed to the darkness of the woods.

"I have a better idea. Come with me," he said, reaching across the space between us to take my hand in his. My hand throbbed with the contact, tiny sparks passing between where we touched and careening up my arm until it glowed with soft white light. It was the first time my Mark had reacted to him so vividly, sending a jolt of shock through me. The dark in his mirrored mine, the faintest hint of purple illuminating the black as his Mark recognized the call from mine.

Something had changed in us; something had shifted, and I was terrified to admit that it might have been my acknowledging the fact that I wanted him in spite of the consequences. Now, my Mark fed on that reaction to his touch.

He led me into the tree line beside us, pausing at the line of thick branches. Peeling back one of them with a mystified smile on his face, he revealed a narrow pathway while I stared in stunned silence.

"I can't believe this is still here. It's been years since I last traveled through the Hollows," he said. The path curved up the side of one of the foothills, disappearing into the darkness of the shaded trees. He pulled me into the pathway, releasing the branch that hid the entrance so that it snapped back into place and disguised it once more.

"What is this place?" I asked, wonder lighting up my eyes as he led me to the very base of the hill, which, standing apart from the other foothills, was more like a butte. Where the path started up the side, curving around to create an easier to manage incline, someone had carved steps into the stone in the areas where it became too steep. More stone lined the path as we rounded the bend to the back of the hill, the surfaces stained with age and cracked from what appeared to be years of neglect.

Trees lined the path on the outside, where Caelum walked beside me, shielding us from view if anyone happened to look up at the butte. On my right, I lifted a hand to trail over the stone of the face. As if the earth itself had melted away to make the walkway, the same stone that lined the steps went as high as I could see when I tipped my head back.

Faces were carved into the surface, ethereal beings with slightly pointed ears and harsh planes in their bone structures. I'd heard that their features were sharper, their characteristics more defined. I couldn't be sure how much of that was emphasized by the stone work and how much was true to their appearance.

The only Fae I'd seen had been transparent, but the members of the Wild Hunt were a breed all of their own within Alfheimr. My fingers ran over the thin lips of a man whose features seemed particularly jagged, his hair surrounded by snowflakes. "According to the legends, these are the faces of the Old Gods," Caelum said, stepping up behind me. I hadn't even realized that I had turned to the rock face, my hands shifting from the man's mouth to the woman at his side. Her hair somehow seemed lighter than the others at her side, as if her presence had been imbued into the rock. "Twyla, The Goddess of the Moon," Caelum said, his hands shifting up to my waist. He dragged my hand with his along the fabric of my dress and then behind me, to the small of my back. The awkward angle of my arm gave me pause, the tips of his fingers pressing into my spine and the swell of my backside as he leaned in until his breath tickled my cheek. "It's said she is the Queen of the Winter Court."

"How do you know so much about the Fae? Your father's library?" I whispered, shuffling to the side. Caelum followed me seamlessly, his body mirroring mine to the point that we seemed to move in synchronization. I touched the Goddess next to Twyla, my fingers sinking into the harsh lines of her beautiful face. Her eyes had been painted, the rock itself glimmering as dark as night with specks of lightness within.

Long hair fell to her shoulders, the color lost to the rocks as if the carver hadn't put as much essence into her likeness as they had Twyla's.

"My father believed that, in order to fight them, we would have to know them. When the rest of the realm sought to destroy the knowledge of our enemies, he collected it. *Studied* it. He taught me about them," he answered, his lips brushing against my skin as he spoke. His words from earlier in the day, the taunt that he knew I would welcome him into my body one day, sat heavy in my mind.

It couldn't happen, and yet there was no mistaking the goosebumps that rose along my skin where he touched me.

"Who is she?" I asked, clearing my throat, determined to focus on the subject at hand. His father's teachings interested me far more than I cared to admit, out of habit. Curiosity about the Fae was condemned, my interest in the Veil enough to have me hanged if I hadn't had the protection of a Lord.

To know about the creatures hunting us, could anything ever be more useful than that?

"The Queen of Air and Darkness," he said, something in his voice compelling me to glance over my shoulder at him. "Mab is the Queen of the Court of Shadows." His face was stern, set into harsh lines as he stared at the likeness of the breathtaking female.

"She's beautiful," I said, my heart sinking at his study of her. Menace lingered in the sharp lines of her face, seeming to stare out at me through her dark eyes.

"According to the books," he said, shuffling me to the side, to the next of the Old Gods. The sun continued to set behind us, casting an eerie glow over the rock face as we passed by the male at Mab's side. "She's the greatest evil the world has ever known."

"I thought that was the Fae in general," I teased, smiling up at him and trying to lighten his mood. His grip on me had hardened, not painful in the slightest but more rigid, as if he couldn't stand to release me.

He smiled down at me softly, turning his attention back to the next God as we sidestepped. "I imagine the Fae are much like people. Some are good, some are bad, and most are just trying to survive. I don't believe an entire species can be evil. Do you?" he asked, the words softly spoken in my ear.

There was a challenge in his voice, a threat to everything he knew I'd been taught. The Fae were the greatest evil to walk the earth, condemning those that were Marked to a life of imprisonment within the realm of the Fae.

There was no freedom in captivity, no choice in the life they offered.

"You said your father thought the best way to fight our enemies was to know about them. If you don't believe they're evil, then why—"

"I believe some of them are evil. The things in the books about Mab would give a grown man nightmares. So long as evil is as powerful as she's rumored to be, then light can never truly reign in their realm. There can never be any hope for peace between our races."

"You think there could be peace without her?" I asked, the idea rattling around in my head as my eyes landed on the God in front of me. The eyes carved from stone felt like they watched me, his unforgiving stare looking down at me, as if the carvers had wanted to use it to intimidate those who walked this path.

"I think the alternative is another war where we destroy each other. I have to hope there's a solution for peace." I had to as well, since the last of the witches had given their lives to create the Veil. We wouldn't be so lucky a second time.

His cheek touched mine, his chest pressing into my back as he leaned forward. His hand released mine finally, his arms wrapping around me to circle my stomach as if he could sense the sudden chill that had swept over me. "Eerie, isn't he?" he asked, rubbing his stubbled cheek against mine. "The God of the Dead has always been the one to scare people away from this place."

Everything inside me froze. Even though I hadn't learned much of the Fae, the Old Gods were whispered about here and there. The God of the Dead more than any of the others.

The stone God staring back at me was the one who had leveled an entire city during The Great Wars, the one who'd killed more humans than any record could track. He was the harbinger of death, the sole Fae who could reanimate the corpses of our loved ones to use against us. If anything could be deemed the most vile of this world, I doubted it was Mab.

It was him.

Caelum sensed my unease, slowly gliding his hands on my stomach until only one arm remained wrapped around my hip. He pulled me into his side, and in the wake of the chill that had swept over me staring at the God of the Dead, I allowed the touch to warm me as he guided me up the walkway and away from the faces in the wall.

We ascended the stone path in silence, my heart heavy with confliction about Caelum's words. Part of me wanted so badly to believe the creatures hunting us weren't all bad, and there could be peace and an end to the miserable fate of being Fae Marked.

Were humans so perfect, if they were determined to slaughter us all because of a Mark on our neck that we had no control over? The answer wasn't the one I wished for.

"Why do humans kill the Fae Marked?" I asked, a hush falling over the woods with my words. It was as if Caelum forgot to breathe for a moment, the tension claiming his body bleeding through to me. "What difference does it make to them if we're dead or taken? Why isn't that our choice to make?"

He sighed, tilting his head down as we walked, and I felt his chin touch the top of my head. "Being mated makes the Fae even stronger. That's what the *Viniculum* is—why it protects us. Somewhere, there's a mate looking for us, seeking to claim us as theirs. The establishment of a mate bond increases a Fae's power. If you can keep a Fae from their mate, you can keep them stagnant. Unable to increase their power, and if you do successfully manage to kill the mate, some Fae don't survive." I'd heard that mates strengthened their Fae, in whispers, but I'd thought them the dramatic whispers meant to cause fear.

"They die with us?" I asked, staring up at him as he pulled his chin away from my head.

"When it's the final death? Sometimes," he answered. "Sometimes they're lost to madness. Sometimes they seem to go mad before they ever find their mate."

"Are mates ever other Fae? Or is it always humans?" I asked, peppering him with questions and not even caring that it implied I was more interested than I should have let on. All the rules of my past were null and void, now that being Marked was my reality.

Knowledge was my only power.

"Sometimes," he said with a shrug. "It happens, but not nearly as often as a mating pair between a Fae and a human. That was the consequence of the witches' curse to maintain the balance between realms. I'm sure you can imagine what mating to another Fae does for both their magic, if a human soul acts as an amplifier. Two Fae being mated is even stronger than that."

"Having a mate who has a very limited lifespan must be terrible, if they have any feelings whatsoever for the human, anyway," I said, hating the thought of belonging to a male who would watch me age and wither and die while he remained eternally young.

"Human mates do not age, Estrella. Once the bond is completed, the life forces of the two are joined. So long as our Fae live, so would we."

"But the Fae don't die," I said. *Unless you stabbed them through the heart with iron or severed the head from their shoulders, anyway,* I didn't add. They could be killed, but diseases and aging didn't touch them. From what I did know, the Old Gods were at least a thousand years old.

"No, they don't," he agreed, walking up the last of the stairs until he reached a plateau on the side of the butte. He took my hand, helping me up the last of the steep steps until my feet fell on the stone landing.

All thoughts of living forever immediately fled my mind at the wonder before me.

18

"What is this?" I asked, staring at a natural pool in front of me. Water trickled down the face of the butte, falling into the steaming pool in front of us. The carvings in the rock walls surrounding the pool were different than those below. A mix of humans and the same faces of the Gods we'd seen on our journey up the path, entwined in positions that left little wonder to the purpose this place had once served.

"According to my father's books, this place was sacred to the Fae, once upon a time. The Old Gods were born from the Primordials, the first beings who didn't have a human form unless they willed it for a time. This mountain was sacred to the Primordials Peri and Marat," he said, gesturing to the couple at the center of the carvings in the rocks. A male and female Fae embraced, her legs wrapped around his hips and her back curved in ecstasy. "They were lovers once, before their only son was killed in one of the first Fae wars between the Seelie and Unseelie Courts. They celebrated his birth every year by coming to the place of his conception and joining together amongst the Fae and humans who joined them."

His fingers swept the hair off one side of my neck, his breath warm against my chilled skin. He chuckled as he undoubtedly watched my skin pebble with his proximity. "I think you can guess how they celebrated."

I cleared my throat, stepping away from him and the canvas of rock that detailed every sordid event. The faces of the Old Gods stared back at me, twisted in pleasure as they toyed with one another or with the humans who had come to partake.

I'd never seen pleasure the likes of which was stamped onto every human's face, with no traces of the pain I would have expected after everything I'd been taught about the ethereal beings. "How old are these carvings?" I asked, glancing at the haunting face of the God of the Dead. He sat on one of the chairs carved from stone at the side of the hot spring, two humans kneeling at his feet between his legs. His hair barely skimmed his bare shoulders, the rippling muscles of his physique bulging with effort. One of his hands was buried in a woman's hair, pulling her toward his bare waist, with the entirety of his swollen cock revealed.

Holy *Gods.*

I turned away from the erotic image, my eyes landing on each of the Gods engaged in similar acts. It wasn't only the male Fae who enjoyed the partnership of more than one human at a time; female Fae were shown grouped off with two to three human men at once, as well.

"I take it the Fae don't believe in monogamy?" I asked, snorting as I gave the carvings my back. Facing Caelum, I watched his eyes drift down from the sexual art on the side of the mountain, a smirk on his lips as he met my gaze.

"What's wrong, Little One? Never been with two lovers at once?" he asked, his lips curving into a full blown smile when I flushed.

"No," I clipped out, sidestepping him and making my way to the hot spring where I knelt down. I skimmed the surface of the water with my fingers, immediately feeling the warmth of the water suffuse my skin. "Have you?"

"I imagine I have done a lot of things you haven't done."

"Eew," I groaned, immediately regretting asking the question as envy consumed me. Men were free to do as they pleased, whether that involved one woman or six. If I'd done the same, they'd have sent me to be purified by the Priests or hung me for my crimes against The Mother.

It depended on Lord Byron and the High Priest's mood that day.

Caelum shrugged, stepping up beside me. He tugged his tunic out of his trousers, tearing it off over his head. With me kneeling at the side of the pool, I was immediately reminded of the humans kneeling for the God of the Dead.

I glanced up at him, finding him staring down at me intently. Swallowing, I held his gaze for a few seconds. Seconds that felt like hours. The tension between us pulled taut, leaving no doubt to the accuracy of his earlier prediction.

I didn't know how I would be able to travel at his side, sleep beside him every night, and never seek out the promise that lurked in his eyes as he watched me. The heat that blazed there was like nothing I'd ever seen: a desire so potent I didn't think I'd be able to withstand it.

He reached out with a massive, calloused hand, cupping my cheek and running his thumb over my bottom lip. The tip sank inside, brushing against my tongue as the flavor of his skin teased my mouth.

"Tell me again how much you don't want me, Estrella," he said, pointedly using my name as he stared down at me. The arrogance of those words snapped something inside of me, my desire fleeing as rational thought returned.

I sank my teeth into his thumb, gratified when it twitched in response to the pinch of pain. When I pulled back, I stood fluidly and glared up at him as he raised his thumb to his mouth and sucked a drop of blood from his skin.

I ignored the last pulse of desire that still throbbed within me, ignored the strange urge to take his thumb into my mouth and suck. He stared at the expression on my face, something dark gleaming in his gaze. "You're a dick," I said, huffing and gathering my hair in my hands. I toyed with the snarled edges, wincing when I realized just how disgusting I must look.

How many days had it been since I'd bathed? Since I brushed my hair?

"Why don't we find out just how much you like my dick, Little

One?" he asked, his hands dropping to the ties on his trousers. He unknotted them while I watched in shock, my eyes caught on the smooth, nimble way his fingers worked the laces apart.

He kicked off his boots, sliding them to the side as my eyes snapped back up to his face. I held his probing stare, my lips pressing into a thin line when he smirked at me and shoved his trousers down his thighs.

I swallowed, compelling myself not to look, not even when he bent forward to push them off the rest of the way, pulling the fabric off his calves and taking his wool socks along with them. He stood up straight in front of me, running a hand through the short blond hair on top of his head. "It won't bite you, Estrella," he said with a grin, taking a single step closer to me.

He didn't touch me, keeping a breath between us as he towered over me. He was so close that I stared at his bare chest, at the swirling lines of the Fae Mark where it wrapped around his bicep and crawled up the side of his neck.

It dipped down, skimming just over his collar bone before it stopped abruptly. From what I could tell, mine did the same, as if it was incomplete and waiting for the last piece to be written. If what Caelum had said before was to be believed, it was waiting for the completion of the bond.

I jolted when Caelum grasped my hand in his, lifting it to touch the place where the edges of the Mark curved onto his chest. His eyes closed at the moment of contact, and a shudder wracked my body as a feeling of comfort overwhelmed me.

Touching his mark, feeling the warmth of it flooding through me, felt more like home than the cabin I'd shared with my family ever had. Like the other Fae Marked were always meant to be my true home, the place where I belonged.

"Most Fae only practice monogamy once they've found their mates," he said, answering the question I'd asked what felt like ages ago. I'd gotten distracted by his proximity.

By his nudity.

"Oh," I said, my brain struggling to keep up with the conversation, knowing that I would see all of him if I only looked down.

"From what my father said, the Fae are very possessive of their mates. They've been known to kill if someone even looks at their mate inappropriately," he said, reaching out to unclasp the cloak from my shoulders. The fabric puddled behind me, landing on the stone surrounding the hot spring. I shivered, the cool air kissing my skin as a sudden breeze blew through the trees.

Caelum smiled and leaned forward to sweetly touch his lips to my forehead. Turning so his arm brushed against mine, he strolled directly to the edge of the hot spring and walked down the slope that led into the water. The steam increased as his cool body touched it, the muscles of his ass flexing with every step.

Gods.

I swallowed, shoving down the images of nails digging into his flesh that erupted through my head in a chaotic mess, and I pushed away the feelings his broad, muscular physique brought. He turned to me suddenly, jaw clenched, with eyes narrowed and so dark they almost looked black.

I'd been so busy staring at his ass, so fixated on the relative safety of that part of him compared to the front, when he turned I got an eyeful of *everything*.

He paused, the water touching just above his knees and hovering so close to where his length hung down his thigh. I froze, my body turning to a statue as my mouth dropped open in shock.

"Gods," I muttered, my hands lifting to cover my mouth as I realized I'd said the word out loud. Caelum grinned, tilting his head to the side as he studied me, and made no move to sink lower into the water. Made no attempt to hide the manhood that must have been the source of his arrogance.

Under any normal circumstances, I'd have said that the man was overcompensating with his bravado for something that was lacking elsewhere. Caelum's were not normal circumstances; his cock something I didn't even know was within the realm of possibilities. I guess the magic of the mate bond had chosen a mate for what would be a very pleased Fae female.

"See something you like?" he asked, finally stepping backward until his lower body submerged, and I was freed from the temptation to continue to admire his cock.

"That looks more like a torture device than an instrument for pleasure," I said, shaking myself and wrapping my arms around my waist.

Caelum chuckled, ducking his head beneath the surface. He ran his hands through his hair when he re-emerged from the water, pushing it back from his face as it dripped down over his chest and the muscles on his stomach. "When the time comes, you'll take all of it and beg me to fuck you harder, Little One," he said, walking through the water until he reached the edge where I stood.

He stared up at me, affection in his gaze that didn't belong; it didn't fit for how briefly he'd known me. If I hadn't known better, I might have compared him to the images of the humans on their knees.

To the complete and utter worship on their faces as they serviced a God.

He reached up, catching me by the ankle and gently lifting my foot off the ground. A shock ran through my body when he touched me, my desire so potent I didn't think I'd ever felt anything like it. But it also came with the knowledge that it wasn't real. It wasn't about Caelum or about me, but about the magic on our necks that marked us as the same. He could have been anyone, any of the Fae Marked, and I suspected my body would react the same way.

Nothing else made sense. Attraction like this didn't exist.

He slipped my shoe and sock off, tossing them to land next to his boots. "What are you doing?" I asked, stumbling back a step until I was out of reach.

"I think it's obvious that you aren't going to come in unless I give you a little push," he said, reaching for my other foot. I kicked out, my bare foot colliding with his wrist with a solid thump that would have hurt most men.

Caelum only grinned at my show of violence.

"I'm not going to come in at all," I said, my lips twisting as I shook my head.

"Baths don't come around often for people on the run, and soon enough it will be too cold for anything that isn't a hot spring. Don't be foolish, Estrella. Get in the water," he said, stepping back from the edge to give me some space.

I eyed the water with desire, wanting nothing more than to submerge in the warmth of it. Even with the steam billowing around me, the temperature had dropped since the sun had set. I bit my bottom lip, considering a way to do it without getting too close to him while I was naked. The spring was big enough for a dozen people. The question was whether or not he would stay on his side.

"Turn around," I ordered, lifting my leg to pull off my other shoe.

"Well that's not exactly fair. You've seen me," he said, a smirk on his face that leaked into his voice, but he walked to the opposite side of the pool, resting his elbows on the edge and facing out over the valley.

I hurried to strip my dress off, splashing through the water in my haste to get entirely submerged before he could turn around. Warmth surrounded me, sinking inside and heating the bones I hadn't even realized were chilled. Every aching joint in my body practically moaned at the feeling of bliss the warmth provided.

I lowered myself until I was submerged up to my neck, not wanting to answer any questions about what he might see. His body was free from scars, flawless in a way mine would never be, reminding me that we weren't the same, and no matter what the Fae had decided we would become soon, our lives hadn't been the same.

"Okay," I said, sighing as I dipped my head back to wet my hair. Letting it soak in the water, I ran my fingers through it to try to get the knots out the best I could without a brush.

"Let me help," Caelum said, stepping closer to me as I struggled to reach a tangle at the back of my head.

"You and the basilisk in your trousers stay right there, thank you very much," I said, snapping to attention the moment he came closer.

He stopped the moment I uttered the command, his face lighting with amusement. "I'm not wearing any trousers."

"And that is the problem. I like my intestines in my stomach and not shoved into my lungs. You just keep that thing away from me," I said, watching as he chuckled and looked at me as if I'd grown a second head.

"I can't say that I've ever heard that one before. Usually women ask me to introduce them to the Gods," he said.

"Gross." I shoved back the surge of jealousy in my veins. "Can you maybe not talk about your previous conquests when you're trying to get me to fuck you? It's rude."

"Jealous, Little One?" he asked, raising an eyebrow at me as he took another step. "Why don't you help me erase the memory of the ones who came before you? We both know they don't matter anymore."

I swallowed, ignoring the confusion that came with his words. He took another step, his growing proximity a far more important topic to dive into than why the others didn't matter. "I swear to Gods if you touch me, I will rip it off and feed it to you, Caelum," I said, backing away a step.

His grin widened as he took another step forward. "I probably shouldn't find it so arousing when you threaten me, and yet I get a little tingle every time." He shrugged as if there was nothing that could be done about it, stepping closer to me with his hands raised innocently. "I promised you I wouldn't touch you in that way until you're ready. I meant it, Estrella. You can trust me with your body."

"I don't even know you," I said, my back touching the edge of the pool. He closed the distance between us, hovering just out of reach. The knowledge that he was so close, the feel of his presence drifting to my skin through the water, was maddening.

It pushed at my self-control, testing everything I thought I knew about myself.

"I know, and we have all the time in the world to get to know one another. For now, turn around. Let me help you with your hair. We don't know when we'll next get an opportunity like this." He lowered himself into the water until only his head was exposed, putting it level with mine. Tearing my fingers free from the snarl I couldn't quite work free, I sighed and turned my back on him. He slid his fingers into my hair, carefully pulling it away from my naked body so that his knuckles only brushed against my skin occasionally as he worked in silence.

"Where is your father now?" I asked, trying to fill the silence that hung between us.

"Dead. Some years ago now."

"I'm so sorry," I whispered, knowing the pain of that grief. A commonality we shared, another link between us that gave us an undercurrent of understanding we shouldn't have felt.

"We weren't close," he said, working his fingers through my hair. His words seemed to conflict with the way he'd spoken of the man who'd educated him about the ways of the Fae and their history. "He was dedicated to his studies and his responsibilities. His wife hated that I existed, and she did her best to drive a wedge between us. It worked more often than not."

I stilled. "His wife wasn't your mother?" I asked, wondering if his birth mother had died when he was young. It was the only explanation; the alternative of him being the child of an affair but raised by the father was unheard of.

"No. My father had an encounter with a married woman when he attended a party. It was somehow decided it would be my father who'd raise me, but his wife never warmed to me. They never had children of their own, so I became the sole heir, regardless of my status."

"That's terrible. To be raised in a home without love..." I trailed off, unable to fathom a life without my family who would have done anything for me. Both my parents and Brann would've given their lives for me in a heartbeat.

He sighed, leaning in until his breath touched my cheek. True to his word, he didn't touch me, keeping a thin layer of water between us as I turned my head to look at him. My hair slipped out of his hands, my lips hovering so close to his, if I moved in the wrong way, they would touch.

Caelum's stare drifted down to my mouth, lingering there before those piercing dark eyes lifted back to mine. "It was as bad as you can imagine." His words hovered on the air between us as a wall cracked inside my heart.

Not all scars were visible.

"But it taught me one thing," he said, reaching out to tuck my hair behind my ear and smooth the tangles on the side of my head. "No matter what my future looks like, nothing will keep me away from the woman I love. Not even death will keep me from her."

I cleared my throat, suddenly overcome with the need to retreat from the intensity of his words. Even barely knowing him, the thought of him one day having that with someone else filled my chest with lead.

With heartache I hadn't earned.

What difference did it make to me if he touched another woman with those gentle fingers that so often stroked my skin? If his breath washed over another woman's cheek while he murmured in her ear? If he tore another woman in two with his monumental cock?

It didn't. It couldn't.

"She'll be a lucky woman," I said, running my hand through my hair as he finished with the tangles. My fingers were pruney, my toes tender as they scraped the bottom of the hot spring.

"I hope she sees it that way," he said, shrugging his shoulders with a smile. As if he knew he was both impossible to deny and impossible to tolerate, all in the same breath.

"I should get out. Do you mind?" I asked, smiling sheepishly as he stepped away. He turned his back to me where he stood in the middle of the pool, leaving me to heave myself out of the water and onto the edge of the spring.

The sudden burst of cool breeze pebbled my skin, everything in my body going still in response. I turned to look over my shoulder, finding Caelum's tense face staring back at me. His gaze wasn't on mine, instead fixated on my naked flesh and the scars covering my back in thick white lines.

When his eyes raised to mine finally, the menace in them stole the breath from my lungs. His jaw clenched, his nostrils flaring, as he took that first step toward me. Water sloshed at his sides as he prowled through the hot spring with a look of pure rage etched into his handsome features. I scrambled, gathering my dress in my hands and covering my body with it as I spun to face him, tearing the sight of my scars away from him and hoping I could somehow defuse the situation and calm the monster that seemed to rattle at the cage of Caelum's skin.

He placed his hands on the stone edge of the spring and, with an animalistic grace I would never hope to achieve lifted his nude body out of the water and unfolded to his full height. Through the steam, his dark eyes glimmered with the promise of violence and retribution. "What the fuck are those?" he growled, something darker echoing in his voice.

As if he was truly part beast, his rage made him vibrate as he stalked toward me. The Fae Mark on his neck glowed with his anger, the black and white swirls of ink pulsing in time with his steps.

I wondered if the Mark stole our humanity, if it made us more feral, like the Fae who claimed us.

"It's nothing," I said, swallowing and forcing a lame smile to my face. Shame heated my cheeks, leaving me wanting nothing more than to pretend the last few moments had never happened. That he'd never seen the consequences for my disobedience as a girl.

"That is not nothing." He crossed the remaining distance between us, his eyes gleaming with a predatory light. All thoughts of his promise not to touch me until I begged for it forgotten, I backed away from him in a panic. Clutching my dress to my body, I shielded myself from his view when he was lost to the anger that danced in his face.

My back struck the rock carvings on the side of the mountain, the stone figures of the Old Gods digging into my spine as Caelum pressed his body flush against the front of mine. His forearm curved above my head, resting against the rock above me as he leaned down and surrounded me.

"Caelum," I whispered, watching as the first snow of the season fell behind him as white flecks against the fading light of the evening sky.

"Who the fuck hurt you?" he growled, his chest rattling in front of my face as I stared up into his obsidian eyes. Something shifted on his face, a rage like I'd never seen taking over as he gritted his teeth when I didn't give him the answer he demanded. "Who?"

"I was a difficult child," I said, shaking my head to try to justify what I knew now had been just another way of the lord grooming me to become what he wanted. "Always getting into trouble. Playing with the boys instead of sewing with the girls. Lord Byron thought it would force me to behave more appropriately for a young lady."

"Is he still breathing?" Caelum asked, tilting his head to the side slightly as he stared down at me.

"I don't know," I admitted, swallowing against the dread threatening to close my airway. "I fled Mistfell when the Veil shattered. It was the only way to survive."

Caelum grasped my chin between two fingers and tipped my head up, dropping his face lower until his mouth was only a breath away from mine when he spoke the vow I didn't doubt he had every intention of keeping. "He won't be for long."

I swallowed, unable to come up with any kind of response in the face of his wrath. No one in their right mind would threaten to kill a Lord for disciplining a girl.

"He will suffer for every mark on your skin, every moment he frightened you, every tear you shed, before I finally put him out of his misery." He leaned forward, brushing his lips against the corner of my mouth. Not quite a kiss, not quite not. Everything in me tightened, the fear of the moment dissipating as I shifted with sudden desire to feel that full mouth on mine.

He stared down, as if he knew exactly what flashed through my mind, how the thought of him murdering my tormentor turned me on just as much of the feel of him hard against my belly.

He stepped back as quickly as he'd come to touch me, turning his back and running both hands through his hair as his muscles tensed with frustration. With control. Because I hadn't asked him to touch me yet, I realized. He'd stayed true to his word, keeping my body safe with him. Even with me naked against him, he hadn't taken liberties the way most men would have.

I narrowed my eyes on a roadmap of scars on his back, horrific marks of lashings far worse than the ones I'd suffered. The thick, raised white lines covered his back, crisscrossing and overlapping over his flesh as if he'd been whipped more times than I could count.

My dress dropped to the ground, forgotten as I closed the distance between us. I couldn't understand how I hadn't seen them before. Had I really been that distracted by his ass?

Yes.

I touched my fingertips to one of the scars in the center of his spine, feeling his body still at my touch. "Who did this to you?" I asked, my voice sounding softer and more broken than I'd ever heard it. Had this been what he'd meant when he spoke of the struggles of his childhood? Of being raised by a woman who hated him?

"Someone who I will *never* allow to touch you," he vowed, spinning back to face me. There was no fabric between us when he pressed against me, nothing but the feeling of skin against skin as he pulled me into his chest.

His hands touched my scars, fingers drifting over the pattern as if he needed to memorize every single one. As if he'd need that information one day soon.

I sank into his embrace, drawing comfort from a moment of solidarity with a stranger. We both understood the blinding pain, the feel of our blood dripping down our backs and over our legs. We understood standing in a puddle of our own blood, slipping in it and hanging from our wrists when we couldn't get our footing.

The snow stopped as quickly as it had begun, but shivers soon claimed me anyway, forcing me to separate from Caelum to get dressed and find a sheltered place to sleep.

I'd never forget the look on his face, the absolute rage on my behalf. My family had loved me, but they'd never promised vengeance for me. No one had ever cared the way he did.

That terrified me.

19

We made our way down past the stone faces and steps in silence. We ignored the tension thrumming between us and the way Caelum's rage simmered in the air. The snow around us fell more steadily as we traveled, leaving a dusting at my feet as I trudged through the wet underbrush to keep up with him. Darkness fell, leaving me stumbling behind him as he led the way through the woods.

The mountains we hugged grew larger as we walked, behemoths that disappeared into the sky overhead. I couldn't see the peaks, couldn't see anything but the bases of them as they changed from tree-lined and welcoming to rocky and jagged before my eyes.

"We're almost to the caves," Caelum called ahead of me as I shielded my face from the wind that seemed to tear through me. I shivered beneath my cloak, wondering how he could even be functioning in this cold. "We need to get you warmer clothes."

I didn't bother to argue that it seemed unlikely to happen, with us leaving the villages behind us in favor of staying in the mountains. It was far safer this way, assuming I didn't freeze to death.

"It's too early for snow," I protested, glancing up at him and defying the gust of wind that threatened to knock me on my ass.

"The Fae are here, Little One. Everything you thought you knew has changed," he said, wrapping an arm around my shoulders and tugging me into his side. He used his body to shield mine, guiding me forward through the darkness.

Like so many nights when I'd snuck out of my bedroom to walk through the woods, something in the darkness around us gave me comfort again, reassuring me that it returned in its own time. It wasn't the unnatural darkness of the eclipse where I couldn't function; not with the moon and stars shining above us to light the way through the gaps in the canopy.

Even though the darkness was our ally, the cold sank into my clothes, and there was no promise of a night on the living room floor next to the fireplace after I snuck back in to warm me up. There was no Loris to show me other ways to keep warm as the snow fell around us.

There was Caelum, the man who I had a feeling would give me all of that and more, if I let him, but I knew instinctively that I would never be the same if he touched me. He'd ruin the memories I had of fumbling hands and urgent touches, the memory of a friend who gave me something sweet in a harsh world determined to strike me down. I'd already killed him, reduced him to snow before he could drive a blade through my heart and end my life.

I gritted my teeth, the memory of the guards' shock as they studied the Mark on my neck. I'd only seen two others, and given that Caelum's matched my own, it didn't seem like they were overly unique, so the reaction made little sense.

Caelum veered toward the rocky cliff face we'd been paralleling and looked for something through the darkness. "Here," he said, taking my hand and pulling me to follow him. The narrow cave entrance we approached was almost too small for him to fit through, as well as opening at my eye level.

He grasped me around the waist, lifting me up to it while I fought back the urge to squeal. I grasped the ledge, pulling myself in and hugging one side of the entrance so that he could hoist himself up and in smoothly. He pulled his short dagger from the sheath on his thigh, rising to his feet as he hunched forward to fit through the tunnel and pass by me. I stood up behind him, letting my body unfold to full height in the enclosed space. Following close behind, I tried to remember to give him enough room to maneuver in the event that something attacked us.

It didn't seem likely in such a small passage, but who knew what it connected to within the mountains. Cave beasts were a very real concern in the Hollow Mountains, and not something I ever wanted to encounter. I'd rather the Mist Guard ran me through than face the ordeal of being eaten alive while foot-long claws shredded me into ribbons.

We made our way down the small tunnel until it widened and the cave got tall enough for Caelum to stand to his full height in front of me. With the increase in size, my worry over beasts increased. Oblivious to my misgivings, he stepped out of the tunnel, dropping down a few steps into a cavern that resembled a room. Across from the tunnel where I lingered, another, wider tunnel threatened, as if an ominous being in itself. It was big enough for the cave beasts to come charging through, I thought. I'd never seen one, but one would have to be enormous not to fit.

"Wait here," Caelum said, hauling himself back up into the tunnel alongside me.

"Wait, no!" I protested, spinning to follow him.

"Stay right here, and you'll be safe. I'm just gathering a few pieces of wood for a fire to keep you warm," he said, touching his lips to my forehead briefly before he darted off, leaving me gaping after him until I spun to stare down into the cave opening.

Without the light of the moon and stars above my head, the only hint of light came through the tunnel at my back and from the glowing rocks down the tunnel on the opposite side of me. I couldn't see anything aside from those two spaces, feeling the vast size of the mouth of the cave more than I saw it.

Anything could be lurking down there, waiting for us to walk right into a trap. I counted the seconds as they passed, waiting with bated breath for Caelum to return.

What if he left me?

I couldn't stand the thought of being on my own, completely alone as I tried to evade the Wild Hunt. I didn't stand a chance without him, and we both knew it.

"Caelum?" I hissed, my voice echoing down the silence in the tunnel.

"Miss me, my star?" he asked, the shadow of his broad form finally reappearing at the entrance of the cave. He hurried through it, wood piled in his arms as he passed me and dropped down into the large space without hesitation.

"What if it isn't safe?" I asked, staying in my little enclosed tunnel.

"Nothing has been here for a long while," he said, striding toward the wall between the two tunnels. He dropped the wood on the ground, the clatter of pieces striking against the stone beneath his feet echoing through the space.

Nothing moved in the moments that followed the noise, nothing struck him or ate him while I waited.

I dropped down, bending my knees to absorb the impact as my boots slapped against the rock. I stumbled toward him, squinting to see through the darkness, until I felt him at my side. The sound of metal scraping against metal erupted through the room, the sparks from his flint glowing against the wood as he tried to get a fire going.

"Where did you manage to find dry wood?" I asked, thinking of the snow outside. The thought of an entire cold season without a store of fire wood made me shiver, knowing that even though we'd been lucky tonight, the nights in our future probably wouldn't be so fortunate.

"The snow hasn't had time to soak into the ground or the fallen trees just yet. We'll be warm tonight, at least," he answered as the sparks caught on the wood. Light filled the space, giving me my first glance at the cave we would call our home for the night.

Whatever Caelum had felt about this cave, he was right. There were no signs of life or any indication that anything had so much as twitched within it recently. He nurtured the fire until it was crackling happily in front of us, the tunnels providing an escape for the smoke.

As soon as that was finished, he leaned back against the cave wall and sighed as the warmth sank into his chilled frame. I moved to sit near him, letting the flames chase away the worst of the chill. Hunger made my stomach pang, but it was far too dark and the weather too cold for us to do anything about it until the morning.

Caelum heard my stomach growl, chuckling as he let his eyes drift closed. "I'll set some traps first thing in the morning and see if we can catch some breakfast before we get moving for the day."

"Okay," I murmured, watching as he readjusted his frame to try to get more comfortable.

"Get some sleep, Estrella," Caelum murmured, laying on his back on the cave floor. He tossed his arms over his head, forming a pillow with his forearms. I lay on my side and huddled in on myself, facing the cave opening with the fire between me and whatever might come for me.

There wasn't much that had frightened me in my life—I knew that was a lie as soon as I thought it. There wasn't much that frightened me enough that I didn't do exactly what I wanted anyway. There were perks to being stubborn, advantages to digging my boots into the ground at my feet and risking everything for a single moment of freedom.

But survival was different. The image of death at the jowls of a beast three times my size would torment me to the point that I couldn't sleep.

"I can hear your thoughts from here, Little One," Caelum murmured, his lips tipping up into a smile as I rolled over to look at him. He opened his eyes slowly, peering at me as I sighed.

"Do tell," I said, using the distraction as I snuggled deeper into his cloak. "I would absolutely love to hear how you think my mind is filled with thoughts of you yet again." The sarcasm dripped from my words with mocking condescension.

"Come here, and I can distract you from such wasteful thoughts. Why think of things that you could have if you only reached out a hand?" he asked, the playful smirk at his lips drawing my attention down to the vivid white of his teeth.

"We're supposed to be sleeping," I argued, turning my head way from the striking features of his face to look at the cave ceiling. He was so disarming, so unrealistically handsome. None of the men in Mistfell had such perfect features. His eyes were darker than I'd ever seen, like shadows painted into his lightly tanned, even golden, skin. His nose was straight and the perfect size over his generous lips. His jaw was square, and his brow strong and stern, despite the playful expression he so often wore.

"So why aren't we?" he asked, drawing my attention back to him. He leaned forward, grasping one of my hands in his. His thumbs ran over my palm, caressing it lightly. "Talk to me."

I sighed, letting my head thump against the stone as shame heated my face. He seemed so fearless, so unconcerned with any of the dangers around us. "I'm afraid," I mumbled, keeping my eyes off of his purposefully.

"What could a star be afraid of?" he asked, the teasing lilt to his voice reassuring me slightly. He squeezed my hand tighter in his, encouraging me to continue.

"It seems like I'm afraid of many things lately," I said, shaking my head as I thought of the way I feared him more than Lord Byron. It made no sense, but Byron had been able to touch my body. He hadn't been able to reach inside me and toy with my soul the way Caelum could.

"And yet you continue on anyway, my brave little star. You burn so bright I sometimes fear the Wild Hunt will sense you from miles away," he said, making the breath hitch in my lungs.

"Then why stay with me? Surely you want to be as far away from me as possible if you genuinely fear that?" I asked, my mind trying to work around the possible reasons he would endanger himself for me.

He ignored the question, smiling gently as he tucked a lock of hair behind my ear. "What are you afraid of?" he asked again.

I sighed, brushing off the moment between us and knowing it was for the best. "The cave beasts," I answered, nodding my head down to the fork in the tunnel where it veered into the network within the mountains.

He followed my gaze, his head nodding as if he understood. "Do you truly believe that I would ever allow anything to harm you? Cave beast, Fae, or human, they'll have to go through me to get to you."

"I don't understand why you would risk so much for me. You hardly know me," I whispered, the words hovering between us.

His face shifted, a heavy sigh escaping between his parted lips. His hand cupped my cheek, and he sank his teeth into his bottom lip. "I don't feel so alone when I'm with you," he murmured, tipping forward to touch his forehead to mine. He dropped his hand to the Mark on my neck, the swirling and writhing ink of his skin brushing against mine and causing a shock to roll through me. "I've spent my entire life feeling alone, even when I'm surrounded by others. I'd do just about anything not to feel that again. You and I are the same." He squeezed his hand at my neck, tightening around the Fae Mark. "This ties us together in ways none of us understand. So you can be scared all you want, Little One, but do it knowing that you'll have my swords at your side until the end."

He retreated suddenly, severing the stifling moment between us as my eyes burned. Settling himself back down to sleep, he stretched his legs with a groan. "What are you doing?" I asked, watching as he patted his stomach with a hand.

"Come here," he said, a chuckle transforming his face and all traces of his seriousness from only a moment before faded away. I didn't linger, letting his good mood wash away the intensity. I suspected men like Caelum didn't want to be vulnerable, and those moments where I saw beneath the arrogance and posturing were something rare, to be treasured.

I quirked my brow at him, glancing down to his trousers pointedly. I'd made my thoughts on his cock known already.

"It's not going to jump out and bite you, Estrella," he laughed. "Rest your head on me, and I'll tell you a story until you fall asleep."

That gave me pause. The only part of Lord Byron's manor I would miss was the library full of books and the stories they contained. The adventures people had lived. "What kind of story?" I asked, narrowing my eyes. "Is this a sex thing? Because I'm not above punching you in the dick."

"Estrella, I promise; you will know when it's a sex thing," he said, patting his stomach again. "This is the oldest story I know." I shifted forward, turning to put my back to him as I lowered myself down. The side of my face pressed against his shirt, drawing in a deep breath of the distinct scent I'd come to associate with Caelum.

He always smelled like wintergreen, like fresh snow falling in the meadow at night. Like drawing an essence sharp and cold into your lungs and letting it burn you from the inside.

He draped his cloak around me, enveloping me in warmth. I didn't have it in me to protest that he'd be cold, knowing from experience that it was as futile as trying not to breathe him in.

He raised a hand, running it through the waves of my hair gently as he hummed softly. "In the beginning, there was nothing." He paused as the strands of my hair fell through his fingers. His voice dropped lower, murmuring the words of his story as he continued on with a lyrical cadence. There was no doubt in my mind the story he wove was one he knew well, one that he'd been told repeatedly throughout his life, perhaps by the father who'd taught him all about things we weren't meant to know.

"The world was an empty void, a place without light or substance or shadows. The world was nothing but Khaos, but he eventually grew tired of being alone and he used the darkness surrounding him to create Ilta. He fell in love with the Primordial of Night, and with the way she shimmered in the shadows she created. They came together and eventually created a son, Edrus, the Primordial of Darkness. Ilta and Edrus grew close, closer than she felt with Khaos, and she jilted her previous lover in favor of her son," he said.

"She what?" I asked, outrage rising in my gut. This *was* a sex thing.

"There were only three beings in all of the world, Estrella. Is it so surprising that familial boundaries as we know them today didn't exist when they were creating, well, everything?" he asked, tapping his finger against my nose pointedly. "Together, Ilta and Edrus had two children, and on and on creation went until there were seven generations of Primordials and the world as we know it came to be. They created the dirt beneath our feet and the mountains that rise into the sky, the sea at the edges of the Kingdom and everything around us. From those

Primordials came the last generation of Gods, the ones humans once worshiped, until they learned the truth."

"The primordials birthed the Fae race?" I asked, yawning as I tried to force my eyes to stay open. "Is that what the Fae believe?"

"It is. They believe in The Father and The Mother in their own way, but they do not worship them the same as the human race. The Fae believe The Father and The Mother are waiting to take you to the after-life after your thirteenth life cycle comes to a close, but they're not ruled by the weight of their choices during their time in this world."

"What happened to the original Primordials? Why would they allow their children to be worshiped as Gods if they were the ones who actually created the world?" I asked, shifting my head on his lap. I lay on my back, staring up at him as he curled himself over me and trailed gentle fingertips down my cheek.

"Curious thing," he said. "You're supposed to be falling asleep."

"When you said you'd tell me a story, I didn't think you meant something from the forbidden texts! I thought you meant a bedtime story. How am I supposed to sleep when you're talking about the creation of the world?"

"I'll keep that in mind for the future. I could tell you a sex story instead? Perhaps one of the ones I've read about the union of Peri and Marat and the celebrations of their son? We already have the visual aid from earlier, and I'm certain we could—"

He grunted when I lifted and dropped my head into his stomach, turning away from him to face the fire. I couldn't bring myself to take my head off him, not with the warmth of his body heating my near-frozen ear.

"I take it back. You're more cruel than curious. A curious thing would want to reenact those moments and discover just why they were so pleasurable."

"Would you shut up or just tell me where the Primordials went already?" I asked, groaning past my annoyance with his antics.

"They disappeared, Little One. Nobody knows where they went or what happened to them. Only that they abandoned this world and those in it. The children of the Primordials, what we know of as the Old

Gods, took over. They put themselves at the top of the hierarchy and lived a life of decadence and sin," he said, continuing on as I snuggled into him against my better judgment.

He spoke of gilded cities, of the lands they'd had fashioned in their own honor, and the temples where they were worshiped. I fell asleep to the image of temples of stone in my head, my eyes drifting closed as slumber finally claimed me.

20

I snuggled deeper into the warmth wrapped around me, rubbing my face against bare skin where the laces of his shirt had parted in sleep. A deep groan startled me just enough that my eyes flew open in shock, holding myself perfectly still as I tried to unravel what had happened.

I'd fallen asleep with my head on Caelum's lap, so why was it his chest I snuggled into? I glanced down at our bodies, wincing when I found my dress hiked up to reveal my bare calf where my leg draped over his waist. My body was half on top of him, sprawled across his as if I could suck the heat from his bones and into mine. With the embers of the fire at my back, his body warmth at my front, and his cloak draped over myself, the cold of the early winter outside was a thing of the past.

Something hard pressed against my belly, the length of him seeming impossible to even speculate on as I bit down on my bottom lip to stifle the shocked gasp that tried to escape. His fingers tightened, bunching the fabric of my dress up further as he squeezed an entire cheek of my ass in his grip. His hand was enormous, covering it entirely and using the grip to pull me tighter into his body as he shifted his hips to grind his erection into my belly.

I looked up into his face, where the lines that were usually taut with intensity and a hint of brutality, or playfully arrogant, were relaxed in sleep. Nothing remained in his expression of the man he projected in his waking hours, only a peaceful expression, giving him the illusion of being somehow...normal.

Of being less intimidating, less exceptional.

I swallowed down my nerves, slowly lifting my head away from his chest to put some distance between us. I must have rolled onto him in my sleep at some point, and I could just imagine his arrogance if he woke to discover me clinging to him like a leech. I lifted my leg off his waist, slowly pulling it back to twist my body off of his without disturbing him.

He moved, rolling me beneath him in a move so smooth and sudden that I squeaked as my back rested against the stone. His weight covered me, his dark eyes seeming to dance with shadows as he opened them suddenly. "Where are you running off to, my star?" he asked, squeezing my ass in his hand more intentionally as his lips tipped into a smirk that made me want to punch him in the mouth. "Did you think I wouldn't notice your body wrapped around mine? That I wouldn't feel you even in the depths of sleep?"

"I loathe you," I mumbled, shifting my hips to try to rub his hand against the dirt beneath our bodies until he had no choice but to remove it. The motion rubbed me against him, my legs spread around where he'd slid his hips in between them when he'd rolled me.

"If this is what your hate feels like, then I can't wait to feel your love," he said, leaning forward until his nose touched the end of mine. He trailed it up, tracing a path over the arch until he touched his lips to my forehead. When he drew back, his eyes dropped to my mouth.

"Love?" I asked, the hushed sound hovering between us as he stared at my lips intently.

"Yes, Little One. *Love*. Did you believe I was aiming to earn your friendship with my hand on your ass and my cock nestled between your thighs?" he asked, grinding forward as if he could prove his point.

"Friends can fuck, Caelum. I would have thought you'd be

completely aware of that, given all your sexual adventures," I hissed, turning my head away from his. He was too close, his face lingering so near to mine that I thought he just might be able to hear the thoughts swirling in my head.

"There's that jealousy again," he teased, a growl of satisfaction rumbling through his chest. "Do friends get jealous of past lovers? Because I cannot promise I wouldn't disembowel any man who has been inside you."

"Well, fortunately there's no need for that," I said, a scowl taking over my face. "He's already nothing more than snow."

Caelum stilled, all the amusement falling off his face as he tipped his head to the side and stared down at me. "He tried to harm you after you were marked?"

"He was one of the Mist Guard they sent to hunt me down and run me through. A good way to prove his loyalty, I suppose."

"He chose his duty over you," Caelum said, leaning his face forward until he nuzzled into the sensitive skin at the hollow of my neck. His breath was warm as it wafted over my mark, the intimacy of it feeling familiar. "He was a fucking idiot."

"Duty always comes first," I said, echoing the words that had been beaten into me from a young age. Duty before family. Duty before love. Duty before *everything.*

Mine had been to bear the next Lord of Mistfell. I couldn't help but wonder what duty Caelum had been saddled with. If I hadn't known better, I'd have sworn he was the perfect candidate for the Royal Army.

"Love should always come first. We've gotten lost as a whole if we've forgotten that. There was a time when people would have burned the world down for those they loved," he said. My stomach rumbled beneath him, drawing a grin to his face as it interrupted the moment.

To have someone love me so completely that they not only chose me, but would have defied everyone and everything to have me—it seemed so impossible in our world. Brann had sacrificed everything to protect me, but even that had felt like there was an ulterior motive. As if there was something I didn't know, that I couldn't know, hanging between us that drove him to protect me.

Because if the most important thing to him was making sure the Fae didn't capture me, why wouldn't he have allowed the Mist Guard to kill me in the first place? It was the only guarantee.

"Come on," Caelum said, removing his weight from me and holding out a hand to help me to my feet. "I'll teach you how to set a couple of traps. We'll wait for a little while and hopefully catch something before we need to get moving for the day."

"Are we still trying to get to the Mountains of Rochpar?" I asked, thinking of the grueling travel through the coldest months. There was no chance we would make it before true winter came, and while I couldn't deny that putting as much distance between us and the fallen Veil as possible would be to our advantage, freezing to death wasn't appealing in the slightest either.

"Eventually," he said, hoisting me up into the tunnel we'd entered through. He followed at my back as we made our way out, finding the weather much more agreeable in the early morning light. The wind had died down, the snow had stopped, and most of it had melted off the ground already. "But with the weather being unpredictable, I think we need to find an alternative to wait out the cold season. There are rumors of a Resistance to the Fae *and* the Mist Guard in the Hollow Mountains. We're going to keep moving in the hopes of stumbling across them."

"How will we find them?" I asked, the idea of a resistance to the Fae seeming out of my wildest dreams. More people like us, more ability to survive if there was a place to ride out the winter successfully.

"You don't," he said, jumping down from the tunnel and reaching up to grasp me around the waist and lower me to the leaf-covered ground. "They find you."

My heel had been tormented enough, the skin that had split long ago and blistered around the original wound, parting to give way to a deeper wound that was much worse than I'd thought it could get. I flinched with my steps, feeling it tear further with every pace.

Caelum lifted his head slightly as he studied me, danger churning in his gaze. "You're hurt," he said, leveling a look at me that I thought might have made grown men wither. "Why didn't you say anything?"

"There's nothing to be done for it. I can't walk without boots," I said, shrugging off the pain in my ankles. One was worse than the other, the slick feeling of blood on my skin driving me to the point of madness.

Well- fitted footwear was of great importance when walking for endless hours every day.

"Your boots are hurting you?" he asked, his brow furrowing. Just a glance at his clothing spoke to the high quality items he'd been accustomed to before the Veil had shattered. The needlework on his tunic and trousers alone probably cost more than I would see in a year as a harvester.

"Yes. They don't fit me right, so the leather rubs at my ankles and bunches up my socks and cuts into me," I explained, watching his jaw clench.

He took my hand in his, guiding me away from the base of the low mountain we'd been hugging, so that we'd have the ability to find shelter in a cave when the sun started to set. "Where are we going?" I asked.

"There's a village not too far from the Hollow Mountains. We'll go find you some new boots there and maybe a cloak while we're at it. You can't keep walking in boots that wound you," he said, his tone feeling scolding as he glared down at me.

"A few blisters are the least of our problems," I said, even though I wouldn't object to functioning footwear and a warm cloak that didn't bear the weight of leaving Caelum unprotected from the elements.

"Did they heal overnight?" he asked, studying me intently.

"Mostly," I admitted. I hadn't wanted to voice the strange healing that seemed to happen every time I got hurt. Scrapes faded quickly; my dislocated shoulder had stopped hurting within hours. Nothing lasted, but every time the blisters healed over, the fresh baby skin that covered the wounds was reopened the next day.

"You'll heal quickly now. If we can just find you some boots that fit you better, your feet will be better in no time. That's important, Estrella. You can't run properly if you're in pain."

"I just don't think it's worth exposing ourselves to the Mist Guard." I sighed, but I followed. He then sighed, stopping his journey to reach behind me and lay a hand across my waist. His other went to the underside of my legs, sweeping them out from under me until I was cradled in his arms with my head resting on his shoulder. "What are you doing?"

"You're slow because you're in pain. We'll move faster if I carry you," he said, striding forward as if he didn't have the weight of a whole-ass person draped over his arms like a rug that needed cleaning.

"Don't be a dick. I can walk myself."

"Can you?" he murmured, raising a brow as he ran his eyes over my torso, down my legs, and to the boots that even I knew were slowly filling with blood.

"Don't make me punch you," I warned, squirming until he finally relented and set me to my feet. My heels protested it immediately, but I pushed forward and walked faster with him at my side.

I wouldn't be carried through the woods like a damsel, not when I knew I was capable of walking myself. To think such a small wound could render me incapable would only make me angrier.

We continued on in silence, both of us stewing in our own frustration through the hours we walked to find the village he'd mentioned. I didn't want to ask; didn't think it wise to try to learn anything more about his background. Not when his life and history only served to endear me to him more and more.

"Was your father a Lord or something?" I asked, unable to stop the burning curiosity.

"You could say that," he said evasively, shrugging his shoulders.

That certainly explained why he'd been tolerated even though he wasn't a legitimate child.

Money could buy many things. Even a bastard child as an official heir.

I quieted down, reading the signs of his unwillingness to discuss more about his father's title. It didn't matter in the end.

Nothing about the world we'd known mattered anymore.

21

"Would you stop it?" I snapped, swatting Caelum's hand away as he tried to snake his arm around my waist.

Again.

"You're still limping," he argued, as if that was justification for his continued attempts to carry me.

"You said it wasn't much farther," I said, nodding my head forward and motioning him on as I passed him.

He growled in response; the sound rumbling in his chest as he stalked after me. His massive hand came down on the top of my head, using it to steer my body more northward than I'd begun to walk. "You have the sense of direction of a hydra."

"Aren't they blind?" I asked, thinking back to the paintings I'd seen in the books that warned of the horrors of Alfheimr when the High Priestess wanted to scare me into staying away from the Veil. They were filled all the creatures we wouldn't ever have to see with the Veil to protect us, so long as I learned to leave it alone. The Fae were terrifying enough, their ethereal bodies so similar to ours but different in all the ways that mattered. The monsters and beasts of Faerie were crafted from nightmares, molded from darkness and all the evil magic brought into the world. The enormous three-headed serpents didn't even have eye sockets.

"Yes. Yes, they are," he agreed, quirking an eyebrow at me as he walked at my side, his pace relaxed so that I could keep up.

As much as I feared the cave beasts, the thought of sleeping exposed to the elements and to the Wild Hunt and others who might kill us in our sleep was somehow even more terrifying. At least when I had Caelum to protect me, the two of us might have been able to escape a cave beast's wrath.

But I doubted the Wild Hunt would let us slip away twice.

"I wish I was a hydra," I teased. "Then I could just swallow you whole and not have to endure your endless hovering anymore."

"My star, you can swallow me whole anytime you—" I smacked him in the stomach, drawing pleasure in the grunt that rolled into a laugh as the strike cut him off.

"There's that tingle." He laughed when I glowered at him.

"You do realize you aren't supposed to *enjoy* being punched, don't you?"

"I can think of worse ways to pass the time," he said, shrugging his shoulders as if my little violent outbursts weren't of actual concern to him. It both infuriated me and intrigued me that he was so unconcerned with my displays of violence, when so many men would've had me beaten for less.

"Do you not worry that I might bite it off if you put it near my mouth?" I asked, braving the dangerous tension between us to continue the conversation I should have left unanswered. His gaze felt heavy on the side of my face, his attention fixated on me when I didn't turn to meet his stare. I focused on my feet, on the way my too-large boots trudged through the leaves and underbrush on the ground.

"Maybe," he said finally, his eyes leaving my face as he turned his attention toward the path in front of us. A building appeared in the distance, the first of the village where we needed to gather supplies. "But I'd know a few moments of perfection until you did."

I scoffed, laughter bubbling in my throat and doubling me over as I tried to catch my breath. "Do you believe the lines you feed to the women you try to bed? How do you say them with such a straight face?"

"Oh, my star, you seem to have misread the situation. I do not tell women lines or whisper sweet nothings in their ears or give them false promises I have no intention of keeping. They come to my bed entirely willingly with a great understanding of what I have to offer them: one night of fun. There is no need for romantic lines or exaggerations."

"Then what would you call the perfection of my mouth? A dramatic half-truth?" I said, letting him guide me off the path itself and into the woods surrounding the village so we could observe.

"I would call it the truth," he said, turning toward me suddenly and trailing the pad of his thumb over my bottom lip. "I think we both know that there wouldn't be many better ways to die than with your lips wrapped around my cock, Little One. The only thing that might be better is if I was between your pretty thighs, sinking inside you while you struggled to take me."

I couldn't breathe. We spoke of his death, of all the ways he could die that would be mixed with pleasure, and yet it was me who felt like I was on the verge of the end. As if my lungs would never draw in air again, not with the filthy words that came out of his mouth and the way his dark eyes seemed to glimmer with understanding as he stared down at me.

"Tell me again how much you don't want me, my star. I do so love the way you lie."

"I loathe you," I wheezed, repeating the words from earlier as a blinding smile claimed his face.

"Hmm," he hummed, leaning forward to touch his lips to the part of my mouth he'd explored with his thumb. My breath caught, a shuddering rasp in my lungs as he took my mouth and made it his. "Why fight the inevitable? We both know where this is leading."

"With me brokenhearted and abandoned when you find something prettier?" I asked, the words escaping before I could rethink them. I hated the vulnerability they showed, the weakness it was to admit that he had the power to hurt me.

No one deserved to have that ability over me.

"I've seen my fair share of women. Trust me when I tell you there is nothing prettier for me than you. The only way this ends is with you as mine," he said, drawing back to stare down at me meaningfully. "Always."

I stuttered as I stared up at him, fumbling over the mess of words that came to my mouth. They all tangled together into a web of incoherence, leaving me with the distinct feeling that he would never stop throwing me off balance.

He enjoyed seeing me flounder far too much to ever allow me to just go about my day peacefully, without fear of making a fool out of myself when he said things I'd never imagined a man saying to me.

He touched a hand to my cheek, running that thumb over the freckles that dotted the arch of my cheekbone. His mouth still hovered just a breath away, the words he murmured brushing the smooth skin of his lips against the junction of mine. "Come out and play with me, my star. I know you're in there somewhere, burning away where you think no one can see you. Imagine how brightly you'd shine if you embraced all that fire."

With his palm on my cheek and his face touching mine, we shared the very air we breathed between us. It seemed to sigh, something tangible arcing through the air as his hand slid down from my cheek to the Mark on my neck. The circle on the back of his hand shone with white light as he turned his head toward mine. His lips brushed over mine in a smooth caress, a glide that seemed to steal the breath from his lungs in the same moment it captured mine.

He groaned, a soft and low noise that erupted through the silence of the woods surrounding us. The village not far off ceased to exist, the potential for someone to see us no longer mattered as he dropped his free hand to my waist and guided me to take a few steps backward. The firm press of a tree at my spine ensnared me into the trap he'd set so quickly I didn't have time to question any of it.

His mouth was a ghost of a thought over mine, almost there but not quite as he held my stare and shifted his head back and forth.

Taunting me. Teasing me.

"I'm going to kiss you now," he murmured, the words brushing against me. They felt like a threat. They felt like a promise. They felt like everything I shouldn't allow.

Yet I couldn't move away, couldn't stop it from happening; not with that intense, dark stare pinning me to the spot. I wondered just how it would feel to burn so brightly that I was reduced to nothing but ashes on the wind.

"I thought you already had," I whispered, immediately cursing myself for my stupidity.

Caelum chuckled in response. "No, Estrella. I haven't even begun to kiss you yet," he said, tipping his head to the side to get a better angle. His mouth pressed more firmly to mine, molding against the seam of my lips as he guided my head back into the tree trunk. My mouth tingled where he touched it with his, and tiny pinpricks of cold static arced between us.

His lips stayed soft, a gentle exploration as he traced every corner of my mouth with his, and as he caressed me gently and found every weakness. When he parted for me, I followed in a well-practiced, synchronized dance that we had no right to know. We'd never danced together, never kissed beneath a canopy of evergreens with branches hanging low all around us, and yet against reason, he felt familiar. He felt like coming home after years away, and the breath he expelled into my lungs was the first true breath I'd taken; one of pure, frosty air.

The girl who emerged from this tree canopy would never be the same.

I opened for him, letting him tip my head back with the hand on my neck and fingers that felt almost too harsh. His groan poured into my mouth and down my throat, his tongue tangling with mine as he drank from me as greedily as he gave. He kissed me fucking senseless, until my name was a thing of the past and my arms were wrapped around his neck. The moment my hand brushed against his Mark, he gasped into my mouth and pressed his body harder into mine.

The distance between us disappeared as he encased me in the safety of the cocoon he created with the tree and his broad form leaning over me. He pressed his hips against my belly, the length of him seeming to sear my skin through my dress, jolting me back to a bit of reality.

We needed to get back to the mountains before night fell.

"Caelum," I murmured, tearing my mouth from his. He sighed his frustration, dropping his face into my neck and trailing his lips over the Fae Mark that was so similar to his. It blazed like ice so cold it burned, the white glow of it shimmering off his skin. "I'm sorry," I added, feeling the need to apologize. I hadn't asked for him to kiss me, but I damn well hadn't stopped him, even though I knew better than to allow it.

With just one kiss, he'd proven everything I'd already known. The man would be the end of me.

"I would wait an eternity for you, Little One. You never need to be sorry," he said, dropping one last gentle kiss to my mouth and backing away. I peeled myself off the tree, turning my attention back to the village as he gave me space.

My lips burned, the flesh bruised from his kiss as the cold air erased the heat of his mouth.

And I still thought it had been worth it.

22

The temple in the village we came across was smaller than the one where I'd spent my days on my knees in Mistfell. The building was still crafted from stone, but there was no tower jutting up toward the sky to reach for the afterlife, only a single story that crouched low to the ground. The windows were plain, not the four-paned windows that had let light filter in through glass, which was far too expensive unless it had been gifted.

We skirted around the edge of the village, hugging the tree line as we kept an eye out for any stragglers who hadn't yet gone to Temple or who risked the wrath of their High Priest for a few moments' delay.

The village was silent, the presence of everyone required inside the weekly Temple, making it the perfect time for us to gather supplies without detection. I knew from experience that even the Mist Guard was severely limited in terms of who took shifts that brought them away from the sacred weekly worship.

Caelum peeked toward the Temple and through the window, his gaze snagging on the worshipers kneeling before the Priestess where she walked with her switch at her side, ready to discipline any who didn't bow to her satisfaction.

"Fucking zealots," Caelum muttered, turning away from the scene in front of us. We made our way further around the village, getting as far away from the temple as we could manage.

"You seem rather interested in the Old Gods," I said, squinting up at him as he moved through the shadows at the edge of the woods. He carved his body through them with well-practiced ease, claiming them as his own and molding himself into them so well that I suspected I wouldn't have been able to see him if I'd been a passing villager. "Some would say that makes you the zealot."

"At least the Old Gods didn't advocate a life of boredom. They lived for the sake of pleasure, not some potential doom that came after thirteen life cycles. I will never understand why people would choose to spend their life on their knees when they could do anything and be anything they wanted," he said, grasping my hand in his and dragging me alongside him to keep up when I wasn't as talented at keeping to the shadows as he was.

"That's a pretty notion, but is it ever really a choice when the alternative to obedience is death?" I asked, stepping out into the yard of one of the houses on the outskirts of the village with Caelum. He grabbed a heavy wool cloak off the clothesline, tossing it over the top of his where it rested on my shoulders, to hold as he pulled me toward the door to the house itself.

"I would rather die on my feet than live in service to something I don't believe in," he said, shrugging his shoulders as he pressed his ear to the door. When there was no sound, he pressed the latch down and pushed it open slowly.

Empty.

He moved inside quickly, tugging me to follow and closing the door behind him. "Boots," he ordered me, gesturing to the few pairs of shoes at the side of the door. I slipped mine off, wincing at the stains of blood that soaked the heel on my socks and leaked down to cover the soles of my feet.

Caelum froze in place where he'd started to move to one of the bedrooms, his gaze snagging on the blood. "The next time you try to downplay your injuries, I'll toss you over my shoulder and carry you whether you like it or not. Is that understood, Little One?" he snapped, retreating into the bedroom as I peeled the ruined socks off my feet, as well.

Caelum emerged, clutching a pair of women's trousers and a pair of socks. "Put these on," he ordered, and I took the pants from him. The fabric was heavy, warmer than I'd ever felt.

"What are these?" I asked, having never seen a woman in pants in my life.

I hiked up my dress, slipping a leg through each of the holes and sighing contentedly the moment the warm fabric wrapped around my legs. "Wealthy women wear them under their dresses when it's cold. They're called leggings," he said, turning his attention away briefly when my undergarments would have come into view. He'd seen it all, but I still appreciated the moment of privacy as the leggings settled around my waist and covered my ass.

I wiped the excess blood from my feet with a rag I found in the kitchen, doing my best not to ruin the new, thick socks that I pulled on before I stepped into the women's boots that I'd chosen. They weren't a perfect fit, but they were far, far better than the ones I'd had before.

"I think you underestimate the power of being raised to believe in something so deeply that you truly fear the consequences of disobedience that will come *after* death," I said, thinking of all the times Bernice had tormented me with what would be waiting for me in the arms of The Mother if I continued to prove a disappointment.

The agony. The abuse. The retribution that I could only pay in blood.

"And yet you do not seem compelled now to attend Temple. You lived your life according to their rules, and what did that get you?" Caelum asked, a shadow passing over his face in a furious expression before he shoved it down. "They don't deserve your loyalty."

"They don't have my loyalty. They never did, despite their desperate attempts to mold me into a Lady," I said, accepting the hand he offered. He guided me out of the house cautiously, taking me to the edge of the woods where he found an axe stuck into the tree stump the owner used to chop wood. He pulled the heavy thing free as we passed, not even pausing in his steps as he wrenched it from the wood.

"Is that why you were so quick to run? You must have been, in order to escape in one piece," Caelum said, glancing back toward the village as we ducked into the trees once more.

"Let's just say the only thing waiting for me in Mistfell was death, even before the Veil fell," I said. His brow furrowed, his jaw tensing for a moment before he grimaced and turned away.

"Stay here," he ordered, ducking back into the village. I nodded, even though he'd already turned his back on me, watching as he darted around the outskirts and gathered supplies from outside of people's homes.

I turned my stare to the sky and studied the position of the sun, readying myself for Temple to end. By the time he returned to my side, there was a pack slung across his shoulders, filled with supplies he'd gathered from the fringes of the village while I observed him from the corner of my eye. He'd snuck in and out of barns and houses, shoving in rope and blankets, more flint, and an extra canteen.

The axe he'd found was strapped to the sheath that crossed his back beneath his cloak. Between his two swords, the axe, and the dagger strapped to his thigh, he cut a formidable figure.

I held out a hand for the pack he'd loaded with the supplies, knowing that all the weapons he carried must have been heavy; not to mention, the pack would only hinder his ability to get to them if we needed them.

It seemed safe to say that day would come eventually.

"Hey! Thief!" a woman's voice yelled as she stepped out of the temple and glanced toward her empty clothesline where her cloak had hung. She turned to the woods, finding us and seeing her forest green cloak wrapped snugly around my shoulders.

Guilt consumed me, knowing that there was every chance she couldn't afford another one for the season, but she had a roof over her head. A fire in her home.

I had the promise of a cold cave and walking through blizzards.

"Run," Caelum instructed, as people started to emerge from the temple to join with her shouts. I turned, running back toward the mountain range hidden behind the trees. I had to hope I was going in the right direction, with Caelum's reminder of my useless navigating skills hanging over my head.

"They went that way!" the woman yelled behind us as I tore through the leaf-covered underbrush. Caelum didn't speak as he followed me, his hand coming down on my spine every now and then to coax me to run faster. To hurry. I knew without a doubt he'd slowed his pace to stay with me, though his long legs were able to eat up the distance far faster than mine could ever hope to do.

"Faster," he urged, taking my hand briefly to shift my path of direction.

More southward, I suspected.

"Return the cloak and you won't be punished!" a man said somewhere behind us. He was close, too close for comfort. I spun to look back, risking the consequence of them closing in. If they caught us, punishment for stealing would be the least of our concerns.

We all knew what the Mist Guard would do to anyone who failed to turn in Marked who crossed their path. They wouldn't hesitate to surrender us. Not with their lives hanging in the balance as well.

"Estrella!" Caelum warned from behind me, his voice erupting through the woods. I heard it over the sound of my heavy breathing, snapping my attention back to him just as my foot caught on a tree root and I went sprawling forward.

He'd somehow seen what I hadn't. There was no ground beneath me, not for what seemed like an eternity as Caelum tried to grasp me by the new cloak wrapped around my shoulders. His fingers slipped through the fabric, grappling for purchase as I fell.

My hands hit the ground first, scraping raw along the harsh brambles covering the ravine. My cheek slid across it next as I squeezed my eyes closed in a desperate attempt to protect them, and then the rest of my body struck. Landing sideways, I rolled down a bank into a ditch until I came to a stop at the very bottom. My hand dropped into a narrow stream, the icy water burning my skin with cold so quickly that I yanked it back and rolled back toward the hillside.

Caelum barreled down the hill, running through the brambles as they tore at his clothes and skin until he reached me. The villagers stood at the top of the hillside, staring down after him while I watched.

None of them braved the drop into the ravine, talking amongst themselves and buying us some time. I planted a hand in the rocks next to the stream, the blood and scratches covering my skin making me grateful that the gloves Caelum had found for me were tucked safely in his pack and not torn to shreds.

I pushed to my feet, my cheek burning and body throbbing as Caelum reached me, wrapping his arms around my waist and lifting me off the ground. "Are you alright?" he asked, studying the wounds on my face intently for a moment as he clenched his jaw. He turned that molten stare up to the villagers, who slowly started to brave the brambles to make their way down.

"I'll be fine. Let's go," I said, nodding toward the path of the stream. I took the first step away from the villagers, my ankle caving beneath me the moment I put weight on it.

Caelum caught me as I fell, growling as his hand twitched toward a sword. He seemed to shake off the moment of fury, the unrealistic belief that he could fight the villagers off on his own. "Put this on," he said, handing me the pack. I did as he told me, wondering why he would give me the extra weight when I couldn't even support my own.

Clarity came the moment he pulled the axe free and lowered himself to one knee in front of me. "Don't be ridiculous," I said, my throat burning with the possibility of being caught. "Even you can't outrun them with my weight. Just leave me."

He spun, pinning me to the spot with a glare so fierce I thought I might shrivel up on the spot. It was worse than any humiliation I'd felt when he'd teased me about the inevitability of being intimate with him.

It was worse than everything.

"Do not ever let me hear you say those words again. Do you understand me, Estrella?" he asked, taking my hand and pulling me closer. He wrapped it around the front of his neck, leaving me to follow with the other one. As soon as I had my hands placed on his shoulders, he reached back and grasped me around the back of each thigh. Hoisting me onto his back, he stood smoothly and without any of the difficulty I'd have expected from something as bulky as an entire person and supply pack. And weapons.

His swords were sheathed in the cross-back scabbards, poking into the spaces between my arms and where he hiked my legs up high on his hips. He bent forward slightly, grabbing the discarded axe off the ground and hurrying forward.

He walked faster than I could typically walk on my own, hurrying as quickly as he could without dislodging me or risking me further injury. The sounds of the villagers trying to make their way over the brambles and down the ravine faded into the distance as he stepped over the stream and walked up into the woods on the other side.

His breathing came harder by the time he reached the top, but still he kept walking, treading along until there was no doubt that we'd left the villagers behind us. Only then did he angle back down toward the stream, keeping a watchful eye for any stragglers that might have continued on in search of us. Finally, when we must have been miles from the place where I'd fallen, Caelum bent forward to lower me to my feet in front of a log that I could sit on.

He stripped the pack off my back, pulling out a bedsheet he'd grabbed. It had seemed foolish at the time, but as he cut through it with his dagger and dipped it into the stream, I understood why extra cloth would probably never be a bad idea.

He touched the cold fabric to my face, cleaning the cuts that I could feel on my cheek. "How bad is it?" I asked, flinching as I thought of the fact that only a few hours prior, he'd said I was the prettiest woman he'd ever seen.

"Worse than I want it to be," he said, cleaning the worst of the scrapes. When he was satisfied that my face was tended to, he rinsed the rag in the stream once more and took my hands in his. My palms were covered in dried blood, having taken the brunt of that first impact.

A glance at the front of his cloak and shirt showed the stain from my injuries covered his clothing.

I winced as he touched the cloth to my hand and cleaned the blood off to inspect the cuts beneath. He glared at the injuries on the first palm as he set it on my lap, moving to the other and starting the process of cleaning that hand. The scrapes weren't horrible enough that I'd die or needed serious attention from a healer, but it didn't take much to cause an infection or make functioning painful.

The worst of the cuts was on the tip of my finger, a deep poke hole that throbbed when Caelum ran the cloth over it. He squinted, setting the cloth to the side and using his fingernails to pry out the thorn that had wedged itself into my skin. I squeaked as he pulled it free and blood welled up in my fingertip.

He leaned forward, drawing my finger into his mouth and licking the blood from the wound as I watched in shock. Warmth spread through my hand, saturating my chilled flesh as his dark gaze landed on mine. Heat flowed through my veins, burning me from the inside in a way that made me want all the things I shouldn't and reminding me of the way he'd rubbed his shaft against me when he pinned me to the tree.

Something simmered in his gaze, thickening the air between us as he slowly pulled the finger free from his mouth and used his teeth to tear off a dry strip of fabric that he pressed to my finger to help the bleeding stop. "Hold that there," he instructed, as if he had no clue that I was aroused by the sight of him licking the blood from my finger.

There was something wrong with me.

He knelt at my feet and grabbed my new boot. He unknotted the laces, pulled it off, and yanking down the sock. Even I saw the purple swelling wrapped around my ankle and the way it seemed to bulge between my leg and my foot.

"Fucking Gods," Caelum muttered, hanging his head forward. He tore off more of the sheet, making strips as he wrapped my ankle in them carefully before replacing the sock.

"I'm sorry," I muttered, knowing that I'd effectively slowed down our pace dramatically. There was no way Caelum could carry me for the days it would take my ankle to heal entirely, and I would be fortunate if I could walk at all the next day.

"Stop apologizing for things that aren't your fault. You didn't intend to fall down a fucking ravine. You were running for your life. I should have just killed them. At least then you wouldn't be injured."

"You can't kill an entire group of people over a cloak, Caelum," I said, shaking my head.

Something lurked in the shadows of his eyes as he turned his attention to my face. "Maybe not, but I would kill an entire group of people for putting you in danger."

I swallowed, sucking back a breath of cool air as he carefully put my boot back on my foot.

"Does that frighten you, Little One? Knowing how far I would go to keep you safe?" He stood and held out a hand, in a way that felt like more than an offer to help me stand. It felt like by accepting his hand, I would be accepting his violence and willingness to kill those who got in his way.

"Yes," I admitted, unable to fathom the reality. I would kill to protect Caelum from those who meant to harm him, but innocent people who just wanted to survive?

That wasn't something I thought myself capable of doing.

"Good. Perhaps you'll be mindful of putting yourself at risk unnecessarily in the future. It's best for everyone that you stay safe. You do not want to consider what I'll do if someone tries to take you from me."

He strapped the pack to his back, placing an arm behind my knees and one behind my back and lifting me into the cradle of his arms as he hiked up the bramble side of the ravine. It wasn't as steep as the place where I'd fallen, and soon the mountains loomed ahead at the top of the ridge. He traversed it, picking his way toward them and the possibility of more caves and, hopefully, a place to hide while I healed enough to travel. Right now, we were losing time with every hour that passed that I was unable to move on my own.

I was a liability to him, and yet, I couldn't bring myself to sneak off in the night.

The thought of what he would do when he hunted me down once

again was enough to keep me by his side, wondering how my savior had somehow become a morally gray man with no boundaries and a distinct lack of understanding how an actual courtship worked.

You didn't just decide a woman was yours to protect after a few days spent together.

Right?

23

I sat outside the caves as the sun set, the shadows starting to dance on the horizon as it faded from the sky. The light it cast through the canopy of branches and evergreen needles bathed the forest floor in an eerie sort of glow as Caelum stalked through the underbrush. Running his palms over tree roots and stumps, he felt for moss and a type of leaf that he said could be made into a poultice to help with the swelling on my ankle.

I'd never expected a man like Caelum to know about poultices, and I had to wonder if that knowledge came from his father's library, too. He went to a cave opening; a much larger entrance that immediately set my nerves on edge. It felt too obvious, less hidden.

Big enough for cave beasts to use it to come in and out under the cover of darkness.

Stashing the herbs and moss he'd collected in his pack, he swung it over his shoulder and onto his back before coming to collect me from the stump where he'd deposited me. He picked me up without fanfare, draping me over his shoulder as he swung the axe on his other side.

"There are kinder ways to carry me," I sniped, lifting my head just enough that the blood wouldn't rush to it and make me dizzy as he ambled through the cave entrance. He whistled as he walked, entirely unconcerned with the body draped over his shoulder like a sack of root vegetables.

"I can drop you faster this way if I need to fight off a cave beast," he said, his steps remaining sure as he made his way deeper into the cave carved into the mountainside.

"Oh, that's much better. I do so love the idea of being dropped onto the stones," I said, feeling the need to argue with him just for the sake of it. I hated being reliant on him. I hated the fact that I couldn't even walk on my own, let alone survive without him to take care of me.

"I'd rather that than see the flesh torn from your bones. It's such pretty flesh, after all," he said, using the hand that he'd wrapped supportively around the backs of my thighs to smack me on the ass.

"Hey!"

"Quiet," he ordered, the word a murmur. "I need to listen."

"Convenient," I grumbled, but I kept my mouth closed after the single word of protest. Arguing wasn't worth leaving him unawares. I, too, liked my flesh on my bones.

Caelum walked through the cave entrance until it curved to the side, offering us protection from the colder temperatures. When we came to an alcove, he lowered me to the ground carefully and pulled the ingredients for the poultice out, along with the wood he'd collected for a fire for the night.

I stretched my leg out in front of me, leaning my back against the cave wall and sighing. We hadn't eaten since that morning, and it seemed like that would probably become the normal routine when the sun was already starting to set by the time we stopped for the day. Maybe the time it would take my ankle to heal would allow us some time to gather food, if we could brave exposure outside the cave during the day long enough to try to find some berries or vegetables or something to harvest.

We'd need to hurry before they died for the season.

Once the fire was established, Caelum grabbed two rocks and used them to grind the herbs. A small splash of water turned them into a paste. "I can do it," I said, protesting when he pulled my boot off. He tugged my sock all the way off, rinsing it with some of the water from a canteen and placing it beside the fire to dry overnight.

He ignored my assurance that I was capable of tending to my own injury, shifting forward to sit in front of me with his side to the fire. He drew my foot into his lap, running gentle fingers over the bruising before he bent it forward and back, testing the movement. Pain shot up my leg with each bend, but I knew without a doubt it was nothing more than a sprain.

I hadn't broken the bone or done anything to damage it permanently.

"I think you'll be okay to walk in the morning," he said, shocking me as he dipped his fingertips into the paste he'd created. "We'll check the traps and eat something before we head out."

"What do you mean I'll be okay to walk in the morning?" I asked, scoffing at him. There was no way the swelling I had would just disappear overnight.

"You aren't entirely human anymore, Little One. The *Viniculum* doesn't just make you stronger or more agile, it makes you heal faster, as well. Your scratches already look better. They'll be gone by morning." I followed his gaze down to my hands and the cuts that had felt like my skin had been torn from my fingers only hours before.

Sure enough, all that remained were slightly swollen pink lines. Something that would have taken days of healing a little over a week ago had magically happened over the course of a few hours.

He touched the paste to the swelling on my ankle, rubbing it across the injured joint. A tingle spread across it immediately, a cooling sensation flowing over the skin as he leaned forward and blew on the paste intently.

"If the *Viniculum* supposedly makes me more agile, why doesn't it stop me from tripping over my own feet?" I asked, glaring at the amused expression he turned up to my face. With his lips pursed while he blew on my ankle and his gleaming eyes staring up at me through his lashes, something low in my belly clenched, the sudden image of that expression on his face while he blew on *other* places taking me out of the moment.

The bastard smirked as if he knew it, too.

"You know how a newborn fawn has to learn to walk on new legs?" he asked, his lips curving into a smile despite the tension thrumming between us.

I gasped, staring at him in shock. "Did you just compare me to something that's never walked before?"

"It isn't an exact metaphor, but it's similar. Your body is different than it was before. You move more swiftly, come upon obstacles quicker. Your reflexes need to catch up and work more efficiently now."

"First, I have the sense of direction of a hydra and now I walk like a stumbling newborn deer. You truly know how to compliment the woman you're trying to bed, Caelum the Marked," I said, shaking my head as a disbelieving smile tugged at the corners of my mouth. The humor dancing in his eyes couldn't be denied, something contagious passing between us as I tried to fight off the desire to return it.

"Tell me which part wasn't true, and I will gladly rectify it, Estrella the Star," he said, raising a brow as he waited for me to argue. I wanted nothing more than to prove him wrong, but knew well enough that I'd be lost within a moment of wandering on my own, and my swollen ankle made it impossible to argue my ability to function on my own two legs. "The silence is positively deafening," he said, his face breaking into a full-blown smile.

"Do shut up. We can't all be perfect men who know how to navigate and fight and walk flawlessly," I said, biting my tongue before I could tell him something about the way his trousers hugged his ass and hips as he moved.

"You're perfect just as you are, Little One, stumbling on awkward legs and horrible sense of direction included. I could spend the rest of the night telling you about all the parts of you that I would never allow anyone to change," he said, his voice dropping to a low rumble as he spoke the words. That tension throbbed between us once more, all brevity of the moment lost to the spark of energy. "But I don't think you're ready for that just yet. One day, I'll whisper it against your skin as I explore every piece of you with my mouth."

"And what would you do if I returned the favor?" I asked, my voice breathless. It felt like baiting a tiger, playing games with a predator as those dark eyes deepened to the blackest of night skies.

"Memorize the way the words felt when your lips moved against me. Control myself as long as possible before rolling you beneath me and sinking inside of you," he said, his voice deep and carefully controlled. As if he knew that in spite of my words and the way I'd walked him into the conversation, he was one wrong word away from sending me scurrying backward in discomfort with how much I *wanted* that.

I cleared my throat, tearing my eyes away from his and shifting my attention back to my ankle, breaking the moment between us before I could do something I might regret.

"Where did you learn about poultices like this?" I asked, making conversation to stifle the awkwardness I felt over his proximity. He leaned forward toward the place where he'd lifted my dress and pushed my leggings up my legs, lingering over the spot where he stroked my calf and shin with smooth caresses.

"My father's personal library," he said, confirming the suspicions I'd had not long before. "He had all manner of book there, most of them very forbidden and worthy of a death sentence if he was ever discovered."

"You miss him. It comes through every time you speak of him," I said, picking up on the melancholy note, and the way he always turned his gaze to the side and never looked me in the eye when speaking of his father. His attention shifted back, a sad smile gracing his lips as he finally met my stare.

"I miss the idea of him. I miss what we could have been if circumstances had been different," he admitted.

"You mean if your stepmother hadn't been..." I trailed off, not wanting to put words in his mouth. The details he'd provided of her had been so sparing, so vague that I couldn't form a realistic picture of the woman who'd helped raise him.

"Cruel? Yes. If she hadn't been so evil, I believe my father would have made the sacrifices necessary to be with my mother. Who knows what my life might have been then?" he asked, shifting his weight so that he stretched his legs out in front of him.

I hated the sadness etched into the lines of his face, the vulnerability lingering beneath the surface of this stunningly handsome man with the playful attitude I wished I could have. His depth was subtle, existing more in the moments when he shifted his expression, when there was no mask to be shown, revealing the raw emotion underneath. If I hadn't watched him so intently, to memorize every detail of the face that I could see myself falling in love with, I might not have even seen it.

My heart would have been safer if I hadn't.

"Will you tell me another story?" I asked, swallowing around the thick feeling building in my throat. I wanted nothing more than to give in to the pulsing attraction between us, and I might have, in a moment of rebellion against the Crown and all it demanded of me, if it wasn't for the way my heart fluttered in my chest every time he met my eyes. I would have leaped, if it wasn't for the way my stomach thrilled with a surge of something between nervousness and excitement every time he laid a hand on me.

If it wasn't for the fact that I could very easily fall in love with this man who could never be mine, because even if he didn't move on to someone else, he would never belong to me in the first place. The Fae Mark meant he had a mate out there, someone who would search for him until his dying day.

I didn't know what happened when she found him, or when the male searching for me found me. Would all previous attachments just disappear? Did it work that way, or was it strictly a physical bond that eclipsed all else? Did humans even feel it, or did they spend an eternity with someone they never loved?

Each possibility was just another reason why Caelum and I had to remain free. I didn't want that for me, but even more so, I didn't want that for *him.*

I was in so much trouble.

"Yes, Little One. I'll tell you another story," he said as he reached into the pack and pulled out the blanket he'd stolen. He lay near the fire, leaving the place directly next to it for me to claim. He tapped the ground beside him, and I eyed the spot nervously.

I hadn't agreed to sleep curled up in his embrace the night before, but even that felt more innocent than doing it tonight. After he'd kissed me senseless, I couldn't help but wonder exactly what would happen the moment I lay next to him.

But it was cold, even with the fire going at my side, and there was only one blanket.

Shoving down my nerves to a place where I hoped he couldn't see them, I moved into the space he'd left for me and stretched out on my back, turning my head to face him. He rolled to his side, facing me and sliding an arm beneath my head to protect it from the packed dirt beneath us. "What kind of story would you like to hear?" he asked, draping his other hand across my belly.

I sucked in a breath, forcing words to come out when all I could do was fixate on the touch. "Do you know any about the Fae and their mates?"

"I do," he said, his voice sounding surprised as he nodded slowly. "The mates came to be a very long time ago. The Fae were cursed by the witches who fought against them in endless wars, their souls fractured in two upon their birth and their other half planted into another person entirely. Some were human, others were Fae as well, but being without their other half was said to be a painful experience. Like being half a person."

"This is more like a history book than a story," I teased.

"Alright, Little One," he laughed. "There once was a Fae who waited over three hundred years for his mate to be born into her first life. This wasn't typical, anything over one hundred years tended to push even the most stable of Fae past their breaking point. A life without half your soul was unthinkably cruel. And then one night, he felt the moment she reached adulthood, and he wept with joy."

"What happened?" I asked, sensing from the seriousness on his face that this was not a story with a happy ending. I'd need to give him that caveat in the future. All romantic stories needed to end with them spending their lives together.

Life was hard and brutal enough as it was. The last thing I needed was a reminder of my loneliness in my bedtime stories that were meant to distract me from my grief.

"The witches shielded her from his view so that he could not get to her. They wrapped her in a cloaking spell, disguising her location and keeping him from her for many life cycles. But the spell didn't protect him from feeling her. It didn't stop him from falling in love with the essence of her every time she reached adulthood. It didn't stop him from feeling every time she died, her life fading away as he wept for another life wasted. On and on it went over centuries. Over thirteen lives, he waited and fought to find a way to get to his mate before she could die the true death and he would lose her forever."

"Did he ever find her?" I asked, swallowing back the burn of tears in my throat. I shouldn't have felt sorry for the nameless Fae male. I shouldn't have felt anything for him, knowing that he would have taken that human woman from everything she'd known if given the chance.

I'd been taught we were nothing but property to them, a being whose desires didn't matter in comparison to the needs of the Fae, but now sorrow pierced my gut at the thought of spending all those centuries alone. Of feeling the other half of my soul die repeatedly. To think that somewhere out there was a male who was supposedly the other half of me was unthinkable; impossible. How could the other half of me exist outside my body?

"He did. She was in her final life cycle when the witches' protection broke and he finally found her. But in order to complete the bond, he had to get her back to Faerie soil so that her life could be linked to his. Without it, she would remain mortal and die the true death," he said, leaning forward to touch his mouth to mine gently.

I drew back sharply, resisting the urge to growl my frustration at him. "Did they make it?"

He sighed, murmuring into the space between us. "I don't know. The story was never completed. They could be living happily in Alfheimr, or they could both be gone. Her to the true death, him to the madness that would have consumed him after losing her."

"Why would you tell me a story that you don't even know the ending of?" I snapped, lifting his hand off my stomach in protest.

He chuckled, replacing it immediately and using it to turn my body to face him . "Because life isn't always tidy. We don't always have the answers we want, and love isn't always pretty," he said, his gaze pointed as I swallowed audibly. "It's messy and painful, but it is always worthwhile. It is always the answer, my star, not the problem."

"You're saying I should love the Fae male who is supposedly my mate?" I asked, my brow furrowing as I thought about the inconsistency with what he'd said in the past. One more tick for the suspicion that we could only be temporary.

One more nail in the coffin of what could have grown between us, if not for the threats looming on the horizon.

"No. I'm saying you should let yourself love *someone*. If it is your mate, then so be it. But do not keep yourself guarded from the possibility of something more, out of fear of being hurt, because it is worth every moment of pain it will bring when it ends," he said, the knowing expression on his golden-skinned face nearly taking my breath away. His words were so close to the very same thoughts I'd had earlier in the evening, an echo of something I'd known deep inside.

"What's the point in loving someone if fate is determined to tear you apart?" I asked, the words a faint whisper that hovered between us. He closed the distance, caressing my bottom lip with his mouth briefly before it curved into the smile.

"Because even just for a little while, we don't have to be alone. There is no guarantee they'll ever find us. No guarantee that we'll ever be taken back to Alfheimr, but if they do, do you want to go never having lived or made a choice for yourself? Or do you want to have enjoyed your freedom while you had it, before they strip it all away from you?" he asked.

It reminded me of the nights I'd spent wrapped in Loris's embrace, risking death for a few moments of the pleasure that was forbidden to me. He hadn't been someone who would have ever been meant for me, but he hadn't been a danger to my heart, either.

Could I really risk my heart in the process? Or had it never really been mine to give?

"I can feel you thinking too hard," he murmured, cupping my cheek in his hand beneath the curtain of my hair. He leaned in, his mouth coasting over mine once again and chasing away all rational thought. He rolled into me, moving me beneath him as his weight settled over me and pinned me to the ground.

Instead of feeling suffocating like it so often had when Loris did it, all I felt was comfort being wrapped in Caelum's embrace. He kissed me, letting one of his hands skim down my body over my dress until he could grasp me around the back of my thigh.

I moaned into his mouth when his fingers brushed against my ass, guiding my leg out and around his waist so that he could sink further into me. So that he could cover me with his body.

I helped him, wrapping my legs around him until the twinge of pain that shot up my ankle drew a startled gasp from me. Caelum froze in place, pulling his mouth away and leaving me bereft, as if I needed to remember how to breathe on my own all over again.

He sighed, reaching back to guide my injured leg to the ground as he lifted himself up onto his forearms and stared down at me.

"I'm sorry. I'll be fine, really," I said, sinking my teeth into my bottom lip. I couldn't bring myself to tell him I didn't want him to stop, that I was ready for all the pleasure he'd offered me on countless occasions.

It seemed a betrayal to myself to voice the weakness he'd brought out in me, and to admit how desperately I needed to feel something after losing everything I'd ever loved.

Caelum's presence was the only thing that made me feel alive, as if I hadn't died with Brann on that cliff.

"You will be, but we have all the time in the world, Little One," he said, rolling off of me and dragging my body to drape me over his. He positioned my injured ankle over his hips, gently depositing it there as if the injury would keep him from disturbing me in the night.

His eyes drifted closed, the only sign he gave me that the time had come to sleep. Disappointment fluttered in my belly, having been so close to crossing the line in a way I could never come back.

It was only a matter of time before I did. That much was clear from my brief time spent with Caelum.

The real question was what would remain of me when it was all over with.

24

My weight shifted suddenly, my body thrown to the cave floor so hard that I drew in a shuddering breath after the wind was knocked free from my lungs. “Don’t fucking touch her,” Caelum warned, his voice filled with malice as I flung my alarmed gaze toward him. The haze of sleep vanished in an instant, my mind suddenly alert as I tried to take in what was happening.

The tip of a sword hovered just in front of my nose; the man holding it stood with his legs spread ever so slightly around mine. I swallowed as I met his cold blue stare, glancing over toward where Caelum struggled against the four men fighting to pin him to the ground.

He pulled the dagger from the sheath at his thigh, pressing it to the throat of one of the men so deeply that they all froze. The man standing over me watched with interest, cocking his head to the side as he shifted his attention back down to me and touched the tip of the blade to my chest.

To the space just above my heart; the spot that could take me to a true death if he pierced it.

“You could kill him,” the man spoke to Caelum, shrugging his shoulders. "But do you think you'll get to her before I run her through?"

Caelum froze, his jaw clenched tightly as one of the other men wrapped their hands around his where it clutched the hilt of his dagger. He let them take it from him, his eyes never leaving mine or that blade pressed to my chest in warning. "When I'm through with you, there will be nothing left to reincarnate," Caelum growled.

The man above me chuckled, his face twisting into mockery. "You've got him properly wrapped around your little finger, don't you, pretty?" he asked, using the tip of his blade to flick the hair away from my neck. My Mark pulsed, drawing a blue glow from his own Fae Mark. He was the only one to wear the Mark, the other four men entirely human as they watched Caelum warily.

"You say that like it's a bad thing," I murmured, peeling my lips back from my teeth as something vicious overcame me. I was so fucking tired of being a victim. Of being treated like I was less than the men around me, because they had a piece of meat swinging between their legs. I touched a finger to his sword, trailing it up the flat edge in a teasing motion. "He has his uses."

"I'm sure he does," the man laughed, his eyes narrowing in on that innocent finger. I pressed a palm against each flat side of the blade, jerking it to the side as I hooked my feet around his ankles and used them to slide myself down between his legs, causing him to stumble forward.

His sword plunged into the dirt above my head, Caelum's shout echoing through the small alcove as I twisted out of the way and jumped to my feet. My ankle gave a tiny twinge of pain but held beneath me; the hours that had passed in the night had given it time to heal with my new abilities.

My boot came down on the man's ass where he bent over in front of me, knocking him further forward. "There are far kinder ways to wake a woman in the morning," I snapped, flinching when another set of hands grabbed me by the hair. The second man yanked my head back, twisting my neck from side to side as he looked at my ears.

Looking for the legendary pointed ears of the Fae, I realized.

I reached up above my head, grabbing him by the shoulders and pulling him toward me at the same moment I bent myself in half and pushed with my legs. He hit the ground in front of me with a thud, his arm landing at his side for a moment before he reached for his sword. I stepped on his wrist, squatting beside him to snatch the weapon away from his fingertips.

Caelum watched with a smirk on his face, distractedly fighting off the three remaining men who struggled to contain him, even when he didn't give them all his attention. I had no doubt that he could have escaped them all if it hadn't been for the risk to me.

It was a good fucking thing I could take care of myself in this way, at least.

"You will unhand my friend if you like yours breathing," I said, putting my assailant's own sword to his throat.

The man who'd first held a sword to my face slowly got to his feet, his hands held out in a peaceful gesture, as if they hadn't actually intended to harm us. I believed he meant it, knowing we weren't the Fae hunting him. "You got anything to add?" he asked Caelum, rubbing a hand over his face.

"I think she covered it, really," Caelum returned with a smirk. He moved with a fluid grace that took our attackers off guard, proving my suspicion that he had only not fought them off for my safety.

That shouldn't have made my stomach clench or butterflies rise up to my throat. Knowing that my safety came before his should have appalled me. Instead, I wanted to kiss him, and I wasn't sure I was ready to be the initiator in our intimate moments.

Not yet, anyway.

He disarmed his attackers smoothly, until every sword was either held within his grasp or flung against the dirt, leaving the men gaping at him awkwardly.

"Perhaps you would like to explain to me what exactly you were planning to do before my love emasculated you?" he asked, weighing the hilt of one of the swords in his hand as he watched the men carefully.

"We're looking for survivors. We had to be sure you aren't one of those Fae bastards. Evan over there knows how to see through glamour," he said, gesturing to the man who laid sprawled out in the dirt beneath me where I'd left him. His attention shifted over me and then to Caelum, studying us in a way that felt somehow invasive.

"The Fae Marks didn't give it away?" I asked, glaring at the man who'd spoken.

"You've never seen a Fae, have you pretty? Those bastards are born with the Mark," he grumbled.

He stared at the friend he'd said could see through Fae glamour, who nodded his head finally, and the men heaved a sigh of relief. The one who'd put a sword to my face came forward, holding out a hand for Caelum. "Name's Jensen," he said, holding Caelum's stern gaze as he looked down at the offered hand with a sneer.

"I am not interested in shaking the hand of a man who chooses mine before the hand of the woman who bested him," Caelum said, nodding his head toward me in acknowledgement of the slight. Jensen had passed me over when he wouldn't have, had I had a cock. Even after I'd proven I was worthy of being treated as an equal, he'd still chosen Caelum. I couldn't blame him entirely, not when Caelum had proven to be the greatest threat in the room.

But still, Caelum advocated for me when no one else would have.

"You know better than to underestimate a woman, Jensen," a feminine voice scolded as the owner stepped around the corner of the tunnel. Her cloak was clutched around her, her hood pulled up to cover her head and hair. She moved through the tunnel with a sort of lethal grace, her steps more masculine than I was used to seeing with the women of Mistfell, who only had value in their femininity.

She drew the hood of her cape back slowly, revealing a beautiful face marred by a scar on one side that slashed through her eyebrow and across her cheekbone. Her blond hair was tied tightly into a braid that extended down over the shoulder of her cloak and toward her belly. A Fae Mark swirled on the skin of her neck, curling up to her face.

She stepped in front of me, glancing toward the two men I'd defended myself against as a wry smirk graced her lips. Her attention shifted toward Caelum, pausing on him as she studied him intently for a moment and then shrugged. "I suppose I don't need to ask if the two of you can fight."

"Unless you like to waste time stating the obvious, it would appear not," I said, glancing down at the hand she held outstretched. I placed mine in it, watching as the Mark on her neck glowed a soft red.

"A tongue as sharp as your blade," she said with a chuckle. "What's your name?"

"I'm Estrella. That's Caelum," I said.

"Welcome to the Resistance, Estrella. We oppose all parties who wish to dictate our way of life. As such, we offer refuge to any who seek refuge from the Fae, the monarchy, or the Mist Guard. My name is Melian, and I highly suggest that you come with me. My scouts spotted the Fae in the area last night. It's fortunate that we found you first," she said, tilting her head to look back to the tunnels she'd emerged from deeper inside the mountain.

"Why would we go with you? How can we trust that we won't wake to another sword in our face tomorrow?" Caelum asked, earning a glare from me. He'd said we had to hope that the Resistance would find us, and they had.

Why would we not want to go with them to survive the coming winter?

"If you would like to hide out in these caves like animals, be my guest. But I can offer you something you'll never find on your own," Melian said.

"What's that?" Caelum asked, glaring at the woman who dared to show no concern for the fact that he could probably gut her before she so much as blinked.

"A safe place to rest your head. A place to live without fear," she answered. "A bed with blankets and food to fill your belly. We'll give you a few minutes to discuss it between yourselves. If you decide you'd like to come with us, we'll be around the corner." She nodded to her companions, supervising as they picked their weapons up off the ground.

The man I'd disarmed stood when I removed my foot from his

wrist, accepting the sword I handed back to him with a tentative smile. They followed Melian as she walked around the corner, leaving Caelum and I to stare at one another from across the distance between us.

"Are you alright?" he asked, his chest rising and falling as if it took everything he had to control himself and push back the anger he'd felt when we were ambushed.

"I'm fine," I said. Even if there had been a brief moment where I wondered if we'd find a way out of our predicament, they hadn't successfully hurt me.

The thought of them hurting Caelum was almost laughable.

"Good," he said, bending down to pick up the blanket that had been left on the floor when they'd pulled him away from me in our sleep. He shoved it into our pack, forcing the rest of his belongings into it and slinging it across his back. "Let's go."

He made his way toward the entrance to the cave, going in the opposite direction of Melian and the others. "Wait, what?" I asked, hurrying after him and grabbing his hand. "You said you were hoping they would find us. If they can give us a safe place, we have to take it."

"That was before they put a sword to your heart, Estrella. We can't trust them." He sighed, glancing back toward the rebels. I knew without a doubt he was curious about them.

It seemed unfathomable to consider that they'd existed before the Veil had shattered, but there hadn't been time to organize anything in the days since.

"You can't blame them for being cautious. If they weren't, they'd probably be dead by now. They didn't hurt us," I said, tugging him back toward where they'd headed. He nodded, but his expression remained guarded and torn. As if he couldn't come up with a genuine excuse why we should keep our distance, he looked back in their direction.

"If they give me a bad feeling, we leave. No questions; you do what you're told, Little One," he said, earning a glare from me.

"I've had enough of men telling me what to do. I thought you were better than that," I said, tugging on my hand to try to get him to release it. If he thought I'd go back to being nothing more than a plaything and the property of a man, I'd leave and take my chances without him.

Freedom was more important than love, even if my heart did stall with the realization that I suspected love was exactly what I felt for Caelum.

"When I tell you to do something, it is because I want to keep you safe. Not because I want to tell you what to do. There's a difference, Estrella. You can be whoever you want to be, as long as you are safe when you do it," he said, the timbre of his voice dropping low enough that I knew he meant it.

"I suppose being at your side is a requirement too?" I asked, glaring at him as he took my hand in his and adjusted his grip.

"Not a requirement so much as very strongly encouraged," he said, guiding me toward where the Resistance had disappeared. They waited around the corner as Melian had said they would, lifting torches off the ground and lighting them with the flint they pulled from their pockets.

Rumbling came up from the depths of the tunnels as Melian turned and led the way with one of the men on either side of her. At the insistence of the remaining three men, Caelum and I followed after her with the others taking up the rear. Caelum's discomfort was palpable, hanging between us as he squeezed my hand tighter in his.

"What's that noise?" I asked, turning to face him as the rumble seemed to grow louder with every moment that passed.

"Cave beasts," Melian said from the front. She held a sword clutched in her hand, the others armed as well. Caelum's had never left his hand, and I felt strangely naked without one of my own. I pulled the dagger free from Caelum's sheathe strapped to his thigh, holding it tightly in my grasp.

"What happens if they find us?" I asked, glancing back to the men behind me.

Jensen met my gaze, a sly smile transforming his face. "We fight. You aren't scared, are you, pretty? I'm happy to protect you, but you should know there are much scarier things in the woods now with the Veil down. Cave beasts are the least of your concerns." His hand came down on my shoulder, making me glance down at the intrusion in disdain.

"If you value that hand, you will remove it immediately," Caelum growled, his voice echoing through the narrow tunnel as Melian stopped in her tracks and stared back at the altercation behind her.

"Or what, pretty boy?" Jensen asked, raising an eyebrow at Caelum in challenge.

"Or I will sever it from your wrist and give it to her as a token of my affection," Caelum responded, his lips peeling back from his teeth ever so slightly even as the tunnel seemed to cool with the rising tension between the two men.

"That's enough, Jensen," Melian said. "You know the rules. You can only touch her if she gives you permission." She resumed her trek down the tunnel that narrowed as we continued forward, so we could only walk two by two. The reason for the torches quickly became obvious as the tunnel grew darker, until all traces of natural light disappeared and only the light of the fire enabled us to see at all.

Melian stopped suddenly, the man next to her dropping to his knees at her feet and lifting a slab of rock away from the ground. He shoved it to the side, revealing a hole carved into the ground beneath it. A manmade tunnel ran perpendicular to the natural cave tunnel, disappearing into the darkness below as the first of the men jumped down.

"Tunnels?" Caelum asked, turning his attention to Melian. "How could you have had time to do all of this?"

"My ancestors were the first members of the Resistance. They were the Fae Marked saved by the Veil all those centuries ago. They knew it was only a matter of time before the Fae returned to this land and came for them again in their future lives, or in their children's lives. We've been here since the Veil was erected hundreds of years ago, preparing for the day that those chosen by the Fae would need a safe place to land," she explained, watching as another of her men dropped into the tunnel below.

"I thought the Fae could track their Marked somehow. Was that not true?" I asked as she stepped toward the hole as if to jump in.

"They can," she agreed. "Which is why it is even more important to have a safe haven that has been warded by a witch. So long as we keep our safe havens a secret, no one ever needs to find us." A small smile graced her face as she plunged into the darkness, calling up for me to follow next.

"Go," Caelum ordered, glancing sideways at Jensen and the other men who remained on the top level. He clearly trusted Melian with my safety more than them. I nodded, shoving my dagger into his sheathe once again, not trusting my coordination enough not to stab myself with it.

I jumped into the hole, falling through air for only a moment before I landed and bent my knees to absorb the shock. My ankle gave a little twinge on impact, but it was nothing compared to the pain of the day before and almost forgotten by the time I straightened. The tunnels were carved into the rock of the mountain itself, making for a much harder landing than it might have been.

Caelum landed at my back, his hand immediately coming down on my spine as he reassured himself I was okay. He took my hand, pulling me out of the way so the others could jump down.

Melian's eyes landed on our hands clasped together, something like disdain filling her eyes for a moment before she turned her attention fully to Caelum when he spoke. "How far do these tunnels go?" he asked.

"They cover most of the Center Channel," she said, referring to the mainland that extended from Mistfell to the Mountains of Rochpar on the other side of the Kingdom. "Each of the Four Auxiliary Lands has its own network of tunnels, as well."

"That's incredible," I said, my voice conveying the awe I felt over something of this magnitude existing right beneath the noses of the Royal and Mist Guards for all this time. These people probably had an entire way of life, an entire history, that the Kings and Lords knew nothing about and had absolutely no control over.

Who would I have chosen to be, if my life hadn't been dictated by societal expectations?

Melian guided us through the passage, our group walking in silence as I stared with fascination at the walls around me, imagining how long it took to dig and carve just one tunnel out of solid stone. Caelum held my hand clutched tightly in his, clinging to me as if the tunnels would sweep me away and force us to separate.

Nothing could have prepared me for the number of people that waited in the main cavern when we finally arrived. There were dozens of them. Some of them were well-equipped and armed, though their faces appeared relaxed as if they were completely at home.

Others were rougher in appearance, looking beaten and downtrodden as if they'd only just escaped the fate waiting for them above the surface. Not everyone was Fae Marked, I assumed the product of generations of living in those tunnels.

"I'll take you to the women's quarters so you can get settled in," Melian said. "Introduce you to some of the younger girls."

"I go with her," Caelum interjected, refusing to release my hand when I nodded to follow her. As much as I hated to separate from him in someplace new, I understood that we were newcomers. We were guests in their way of life.

"The men and women bunk separately. You're more than welcome to see her whenever you like," Melian explained, gesturing around the main cavern that I understood must have been the common area of sorts.

"Then we're leaving. Either we stay together, or we do not stay at all," Caelum said, ignoring my look of exasperation.

"I think you've forgotten who needs who in this scenario," Melian said, crossing her arms over her chest. "I have the safe haven you need. What do you have to offer?"

"A fighter who can help you stand against the Fae to protect these people, if it comes to it," he said, raising an eyebrow at her in challenge. "We both know I am the best fighter you have now. You wouldn't have gone up to the tunnels yourself without the best of your men at your disposal."

Melian sighed, hanging her head. "Getting romantically attached now that you've been Marked is foolish," she said, turning her attention to me as she issued the warning.

Too late, sister. I already knew it and my heart throbbed in response.

"But fine. We have a few private alcoves that are usually reserved for our higher-ranking officers. The two of you will make yourselves useful, or I will give it to the next person in line. If I need you with me for a retrieval? You're with me," she said, glaring at Caelum for a moment before she turned down one of the corridors. It was lined with doorways carved out of the stone, blankets draped to cover the ones where people apparently wanted their privacy.

The blanket was drawn open on the second to last doorway, the room empty except for a bedroll laid out on a low wood platform. "I'll have a second bedroll brought in for you," Melian said, shaking her head. "Take the rest of the day to get acclimated and introduce yourselves. Tomorrow I'll put you both to work."

She disappeared out the open doorway, leaving me to the fight I felt brewing with Caelum.

One of these days, I was going to stab him in his pretty face.

"You don't think I'm capable of taking care of myself," I snapped, crossing my arms over my chest as I glared at him. He removed the cloak from his shoulders for what seemed like the first time in days. The stained fabric of his tunic hugged his chest and broad shoulders, showcasing the breadth of the body that was too often concealed. He hung the cloak on a peg sticking out of the stone wall, stepping toward me to unclasp my own from under my chin. While his fingers brushed against the hollow of my throat, I shoved down the tingle of awareness that always came when he touched me.

My body was a traitorous bitch, but she needed to know when I meant business.

"Of course I think you can take care of yourself. I just watched you knock two men on their asses," he said with a chuckle, turning away to hang my cloak on top of his. The tunnels were warmer, protected from the cold weather aboveground. I wondered briefly if there was some kind of heating system through them, because I hadn't seen a single fire in the common area or any of the open alcoves.

"Then why is it that I am not allowed to sleep with the rest of the women?" I asked, glaring as he made his way around the small alcove that would be ours. The sleeping platform in the back corner of the room was tucked against the wall. It made me immensely grateful that Melian had said she would grab us a second bedroll.

Sleeping with Caelum had proven dangerous enough as it was; having a space of our own in any way seemed even more dangerous.

"We look after one another, Estrella. You promised me we would stay together no matter what. Are you already trying to renege on that promise? I'd hoped you were more loyal than that," he said, a bitter grimace on his face, as shock claimed me.

"How is sleeping in a different room reneging on a promise to stick together? I'm not speaking of going our separate ways and never seeing one another again, Caelum," I protested, shaking my head in disbelief. "There is a difference between loyalty and dependence."

"Do not speak to me as if I know nothing of loyalty, my star. You cannot imagine how deep mine runs," he warned, taking a few steps toward me until he closed the distance between us and stopped so close that his stomach brushed against my chest. His eyes gleamed as he stared down at me, something cold sharpening his features.

"If you put me in a cage at your side, then you're no better than the man who tried to make spreading my legs for him my life's purpose. I need to be more than that. I need to do more than that, Caelum," I sighed, hoping I could break through to the rational, understanding version of him that I knew existed somewhere beneath this...brutal possessiveness.

"You already are more than that, Estrella," he said, his voice softening as he reached up to cup my cheek with his hand. "There has never been a moment in the time I've known you when you've been anything less than extraordinary."

I cocked my head to the side, the corner of my mouth tipping up in amusement. "Even when I fell down the ravine?"

"Okay, maybe you were less than extraordinary then," he chuckled, releasing some of the tension between us.

"I need you to be okay with me going my own way during the day. There's no chance that we can have a life here and not ever separate. We'll have different purposes and duties; I want to contribute to their cause. To our cause," I said, correcting myself. I may not really be a part of the Resistance yet, but I was one of the Marked that they stood to protect.

I wanted to help the people like me who stood no chance of escaping the Fae on their own. The ones who'd lost everything they'd known and loved when their entire villages turned on them.

Caelum clenched his jaw, leaning forward to touch his lips to my forehead before he spun and stripped the weapons from his body. He laid them down next to the bedroll, even though there were still hours left before night fell. "Alright, Little One, but I have some conditions of my own." He patted the space next to him as he dropped onto the bunk, giving me precious little choice but to hear him out.

Relationships were about compromise; the least I could do was listen to his version of it. The thought was jarring, as I realized that, at some point in our traveling together, I had started to think of this as a relationship.

Fucking damn the Gods.

I strode forward, taking the seat next to him even as my heart throbbed in my chest. I shouldn't have had feelings for this testy man who seemed to piss me off as much as he made my heart flutter. "No matter what tasks the day takes us to, we spend our nights together. If one of us is needed on a trip outside the safety of these tunnels, we both go together. If we die, we die together," he said, the words echoing through the room with something that felt significant. The air seemed to still momentarily in acknowledgement of his vow, as if the ancient witches themselves had heard him and lent their power.

"Together," I said, agreeing to those terms with only a moment's hesitation. I couldn't recall when it had happened, couldn't identify the moment he'd taken my heart, but I no longer wanted to think of my life without him in it. As long as I had the freedom to be who I wanted, I could sleep by his side at night.

It was scarcely a hardship.

25

Caelum pulled back the curtain to our private room, sewn from scraps of fabric and thick enough to block light and some sound, stepping into the warren of tunnels. I followed behind him, keeping close in my uncertainty with the new place, and with the new people who would be our neighbors if we stayed. Being a woman had taught me more than I cared to admit about needing to read the room and figure out where my place would be with those around me.

In Mistfell, most of the time I'd needed to pretend to be a demure lady, saving herself for marriage, but every now and then I'd found companionship with people who allowed me to be myself.

With my family. With Loris.

My heart panged with the loss of all of them, hoping that my mother was coping and surviving in the chaos that must have come after the Veil shattered. There was no one left to protect her; not when Brann had come with me and died for it. He'd have been better off staying with her and trying to hide from the army of Fae that had most likely descended upon Mistfell.

"You alright?" Caelum asked, touching a gentle thumb to the side of my jaw. I nodded, not quite able to find the words to answer him. I would survive, but it was hard not to feel like I'd left the girl I'd been back home.

We continued down the hall of doorways and alcoves, the only light in the space coming from the torches that lined the stone corridor. The walls pressed in on me, oppressive and nauseating. I'd always loved the darkness, but something about being locked away under the ground was unnatural—unnerving.

I trailed a hand over the rough surface as I took a deep breath of humid air. The warmth inside the tunnels was a blessing; my cloak had been left behind in our shared bedroom as I wouldn't need it, but I craved a lighter dress, as well, or a shirt like the men's to pair with the leggings, instead.

We finally emerged into the common space where most of the Resistance appeared to congregate. The room was circular, with the ceiling in this part of the underground cavern curving to an apex at the center. Wooden posts acted as support, wedged between the rough stone floor and the high ceiling above. The space felt less claustrophobic than the tunnels we'd traveled to get here or the small bedroom Caelum and I shared, the space above my head serving to give me room to breathe.

I paused to look around, taking in the dozens of people socializing and talking over wooden tables with maps laid out on them. Caelum and I exchanged a glance between us as we debated whether we should introduce ourselves or wait for someone to notice us.

It didn't take long; only a few moments passed before the people who hunched over the tables and the documents spread out on them sensed the strangers in their presence. Most of them had seen us come in earlier, but they hadn't made any move to approach, as if they knew we weren't both enthusiastic about being here.

Caelum's steps faltered as we walked into the center of the space, making our presence fully known and waiting for someone to approach. I was far too uncertain to make myself at home and introduce myself, especially with the tension rolling off of Caelum that set me on edge.

I turned to look at him, following his pointed stare to a woman who stood lurking in the background of those bent over the tables. One of her eyes glowed like moonlight, shining out from her umber skin, whereas the other was as dark as the night sky. Her hair fell in long waves, curling around her shoulders like freshly fallen snow. She was absolutely, heartbreakingly beautiful with flawless skin and lips painted red.

She raised a hand to the moon that shone on her forehead, casting a soft glow on her fingers that were tipped in darkness, shimmering like the starlight of the Veil itself.

Those eyes were fixated on Caelum, returning the intensity he gave her. My attention shifted between them, feeling something pass that I didn't understand.

My suspicions rose, my stomach dropping like lead. *They knew each other,* I realized with another twist of my gut.

Caelum turned to me, wrapping an arm around my back, soothing parts of me that he shouldn't have been able to touch; the wounded girl who didn't want to admit I wouldn't stand a chance of holding onto him.

It was why I never should have let him under my skin in the first place.

He buried his face into the curtain of my tangled hair, his lips brushing against the shell of my ear. "She's a witch," he murmured, his voice low enough that I knew he didn't want the others to hear.

The glowing mark, the fingers that had been dipped into the shadows of the night itself, the eerie mismatched eyes: all of it made sense with her being *Other.* Her eyes fell to me, studying me intently as she pursed her lips briefly before smiling.

As quickly as she'd studied us, she turned her attention back to the maps on the table, closing us off as if she hadn't examined us from the inside out. "That's Imelda," a woman said, stepping up in front of me. I forced my eyes off the witch to meet the kind, gray-eyed gaze of a human woman. "And I'm Amalie. She's taught some of us to see through Fae glamour, but no one is better at it than a witch."

"A witch?" I asked, pretending Caelum hadn't recognized her for what she was. I couldn't be certain that his knowledge wouldn't be used against us or make us look suspicious, having questioned it myself when we first met, as well.

Brann had been cautious in the face of Caelum's knowledge, leading us straight to his death out of that fear. My heart faltered in my chest; with the promise of a safe place to rest my head that night, the pain of the loss of him seemed more blinding. I didn't have to focus on keeping my feet moving, or on where my next meal would come from. I didn't have the same kind of life-changing distractions.

"Yes. She is how we keep the tunnels warded," the woman said, the explanation bringing that multicolored stare back to us. "They draw their power from the nature around them, and their magic isn't tied so directly to Alfheimr, like the Fae."

"I thought they were all dead?" I asked, thinking of the stories that told of how the last of the ancient witches had given their lives to create the Veil, to protect humans from the wrath of the Fae.

"Most of them are," Imelda said, raising her chin to meet my inquisitive stare. She stepped around the edge of the table, coming to stand next to the woman who had greeted us. "But there are some of us here, some of us alive in Alfheimr, as well, I suspect. The Crown tried to kill off the rest of us who survived the Veil to fit their narrative of events, but we're still here."

She leaned into me, her face stopping only a breath from mine as she looked down my body. She drew air into her lungs, smelling me as her brow furrowed and she tilted her head to the side. "Death is calling to you," she said, her words echoing what had been foretold in the woods on Samhain.

I swallowed when Caelum's hand tightened around my waist, his arm twitching against my spine. "Is that a threat?" he asked, his voice dropping low in warning. Only he would be foolish enough to think he could stand against a witch.

The mark on her forehead pulsed with light, answering the quiet violence hidden in his words. "I don't mean either of you any harm. Death stalks her, as if she is halfway to the grave already. From the look in her eye, this is not the first time she has heard such a thing," Imelda answered, turning her back on us and vacating the common space.

Caelum's stare burned into the side of my face as I ignored him, smiling gently at the woman who'd been kind enough to greet us. I didn't want to speak of the night in the woods or the death that I felt pacing at the edges of my life, waiting for me to make one fatal mistake.

Waiting for the knife to press against my throat once more, to take the life the Fae had denied it when they broke through the Veil.

"Sorry," the woman said with a little laugh, shaking out her chestnut hair. "She can be a little intense."

"So can he," I said, nodding my head toward where Caelum refused to release me.

A child raced up to the woman, grabbing her around the legs and gazing up at her with all the affection I'd given to my own parents as a girl. She knelt down to tend to the child while we watched, smiling apologetically when the young girl refused to release her. The fact that there were children living in their community brought a smile to my face, the bittersweet reality of their survival and relative freedom from the harsh life above the surface tempered by the fact that they probably rarely got to feel the sun on their skin.

Jensen crossed the distance, emerging from behind the table and coming to stand in front of us. "We got off on the wrong foot, but you must be hungry. Let me take you to get something to eat."

He gestured for us to follow him, and Caelum and I did so silently. The pessimistic part of me wondered if we should trust food provided by people we didn't know at all, but my stomach grumbled with hunger as if to protest my thoughts of turning down an opportunity for a meal.

There'd been nothing but wild hare and fish in the days since Caelum and I had started traveling, because while I didn't doubt his ability to hunt or snare something larger, the time it would take to butcher it wasn't worth the risk.

Walking through the maze of tunnels and descending down stairs carved into the rock itself, we curved around a center room. "How is it so warm in here?" I still hadn't seen any sign of a fire or stove and given that they could cause a risk of suffocation, I would have been surprised.

"These mountains are warm in general. All the springs surrounding it are hot springs. We aren't sure why it is, exactly, but the further into the center of the mountain range you go, the hotter it gets. The core of the central mountain is hot enough to make you sweat," Jensen answered, pushing open a door as he stopped at the bottom of the stairway.

The scent of food immediately wafted through the doorway, the heat of the kitchen seeming stifling as a handful of women labored over the fireplaces.

"What have I told you about sneaking down here before mealtime?" one of the younger women asked, raising a wooden spoon from the pot she'd been stirring to wave it at him as she scolded him. Above the stove, there was a little alcove carved into the rock for the smoke to vent upward. Cool air filtered in from the corridor, so a breeze flowing through brought fresh air and ventilated the kitchen.

"It isn't for me this time, Skye. I swear," Jensen said, reaching back to grasp my hand and tug me further into the room. Caelum's eyes narrowed on the contact, and Jensen released me immediately upon seeing the glare for what it was. "They've just arrived from above ground."

"Oh! You must be starved. Sit, sit," Skye said, fussing as she grabbed two bowls off the counter and ladled soup into each one. Setting them in front of us, she pointed Jensen toward the metal spoons off to the side and he grabbed one for each of us as Caelum and I pulled out the chairs and lowered into them slowly. Skye cut a wedge of bread off the loaf, dropping it onto the table in front of us as the aroma of freshly-baked dough made my stomach growl.

I lifted the bread to my nose, inhaling the scent for a moment as I tried to pretend to just enjoy the smell, but also tried to detect any of the poisonous plants I was familiar with. If a Lord could slowly poison his own wife, I would put nothing past a community of people I didn't know.

"You really think I'd be ballsy enough to poison that oaf of a man next to you?" Skye asked, drawing my attention up to her. Her hand dropped to her hip, head cocking to the side as she raised her eyebrows at me in challenge. "I'd need to feed him the whole loaf, you hear me? Eat."

"Sorry," I mumbled sheepishly, taking the first bite of the bread as Caelum chuckled at my side and lifted the hot stew to his mouth.

"I feel like I should take offense to being called an oaf. I am not stupid or clumsy," he said, earning a smile from the woman as she laughed under her breath.

"Apologies then. You're too pretty to be smart. I shouldn't have assumed," she said, turning back to the pot of stew as her cheeks turned pink. I swallowed, the loaf of bread feeling like a heavy weight in my stomach.

Had she been flirting with Caelum? More importantly, had he been flirting back?

Maybe being on our own *was* preferable to having others like us around. It would have been difficult for him to stray if there weren't other women around, but now that there were...I sighed.

Caelum dropped a hand to my thigh, his fingertips digging into the fabric covering my skin as if he could sense the squirming, throbbing jealousy that threatened to make me sink into my bedroll and never reemerge.

I hadn't wanted this. I hadn't wanted to *want* him. I definitely hadn't wanted to get so attached that the thought of him touching another woman made depression swirl in my gut and threaten to overwhelm me. The bastard had worked his way beneath my skin with what were probably false promises, and there would be nothing left of me when he tossed me aside.

"Eat, my star," he said, leaning into my side. His mouth hovered just above my ear, his words sinking inside me along with the proximity I'd come to crave.

"That has got to be the sweetest nickname I think I've ever heard," Skye said, turning back and staring at us. "You don't look like siblings. How do you two know each other?"

Jensen's eyes felt heavy on the side of my face as I lifted my spoon to my mouth and ate a bite, using it as an excuse to give Caelum the opportunity to define us. As much as I wanted to stake my claim, it seemed far smarter to let him put a label to what was happening between us.

"We aren't siblings. Estrella and I are together," he answered, the words soothing the part of me that I hadn't wanted to be frayed in the first place.

"Oh!" she said, glancing out the side of her eye to where Jensen stared at me. "We tend to be more...open in our relationships. You should probably be ready to bathe him in piss if you want the other girls to know they aren't able to take him for a ride," she said, a teasing lilt coming into her voice.

I didn't have any desire to mark my territory. Okay, I did, but I didn't want to have to. Any man who couldn't be trusted to label himself as off-limits wasn't worth my energy.

Caelum could have just about anyone he wanted. I'd never be able to stop him from wandering unless it was what *he* wanted. Understanding that brought me a certain measure of peace, knowing it would probably be inevitable for us to end, giving me a twisted satisfaction.

He was jealous enough that I could just imagine his rage over seeing me with someone else if that ever happened. I'd enjoy every minute of tormenting him, in that case.

"I'll keep that in mind," I said instead of voicing my bitter thoughts.

"It won't be an issue," Caelum said, reassuring both of us as he dug back into his stew. I dunked my bread into the broth, lifting it my lips and taking a bite. The flavors and herbs of the two combined to create a symphony in my mouth.

I was certain the foods Lord Byron had fed me in the privacy of his library at night had been more decadent, but there was nothing like the first bite of actual flavor after weeks of near-starvation and bland, roasted meat. "This is really good," I said, swallowing the bite in my mouth.

Skye turned a bright smile my way. "She has manners. Imagine that." The sly look she leveled at Jensen erased any of my worry that she might have thought me rude in the moments leading up to the compliment.

"It isn't his fault. Men have no need of manners," I said, shifting in my seat to look at Caelum from the corner of my eye.

He set his spoon into his bowl loudly as he finished shoveling the stew into his mouth. "What are you trying to say?"

"That you're more beast than man half the time, clearly. Don't be daft. You just told Skye you had a brain; now isn't the time to prove yourself wrong," I argued, smirking at the mock-incredulous expression he wore on his features.

"That's rich coming from you," he said. "I seem to recall you putting a knife to my throat when we first met. I hardly think that's a polite way to greet a newcomer."

"You intruded on my shelter for the night," I said, taking another bite of bread and chewing thoughtfully. If we'd just stayed like I'd wanted, would Brann still be alive? Would he and Caelum have found a way to coexist?

I swallowed. Not if Caelum had insisted on being intimate and touchy with me. Brann would have castrated him while he slept.

"I believe I was there first," he said, picking up the spoon I'd abandoned in favor of my bread. He scooped a spoonful of it and lifted it to my mouth, touching it to my lips as I parted and let him feed me. It again reminded me of the day when he'd fed me fish so I didn't have to touch it with dirty, bloodstained hands.

It should have reminded me first of Lord Byron's aged fingers feeding me delicacies I'd never asked for and calling it a gift. But nothing Caelum could do would ever feel as slithering and disgusting as the actions of the Lord who'd tried to groom me from childhood. Who'd made me watch the High Priest sacrifice my father, and then tried to force me into his bed.

I shivered, chewing the stew that suddenly tasted like ash in my mouth.

He continued to feed me while Skye and Jensen watched, the moment between us feeling far too intimate for their prying eyes. It was such a simple thing—letting him guide nourishment to my mouth and swallowing what he gave me—but the gleaming expression on his face was haunting.

As if feeding me appealed to him on an animalistic level, his need to provide for me rose to the surface with the uncertainty and risk of death behind us. He scraped the last of the broth out of the bowl, resting the spoon on my tongue and letting me swallow the liquid down while he stared at my mouth in fascination.

Skye cleared her throat, turning her attention back to the pot behind her as Jensen snapped out of whatever trance he'd gone into while we had our moment. "I'll show you to the baths in case you'd like to get cleaned up. We'll see if we can find something more fitting for you to wear, Estrella. Dresses are fine in the caves, but if you ever go to the surface, we recommend all the women skip them and just wear pants. They're warmer and easier to maneuver in."

I stood, letting Caelum take my hand in his grip as we followed behind Jensen. His possessiveness in the face of a man who'd expressed a tiny inkling of interest wasn't lost on me, and I let it warm me from the inside. I had to hope it meant he didn't intend to mess around with other women, especially now knowing I could have options, as well.

We passed by the members of the Resistance as we made our way even lower into the caves. The cave complex seemed to go on forever, curving and twining until the air grew humid. "There are far fewer women than men here," I observed, noting every person we passed.

Jensen turned back to me with a sad smile. "Most women aren't taught to be able to protect themselves. It's much more difficult for them to escape when the Mist Guard comes for them. Most of them never so much as made it out of their villages before they were cut down. We've had lots of Fae Marked men join our numbers since the Veil fell, but only two women have made it to the Hollows that we know of."

"But the *Viniculum* should have protected them, shouldn't it?" I asked, glancing toward Caelum. He nodded, but his face dropped with sorrow.

"There are ways to prevent the magic of the *Viniculum*. Faerie magic cannot survive the touch of iron. If they managed to capture them with iron somehow, the Marked would be defenseless entirely." I thought back to the collar the Mist Guard had placed on my neck and the way it had drained my energy away from me, rendering the snowy magic useless. My stomach filled with dread, thinking of being hunted down and killed with that heavy collar on my neck and no brother to help save me.

"The Mist Guard has had centuries to devise ways to entrap the Marked when the time came again, and other ways to fight the Fae. Everything has changed since the war before the Veil," Jensen agreed, shaking his head sadly. "Our only hope is to bring as many of us here as we can, and to wait out the worst of it."

He walked through an open archway, stepping into what I knew had to be the bathing room. Steam billowed off the underground spring, filling the air with humidity and warmth. But that wasn't the most shocking part of the bathing room.

Men and women bathed in the water together. Some of them minded their own business and kept to themselves. Others coupled off. A few were joined in groups of three or more.

"Gods," I mumbled, cursing myself when both Caelum and Jensen turned to look at my flushed face. It was worse than the statues carved into the stone at the place Caelum had taken me to.

These people were real. They moved and writhed together.

"You'll get used to it," Jensen said with a laugh. "I'm sure it's quite the shock compared to what you're used to."

"This is going to be a problem for us. I don't relish the thought of other men looking at her. Is there nowhere we can bathe in privacy?" Caelum asked.

"The springs are limited in number. You'll just have to try to time it so that they're less crowded, if that's your preference. While I'm sure many people wish we had springs where we could afford privacy to everyone, it just isn't feasible with this many people using one bath."

"Of course not," I said, tearing my eyes from the scene in front of me. I didn't want people to see me naked, but I wouldn't be that spoiled and entitled brat who protested their way of life and acted as if I was above it. If this was to be my home, I'd need to assimilate to it sooner than later.

"Estrella, you don't have to do something you aren't comfortable with," Caelum said.

"We'll come when it's more likely to be empty until I get used to it.

I'm more concerned about your snake drawing too much attention," I said, brushing off my nerves in favor of pretending I was unaffected.

Caelum would fixate if he knew how much my insecurities threatened to surface.

The naked women in the bath and at the edge of the spring were beautiful, with healthy and striking bodies. Not scarred and too thin to be appealing.

"Thank you for showing us the way," I said, turning my attention to Jensen quickly.

"Melian has asked that Caelum report to the commons at first light for training exercises. You'll need to consider what skill set you might have that could be useful here," he said, turning his attention back to the baths, as if he wanted to convey something meaningful.

"I was a harvester," I said, knowing that my skills with plants could come in handy.

"That will be very useful—when the warmer months come. As of now there is nothing left to harvest and the ground is too frozen to plant. You'll need to find something you can contribute until then." He glanced over his shoulder again. "Melian wouldn't like me mentioning this so soon, but some ladies find the pleasures of the flesh to be a very worthwhile way to make themselves useful. With numbers uneven and more men being here than women, we have to consider things most groups of people don't. Having a bunch of men locked up without something to fuck doesn't benefit anyone. You'd be treated well."

"I think it best that you shut your mouth before I break your jaw," Caelum snapped, and for once I couldn't force myself to protest the threat of violence. I had nothing against women using their bodies in such a way if it was what they truly wanted. I didn't even begrudge the Resistance for needing such a service in the first place.

But that didn't mean that I had to become a Lady of the Night myself.

"I can fight," I said, interjecting myself into the conversation that centered around me. "I'd be much more useful at that than.... I wouldn't even know how to begin with being a Lady of the Night."

"I think you would find that our men are very capable of guiding you through exactly what they expect of you. You're beautiful. It would be a shame to waste that face on fighting, where it's likely to take a beating. Just think about it. If my choice was a life of pain and war or a life of pleasure and fucking, I know which one I would choose."

"Stop," I demanded, my face twisting into a glare. While I appreciated Caelum standing aside during the exchange of words, having now made my desires known, I did *not* appreciate the attempt to bully me into something I wasn't comfortable with. With the way Jensen looked at me, I had no doubt he intended to be my first customer. "Caelum and I are monogamous. I'll not be entertaining any other men."

"Perhaps when he's done with you then," the rebel said, huffing a laugh as he turned on his heel and strode off, leaving me with a very pissed off companion at my side.

"One of these days, I will enjoy watching him bleed to death."

26

We hadn't lingered near the baths, instead choosing to wander through the tunnels and explore what we could for the rest of the day. We found an armory that made Caelum's eyes gleam with satisfaction at the room stuffed with all manner of weaponry. The training rooms where he would need to report the next day weren't far, just a few steps away down the labyrinth of tunnels they'd carved over time.

We'd grabbed food from the kitchen again, sitting at Skye's table in relative privacy and avoiding the public area where the others dined together. Given my rather jarring introduction to the people of the Resistance, I wasn't entirely certain that I felt up to dealing with more new faces in one day.

The privacy of our little bedroom felt like a welcome reprieve I didn't want to admit, out loud, I'd needed. Not after fighting for the ability to bunk with the other women earlier in the day. Still, as Caelum drew the curtain closed, I dropped down onto one of our bedrolls with a contented sigh.

"You look tired," Caelum said, moving to the other bedroll on the low, wood platform. I'd gotten used to sleeping wrapped up in his arms, but without the need for body heat, it felt even more intimate to choose to sleep that way.

There was no excuse that we were doing it purely for survival any longer, the only cause for us to sleep entwined being that we wanted to. Having stunned myself with the realization of the depths of my feelings for him as they grew, I didn't know what to expect from myself in this situation.

I was fairly certain I knew what to expect from Caelum, and that didn't help matters.

He laid himself out on his bedroll, stretching his arms over his head as I turned to face him. He looked as relaxed as could be, as if there was no place else he could possibly belong but at my side. I wished I could have his self-assurance.

"I am. I want to sleep for a year," I said with an awkward chuckle, lying on my back on the bedroll. His arm was angled above my head, leaving me to fill the space at his side. As tired as I was, my eyes stayed open to stare at the roof of the cave, feeling the weight of his presence beside me.

My ghosts lingered in the room, riding the waves of grief threatening to crash over me. In the previous nights since the Veil had shattered, my body had been all but broken by the time I closed my eyes for the night, exhaustion dragging me into sleep, accompanied by the sound of Caelum's voice weaving the words of whatever story he told me.

Tonight felt different, the bone deep exhaustion not quite enough to pull me under on its own. All I could see was Brann's judgmental stare, his warnings not to trust anyone echoing in my head and feeling as if I'd disappointed him with the choices I'd made after his death.

Caelum hummed thoughtfully, watching me as I twisted my lips. "Did they ever teach you about the Seelie and Unseelie Courts of Faerie?" he asked, reaching out to tuck a strand of hair behind my ear. I turned my attention his way. The sympathy in his gaze was too knowing, too aware of my emotions as they clogged my throat.

Brann's judgment had been too quick, because how could it ever be wrong to have someone look at me as if I hung the moon from the night sky?

"They didn't teach us anything about the Fae aside from them being evil and tales of the destruction they caused in the war," I answered. I'd spent many evenings hunting for any hint of information in Lord Byron's library, anything forbidden I might find, but there'd been nothing to further my knowledge about the beings, who would now drag me back to Alfheimr if they found me.

"Alfheimr has two main Courts: the Seelie and the Unseelie Fae. Each of those has their own ruler and a ruling system beneath them. The Seelie Court claims the Fae of the Spring and Summer Courts, while the Unseelie has Autumn, Winter, and the Shadow Courts," he said, rolling onto his side. His fingers trailed over the fabric covering my arm, sending a shiver through me in spite of the barrier between our flesh.

His obsidian eyes glimmered intently, watching my face for any hint of a reaction. "From what I know, the Seelie and Unseelie Courts have been at odds with one another for most of history, but very rarely do they engage in outright battle. They're more likely to undermine one another through subterfuge and trickery than they are to fight in pointless wars. The curse the witches placed on the Fae has made them value life above all else."

"The same curse that created the Mate Bonds?" I asked, recalling his story about the way the Fae had their souls splintered to share with another being.

"That one. According to the books, it also rendered the Fae unable to reproduce unless it is with their mate. It stunted the population, and with the Veil separating most of the Fae from their mates…" He shrugged his shoulders as the meaning of the statement hung between us.

"There haven't been any children?" I asked, unable to imagine how quiet the world must have become with the lack of offspring to run around and terrorize their parents.

"I'm sure there have been some. There are the pairs who had already completed the mate bond before the Veil formed, and those few who were mated to another Fae, but the Fae have centuries of life. They were cursed to only have two children for each pairing, to control the population that could have vastly outnumbered humans."

I twisted my lip, mulling over the information and what that might mean for my future. I'd never given any thought to having children of my own, outside of the reality that they would be expected of me. If it wasn't something I had to do for some prospective husband I didn't want to marry, would I want them myself? "Does that mean none of us can have children outside of our mate bond?" I asked, glancing toward the curtain blocking our door. There were a great many Fae Marked within the protection of the Resistance, their marks peeking out from the fabric of their clothing as they curled up their necks. The humans vastly outnumbered them, and I didn't doubt their ability to keep the population strong enough to thrive, but to think of wanting a child and being denied one was agonizing.

"Unless the bond is completed, humans are still able to reproduce with other humans," he said, quirking a brow up at me. "So two Fae Marked could live an entirely human existence together, complete with children and family, so long as they never finished the bond."

"The Fae Mark itself doesn't mean we're bonded to them?" I asked, my hand reaching up to touch the swirling black and white magic on his skin. It danced over his flesh in response, writhing and drawing a pulse of light from the black circle on the back of my hand.

"It connects the Fae to the Marked, in a way, so that they can find one another. But until the ceremony is completed, life forces do not join and humans don't become eternal," he explained, leaning forward to touch his lips to my forehead gently as I covered a yawn with my hand.

I shifted forward, curling my body into his chest. The moment his arms wrapped around my back, sleep threatened to pull me under as I drowsily asked, "What's the ceremony?"

"The Fae have three days to complete a quest to prove their worth and bring back a gift their mate will treasure for eternity. They then make love on Faerie soil in a place surrounded by the magic of the Court. The Spring Fae have sex amongst fields of flowers. The Winter

Fae have a sacred place where they're surrounded by snow-capped mountains and frozen waterfalls. Summer Fae are surrounded by tropical waters and sandy beaches, and the Autumn Fae have sex at the tops of trees as tall as the Hollow Mountains," he said, his voice getting quieter and quieter until it trailed off into a whisper as I fought to keep my eyes open.

"What of the Shadow Court?" I asked, just as I shut out all traces of light.

"Something far more sinister," he murmured, his fingers tightening against my spine. "They hunt their mate in a cove, with all the monsters of Faerie to bear witness to the claiming when they catch him or her."

I drifted off, my thoughts filled with the worst imaginings of what a monster of Faerie must look like, wishing I'd stopped him at the Autumn Court and fallen asleep to dream of people balancing in the treetops.

I jolted awake.

Springing to a sitting position with a hand pressed to my chest, I heaved in deep lungfuls of air in my desperate need to catch my breath. The darkness of the room pressed in all around me, the shadows of my nightmare lingering at the forefront of my mind. Macabre images of shadow monsters devouring Brann's body while I watched haunted me even with my eyes open.

I reached back to touch Caelum, hoping to soothe myself with his presence, only for my hand to find his bedroll empty. I turned slowly as my eyes adjusted to the darkness, looking around the small, dark cavern where the only light came from the torches in the tunnels outside the curtain that was parted slightly. There wasn't a single sign of him in the room he'd insisted we share, the surrounding space empty.

I swallowed, sinking my teeth into my bottom lip as I threw back the light blanket he must have draped over me after I'd fallen asleep. My body felt slick with sweat from my nightmare, tricked into thinking it was trying to escape the monster chasing me down.

I moved to the end of the bedroll, getting my feet underneath me and slipping them into my boots. Standing slowly, I crossed to the curtain at the entrance of the room. Peeking through the crack into the empty hallway, I warred with myself.

I would feel ridiculous if he'd left me to go to the latrine. Wandering around to try to find him with my heart in my gut and feeling like something was very, very wrong would be sad if it turned out to be nothing.

Still, I pulled the curtain back a little more and stepped out into the tunnel. The torches lining the wall lit the way as I followed them back to the common space where all the bunk rooms fanned out in a sunburst fashion.

The tunnel was silent. Everyone in the Resistance slept the night away, the soft padding of my boots echoing through the enclosed space so loudly that I wanted to cringe. It seemed to take forever to reach the commons, the faint sound of voices whispering quietly drifting through to the mouth of the tunnel where I stood. I watched as Caelum ran a frustrated hand over his forehead. I hugged the side wall, making myself as small as possible, as he drew his hand away and spoke to Imelda.

The witch grimaced, her eyes pinching closed as she nodded up at him. She reached out slowly, grasping his hand in hers for a brief moment as she whispered something to him. Beyond the hush of her quiet voice, the low tones barely reaching me, I couldn't make out the words.

I only knew, beyond a shadow of a doubt, that they had not been meant for my ears.

Caelum's fingers closed around hers briefly, a gentle squeeze that seemed to wrap itself around my heart before he pulled back and severed the connection. He whispered something, his face hard and unyielding in a way that I hadn't seen on him very often.

I knew he had the harsh side that I'd seen glimpses of, and he'd shown when he saw my scars, but I'd never seen how intense it became when he used it against other people. There was no wonder that I withered under the weight of his stare.

He turned away from Imelda, coming toward the tunnel where I waited, watching the interaction. His steps faltered as his gaze landed on me, that smooth gait of his disrupted by the shock of his features before he relaxed the irritation he'd shown Imelda from his face.

He closed the distance between us, reaching up to lay his hand against the side of my cheek. It took everything in me not to jump to the conclusion rattling around in my mind, not to flinch back from the same hand that had touched hers. "What are you doing up, my star?" he asked, the gentleness in his voice feeling like a deception.

Like a punch to the gut, confirming everything I'd already known would happen, Caelum was already keeping secrets with other women.

"I feel like maybe I should be the one asking that question," I said, tilting my head to the side as I stared up at him. My throat burned with the rawness of impending tears, and the feeling that the one thing I'd found that I wanted to keep had been torn away.

"We were discussing the warding on the tunnels. I needed to be sure it was safe for you here," he said, brushing his thumb over my cheekbone, as if he could see the tears that I clenched my teeth to prevent, and the dread settling into the pit of my stomach.

"In the middle of the night?" I questioned, pulling back from his caress. His hand fell from my face, hanging in the air as if suspended in his disbelief that I didn't want his touch. That I didn't crave his torment, when my heart felt so close to shattering.

"Your jealousy is showing again, Little One. You know how much I like it," he said, his lips tipping up as if he could diffuse the tension rolling between us with teasing.

"Is that why you snuck out of the room *you* insisted we share in the dead of night? To make me feel like this?" I asked, taking a step back and putting more space between us as I wrapped my arms around myself. The warm air felt too cool against my sweatslicked skin, drawing Caelum's attention as he stared at me inquisitively.

"Did you consider that perhaps I like your jealousy because it's the only way you show me you care for me the way I do you?" he asked, dropping his hand to his side finally. "You've made no attempt to claim me as yours. In fact, you've denied this at every opportunity when I've made my intentions toward you very clear. I want you in a way that should terrify me, that consumes my every thought. I want you in a way that I know I will slaughter anyone who dares to hurt you, to touch you," he said, pausing to run a hand through his hair. He took a small step toward me, hesitating to close the rest of the gap. "I will not watch you with other men. I will not watch you deny what is between us in every moment that my mouth is not on yours, and still act the part of a jealous lover."

"Caelum," I murmured, my face pinching with his words. He was right; I knew it as well as he did. My fear of being hurt stopped me from taking the plunge with him, from accepting what my heart already knew.

"I would burn the world to the ground and lay it at your feet if you so much as asked it of me, and yet you give me nothing. You've never once told me that you feel the same way I do." He closed the distance between us, stepping into my space until he could trail his knuckles over my cheek. He leaned over me, his body enveloping mine and forcing me to look up into his piercing eyes as the first tear fell down to touch his fingers. He brushed it away, curling his knuckles down my jawline until he grasped my chin gently and held me still. "All you need is to say the word, and I am yours. So tell me, my star. Do you want me?"

My ears rang in the silence that stretched between us, his glimmering eyes waiting for my response.

"Yes," I whispered, the word feeling torn from my soul, as if it splintered me inside to admit it, cleaving who I'd been in half. Half of me belonged to the mate hunting me across the Kingdom, but the half that I knew, the half that was Estrella Barlowe of Mistfell—she belonged to Caelum.

Mate be damned.

He curled his free hand around the back of my head, pulling me toward him at the same time he lunged. His mouth crashed down onto mine, his lips parting as he shared his breath with me. He entwined us, his arms surrounding me and his body backing mine into the stone wall of the tunnel.

My head pressed against the unforgiving wall, causing Caelum to pull his lips from mine. His breath came in deep, controlled sighs as he trailed his mouth over my jaw and laid kisses to the side of my neck. The pinch of his teeth came at the skin there as he sank them into my skin, squeezing in a bruising grip as bindings inside me slackened.

My body gave in, the space between my legs throbbing and begging for his touch as his hands skimmed over my waist, and he explored the body he'd conquered. "You're going to break me," I whispered, not having meant to speak the words out loud, but there was no boundary between us, no part of me that wanted to take back the words I should have kept to myself.

He pulled back from my neck, my skin throbbing where he'd bruised me. He stared at it for a moment before finally turning his attention to my face, his clenched jaw fading into something so tender it made my heart stall in my chest, and I couldn't help but wonder if it was always like this. Did falling in love always come with the knowledge that we were no longer alone? Was it always more than stolen kisses in the night and two bodies coming together for a few moments?

"No, Little One. I'm going to love you," he said, touching his forehead to mine. His dark eyes glimmered, tiny specks of light shining in the obsidian, like the stars that had become my namesake. "Until you forget what it is to hurt and then long after that. Until the scars you wear like armor have faded from memory, and only we remain."

27

I woke wrapped in his arms the next morning, his heat surrounding me and enveloping me in a cocoon of sheer comfort. Even the bedroll beneath my body seemed more comfortable than the lumpy, straw-stuffed mattress I slept on in my home. It was the bed that had belonged to my parents, before my father died and my mother spent her nights sleeping in her chair.

Caelum's stomach was pressed into my spine, his long, muscular arm draped over my waist and stretching up toward my neck, nestled into the valley between my breasts, shoving my dress against my skin to get there. His hand rested against my heart, feeling it beat against him as he held me tightly to his body.

I sighed, letting my eyes drift closed once more and enjoying the rare comfort of waking up next to him. He'd always been up and moving before me, letting me have a few more moments of precious sleep while he got ready for the day's travel and found us food.

There was no need for that in the tunnels, though; not with food only a short walk away and the lodging more permanent than the caves we'd sought refuge in.

He pressed himself tighter to me in his sleep, his fingers splaying out over my chest and the tips of them brushing over the base of my throat. The bite he'd left me with the night before seemed to throb in awareness, tingling alongside the Fae Mark that contradicted the claiming mark he'd given me.

He groaned, the deep sound bringing a flush to my cheeks as the length of him pressed into my ass in time with that near-growl. "Good morning, my star," he said, using his nose to brush the hair away from the side of my neck. He lingered over the bruise, drawing in a deep breath of me as he moved his hand closer to my face. His fingers curled around the front of my throat, tipping my head back so he could get a better angle to lick my bruise. "Aren't you going to say good morning?" His lips tipped up against my skin, the arrogance of his voice sending a shiver through me.

The man knew damn well how much he was tormenting me, even while he barely touched me. Even with layers of clothing between us, I clenched my thighs together to stop the burn he created so easily.

"Good morning, Caelum," I sighed, my voice coming out far breathier than I'd intended. I'd given in to what I wanted, admitted that the feelings between us stretched both ways, but still I felt the need to hide just how far that want went.

I still didn't know how to walk the line between being a lady and being the new me; between embracing all that had been forbidden and being too forward. Nothing in my life had prepared me for Caelum.

"Rise and shine!" a voice called from the commons, disrupting the moment while I tried to find a way to communicate what I needed from him. What I wanted more than anything was to feel alive, for even just a few moments, and to remind myself that I hadn't died back with Brann. The future sprawled in front of me, just waiting for me to find my place in the world.

He sighed, hanging his head farther until his breath tickled my skin. Then he stood, moving to the corner and cleaning his teeth quickly with one of the small brushes and paste they'd provided for us. I followed, doing the same as I tugged on my boots, and immediately felt grateful for how much more human it made me feel to have a clean mouth.

We emerged into the hallway as soon as that was done, walking down it somewhat hesitantly as we followed the small crowd of people who'd been given private rooms. I clutched Caelum's hand in mine, all my previous fighting words about going my own way during the day forgotten in the face of Jensen's thoughts of how I should spend my days, serving the men.

I didn't know what my strength would be in my new life, but I wanted it to be more than what the world would have assigned to me. I wanted to be more than a thing for men to use.

"I'll look after Estrella," Melian said, stepping up to us as we emerged into the commons. "You go with Jensen to the training rooms."

The other man gave me a cursory nod before he turned away, waiting for Caelum to follow. Caelum pulled the dagger from his thigh sheath, handing it to me meaningfully. "Make sure you aim for the throat," he said, leaning down to touch his lips to mine briefly before he sighed and followed after the one man he now probably wanted to kill.

"He's feeling extra stabby this morning," Melian said, nodding her head as she started walking down the tunnel toward the center of the mountain.

"He wasn't fond of Jensen pushing for me to become a Lady of the Night yesterday," I said, following at her heels. "I can fight. I may not be Caelum, but I disarmed two of your men."

She paused mid-step and turned to stare at me with a sigh of frustration. "Jensen shouldn't have said anything. We don't have Ladies of the Night here, and we certainly don't pressure women into becoming them. We have a few women who offer such services because they enjoy it, but it isn't a shameful position, as it is above the surface. They're respected positions. The women have private rooms, for obvious reasons. They're pampered, and while I completely understand wanting a different life for yourself, one which isn't dictated by your pretty face and the men who want to fuck it, you should know what you're turning down." She resumed her pace, leaving me to follow after her. "You would never have to leave the safety of the tunnels. You would never have to expose yourself to danger."

"Even if I wanted a life of pampering like that, my relationship with

Caelum would never allow it. It was an insult to him to ignore that. I'd rather be a fighter," I explained.

"I think some distance between you and Caelum might be beneficial. You're too attached. The Fae don't just Mark our bodies with their mate bond. They steal our hearts. We're not capable of the kind of life we might have had before them, and if he ever were to encounter his Fae on a mission above-ground, he would be unable to resist the call of her. As would you be, if you were to encounter your mate.

"Between the potential of the two of you finding your true mates and the very real possibility that death will take him away from you, I say this with your best interest in mind, Estrella." She paused to take my hands in hers. They were as cold as ice, despite the warmth of the air surrounding us, and her intense gray eyes stared down at me as she tried to compel me to see the logic of her words, but my heart didn't care about logic as she continued speaking.

"Play with him. Take him for a spin or ten; nobody would blame you. Our ways are much more fluid than above ground. We don't save ourselves for some archaic concept of uniting two people in the eyes of the Gods. We try to discourage romantic entanglements with the Fae Marked now, for the benefit of everyone involved. Sex can just be sex, and you're more than welcome to enjoy as many of the men here as you like. I guarantee the other girls will be looking to take Caelum for a spin."

Jealousy thrummed through me, all-consuming and overwhelming with the constant reminder of what the other women in the tunnels would do to throw themselves at the man I already believed was too good for me.

"You're wrong," I said, my voice stumbling as if I wasn't quite certain if I was trying to convince myself or her. "I have feelings for him. Strong feelings. That wouldn't be possible if what you are saying were true."

"Just guard your heart. This will only end in heartbreak, if you continue down this path." She guided me further into the mountain, leaving the hustle and bustle of the busy community behind us in favor of the warmer central tunnels. I didn't acknowledge her words that my relationship with Caelum would end in heartbreak. How could I argue against them when I'd thought them myself time and time again?

Caelum would ruin me. He'd tear me apart. I just had to believe he would still be standing there, ready and willing to help put me back together when it all came crashing down, but Melian's words about him abandoning me in favor of his Fae mate would haunt me. I'd spend every night wondering if it would be our last. If he would be torn away from me in the morning, and, even worse, not even care about what we'd had or what we'd lost.

"Tell me about your life. Jensen said you were a harvester. As much as I would love to put you to work in the gardens, they're done for the winter and putting you above ground comes with risk. We try to make sure the people who work on the surface in one place consistently aren't Marked, otherwise..."

"They could lead the Fae here," I said, nodding as I considered her words.

"Precisely. Many of our warriors are Marked, but they only go above ground when they're planning to keep moving. It's still a risk, but historically the Fae Marked make the best fighters. The *Viniculum* protects them against the Mist Guard, and they also have the advantage of quicker-than-human healing and a sort of boost in muscle mass and strength."

We walked beyond the cavern that housed the baths. My body ached to soak in the warm spring, but I knew without a doubt that Caelum would never approve of me going there alone. I couldn't blame him, because the thought of the other women watching him without me there made me murderous.

"I lived in Mistfell," I said, to redirect my wayward thoughts. "My family wasn't well off, but Lord Byron had me tutored privately in the Mistfell Manor. I can do basic arithmetic and read."

"You can read?" she asked, a small smile taking over her face. "That is quite rare, indeed. A woman being taught." She veered to the side, leading me through one of the side tunnels until we came to a wooden slab that served as a door.

Heaving it to the side, she opened up a private cavern filled with handmade shelves. On every one of them, books upon books were stacked. Scrolls covered the table, unorganized and haphazard, as if the space had fallen into disuse.

"What is this place?" I asked, stepping inside and running my fingers over one of the dust-covered scrolls laid out on the table. It was a map of Nothrek, and my fingers traced over the cities as I stared down at it. The cities like Calfalls, Tuevine, and Pralis, that had been destroyed in the war, were crossed out with red. "Is this from the war? How is that possible?"

"Our ancestors built this refuge during the war. The Marked couldn't trust the King to keep them safe, so we did it ourselves. For the most part, they tried to stay out of the fighting and just keep to themselves as we do now. But they liked to document everything, and they kept it all here. These books are entire histories from before the war, and what we've been able to collect since," she answered, watching as I stepped away from the table and moved to the rows of books on the shelves lining the walls.

I slowly pulled one out, the weathered binding cracking beneath my touch as I set it gently on the table. The lettering on the front of the book was like something from a nightmare.

Creatures of Alfheimr.

"This is a forbidden book," I said, flipping the cover open gently. The drawings within were horrific, my fingers running over the image of a monstrous creature that was half man and half scorpion. His pinchers and tail were dripping blood while his mouth curved around the throat of a victim.

"A great many things you'll find in these tunnels are forbidden. Unfortunately, most of this knowledge is wasted on us. Not many can read at all, let alone in a way that would allow them to understand these books. Do you speak the Old Tongue?" she asked, tipping her head to the side as I stared down at the name for the creature at the top of the page.

"Some," I admitted. "I'm not sure how much of this I would be able to understand. If all these books are in the Old Tongue..."

"Only the oldest ones, but it would be very helpful if you could translate them to the best of your ability. I'm sad to say that I've been trying to do it slowly, as one of the last people who speaks it, but there's only so much I can accomplish with everything else requiring my attention. My sister was our family historian, and she was the one who was working to translate the old texts." She moved to one of the shelves at the side, which seemed removed from the rest. "These are the books she managed to get through before she was taken from us."

"What happened?" I asked.

"We were on a supply run to gather new books when we encountered a man who needed help. He was half-starved, so we offered him food and a place by our fire for the night. We didn't realize that he had the flesh-eating fever until we'd already returned to the tunnels the next morning. We lost half our numbers over the course of the next week, my sister and the other historians among them."

"I'm so sorry," I murmured. I'd seen the damage the fever had caused when it tore through my village when I'd been a girl. It was the one time that living on the outskirts of the town had worked to our advantage, sparing us from the nightmarish sickness that killed almost everyone it touched.

"This is far more valuable to us than another fighter or a harvester. Perhaps at some point I can choose someone for you to teach and we can rebuild our historian numbers. Knowledge is power, Estrella. What you can give us is a far better weapon than your hand on a sword," she said, stepping back toward the doorway. "Think about it. Spend some time with the books. I'll check on you in a little while."

She retreated out, leaving the door pulled back so I could leave if I wanted to.

But I didn't want to. I turned back to the shelves of books behind me, perusing the spines until I found one of the biggest volumes. It drew me to itself, compelling me to pull it out and gently set it on the table. The pages were worn at the edges, as if someone, sometime, had spent a great deal of energy leafing through them.

Libnor non Diathar.

The Book of the Gods.

Opening to the first page, I read the words aloud, translating them slowly as I went. It had been years since Byron had instructed my tutor that I would have no need of the Old Tongue anymore, and that it was a relic she should stop teaching. He was too late; deep down it lingered within me, the harsh sounds so different from the New Tongue that had been adopted as our official language centuries before.

Even before the war.

"In the beginning, there was nothing," I murmured, the familiar words touching something inside me. They were the exact same words that Caelum had told me, the beginning of his story that night by the fire. The drawing on the first page was a swirling mass of shadows. An inky darkness so black that nothing seemed to exist within it.

There was no man, no face to the ancient Primordial, Khaos. He existed in nothing. He *was* nothing, and he'd been the very first thing to exist, until his loneliness drove him to create his wife. I flipped through the pages, every word confirming the story Caelum had told me.

The Primordials passed me by, each of the eighteen original Gods striking in their own way. As the generations continued, they became more human in form. These were not the Gods we'd worshiped. These were the Gods the Gods worshiped.

I continued through, uncertain what I was looking for until the moment I landed on her page. Mab's drawing was stunning, with her long raven hair falling to her waist. Despite the lack of color on the page, her lips and eyes were shadowed in darkness. Upon her head, a bright crown gleamed, shadows seeming to drip from it and blend into her hair itself.

I shuddered, slowly reading aloud the words scrawled onto the page beneath her likeness.

"The Queen of Air and Darkness is the sister to the Seelie King, Rheaghan of the Summer Court. According to Faerie legends, when the two siblings were children, the dwarves of Elesfast brought a glittering dark gemstone to the castle as a peace offering during a time of war. Mab was immediately taken with the gem, requesting it be placed within the crown atop her head. Her mother would have done anything to please her daughter and arranged for it to be done. The gem had been fashioned by Edrus, the Primordial of Darkness himself, and it slowly corrupted the Seelie Princess until there was nothing but the cold, unfeeling shell of a girl who sought power above all else."

Raising my eyes back to the sketch, I stared intently at the dark gem glittering at the center of her crown. Swallowing down the pit in my stomach, I moved on to the next page. I'd read enough of Mab already, not even daring to dive into the atrocities she'd committed.

I'd heard of the Fae horrors. For Mab to be the worst of them all, she must have been a truly vile creature.

The likeness on the next page stole the breath from my lungs. The God of the Dead's hair was sketched a mottled light-gray, as if they couldn't quite achieve the proper color of his rumored ashy silver waves that fell to his shoulders. His eyes were light, glowing from his severe face. His crown matched the same tone, except for the shadows that fell from it onto his head. His pointed ears were hidden beneath his hair, as were the swirling tattoos of white and black, of which only the tips crept up from the collar of his armor and leather tunic. They seemed to glow from the page with a pulse of magic.

My fingers traced the ends of his mark hesitantly, unable to turn my attention away from the drawing and focus in on his history and the atrocities he'd committed.

They were the same color as mine—and Caelum's.

"I didn't expect to find you with your head in a forbidden book, my star," Caelum said, snapping me out of my trance as I stared down at Caldris, the God of the Dead. He glanced down at it as I shifted the cover closed, feeling somewhat guilty for reading about the very God that we'd discussed.

The one I'd seen a likeness of reclining casually with two women kneeling at his feet. I couldn't look at anything to do with him without remembering that scene. His casual ease and comfort with himself, knowing that the women would have done anything to please him.

"Where's Melian? She said she would keep an eye on you," Caelum said, lifting his dark gaze from the book on the table.

I forced myself to smile, shrugging off the blush that had stained my cheeks. "She brought me here when she discovered that I know how to read. She wants me to translate the texts from the Old Tongue."

"You speak the Old Tongue," Caelum observed, tilting his head to the side thoughtfully.

"I'm far from fluent, and I don't think I could hold a conversation, but I can read it if given the chance. I was just looking through the *Libnor non Diathar*. I never realized just how many Gods there were—"

I was cut off the moment Caelum grasped me around my arms, lifting me out of my chair. He pushed my back against the shelves, his mouth lowering onto mine forcefully. He bruised my lips with his, but as I wound my hands around his neck, I couldn't make myself care.

His chest rumbled against mine as a low growl sounded in his throat, while he gathered the fabric of my dress with his fingers. He lifted it, hiking it up slowly as he kissed me.

"Caelum," I gasped, pulling my mouth away from his when his fingers found the bare skin of my thigh. "We should stop. This isn't the place." His sudden, greedy assault on my mouth had left my lips stinging, wondering what had possessed him.

"Everywhere is the place that I want to touch you," he murmured, dropping his mouth to the top of the Mark on my neck. His tongue teased the sensitive skin there, his fingers working closer to the apex of my thighs. "I'll stop if you really want me to, Little One, but I want to finish what I started this morning. What's it going to be?"

His thumb brushed against my core, the simple, barely-there touch lighting me on fire as I threw caution to the wind. I turned my head, capturing his lips with mine as he groaned. That wandering hand beneath my dress shifted between my thighs, stroking me while I whimpered into his mouth.

He slid his fingers through me, pressing one to my entrance and guiding it inside, carefully at first. My body wasn't ready for the invasion, muscles clamping down and protesting it while he stroked my clit with his thumb and tangled his tongue with mine.

Slowly, I welcomed him inside. He growled when he felt me give way to him, adding a second finger to join the first as he pumped them into me with painful slowness. I wanted it faster. Harder.

More.

I was starved for him and the touch I'd denied myself, as if a gate had opened and only his hands could close it. Yet he deprived me of the orgasm that was building within me, keeping me from falling over the edge with expert torture.

"I suppose this would be an inappropriate time to tell you that I intend to kill every man who has felt you like this. Who has had the pleasure of your body wrapped around him?" he growled, leaning forward to sink his teeth into the sensitive skin on the side of my neck where he'd bitten me the night before.

"You can't kill a man just for having fucked me, Caelum," I argued, unable to force myself to push him away. Even when he was acting ridiculous, I'd have done anything to pull him closer. To take him inside me and make me burn. "Think how many women I would have to kill."

He pressed his hard length against my thigh as he worked me with his hand, building my orgasm higher as he pulled back to stare down into my face. Malice lurked in his gaze when he met my eyes. "I would love to see that, my star."

"That's not normal," I argued, my body jolting when he applied more pressure to my clit.

"I assure you, I do not give the first fuck what is normal when it comes to you. If you want to watch the world burn, I'll set it on fire for you. If you want to slaughter every woman who has ever taken what is yours, then I will gladly sit back and watch you play," he said, a twisted smile toying about his lips as he dropped his mouth to my lips and sank his teeth into the plump flesh. "Now fucking come for me, Estrella."

"Caelum," I gasped, then I shattered beneath his touch as he worked me, my legs feeling like they would have caved beneath me if it hadn't been for his support holding me up and the knee he shoved between mine.

"These lips were made to moan my name," he said, leaning down to kiss them gently as he pulled his fingers free from my pussy. He returned my dress to normal, letting it fall flat and cover me from view as he kissed me sweetly.

He made no move to ask me to return the favor, simply imparting a gift upon me for whatever reason. He could give me that gift every day for the rest of my life and I suspected I would never tire of it.

28

Another night passed without Caelum doing anything more than kiss me in the privacy of our shared room. After our moment in the library when he'd touched me, part of me wondered if something had happened to take away his sense of urgency. The other part of me was grateful, because I still hadn't worked up the courage to bathe with an audience just yet and had to settle for a few awkward sponge baths instead.

That would change today; I knew the activity of the morning would drive me to need a true bath, as I followed Caelum to the training cavern. Even knowing that Melian may not be pleased with the decision to come here, and at the end of the day I would still return to those books and the knowledge they contained, I couldn't not have some form of activity.

I couldn't sit on my hands and eat the food Melian had delivered to me as I read, letting my body fall into disuse. I'd been easily exhausted and unable to run when I'd needed to escape Mistfell.

I wouldn't allow it to happen again.

We made our way through the commons, accepting the light breakfast of buttered bread and the tea they gave me, made from lily of the valley plants, to prevent unwanted pregnancy. I ignored Caelum's pointed stare while I downed the drink, handing my empty cup back to the woman who passed them out to any who wanted it.

We continued on our way, and I winced when all eyes turned to me the moment we entered the caves where the fighters trained, and I knew there had been conversations about me since Melian had assigned me to the texts. I didn't belong here; not when I had another task that needed my attention.

"She can't expect you to spend all day locked up in that cave alone," Caelum murmured at my side. His voice dropped lower, his tone becoming scathing. He didn't approve of the task Melian had given me; rather, he didn't approve of the fact that I would need to do it alone, away from him. "Perhaps I should mention that I can also read the Old Tongue. If translating these texts is so important to her, surely my time is better spent there than having me train with her fighters."

"She believes we need to be kept separate as much as possible. I highly doubt she'll approve of giving us more time together," I said, scoffing as Caelum guided me toward the center of the training space. He hefted two practice swords off the rack, tossing one to me that I stumbled to catch by the hilt.

I hadn't been able to lift Loris's sword when he'd taught me how to defend myself, so we'd focused on daggers and my own body being my weapons. The wooden practice sword was weighty, but not to the point that my arms ached. Or perhaps that was due to the changes in me since being marked, since the increased strength had changed me from human into something more.

Caelum lifted his sword, eyes bright as he waited for me to strike. It went against everything I knew of fighting for me to make the first move, because my smaller body would always be at a disadvantage. I didn't know how to fight when my opponent didn't think me incompetent, and was prepared for even my minimal level of skill.

I spun the sword in my hand, testing the weight and adjusting to the unfamiliar object. I hated to think that my first time truly fighting with a sword would be with an audience to judge me, but I would not allow myself to be discovered helpless.

Never again.

"Come on, my star. Show them how bright you burn," Caelum murmured softly. The soothing intensity of his eyes on mine shoved away those insecurities, bolstering me. The point of the exercise wasn't to show off the skills I already had. It wasn't to prove something to anyone but myself.

It was to learn.

I struck, moving my body in the way I'd so often seen the men do when they trained at the barracks at Mistfell. Caelum blocked the blow with a swift swipe, knocking my sword to the side.

I did it again, feeling awkward with the too-long weapon in my hand, trying to find a way not to have my weight thrown off balance.

"It is an extension of your body. Your sword is a part of you, Estrella. Not the most important part, not even your sole focus. You have the movements and the ability to fight inside of you. I've seen you disarm men with no weapon at all. This is just another tool. Nothing more, nothing less. Sink into that place you go when your life is actually in danger," he said.

I inhaled deeply, letting my eyes drift closed as I reflected back to my terror in the woods on the day I'd lifted the tree branch to fight the Wild Hunt, and to the ghostly rider I'd stabbed with his own weapon. To the fear I'd felt in the caves the moment I'd awoken with a sword pressed to my chest.

I moved then, twisting my body with the fluid grace I hadn't been certain I possessed. My body was small, and I was able to curve through spaces with more natural rhythm than a larger person could use. I jabbed the sword toward Caelum as if I might aim for his chest, dropping to my knees and spinning on them in the dirt as he moved to block the blow to his chest that no longer came.

I cracked the flat side of my wooden sword against his knee cap hard enough that the smack echoed through the room. Caelum grunted, a chuckle rising in his voice as I leaped to my feet and backed away as quickly as I'd attacked.

"There she is," he said, his voice dripping with approval and physical attraction.

"It really isn't normal how much you enjoy it when I hit you," I said, taking a step backward when he came toward me slowly. I forced myself to hold my ground, tightening my grip on the hilt of my sword and readying myself for the attack I knew had to be coming.

"If you can hit me, you can hit anyone," he said, stabbing toward me with a quick jab. I bent backward to avoid it striking me in the chest. "And I will very much enjoy watching you cut down our enemies at my side one day."

His second stab came toward me to accentuate those words, and I raised my sword in a quick arc to shove his to the side. Caelum went on the offensive, stabbing and swiping at me so rapidly that all I could do was deflect his blows. There was no time for me to go on the offensive myself when I could barely defend myself against his attack.

"Come on, Estrella," he pushed, aggravation tinting his voice as he urged me be faster. To be stronger than I was. "Sink into it and *burn*."

I fought to regain my composure, searching for that place inside me where the flame of a star blazed, and for the ability to defend myself when I was too worried about death to fear a potential injury.

What I found inside me wasn't a light. It didn't burn with the brightness of a thousand stars in the night sky. What I found at the center of my body was a place so cold it burned as icy waters in the depths of winter burned, so far from the surface that nothing but inky darkness surrounded me.

I sank into that cold hollow inside of me, letting it wrap me into a familiar embrace. My fingers burned on the hilt of my sword as I shoved Caelum's sword to the side, stepping toward him quickly and lifting my leg to press into his chest between his attacks.

I pushed him with all the strength in that leg, watching as he stumbled backward. He caught me by the ankle as a grin claimed his face, holding it so the bottom of my boot pressed to his chest. I bent my leg at the knee, leaning my weight into him and using it to drive him further away. Just enough that I could get my ankle loose from his grip and stand on my own two feet once more.

I hurried to strike while he was off balance, landing a sharp smack against the flesh of his belly as a woman's laughter echoed through the room. Caelum paused, turning his attention to where Melian strode up to face us.

"It's funny; this doesn't look like my library," she said, lifting her chin toward me in challenge. Her lips curved up into the hint of a dare to defy the challenge, as if she found me amusing in her own way.

"I can fight. It would be foolish for me to lose that ability while studying books that will still be there in an hour," I said. My breath came in deep pants, the exertion of our sparring making me feel heavy as I pulled out of the space inside of me and returned to reality.

"I've no issue with you getting physical activity down here, Estrella. All that matters to me is that you continue your work with the texts. Your value is not as a body to be cut down by our enemies, but in the mind that holds information most of us lack." Though her voice soft and soothing, there was the gentle thrum of a command in it, as if she couldn't quite turn off the leader, but it wasn't harsh or cruel.

"That's funny. I thought my worth was in spreading my legs and letting your men fuck me. According to Jensen anyway," I said, the words carrying through the room. The first judgment of my usefulness would never go away. Her assessment would never erase that someone had thought to use me in the same way men had tried all my life.

"Jensen is being dealt with for his inappropriate behavior toward you. That I can promise you, Estrella. You will not be pressured to become something you do not want to be. Not here," she said, the sadness in her voice bringing a pang inside me. To exist somewhere that I could be more than just a body to fuck or breed was still unfathomable to me, when that was all I'd been raised to believe was my future.

I had no smart reply in the face of knowing the man who'd made me uncomfortable would be dealt with, nothing else I could say to make my stance known.

"Come. You'll train with me," she said, nodding her head over to one of the other unclaimed spaces. I glanced back to Caelum, wincing when I found his glare on her.

"I think I'm perfectly capable of training her," he said, sneering at the woman. He left me with no doubt that the two of them would remain at odds, even with the misunderstanding with Jensen behind us and being addressed. I wanted to like her, even admired her for the fact that she'd come to be in power in a movement that was filled with men and women alike.

"You're holding back," she said, cocking her hip to the side and crossing her arms over her chest as she met Caelum's glare. "I have seen you cut through four of my men at a time. Estrella can fight, and she has the potential to be a great warrior one day if we teach her appropriately, but you will do her no favors by babying her. Her *Viniculum* will protect her against the Mist Guard unless they manage to trap her in irons. It is the Fae she needs to train for, and they are far greater fighters than you," she said, stretching out a hand and catching me by my free one. She braved Caelum's wrath to pull me away from him, taking me over to the space she'd gestured to before. A dummy sewn from cloth and stuffed with straw sat there waiting, the pointed ears on each side of its head leaving no doubt as to what it was meant to be.

"He won't be happy with you," I mumbled the moment we were out of earshot from Caelum. I pursed my lips together tightly to try to suppress the grin and chuckle that threatened to surface at the look she gave me.

"It's cute that you think I care, but I promise you I am very much used to people not being happy with me. Such is the life of a leader who has to make the hard decisions when the consequences can mean life or death," she said, her thin lips tipping up as she smiled down at me. "There are two ways to kill a Fae."

She stepped up behind me, raising my practice sword to tap the dull edge of the blade against the neck of the dummy. "Cut off their head or stab them through the heart with iron. Anything else they can and will heal from in time," she explained, pressing the tip of the sword to the spot where the dummy was marked with a bullseye.

"But iron weakens us, too," I said, thinking back to the shackle that had been placed around my neck. I couldn't imagine carrying something like that around all the time, dealing with the heavy feeling as it sank into my bones.

"Iron makes it so that our *Viniculum* cannot protect us," she said, nodding in agreement. "Some of the Fae have spelled swords that do not weaken them, but they are few and far between, even among the Fae themselves. We have no such luxury, but you can render them immobile long enough to sever their head from their shoulders if you stab them in the heart with a silver sword. That is your goal, and the easiest way for you to deal with them."

"Have you ever killed one of them?" I asked, turning a stare at her over my shoulder. I hadn't seen one, had never laid eyes on them aside from the Wild Hunt.

"One," she said, a shadow passing over her face, as if the memory was too much for her. "It took three of us to take him down when we went on a raid to a nearby village just after the Veil fell. Trisha cut down his legs. Jensen stabbed him in the heart. I took his head. He was Trisha's mate, tracking her through the Kingdom when we were out for too long."

"Do they all look like the Wild Hunt?" I asked, even though I felt fairly certain they didn't, from the likenesses I'd seen in the texts and the statues at the hot springs. I needed the confirmation that the male coming for me would be different than the ghostly beings I'd seen, even if I didn't want to know my mate, and never wanted even the misfortune of encountering him.

"When did you see the Wild Hunt?" she asked, going still.

"After the Veil fell. They almost found my brother and me, and then again a few nights later," I explained. Her eyes drifted closed as she undoubtedly put together the pieces.

I'd had a brother with me. I didn't anymore.

"Caelum saved me," I said, giving her a soft smile and knowing it would partially explain my attachment to him. I'd have been taken by the Fae if he hadn't intervened; already in the arms of the mate I didn't want.

She nodded, turning to regard Caelum less severely than she usually did. "No. The Wild Hunt comes from the Shadow Court and is tasked with collecting the Fae Marked to bring back to Alfheimr. The Old Gods are humanoid, the children and sometimes grandchildren of the Primordials. The children of the Old Gods are known as the Sidhe. The Sidhe and the Old Gods look just like us, except more," she said, her voice dropping lower.

"More what?" I asked, allowing her to guide my arm through the proper motions of swinging my practice sword.

"More everything."

Sweat soaked my skin as Caelum led me through the tunnels. We went higher, climbing toward the surface but on a different path than the one we'd taken when we first joined the Resistance.

"Where are we going?" I asked, glancing over at him. His body was positioned slightly in front of mine as he approached one of the hatches that led from the hidden tunnels up into the caves themselves. This one had steps carved into the rock wall, enabling him to release my hand and climb up so he could shift the stone cover off the hole.

"Somewhere we can get cleaned up without an audience to watch," he answered, hauling himself up and out of the tunnel. "Come on."

I slipped my hands into the holes in the wall, lifting myself up and letting my feet follow. Caelum's hand waited for me when I reached the top, taking hold of me and lifting me free from the tunnel. He replaced the hatch, taking my wrist in one hand to entwine our fingers together.

With his other hand, he unsheathed a sword, gripping it tightly as the distant rumble of cave beasts came from the caves to the left. Caelum led me to the right, seeming sure in his steps.

As if he knew exactly where to go.

"Is it safe? What about the warding?" I asked, my worry overwhelming me. The last thing I wanted was to lead the Fae right to us just because I was a little shy with my own nudity.

"We can't come up here every day by any means, but it's safe to do every now and then as a special treat," he answered, guiding me up a set of steps carved into the stone, which curved around a central beam.

When we finally emerged into the light of the moon, it was to a small, private hot spring hidden on a ledge next to the mountain. The air that met me when we stepped out onto the ground was harsh and cold compared to the insulated tunnels, a single gust of wind instantly making my cheeks burn.

Resting just inside the doorway to the caves was a basket filled with tiny bars of soap, and Caelum grabbed one of them on the way out. He set it at the edge of the pool, unknotting the laces at the top of his tunic as he faced me.

I swallowed, fearing I wouldn't like the answer. "How did you know about this place?"

His fingers paused for a moment, his head tilting to the side as a smirk graced his lips. "Jealous, Little One?"

Nausea churned in my gut. I'd left shortly after Melian worked with me until the muscles in my arms felt so tired I couldn't lift my practice sword any longer, my increased muscle mass since becoming Fae Marked only going so far with hours of repetition.

It appeared he'd been busy in the time since I'd left him earlier in the day. I'd spent the rest of it translating pages and pages of texts until my hand cramped and my fingers swelled from how I gripped the quill.

"I think I'll take my chances in the bathing cavern," I said, swallowing back the urge to be sick. All of Melian's words came rushing back; all of my reminders to myself that I couldn't satisfy him.

I'd known exactly what would happen and still let him convince me otherwise.

Caelum chuckled, stepping toward me as he tugged the tunic over his head and deposited it on the ground next to him. "You get this twitch underneath your left eye when you think I'd let someone else play with me," he said, moving forward until he reached out and touched his thumb to the spot in question. "I think it might be the cutest thing I've ever seen."

"Fuck you," I snarled, jerking my head away from his hand. If he thought I'd sit around and allow him to be with other women without ever allowing another man to touch me, he had another think coming.

We could be faithful, or we could not be. But whatever standards he set would go both ways, even if that meant I had to swallow my nausea and go find Jensen to take him up on his offer to be my first romp within the Resistance.

Caelum grinned, grasping my chin between two fingers and tipping my head up so that he could stare down at me intently. "No one but you has touched me since we first met."

"Then how did you know about this place? I can just imagine what it's used for," I said, trying not to allow all his bare, golden skin to distract me. I wouldn't be dumbstruck by a handsome face and sculpted muscle.

I was more than a body without a brain.

"There were offers," he said, making me swallow down my rising rage once more.

The idea of somehow marking him as my territory became more and more appealing with every word he spoke. "Offers. As in plural. What are you doing with me, then? You could be having another threesome."

Caelum chuckled. "I could be, and I would be if that was what I wanted, but I have no interest in anyone but you, my star. I don't know how much more clear I can be about that. You are the only one for me. Women may make offers, but my answer will always be no. I expect the same in return."

I swallowed as he rested a hand on my shoulders, inching his fingertips under the fabric there and sliding it down toward my arms. With the laces unknotted at the front, it would fall to my feet the moment the sleeves slipped down.

"Caelum," I said, making him pause as I bit my lip. I had no doubt where this would go between us if my dress fell. He wouldn't turn his back this time and wouldn't be distracted by the scars on my back.

"There will be no going back from this once you've taken me inside you, Little One. Take care to understand just how sincerely I mean that. Once we cross this line, you're mine," he murmured, toying with the fabric as he stared down at me. His focus didn't move as he waited for my response, his features patient and relaxed despite the urgency in his gaze.

"I thought I already was," I said stupidly, unable to think of what to say in the face of all his intensity. He leaned forward, touching his lips to mine as he brushed my sleeves off my shoulders.

The dress pooled at my feet, leaving me naked except for the socks and boots on my feet. Caelum kissed down my jaw, trailing his lips over the front of my throat as he lowered himself to his knees in front of me.

He was tall enough that his head was level with my breasts, his mouth caressing softly and drawing goosebumps to my skin. His fingers worked at the laces of my boot as he pressed a kiss to the peak of my nipple, opening his mouth and wrapping the wet heat of it around me.

I gasped as he finished untying my boot, and wrapped one hand around the sensitive skin on the back of my knee, lifting so he could pull the boot and sock free while his tongue slowly flicked my pebbled nipple.

He kissed his way over the valley between my breasts as he switched to the other boot, drawing my other nipple into his mouth with more urgency. He sucked hard enough that my back bowed as he finally stripped off the other boot, rising to his feet in front of me and pressing his bare torso against me.

He kissed me, his tongue tangling with mine and threatening to consume me. I knew in that moment I would do anything to keep him.

His nostrils flared as he pulled back, reaching down to grab my ass in both his hands and squeeze. "Get in the water, my star," he said, his voice dropping low with the command as he took a step away and dropped his hands to the laces on his trousers.

I moved to do just that, escaping the cool air in favor of the comfort of the hot spring. I lowered myself into the pool slowly, letting the warm water envelop me. I dropped my head below the surface, floating there for a moment before I resurfaced.

Caelum lowered himself into the water, dunking his head under until his blond hair turned darker from the soaking. He grabbed the soap off the edge of the pool, stalking toward me slowly and lathering it in his hands.

"The Resistance doesn't appear to have products for hair specifically," he grumbled, touching his soapy hands to the top of my head and working them through my hair methodically.

"I'm used to that," I said with a little chuckle. Soap was universal when you were poor. Only the richest among us could afford anything else.

"You deserve the best of the best. Specific formulas to wash your hair, oils to keep it soft," he murmured as he worked the lather through my hair. His fingers massaged my scalp, and I flushed as I thought of what a mess I must look like compared to what he was used to.

If the women he'd been with before usually had those kinds of products at their disposal, I was nothing compared to that.

He tipped me back, helping me rinse the soap from my hair carefully before he ran the bar across my neck and shoulders. His touch was slow and lazy as he explored every line marked into my skin. Washing the dirt and sweat from my body, his attention fixated only on where the soap and his hand touched me.

Watching the grime wash away to reveal my skin beneath it, the girl I'd once been was revealed just a bit more with every pass of the soap. By the time he finished with my arms and made his way down to my breasts, I thought I might combust.

He cleaned them thoroughly, running the soap over my stomach and eventually touching it to the apex of my thighs.

"I can do it," I said, flushing as I thought of him cleaning the most intimate part of me.

"I had my fingers inside you only yesterday, my star. Do you think I would hesitate to wash your cunt before I bury my tongue inside it?" he asked, rubbing soap-lathered fingers over me. He forced my legs wider, spreading me as he ran his hand over me and cleaned me.

I whimpered, the heat within me building as he stroked between my legs. He moved on to my legs as soon as he was satisfied, lifting them one at a time and washing them methodically. I was a mess of need by the time he turned me around and began to wash my back, his fingers hesitating on each and every scar.

He leaned down and pressed his lips to the worst one, kissing the sensitive skin that seemed to tingle any time someone touched it. The kiss felt like a promise of retribution, a reiteration of the vow he'd made to see the man who'd harmed me dead.

He touched a hand to my ass cheek, gripping it with bruising fingers as he lowered the soap. I jolted away from his touch, spinning to face him as he grinned at me. "I think not."

He shrugged, rubbing the soap over his chest as if the boundary didn't matter to him. "I'll fuck you there one day too, my star."

I blanched.

Was that even possible?

The serious look on his face gave me all the answer I needed, so I just shook my head and took the soap to finish washing myself there. Maybe with a normal man, that could be physically possible, though I doubted pleasurable. But for a man with a cock that seemed to hang down to his knees?

Hard pass.

I brushed off my moment of embarrassment, stepping toward him and lifting the soap to his body. I wasn't willing to let the moment pass me by, knowing that our baths would normally be fraught with company watching our every move. This might be the only time in the near future where I could take the time to learn the contours of his body with my own hands while we were submerged in warm water.

I ran it over the muscles of his chest, staring at the place where my fingers ran over his golden skin. His gaze felt heavy as he watched my face, but something in me couldn't force myself to look up and meet it. I knew that the moment I looked at him with my hands on his skin, my time to explore would come to an end.

I passed the soap over his shoulders and the scars almost covered his body in a way I wouldn't have expected for a man situated to know of wealthy items for women's care.

There was so much I still didn't know about Caelum and the life he'd lived, but I couldn't bring myself to ask with the steam in the air around us and his skin against my palm.

His muscles twitched against my hand as I trailed them down to his stomach, making me look up at him finally as I cleaned the grooves between each of the muscles carved from his abdomen. Only when that was finished did I drop my hand lower, cleaning the lines between his torso and the corded muscles of his thighs.

He hissed when I shifted my hand sideways, rubbing the soap against the top of his shaft. My fingertips brushed against his length, and I watched as he gritted his teeth. My other hand joined the first, wrapping around his cock as I ran the soap over him tentatively. The moment my fingers gripped him, he groaned. "*Fuck.*"

I washed him, sliding my hand up and down his shaft as the soap cleansed him. He'd already been hard by the time I took him in my hand, but there was no denying the way he hardened more in my grip, until he was like a rock, unforgiving, and I knew he would break me when he pushed inside me for the first time.

"Enough," he grunted, covering my hand with his. He guided me, stroking himself with it twice more before he finally pulled it away and took the soap to finish washing himself.

I hesitated, wondering if I'd done something wrong or crossed some sort of line. I didn't understand how I could have misread the situation. "Sit on the edge, Estrella," he ordered, making me swallow back my nerves. I moved to do as he instructed, walking to the edge of the pool.

"Did I do something wrong?" I asked, staring at him as he turned his attention back to me. Danger glinted in his eyes, something animalistic rising to the surface as he prowled toward me. He deposited the soap onto the edge of the pool, grabbing me around the waist and placing me on the cold stone.

I shivered as he spread my legs, inserting his shoulders between them and staring at the center of me as if he wanted to devour me.

"Did you do something wrong?" he asked, tilting his head to the side as he carefully pulled my ass so close to the edge that I felt like I might fall into the water. One of his enormous hands touched the center of my chest, pushing me back until I leaned onto my elbows and stared down at the rugged lines of his handsome face. "If you didn't stop, I was going to bury myself balls-deep inside you while you screamed. I only have so much control when you have your hand wrapped around my cock, my star."

"Oh," I murmured softly, watching as he slid an arm behind each of my thighs and gripped them. He shoved them wide, tilting me further until my back touched the cold stone beneath me.

"Oh," he repeated, as if I was an idiot for being totally unaware of the effect I had on him. He leaned forward, dragging his tongue through me from entrance to clit.

"Oh Gods," I whimpered, my back arching from the wet heat of his mouth.

"I'll be your God any day, my star," he murmured, burying his face into me. He licked and stroked every inch of my skin, sinking his tongue inside me and fucking me with it. When his hand joined in and he pressed a finger in while he circled my clit with his tongue, I thought I would explode.

No one had ever touched me like this; had ever made me feel things like this.

"Caelum," I whimpered.

"What happened to God?" he teased, nipping at my clit as he slid a second finger into me.

"I want to feel you inside me," I moaned, thrusting a hand between my legs to grip his hair. I pulled him closer and then pushed him away, guiding his mouth where I wanted it even as I wanted *more.*

"Then come so I can fuck you," he growled, sucking my clit between his lips and reaching up to pinch my nipple with his other hand. I came, clenching around his fingers and forgetting my own name.

I was still lost in a haze of bliss when he pulled me down from the ledge, the warmth of the water enveloping my skin that felt frozen and overheated all at once. He moved to the shallows and pressed me against the edge of the pool, wrapping my legs around his waist, with my pussy suspended in the cool air.

His cock pressing against my entrance snapped me out of the haze, bringing me back to my senses as he pushed inside me slowly. My pussy squeezed around him, protesting the too-large invasion of the cock that seemed impossible to fit.

He drew his hips back while I curved myself into him, burying my face in his neck as I felt like he would tear me in two. He moved in slow, shallow thrusts, opening my body for him bit by bit.

I felt every inch of him inside me, gliding over my swollen flesh until he finally pressed against the end of me. His balls rested against the curve of my ass, his strangled groan rumbling in my ear as he paused and stayed planted inside me.

"Like you were fucking made for me. You're mine now, Little One. Do you understand?" he growled, burying a hand in my hair and tugging my head back. He stared into my face intently, waiting for the only response I could give as he started to move. Slowly pulling his hips back, he drove in sharply and drew a whimper from me.

I nodded. "I understand."

"You don't, but you will," he said, possessing my mouth with his. He fucked me into the wall with slow, deep thrusts that consumed me. My back scraped against the rough surface, but all that mattered was him pressed to my chest, his cock driving hard and deep between my legs and filling me for the first time in my life.

Caelum's body was the lifeline I clung to while he unmade me from the girl who had existed before his possession. He imprinted himself on my soul and my body, filling me with him until I came violently, crying out as my pussy clenched down on him, trapping him inside.

"Who is fucking you, Little One?" he asked, touching a hand to the front of my throat and bending me back over the edge. He kept fucking me through my orgasm, moving with a faster pace as he sought his own release inside my body.

"You are," I whimpered.

"And who am I?" he asked, planting so deep I saw a void of all life as my eyes drifted closed.

"Caelum."

"Who am I to you, Estrella?" he asked, his meaning coming into focus as my eyes opened to the dark wells of his staring down at me.

"You are mine," I whispered, feeling him flood me with heat the moment I spoke the words. He shuddered, his body going still as he shoved deep and planted himself inside me. He held me still, dropping his mouth to trail his lips over my neck and breathe me in as if I could become a part of him.

When he pulled back and smiled down at me, those dark eyes gleamed in the moonlight.

And I knew I would never be the same.

29

I translated the page, writing a few lines before I gave my hand a break to stretch away the ache. My fingers throbbed every time I bent and straightened them, after only a few days of abuse.

I stood from my chair, giving my legs a chance to move while I tried to work the blood back into my fingers. I needed to teach someone how to write just to have a person to alternate with. Walking over to the books on the shelf, I perused the spines once again to decide which book I would do next, if I ever finished my current one about the creation of Alfheimr.

The knock at the doorway made me spin to face it. Only Melian and Caelum came to visit me in the library, the others seeming to have little use for the tomes that they couldn't read.

Jensen stood in the doorway, leaning his shoulder against the arch carved into the stone. His face was twisted into a smile that didn't seem wholehearted, like it was all part of the ruse he'd created to get what he wanted from the people of the Resistance.

"I see Melian found a use for you after all," he said, stepping into the room. He ran his hand over the scrolls rolled up and stored in boxes on the floor as he moved toward the table where I worked every day.

"It appears that way," I said, barely restraining my grimace. I had no doubt he would have rather I accepted his first proposal for my occupation. The unfortunate reality was that Jensen was far from unattractive. He was someone that I might have taken casual comfort in, if it hadn't been for Caelum. At least, if I'd never seen the less appealing aspect of his personality. I doubted he lacked female companionship somehow, in spite of his toxic, slimy words anytime he opened his mouth.

"Do you know what the ratio of men to women is here now?" Jensen asked, stepping around the edge of the table until he was in my personal space. I remained at the bookshelf, but the way he leaned his ass into the edge of my table meant I wouldn't be able to get around him or return to my task.

"I don't," I said, shaking my head.

"Women make up less than one fourth of our numbers. There is good reason why I wanted you to take other men to your bed. It isn't healthy for so many men to have to share so few women," Jensen said, reaching behind him to grip the table where he rested his ass. "A lot of us don't think it's fair that Caelum gets to have you all to himself. It isn't as though there are children involved yet, are there?" He gave a glance toward my stomach, making my eyes narrow as I fought to retain my composure.

"That sounds like a personal problem, Jensen. My body is not for public use, regardless of my relationship with Caelum. I would never allow men who feel entitled to my body to use me. I'd be better off with the Fae," I said, pausing to cross my arms over my chest. "At least they don't share," I added, glaring at him and the audacity he'd had to come here, spewing his nonsense and acting like it was my duty to spread my legs for the good of the Resistance.

I snorted at his nerve.

"Monogamy won't work here any longer, because we don't have the numbers to sustain it. Think of what will happen if some of the Fae Marked girls see your relationship with Caelum and think they can have that too. One less pussy for the rest of us to fuck, and when men are locked up together with nothing to fuck, we fight. We will kill each other, Estrella. You're being selfish by not doing your part to keep the peace."

"Fuck you," I snarled. "Do you harass all the women here this way? Or am I just lucky?"

He ignored my question, focusing on the vulgarity as he leaned closer. "I would love that, sweetheart. You're the one playing hard to get. All you have to do is come and sit on my cock. I'll make it good for you, too," he murmured, lowering himself into my chair and patting his lap. He dropped his hand to the laces of his trousers, unknotting them slowly as if he actually thought I would behave like a dog and service him. "I don't even mind that your pussy is probably still filled with his cum from when he made you scream this morning. It feels better that way."

I resisted the urge to throw up all over him, holding completely still as I thought through my options. I didn't know Jensen well enough to know if he would go far enough to force himself on me if I said no or tried to slip past him and get out.

What I did know was that the main tunnels and the commons were too far away for anyone else to help me if he did.

"I would sooner walk naked into a blizzard and welcome frostbite than allow your vile cock to touch me," I growled, watching as all pretense of civility fell from his face.

He stood from the chair slowly, stretching to his full height as he approached me. My back hit the shelves, his hand coming to rest on the one next to my head as he leaned into me. "Don't be such a prude, Estrella. It will be fun."

"I said no," I reiterated, wrapping my hand around the spine of a book. If he pushed the issue, I didn't care that I would probably destroy the ancient text. All that would matter would be his broken nose.

"Your mouth said no, but should we find out what your body says?" he asked, touching a hand to my waist.

"I believe the word her mouth spoke is the end of it for you," Caelum said, his deep voice echoing from where he stood in the doorway. He crossed over the threshold, the air in the room seeming to drop in temperature as soon as he was inside with us.

Jensen didn't move from where he leaned into my space, turning his head to face Caelum but keeping his body close to mine. "Surely you understand the women here need to fulfill a certain purpose. Keeping just you entertained is hardly fair when there are so many of us who have needs too."

"Why don't you run and tell Melian that she isn't serving her purpose because she isn't fucking you? I'm sure that will go over well," Caelum said, earning a sharp laugh from me. The older woman would knock Jensen on his ass if he ever proposed that she owed him sex.

"She at least fucks several of the men. At once, I'm told. I'm happy to let Caelum join the two of us if that is what you'd prefer?" Jensen asked stupidly. How he could miss the violence thrumming through Caelum's body, the barely restrained rage that made him look more weapon than man.

"Unhand my woman. Now," Caelum ordered, leaving little opportunity for argument. He stepped closer to Jensen, waiting for him to comply. He did, taking his hands away from me and stepping away.

"Not even fucking worth the trouble. Melian has me cleaning floors for a week because you ran to her the first time," Jensen said, spitting on the floor at my feet. The rude gesture was the last straw for Caelum, growling a curse as he lunged for Jensen. The two men toppled to the ground, then Caelum straddled Jensen's hips and punched him in the face.

Blood burst from the other man's nose, staining the fabric of his tunic as I stepped forward and tried to pull Caelum off him. "She is worth more than you will ever understand, you vile piece of shit."

"Caelum!" I warned, trying to get his attention as he struck Jensen again. "Stop."

I didn't know the Resistance's position on fighting among members, but I couldn't let a snake like Jensen be the reason Caelum and I were on our own in the woods again. We needed a safe place to stay. We needed the wards that protected us.

He stopped finally, standing and coming over to check on me. He took my hand, guiding me out of the library and into the tunnels. Instead of going back toward the commons, he turned to go up the back side of the hollows within the mountain.

"You can't just go hitting people here," I objected as he hurried me along the path. I didn't know where he was taking me, but I suspected it would be somewhere that he could cool off before we had to face the consequences of his violence.

"He touched what's mine," he said, as if it was the answer for everything. The part of me that suspected I might have done the same found joy in that, but something stopped me from enjoying it entirely.

"Do you mean to tell me that none of the women here have touched you at all?" I asked, tearing my hand out of his grip.

"They respect the word no. Unlike him," he said.

"But I haven't hurt them is my point. By your standards, I should have broken the nose of every last woman in here at this point, but I trust you to handle it. You have to trust me to handle it too. I am not a piece of property, Caelum. I'm your partner. I just want to feel like you see me that way." I said, shaking my head in exasperation.

I liked Caelum's jealousy. It heated the blood in my veins and brought me joy to know that he wanted to keep me to himself, but that didn't mean I didn't feel the other edge of the sword, as well. It didn't mean I didn't feel like I might suffocate under the weight of his possession.

In a world that was determined to make me a piece of property, I just wanted to feel free with the man I loved at my side.

"He didn't take no for an answer, and you want to claim I am no better than him?" He shook his head vehemently. "Have I ever made you feel like you do not have a choice with me? In fact, I would say I've been very accommodating, allowing you to make your choice about whether you wanted me or not," he said impatiently, reminding me of the fact that he'd never touched me until I gave him permission and agreed we would be faithful to each other. "But now you've made that choice. If I had it my way, I would have fucked you in that barn before your brother came back and tried to take you away from me."

A part of me delighted in the words, knowing that he'd been drawn to me as quickly as I had to him. But the other part of me craved my freedom and didn't want to go straight from one man's authority to another.

"I made my choice, but I made it thinking I would gain a partner.

Not a keeper. You need to find a way to claim me without turning into a beast and risking our place here," I said, continuing down the tunnel. He walked at my side, his fingers brushing against mine in the same way they had that day in the barn when we'd lain side by side in the straw.

"You are my partner, my star. You own me just as much as I own you."

"We need to stay here. We aren't safe anywhere else. There has to be a way to lay our claims without risking expulsion for violence," I mused thoughtfully. We fell into silence as we continued the way Caelum had led us.

I didn't know where we were going. Only that I would follow him anywhere.

30

Caelum guided us through the tunnels, emerging into the caves above the lower levels as we walked quickly. "I don't think we should be up here again so soon," I said, thinking of the warding that wouldn't protect us outside the tunnels.

"Just for a little while," Caelum said, heading for the light shining in through the cave entrance carved into the side of the mountain. We emerged into the sun, facing the ocean that surrounded the Kingdom. The water crashed onto the shore far below, the rocks and sand heaving with the force of the turbulent waters on this side of the Kingdom.

The ocean in Mistfell was hidden beyond the Veil itself, obscured from view. I'd never actually seen the waves strike against the shore, the force of them battering into the Kingdom.

The water all around the Kingdom faded into the mist, the wall of haze blocking everything else from view, but the sight of the water itself was enough to make melancholy flash through me, the loss of my brother feeling closer than ever.

The last time I'd seen sand had been when I'd stumbled through it trying to find him on the beach.

Sometimes, it was easy to forget the life I'd left behind. Easy to pretend it wasn't my past at all, because the urgency of my new life was so different from that simple world, where my greatest concern was a man who wanted things he shouldn't from me.

I turned away from the water, my brother's words flashing in my mind. I would have to die before I ever allowed the Fae to take me; my brother's instructions for me had been clear. There'd been something else in his warning, something more menacing than I dared to even consider.

Caelum had convinced me that there was a reason to live, but he'd have to understand that I was better off dead than in Alfheimr, if the time ever came.

Pressing my face into his chest, I couldn't bear to look at the water any longer. Couldn't bear to stare at it and wonder if the tide had swept Brann out to sea and left him somewhere nearby.

The part of me that would always search for him wanted to scour the rocks below for any signs of a body, but I knew well enough to know that I wouldn't find him.

I'd never see him again.

"I miss my family," I murmured, feeling tears sting my eyes. I missed my mother and wondered if she was alright and being treated well in our absence. I missed the brother who had died trying to save me from a life of misery.

I missed the father they'd killed while I was a girl.

Caelum gripped the back of my neck gently, squeezing his fingers ever-so-slightly until he was able to pull my face out of his chest and stare down at my tear-streaked cheeks, as if he wanted to eradicate the very things that had hurt me.

He brushed a thumb over the falling tear, wiping it away as he pressed his lips to my forehead. "I'm your family now," he said gently, the words soothing a small part of me that felt like a lone ship lost in the mist and floating without a destination.

I wanted to tell him that it wasn't the same, that we would never truly be family to one another; not when we could be taken at any moment, and the thought of leaving a child behind was unfathomable. I couldn't make myself say the words, though, wanting to sink into his assertion and believe in the distantly happy, if delusional, picture.

Even if just for a little while.

"I love you, my star. I think I've loved you since you put a knife to my throat. Nothing will ever change that," he murmured, the words lighting something inside me aflame with a cold fire. They were impossible, but I couldn't deny the way I felt in return.

"Melian says it isn't possible for us to love anyone but our mates, because being Marked changed us," I said, staring back at him. Giving him the opportunity to take back the words, even while I prayed he meant them.

I couldn't imagine my life without him after only a few short weeks with him at my side, our bond ingrained in me so fully that I didn't know who I would be without him anymore.

Caelum lowered his body down the wall outside the cave, taking me with him as he sat and leaned against it. Staring out at the water and pulling my head into his shoulder, he seemed to revel in the feeling of the sun on his skin and the freedom that came from being outside the tunnels.

"I have no doubt that Melian believes what she says," Caelum said, taking my hand in his and lifting it to touch where his heart beat in his chest. "But I promise you, my heart beats for you."

My resolve crumbled, falling around us as I stared into those obsidian eyes until the moment his lips touched mine. He kissed me softly, gently, as if I was the only thing precious in his world.

But I couldn't say the words back yet, even though they resonated within me. To admit my love was to give him power over me, the power to hurt me, and I wasn't ready for that last step just yet; not after enduring so much pain the last few weeks and so much I still didn't know about him.

He pulled back, smiling down at me knowingly, not waiting for me to say the words back to him. "We have all the time in the world, Little One," he said, settling in to feel the sun on his face.

"Will you tell me more about your life before the Veil dropped?" I asked, feeling like the question might give him the opportunity to open up to me more. If he could do that, then maybe I would be able to let go of the unrelenting fear that he would hurt me.

If I could know him, maybe I could let myself love him.

"What do you want to know?" he asked, his body stiffening for a moment before he forced it to relax. He shifted his legs, getting more comfortable, and I knew without a doubt that talking about his life wasn't something he would do readily.

Everything I wanted to know about him, I would have to pry out of him with probing questions. "Anything. Did you have any siblings?" I asked, watching as he flinched.

"No. My birth mother never had any other children, and neither did my father. My step-mother did bear a child from another man out of wedlock, but she disappeared when she was only a few weeks old," he said, shrugging his shoulders as if it was inconsequential to him.

"That's terrible. Did they ever figure out what happened to her?" I asked, swallowing back the sickness I felt over the thought of a child being stolen.

A baby, at that.

"No, but I have to think she was better off. My stepmother was a vile woman, and that poor girl would have suffered having her for a mother. I would know," Caelum said, shuffling his legs once again.

"What about your birth mother? Did you ever meet her?" I asked, and he sighed, his eyes drifting closed.

"In passing. My family was involved in politics, as was my mother. Our paths crossed because of that frequently, but she always kept her distance because of my stepmother."

"Nothing could keep me from my child," I murmured, not pausing to consider that it sounded like his mother didn't love him enough. It hadn't been my intention.

"There are some evils in this world that use love against you. Keeping your distance is far safer in those circumstances. I hope you're never put in that situation, my star," Caelum said, not seeming to take offense to the words. "We should head back," he added, sighing and getting to his feet. He left me with the distinct feeling that we would have stayed in the sun far longer had it not been for my difficult questions, but I couldn't apologize for wanting to get to know the man who supposedly loved me.

He took my hand, guiding me into the tunnels once again and leaving the light of day at our backs. The descent into darkness seemed more jarring the second time, returning to shelter but leaving something else important behind. I wondered if it was the pulse of awareness coming from my mate, through his ability to feel me from somewhere out there. Hunting me. Searching for me throughout the Kingdom.

I swallowed, suddenly very happy to be returning to the warded tunnels that would protect us, as Caelum grabbed the torch off the wall. We headed toward the closest hatch to go to the lower levels, the silence of the caverns feeling like nothing out of the ordinary as we rounded the corner, me leaning my weight into Caelum's side as we walked.

He froze solid at the intersection between two of the pathways, his grip tightening on my waist, and I followed his gaze, staring into the tunnel straight ahead of us. I saw nothing, felt nothing, until the cavern shook with a force as a taloned foot appeared from the shadows further ahead.

A thick leg emerged next, the hulking form of a cave beast appearing from the darkness as it stepped into the circle of light from Caelum's torch. He put it in my hand, wrapping my fingers around it as he reached for one of the swords strapped to his back at all times.

I stared on in horror as the creature's face came into view, its glossy black eyes too large in its face. It had no lips, only two rows of enormous pointed teeth that protruded from its snout. It stretched out a hand covered in mottled gray skin, jagged and sharp nails at the end of almost human-like fingers. It stood on two legs, thighs as big as my torso, and its ears pointed like horns toward the sky through the hair that sprouted out of the top of its head. When it took another step, the tunnels shook, knocking me sideways with the force of that step as it opened its mouth and roared.

"Run!" Caelum ordered, pushing me toward the other tunnel that would lead to the hatch to get into the safety of the Resistance tunnels below.

"No!" I protested in spite of the fear surging through my body. Our vow stuck in my head.

We lived together. We died together.

"Estrella! *Go NOW!*" Caelum roared, something Other flashing briefly in his eyes as he leveled a glare at me. The creature charged at Caelum as my feet carried me away from the fight. I hadn't even realized I'd made the decision to run, meaning to stay with him, but my legs moved against my will, terror thrumming through me as I raced down the corridor.

He was the best fighter I'd ever seen. If anyone could survive long enough for help to get to him, it was Caelum. I sped around one of the corners, dropping the torch as I fumbled with the hatch and tried desperately to heave it back. The stone was heavy, threatening to crush my fingers as I shoved it to the side and lowered myself in. The compulsion to flee left me the moment I was tucked within the tunnel hatch, leaving me gasping for breath as I turned to watch for Caelum.

I reached back up to grab the hatch, ready to seal it behind me at a moment's notice. The roar of the cave beast echoed down the cavern toward me as I watched for any sign of life from Caelum.

Listening.

An animalistic roar answered the beast's bray, thunderous and murderous, making the tunnel walls around me shake.

I stayed with my head poking out of the tunnel entrance, rooted to the spot and unable to move and get help as I watched the shadows dance in the distance. In terror, I watched the dark blood splash against the cave walls and heard heavy footfalls land on the ground with every step they took.

The fight continued on, giving me just a moment of hope that Caelum was still alive, but even if my body seemed unable to return to his side, I couldn't leave him, either. When silence fell in the tunnel, I slid aside hatch the rest of the way and pulled myself up, staying close to the entrance in case what came around that corner was the beast that would haunt my nightmares.

The sounds of what had been fighting faded into the distinct squelching of tearing flesh, and my heart leapt into my throat with a strangled sob. I couldn't make myself walk away, not even when blood ran down the tunnel toward me, staining the ground with the macabre scene.

I stepped forward, needing to see for myself that he was gone, disbelieving that my new reason for living had been taken, too. I didn't know who I would be, what I would do without him, and I immediately regretted not giving him the words he'd said to me, not letting him know how I felt before I lost him.

Steady, soft footfalls came from around the corner of the tunnel. Caelum's fingers gripped the cave wall as he pulled himself along around the bend and toward me. He was drenched in blood, his clothing stained and his hair turned red with the blood of the creature that seemed larger than life.

I raced forward, touching trembling fingers to the sides of his face.

"What happened?" I asked, trying to glance around him to see what remained of the cave beast.

"Dead," he groaned, drawing my attention back to him. I dropped my eyes to his blood-stained tunic, peeling apart the fabric of his shirt where it gaped at the front. Three enormous slashes cut through his clothing from where the beast must have swiped at him, the skin torn and bleeding.

"You're hurt," I said, wrapping his arm over my shoulder. "You need a healer."

"Not that bad," Caelum said, shaking his head. "We aren't human anymore, remember? It will heal."

"What do you need?" I asked, helping him down the hatch and into the tunnels, pulling the stone closed over my head. We turned back toward the main caverns, making our way toward the sure punishment, for his beating of Jensen, that would wait for us.

"To clean it before it heals," he said. I nodded, trying not to think of what would wait for us as I guided him toward the bathing cavern. The risk of infection was far more important than the risk of other women seeing him naked.

I'd find a way to deal with the jealousy festering inside of me if it meant Caelum himself wouldn't fester and die. "How are you alive? I don't understand," I murmured as we walked.

"*Viniculum,*" Caelum said, the explanation somehow making sense. I'd seen what mine could do, turning a man into a pile of snow, but where mine seemed to be connected to the winter, something in Caelum's appeared delighted in the butchering of life.

In dismantling it bit by bit.

His hands were drenched in blood, as if his body had been as involved in the fight as the Faerie magic coursing through him. Or maybe it was his own blood staining his skin, his own blood and bits of flesh embedded under the edges of his nails.

We stepped into the bathing cavern, all attention turning to the man covered in gore as I guided him to the side of the pool. People scurried all around us as I tore his ruined tunic down the front, shoving the scraps of fabric off his shoulders and kneeling at his feet to tug off his boots and socks. He stumbled slightly as he untied the laces of his pants, shucking them down his thighs and stepping down the steps into the water.

Even bathed in blood, he cut an impressive figure that the women nearby couldn't keep their eyes off of. "Estrella," one of them said, stepping up beside me as I watched Caelum lower himself into the water. "Are you hurt?" she asked me, glancing down at my bloody clothing and my hands that were covered in Caelum's blood.

Or the beasts. I didn't even know.

"He protected me," I said, shaking my head as he emerged from the surface of the water and turned to look at me. He pinned me with an intense stare, rubbing his hands over his skin to wipe away the worst of the blood.

"What happened?" the woman asked.

"We had an encounter with a cave beast above the tunnels," I said, shaking my head. If I had it my way, we would never go on another excursion outside the protection the mountain offered. We'd live our lives in peace without the violence above the surface. I couldn't risk losing him again.

The woman nodded, her attention snagging on one of the men

waiting at the mouth of the bathing cavern. He darted off, probably to alert the guards so they could make sure the tunnel entrances were secure.

"He'll need help getting clean. He's made it clear that no one but you is permitted to touch him," she said, holding out a bar of soap for me to take.

I glanced around the cavern, at the men gathered in the room. Several of them were within the waters of the hot spring itself, others bathing in the mouth of the stream that led down into the cavern from the top of the mountain. The water cycled out the side of the bathing cavern, trailing slowly over the notch carved into the edge of the pool.

With a sigh, I held Caelum's gaze as I kicked off my boots and socks while I untied the laces of my dress. I shoved the sleeves down off my shoulders, letting the fabric drop while I took the soap from her outstretched hand and tried to ignore the feeling of eyes on me.

Caelum's eyes burned, glittering with menace as he challenged the men watching me with a glare. I stepped into the water slowly, letting the bath warm my overly chilled skin as I approached Caelum. I touched a hand to the gashes, gathering water to rinse it off with my hand, then lathering the soap so that I could wash it into his wound.

He caught my wrist in a gentle vice, stopping me from touching his skin. "I'm not in control right now, Little One. I won't be gentle with you."

I glanced around the cavern and the collection of people going about their business. Some still watched us, undoubtedly drawn by the red-stained enigma of a man at the center of the bathing pool. "There are people here," I murmured, swallowing past my unease.

"Then I suggest you let me wash myself, unless you're comfortable with having an audience," Caelum rumbled. "And that you stay in this water. Because if I see your body one more time, if I watch them look at you again, I will not be held responsible for what I do to you. Is that clear, my star?"

I swallowed again, looking around once more and trying to decide if I could tolerate the feeling of eyes on me while Caelum fucked me. If I could allow men to see me in the throes of passion with him.

The idea of women staring at him bothered me, but it was somehow okay when it was tempered with the knowledge that they'd only see him before he plunged into me. Then they'd see me own him, claim him, as mine.

I drew a ragged breath, lifting my eyes to meet Caelum's intense stare where he searched my face for any sign of what would be my answer.

I touched my hand to his chest.

31

I hadn't been expecting the growl that rumbled in his chest, making it shudder against the flat of my palm on his skin. I pressed my soapy hand into the slashes on his torso, gently washing away the blood and gore from his injury. I focused my attention on my job of getting it clean before it could heal, my heart thumping in my chest uncontrollably.

I looked back up at him through my lashes, finding him staring down at my face, watching me. He didn't move, didn't so much as twitch, even as I cleaned the wound that must have been incredibly painful.

A human wouldn't have survived without being sewn closed, but already the signs of his flesh knitting back together were evident. Pink skin formed over the very edges of the wounds, healing while I cleaned him.

His dark eyes sparkled with the light of a thousand stars enrobed in the shadows of the night, his gaze heavy lidded and jaw clenched. "Are you afraid, Little One?" he asked, something deeper echoing in his voice. An element that tasted like power coated my skin, making my flesh pebble as if the cold of a winter's storm brushed over me.

"I'm not afraid of you," I murmured gently, feeling the truth in those words. At least physically; I had no doubt that my body was safe with Caelum. He would never hurt me, never allow anything to harm me. He'd been willing to sacrifice himself to a cave beast to buy me the time to get away to safety.

If I'd doubted his confession of love before, could there ever be any doubt after that?

His answer was quiet, the words hanging in the air with gentle menace. "You should be."

I swallowed down my nerves and finished cleaning his wounds, shifting my attention to the blood on the rest of his skin and trying to ignore the threat that seemed to hang between us.

No matter what he said in the moments after his battle, I couldn't bring myself to heed the warning.

He tipped himself back, lowering his hair into the water so I could run my fingers through it and wash it free of the creature's blood. When he was finally clean, he gleamed like new gold. Something about him seemed stronger, better, after the battle with the monster who would have made a meal out of him.

As if he danced on the edge between something human and something...not.

"When I put my hand between your pretty thighs, will I find you already slick for me?" Caelum asked, the words more a growl than his true voice. I glanced around, my nerves rekindling as I realized that the majority of people who remained in the room watched us intently.

I couldn't fault them, not with the energy rolling off of Caelum. I couldn't decide if I was about to be part of a sexual exhibition or a sacrifice.

If he'd fuck me or bleed me.

If I hadn't trusted him not to hurt me, I might have run, but as it was, I couldn't make my legs move away. I worried my bottom lip, reconsidering my choice to touch him in the first place.

There were too many eyes, too many witnesses, and I realized with horror that more people had filtered into the bathing cavern as I'd washed him. "You had your chance to walk away," Caelum said, touching a gentle hand to my cheek. He brushed my hair behind my ear, taking a single step closer until his body pressed against the front of mine.

He was already hard, his length teasing the flesh of my stomach. "But you haven't answered my question, Estrella. Are you wet for me? Does the idea of them watching me fuck you turn you on as much as it does me?"

"I didn't think you wanted them to see me," I whispered, trying to align his desire with his possessiveness. It didn't make sense, leaving me with the distinct feeling that I was missing something very vital.

"I don't want them to see you, but I have no qualms with them seeing you take my cock like you were made for me," he growled, glancing up at the men who watched. His gaze paused, snagging on someone as I turned to follow it. Jensen stood at the edge of the bath, watching intently while I gulped. His nose was a crooked mess, the skin around his eyes blackening. "Because by the time I'm done with you, they'll know exactly who you belong to."

Caelum's hand brushed over my mark, drawing a startled gasp from me that he swallowed when he crashed his mouth onto mine. He tilted me to where he wanted me, maneuvering me while I struggled to breathe against the force of his assault.

His lips were bruising mine. His fingers were harsh where he gripped the back of my neck in a controlling hold that left me no argument. No place to run, no escape from him.

His hand drifted between my thighs, shoving them wide enough for him to feel me. He took the answer I hadn't been ready to voice, the distinct slickness of me coating his fingers as he shoved them inside of me and worked my pussy open for the cock that would tear me in two.

He growled into my mouth, the sound resonating through him and into my chest as he walked me backward to the edge of the bathing pool. He lifted me, setting me on the ledge as he had the night he fucked me for the first time. There was no patience in his movements as water sloshed onto the cave floor around me, his hand shoving me until my back struck against the stone floor.

My nipples pebbled with the shock of cooler air, my attention straying as the feeling of eyes on my body threatened to overwhelm me.

I squeezed my legs shut, moving to sit up as Caelum's hand shifted from where he'd pushed me into position to gripping my entire breast in his hand and kneading it.

A strangled moan came from me as I fought to sit up, that punishing grip pressing down firmly enough to keep me rooted to the spot. Pinned in place and on display.

"Show me my fucking cunt," he ordered, slapping his free hand down on the outside of my thigh when I didn't immediately relent. "Show them what they will never have."

I sank my teeth into the inside of my cheek, biting down sharply and squeezing my eyes closed as I slowly spread my legs to Caelum's invasive stare. He stared down at me, at the space between my legs, and touched gentle fingers to my core that were so at odds with the predatory way he watched me. "Good girl," he said, sliding those fingers inside of me. He leaned forward, burying his face into me without pretense.

My back arched, my breasts shoving high toward the ceiling as he devoured me. A low keening sound filled the room, and it took me far too long to realize it came from me. He fucked me with those fingers so relentlessly as he licked my clit, I was rushing toward the precipice of an orgasm immediately.

"Caelum," I gasped, thrusting a hand into his hair and holding onto him. My hips moved, rising and falling with the motions of his tongue, riding his face as he brought me to pleasure. He nipped at the flesh around the bundle of nerves that he owned, making the skin sting for just a moment before he groaned into me.

My orgasm came like a siege, stealing the breath from my lungs and taking everything from me. All conscious thought was gone as my legs tightened around his head, a scream tearing from my throat as he sucked at my clit and made my climax seem to last forever.

"*Mine*," he growled, pulling his face out of my pussy. His golden skin gleamed with my essence, his lips flushed and swollen as he reached rough hands beneath my ass and flipped me in place. My breasts rubbed against the rock as he grasped me around the hips, his fingers digging into my skin in a way that I knew would bruise, had my body not healed faster.

He lifted me off the stone and pulled me toward him, barely allowing my front to touch the stone as my legs slid back into the water. Lower and lower he pulled me, positioning me as he went so that his cock pressed against my entrance.

He left me there, hanging suspended from the ledge with only his hands on my hips to support my weight. He curled his chest over my back, finding my ear with his mouth. "This is the part where you should be afraid, my star."

I turned to look at him over my shoulder, our eyes connecting for just a brief moment before he thrust forward sharply and pulled my body down at the same time. He impaled me on his cock, filling me so suddenly that I screamed, hanging my head forward.

There was no slow adjustment like he'd given me the night before, just sharp thrusts of his hips as he forced my body to part for him.

I clung to the ledge, grappling for purchase along the rocks as my body jolted with every one of his drives inside me. "Fucking Gods!" I whimpered, my body squeezed between him and the rock at the edge of the pool. He pressed me flush against it with his brutality, his hands at my hips tipping my ass back to let him get deeper.

Driving between my slightly spread thighs, he fucked me into the wall. One of his hands left my hip, raised to gather my hair in a fist and tip my head to the side and back, so that he could lean in and lick a path up the Mark on my neck and flaunt the bite mark he'd given me there.

"Do you see them watching you?" he asked, murmuring in my ear with a soft, mocking voice that tormented me. His cock stroked in and out of me, battering at my pussy with speed that seemed inhuman.

Uncontrolled. Wild.

I glanced around what little I could, forcing my attention to focus on the people loitering around the room. "Yes," I whispered hoarsely, unable to force more sound from my throat. It felt scraped raw, as if I'd been screaming for hours and hadn't even noticed.

"Tonight, when we're in bed and I've got my cock between your legs again, they'll be lying in their bed, jerking their cocks to the memory of me fucking you. They'll be wishing they were able to make you scream the way I do, and do you know what I'll do?" he asked, punctuating the words with a sharp drive against the end of me. "I'll fill you with so much of my cum that they can smell it on you tomorrow and remember exactly who you belong to."

I gasped as he shifted the hand that held me around my waist toward my clit, stroking the swollen flesh until I whimpered in his arms, "Gods."

"If I'm a God, then you have to give me a gift. Those are the rules," he said, teasing as he moved more slowly inside me. His strokes were still rough, battering hard enough he would likely bruise me, but he moved slowly, giving my body time to build toward a second orgasm that might make me forget my own name. "Do you know what I want?"

I couldn't form the words to give him a response, couldn't shift my focus off the heat building inside of me.

"I want you to come. I want you to clench that tight little pussy around my cock and milk the cum from my balls until it's dripping down your thighs. That's the only gift I want," he said, pinching the sensitive skin of my clit and rolling it between his fingers.

I came, my body twitching in his arms as my throat clenched around a silent scream. Caelum groaned, shoving deep inside of me and letting my orgasm do its job, giving him the gift he'd asked for. Heat filled me as he followed me into bliss, his release coating my insides as he brushed a gentle kiss against my cheekbone.

I swallowed, trying to catch my breath. My eyes stayed closed, pushing away the reality of our audience that would make me undoubtedly regret what I'd allowed to happen, and then reveled in.

Caelum seemed to sense that I needed to retreat, as, in the wake of my orgasm, the eyes watching me were too much. "Come, my star," Caelum murmured, pulling out of me and drawing away. I followed at his heels, keeping my eyes down as I strode up the steps from the bath.

People stared and a woman handed me a towel but kept her eyes averted from where Caelum's cock hung down his thigh.

She nodded to me as she helped me wrap the cloth around my

body. Caelum stared intently at the inside of my thighs and the mix of water and cum that dripped down my skin until it disappeared from view. He wrapped another towel around his waist, hiding himself from view.

"I'll have a spare set of clothes brought to your room for each of you," the woman said, smiling kindly. She was the same one who'd handed me soap when we came in covered in blood. "Go on then. Let the rest of us deal with the storm you've created," she said with a smile, stepping away from me and walking toward one of the men in the room.

He caught her by the waist, bunching the fabric of her dress and tearing it off over her head.

We left, the first sounds of the woman's moans coming from behind us, accompanied by male grunts of pleasure.

32

I backed off the bedroll. Sleep evaded me, driving me to shove my feet into my boots and wrap the spare blanket around my shoulders. The dress the woman from the baths had sent was more revealing than I was used to, designed for the humid temperatures within the caves. Thin straps hung off my shoulders, leaving my arms and a line of cleavage revealed.

It wouldn't have bothered me under normal circumstances, but I still struggled to cope with the feeling of eyes on me while Caelum had pushed me up onto the ledge for everyone to see. I'd agreed to it, been turned on by it, but the shyness that came in the aftermath was very real.

I pulled back the curtain that gave our room a hint of privacy, but had done nothing to keep in the noises when Caelum woke me in the middle of the night, pressing his cock between my legs and murmuring in my ear.

I didn't have much experience, but I wasn't certain that his level of insatiability was normal. Combining that with his almost feral nature after his fight with the cave beast left me curious about the ways being marked by the Fae could change us.

Did we become more like them in ways other than just our

strength? Our healing? The frenzy that drove him to spend every moment inside of me?

I walked through the tunnels, grabbing a torch from the commons and lighting it on my way to the library that consumed so much of my waking time. The books, even while they hurt my hand, had become a welcome respite.

Knowledge was power, and I wanted to have every opportunity to fight. I trained with Melian and the other fighters in the mornings, but Caelum was very rarely an active part of that. After he'd survived a cave beast, there could be no doubt that he'd pulled his punches where I was concerned, just as Melian had said.

It touched me and made me angry all at once, but he hadn't hesitated to unleash his violence on me during sex. To claim me so fully I could still feel the ache of him inside me hours later.

I entered the library, setting my torch on the wall next to the table where I worked. The book I'd been translating the day before sat open where I'd left it when Caelum and I hurried out of the room after the altercation with Jensen.

I didn't know what I wanted to research or where to even begin, but nausea churned in my gut, telling me there was something wrong. I moved to the shelves, running my fingers along the spines and waiting for one to jump out at me. It was how I'd chosen the first books I translated, randomly diving into them one at a time.

A less-weathered book called my attention, beckoning me to pull it off the shelf. I stared down at the name on the front, the words written in the New Tongue.

A Historical Account of the Creation of the Veil.

It wasn't the same text I'd seen in Lord Byron's library; this one was far older. I flipped to the front page of the handwritten tome, skimming through the words in an effort to convince myself that this was simply the original version of what had become common knowledge.

When I delved into it, though, the tale this book painted of the witches who'd formed the Veil was vastly different from the one I'd learned as a child. I'd always been told the witches sacrificed their lives to form the Veil so they could protect humanity from the Fae, who slaughtered us in droves.

This told the story of the witches who were neutral to the war between the Fae and the humans, indifferent to either race in their quest to maintain the balance of the world. It told of the curse they'd placed upon the Fae centuries before the Veil, dooming them to having their souls split upon birth. The mirror of themselves would exist inside another person, most often a human, so the Fae would have a reason to stop the enslavement and torment of the humans of the Kingdom of Nothrek.

Children outside of that relationship were an impossibility, further limiting their opportunity to grow their numbers. Birth within the relationship was rare itself, a natural characteristic of their race.

But one line of witches was tied to the land of Faerie, their magic drawn from the soil itself and the elements of nature around them. Those were the witches who'd cast the curse upon the Fae in name of the Primordial of Nature. They had died out quickly after they erected the Veil, because their magic faded without the connection to the land of Alfheimr.

It left me with one single question, something that I couldn't reconcile and just didn't make sense.

Why would that line of witches have formed the Veil at all, knowing they would be trapped on the opposite side from their magic? The book recorded it as a great sacrifice they'd made to protect something they'd stolen from the Court of Shadows. But it made no mention of what it was they'd stolen, or why a neutral party would care so much for the object.

The story I'd always known was that the witches had sided with the humans in the war and sacrificed themselves to form the Veil so that we could have a chance to survive the Fae beasts who wanted to kill us. I'd seen horrific photos of them in the history books as a child, but none of the drawings in the *Book of the Gods* even remotely resembled the horrors in those books.

The Fae in the *Book of the Gods* were breathtakingly beautiful. They were ethereal and magnetic. They were everything the monsters were not.

A thought danced just out of my reach, a nagging image that I couldn't capture tickling at my mind.

A memory from my childhood. A moment of teeth on my skin.

"What are you hoping to find in these dusty old books?" Caelum asked, making me spin to face him.

I pressed a hand to my chest as I startled. "You scared me."

He tilted his head to the side, coming into the space and stopping beside my chair. Touching the backs of his fingers to my cheek, he searched my face for a moment before he smiled. "You scared me when you were gone from our bed."

The knowledge that the bed that was ours, after our irrevocable claiming of it, washed over me and filled me with warmth despite the chill to my skin.

"I couldn't sleep," I admitted, shifting my legs. I couldn't bring myself to admit that I felt there was something off about us and our relationship; something nagging at me that I couldn't explain. "I may not be able to fight a cave beast like you, but knowledge is power. Maybe if I know more about what I'm up against, I'll be able to protect myself better."

"That's why you have me," he said, running a thumb over my bottom lip, then, "I was too rough with you." He cast a pointed glance down to my lap where I couldn't seem to stay still.

"No," I said, shaking my head. He lifted a skeptical brow. "Maybe a little, but you did warn me."

"I did, but fucking you two more times in the night was unkind to your poor pussy," he said, using that thumb to drag my lip to the side. "I can't seem to get enough of you. Sometimes I forget how new you are to taking my cock, my star." I swallowed, my mouth opening to speak. The tip of his thumb sank inside, pressing down on my tongue pointedly. "I'll have to make use of this part of you as well. Will you wrap your lips around my cock for me while I torment your pussy? Will you sit on my face and suck me off when you just can't take me in your cunt anymore?"

"Gods, the things you say," I said, pulling my head back from his thumb. He smirked down at me, enjoying the flush that stained my cheeks.

"I want to worship you like you're my Goddess. I want to spend my days between your legs, making you come so many times you can't stand up when I'm through with you," he murmured, that smirk transforming into a full-blown smile as he stared down at me. "But I want to fuck your mouth and shove my cock down your throat, too." He shrugged, as if the filthy talk was just a part of who he was and I needed to get used to it.

I'd thought he tormented me and teased me before he'd ever touched me, but I was quickly learning that his innuendos had been vague and nothing compared to the things he said while I writhed beneath him on our bed.

"I'm sorry to interrupt," Melian said from the doorway, suppressing a smile as she stepped into the space.

Caelum hung his head, muttering as he dropped his hand to his side and his mouth twisted into a pout. "No, you're not," he grunted.

"I'm pleased to see you making good use of the books, Estrella. It's very helpful for future generations," she said, smiling at me briefly before she turned her attention to Caelum. "But I'm actually looking for you, for once."

The two of them clearly still disliked each other. I rolled my eyes, turning my attention back to my book.

"What do you need?" Caelum asked, crossing his arms over his chest. Despite my presence in the library, it was the middle of the night. I doubted she would have hunted him down for anything that wasn't important, and Caelum seemed to reach the same conclusion.

"We received word of a group of Fae Marked hiding in Calfalls. I'm leading a team to retrieve them at first light. We could use your skill with a sword in case we run into trouble," Melian said, nodding her head at Caelum. The uneasy alliance between them was based entirely on his skill and the abilities he had that might make her team more likely to survive.

"I'll go," he said, turning to me. "You will stay here and stay out of trouble."

"Like fuck I will," I snapped, standing from the chair. "You promised that we would stay together. You can't spew those words at me when it's convenient and then keep me tucked away like a fragile princess when it suits you. We're either together in all things, or we're not, Caelum. Which one is it going to be?" I asked, crossing my arms over my chest.

"You're safer here. What if the Mist Guard caught you in irons?" Caelum asked, staring down at me as if he could compel me to see reason. To just listen.

Fuck that.

"And what if they catch you? We go together, or we aren't together at all," I said, letting the words hang between us.

He didn't miss the meaning, all too aware of the fact that he'd be leaving me in a bunker full of men. "Fine," he growled finally, clenching his jaw. "But you do what I say."

"Good luck with that," I said, smiling at him as I patted his arm and made for the door. Melian chuckled as I moved past her, her amusement bringing a smile to my face that I didn't allow Caelum to see.

If we were leaving at first light, I needed to get some sleep.

Melian came for me as promised. The tunnels made it impossible to tell what was morning and what was the dead of night, always bathed in darkness and cloaked in the shadows thrown by the torches twinkling on the wall. The other fighters had swept Caelum off much the same way, taking him to the armory to equip him for the rescue mission I suspected none of us were prepared for.

I'd heard whispers in passing of other missions to rescue Fae

Marked, who were in danger of either discovery by the Mist Guard or the Wild Hunt tracking down the mates to bring back to Alfheimr.

She brought me to her private rooms, where I eyed the wooden clothes dresser pressed against the wall, a remnant of a life of luxury I'd never known. I suspected it was probably out of her understanding that I'd only owned two dresses, at most, at any given time. She pulled a pair of black pants from the drawer, tossing them to me.

I caught the bundle against my chest, turning my stare down to the gauzy, light dress they'd given me to wear in the heat of the tunnels. "Have you ever worn pants before?" she asked, smiling at me from across the room, as if I was entertaining. A thick, black tunic followed, and I turned to set the clothing on the bed before I shoved the straps of my dress off my shoulders.

I gave her my back as I dealt with the twinge of discomfort I felt over being naked in front of another person, but after the display Caelum and I had put on the night before, it hardly seemed worthwhile to ask for privacy.

Her sharp intake of breath came the moment she saw my scars, and I glanced over my shoulder at her briefly before I stripped off my boots and shoved my legs into the thick, wool-lined leather pants she'd given me. "I've worn leggings beneath my dress," I said, hurrying to arrange the fabric of the tunic so that I could pull it on over my head.

"What happened?" she asked, her fingertips brushing against the sensitive skin of my scars ever so slightly. They barely touched my skin; it was the echo of a different person near them making me arch away from her touch reflexively.

"I will not be owned. Never again," I told her, shrugging the tunic on finally. The heavy linen settled around my breasts and hung down to the middle of my thighs, giving me plenty of room to maneuver while still not making me stand out too much outside the tunnels.

I turned, meeting her eyes as she stared at me with a pity-filled gaze. "Never again," she said, swallowing as she dropped her hand to her side. She walked to the dresser and pulled open the top drawer to remove a small vial of purple serum. The glass was clear, the cork stopper at the top seeming ominous as she reached out and took one of my hands in hers. She pressed it into my hand, holding it for a moment. "Belladonna serum," she said, answering my unvoiced question.

I knew looking at the vial that it was enough to be a lethal dose. "Does this even work on us now?" I asked, huffing a laugh as I tried not to think about the ways I could commit suicide if I needed to. It had been the plan to die alongside Brann; how unfortunate it would be to make it this far just to end up the same.

"So long as you take it before they get you back to Alfheimr and complete the bond, it will end this life for you. It won't stop you from reincarnating into your next one, but perhaps in that one you'll stand a chance of being free," she said, releasing my hand and stepping back. She was already dressed warmly, swinging her heavy black cloak over her shoulders and pulling up the hood as I donned the warm socks she tossed my way and shoved my feet back into my boots.

She grabbed a spare cloak off the back of a chair in her room, stepping forward to help me arrange it around my shoulders and pull up the hood. When that was finished, she moved to the weapons on one side of her room. Grasping a dagger and strap, she handed them to me so I could buckle the leather around my thigh. I sighed with pleasure the moment I had the weapon, knowing I wouldn't be entirely defenseless as we ventured out into the dangers I'd been so happy to escape only days prior.

It seemed impossible how little time had passed, and yet everything had changed.

"I would give you a sword, but I think you're far more capable with that," she said, strapping her sword and scabbard to her waist.

"I am. Thank you," I said, tucking the vial of belladonna serum into the pocket of my cloak. Another reassurance—another thing I shouldn't want to have. It said something about how vile this world was, when having a way to end my life was considered a blessing.

"Promise me you'll be careful," she said, meeting my eyes earnestly. "I know your Caelum will do his best to protect you, but you are far more valuable to me here with the books. It goes against everything in my nature to allow you to accompany us today, but I feel as if I am left with no choice. You were quite determined to join us."

"I still am," I said, holding true to what I'd said to Caelum. He wanted us to live together, to die together, to stay together. I'd hold to that promise, because everything I wanted in this life was with him now, anyway.

"Stubborn," she said, shaking her head in amusement. "Come. Imelda will ward each of us against our mates before we go. It buys us four days before we need to worry. That's plenty of time to get to Calfalls and back, assuming we don't run into any trouble along the way."

I nodded, grateful at least for that one assurance. "What about the Mist Guard and the Wild Hunt?" I asked, watching as she shook her head and led the way from her chambers.

"The Mist Guard we kill, but if we encounter the Wild Hunt, the only thing you do is run. None of us stand a chance against them." That elusive thought danced through me again, the reminder that the Hunt was one more thing Caelum had survived that was supposed to be impossible.

All because they'd been looking for me.

I did the only thing I could do in the face of that, protecting the secret of their interest specifically in me that even I didn't understand.

I kept my fucking mouth shut.

33

The cold sank into my bones despite the warm clothes designed to protect me from it. After spending days in the humid warmth of the tunnels, I didn't know if I would ever be able to tolerate the cold again in the same way. I'd spent my entire life being well-acquainted with the winter and never having enough warmth, but there was something about it now that reached inside me much more easily, as if that cold hollow at my center called to the wind itself.

We'd been walking all day, first in the labyrinth of narrow tunnels that extended through the entirety of the Hollow Mountains. They weren't the same as the tunnels within the Resistance camp itself, but far smaller and more suffocating. Only wide enough for us to walk in a single-file line, the walls pressed in on us as we passed through. I'd taken in a deep, shuddering breath of frosty air the moment we'd emerged into the sun, more grateful than I could explain for the space at my sides and above my head.

We'd emerged on the other side of the Hollows from where Caelum and I had traveled, the deep chasm of the strait between the Main Continent and the Isle of Ruin at our side. The pathway between the mountain range and the rapidly flowing body of water that stretched on and on left just enough space for us to walk comfortably, without fear of slipping on the snow-covered ground. It was only a dusting, the first hint of the coming cold season that lay atop the grass, but it was enough that we would leave footprints for any who found themselves on the mostly abandoned side of the Hollows.

Caelum walked ahead of me with some of Melian's personal team, discussing strategy about infiltrating the city. I followed behind at a slower pace with Melian at my side, trying not to walk funny from the unfamiliar feeling of pants covering my legs.

"There's something off about this Caelum of yours," she said, knocking into my shoulder with hers as the front row of men walked further ahead. There were still guards of Melian's at our back, protecting their leader from all threats as the others led Caelum away from whatever she needed to say to me. As if they'd prepared for the conversation she knew we needed to have.

In the time since coming to the Resistance, I'd had a few moments where I'd bonded with Melian despite Caelum's protests. She was blunt to a fault, but I found I appreciated the fact that she didn't play games. I always knew where she stood on an issue, for better or worse, and while I didn't always agree with her stance, I could respect it was one she'd taken for the safety of everyone she was responsible for.

"I'm sure that has nothing to do with the fact that you know we've been intimate, and that I've not taken any of your men to my bed, despite your warnings about getting too attached," I said, turning a saccharine smile her way.

She snorted, huffing back a laugh as she lifted a hand and flicked me on the nose. "Such a smart tongue. It will get you into trouble one of these days."

"It already has," I laughed.

"But I am serious, Estrella. I don't trust him, and I'm not certain you should either," she said pointedly, watching as Caelum guided one of her men through a move he used often in their sparring sessions, continuing to walk as he did it with a coordination I envied.

"You don't have to, because I do. He sacrificed himself to save me multiple times. How could I not trust him after that?" I asked.

"Have you ever known a man who could single handedly destroy a cave beast? You didn't see the carnage after that fight, but I did. There was nothing left, Estrella. He reduced the creature to strips of meat not even fit for a stew," she argued.

A cool wind kissed my cheeks as we strolled through a break in the tree line. We wouldn't arrive in Calfalls until the next day, and the prospect of enduring another one of her lectures sounded more exhausting than trekking through Nothrek itself.

"His *Viniculum* protected him, and he's gifted with a sword. Those are hardly crimes, and you don't seem hesitant to use them to your advantage when it suits you. Otherwise, we wouldn't be out here accompanying you to Calfalls," I said, glancing over at her. "If you don't trust him so much, why did you bring us?"

"Better to keep an eye on him myself than leave him with my people," she said, kicking the snow with her boots as she walked. "If anyone should suffer the consequences of trusting the wrong man and allowing him into our midst, it should be the ones who made the choice in the first place. It should be you and I."

I reached out, gathering a clump of snow off the stone side of the mountain. It melted against the fabric of the gloves Melian had lent me, the unique flakes disappearing quickly. "What is it that you think he's going to do exactly? Kill me? He's had hundreds of opportunities. Give me to the Mist Guard? He could have easily done that before we arrived at the mountains. There is no other purpose or ulterior motive. He just wants to be with me. Is that really so hard to believe?" I asked, letting a rare moment of vulnerability shine through.

Her face softened for a moment of understanding as she shook her head. "It isn't hard to believe at all that he would want to be with you. That isn't what drives my concern. I only worry that you're so blinded by your feelings for him you aren't thinking clearly. I can't help but think you're keeping things from me to protect him," she said, reminding me of the information that I had, actually, kept from her. Caelum had said he'd escaped the Wild Hunt because of their desire to find me. Whether or not that was true, I couldn't say, but surely nothing good would come of admitting it to her.

She would either condemn him for doing the impossible or kick us out because of the potential danger I posed to them.

"What could I possibly be keeping from you? I don't understand what you think there is to know about him that matters," I said, my exasperation leaking through my voice. Whatever secrets he kept about his twisted childhood aside, what could possibly be important enough that Melian thought it meant she couldn't trust him.

"Then tell me about him," she said, pursing her lips as she pierced me with an intense stare. "What town was his home before the Veil fell? What's his family name?"

I paused, heat tinting my cheeks red when I couldn't answer either of those questions. "He's the bastard son of a member of the nobility," I said, providing the only information I had.

"What line of nobility?" she asked, crossing her arms over her chest. She saw the weakness she'd exploited, realizing how little I truly knew of the man I'd taken as my lover. "You don't know even that?"

"He doesn't like to talk about his family," I said, rubbing a hand over my face. That much was true. I'd seen the melancholy on his face when I tried to pry into his life with his family.

"He is feeding you vague bits of information to keep you satisfied, without ever providing anything of use for identifying him. If that doesn't tell you there's something off about him, then I don't know what will," she said.

"What? What could possibly be so wrong with him that we need to worry about our safety? He's not Fae," I snapped.

"He could be working with the Mist Guard," she said, eyeing the swords strapped across his shoulders.

"He would have killed me long before we reached the Hollows if that was the case," I said, my disbelieving chuckle hanging between us. "I've had the misfortune of encountering them a few times. They don't generally let the Fae Marked just walk away."

"What if the Mist Guard somehow heard of our existence? They would know that we wouldn't turn away a Fae Marked person in need of refuge, or at least they'd suspect it. He could have bargained for his own life, promising to help them find more of us. People will do anything to save their own skin, Estrella," she said, the words such an echo of Brann's concerns about Caelum that my heart stalled in my chest.

"He's not working with the Mist Guard," I said, feeling the truth of my words in my soul, despite the pain that lanced through me at the thought.

"So stubborn. I just hope it isn't the death of us all," she said, shaking her head to signal the conversation was over as Caelum glanced back over his shoulder at us. He leveled a look that did nothing to ease her distrust, something in his eyes twinkling knowingly.

He was far enough away that it was impossible he'd heard her.

Right?

In the dark of night, Jensen dropped down from the thick branch of the tree, landing on the snow-covered ground and bending at the knees to absorb the shock. "The meadow is crawling with members of the Mist Guard," he said, rising to full height. He only spared a moment to glare at me before turning his attention to Melian. She raised her brow at him, conveying that she would deal with him personally if he didn't pretend I no longer existed.

"We'll have to go through the city to get to the tunnel in the tree line on the other side, so we can make our way to Calfalls," she said, her chest heaving with a disgruntled sigh. "This was far easier before the Veil fell, when we were just raiding the deliveries sent from the Royal Guard."

"What do you mean we'll have to go through the city?" Caelum asked, glaring at the stronghold on the other side of the strait. "It has to be crawling with Mist Guard."

"We can't take the bridges across the strait for obvious reasons. That leaves us with no choice but to cross here, because the flow of water isn't so strong that we'll be swept away with the current. With the Mist

Guard surrounding the city walls, we won't make it around the perimeter. What else would you propose we do in this situation?" she asked, returning his glare with one of her own.

The two of them would be the death of me.

"Turn back. We are of no good to anyone if we're dead ourselves," Caelum answered, earning a sharp gasp from me. He was always so focused on our safety and protecting us from the things hunting us down, sometimes it was easy to forget that he did not extend that kindness to others.

"You would leave half a dozen Fae Marked to die, in order to save yourself?" Jensen asked, the steel of his voice putting me on edge.

"No," Caelum said, turning to the man he wanted to bleed with a fierce glower that made even me wither on the spot. "But I would do it to save *her.*" All eyes turned to me, waiting for my response. I wanted to condemn Caelum for being willing to sacrifice so many for my sake, but there was something about being the most important person in his world that rendered me unable to voice the words.

His willingness to leave them to die was wrong. It spoke of something lacking within him, that he didn't care enough to save them, but he didn't do it out of heartlessness.

He did it because he loved me. Because my life was all that mattered.

"I don't want to leave them," I murmured, keeping my face gentle as I stared back at Caelum and silently begged for him to understand. Those people were like me. They were what might have become of me, if he hadn't found me and saved me.

They needed a Caelum to protect them, and for once in my life, I wanted to be a part of something bigger. I wanted to be one of the ones helping instead of the person who needed rescued.

Caelum clenched his jaw tight, the frustration bringing out his chiseled square jawline. "If you get hurt..." His narrowed gaze and the fury rolling off of him were just as threatening as any words he could have uttered.

He would blame any and everyone involved, whether it was Melian or the Mist Guard. I wouldn't want to be on the other side of that wrath.

He closed the distance between us, laying a hand on the side of my neck. His thumb tipped my head up, uncaring of the audience of four, who watched us intently.

"You will not do anything foolish or put yourself at risk. Do you understand me?" I narrowed my eyes, attempting to tear my neck away from his grip, but he followed.

His eyes flashed with warning, as if pushing him too hard on this would be a fatal mistake. "Caelum," I said, my voice dropping into a low warning of my own in response.

"You will do as I tell you to do, or I will drag you back to the tunnels, even if I have to carry you," he said, crowding his body into mine as he towered over me. "And if you growl at me again, I can tell you *exactly* what we'll be doing the moment we get there."

I swallowed past the desire his low threat created, my throat dry as I forced myself to concede. "Fine." In addition to the Fae Marked hiding in Calfalls, my curiosity about the legendary Ruined City itself served to drive me forward. The destruction caused by the God of the Dead during the war had been the perfect cautionary tale to make us fear the Fae.

"I don't have good feelings about his resolve to get the lot of us through Tradesholde alive," Jensen said with a grimace, turning away from us as if he couldn't stand to watch the display any longer. Melian's personal guards, Beck and Duncan, followed after him in stoic silence, grabbing the pile of brush that disguised a boat tied to a tree by the shoreline.

"Get in if you're coming; turn back if you're not, but stay out of my way," Melian barked at Caelum as the three men turned it around and held it steady at the shore. She climbed into the large rowboat, taking the front seat and looking out over the strait.

"Shouldn't we at least wait for daylight?" I asked.

"Until we have the cover of trees, moving at night is better. We'll find a place to sleep for the night on the other side of Tradesholde," Beck answered, climbing in after Melian. I followed after him, moving to the middle seat with Caelum at my side. Jensen and Duncan took up the rear, pushing the boat off the shoreline as they hurried to scramble inside. Melian passed back oars, handing one to Caelum and Jensen respectively so the two men could paddle on opposite sides.

The current threatened to sweep us away, even in the place where the strait widened and it became less forceful. I wrapped my fingers around the edge of the boat, looking over the side into the dark waters beneath us.

It was as if there was no bottom, and it plunged into a chasm that connected to the home of tortured souls who displeased The Father and The Mother. The bridge across the strait wasn't far enough away to leave me with any sense of comfort, knowing that one strong current would be all it took to expose us to the Mist Guard waiting downstream.

The walled city on the other side of the strait was bigger than anything I'd ever seen, jutting up out of the barren landscape with gleaming torches to light the stone. It made the Mist Guard fortress at home seem like a playhouse, and it wasn't even the capitol.

We hurried out of the boat the moment we touched the shore on the other side, the men rushing to cover it with brambles to the side of the beach area. Jensen swore as one caught the skin of his wrist, drawing it into his mouth to stem the flow of blood before he could leave a red stain on the snow.

"Let's go!" Melian whispered, taking my forearm in her grip. She pulled me toward the stone wall of the city, shoving a moss-covered stone out of the way to reveal a narrow passage. We stepped inside the darkened tunnel, the walls oppressive as the men followed behind us and pulled the cover closed to disguise the entrance.

"How do you know about this?" I asked, keeping my voice quiet.

"Cover your marks," she said, urging Caelum, Jensen, and I to pull our hoods tighter about our necks as she did the same. Beck and Duncan weren't Fae Marked, and far more able to pass any inspection the Mist Guard might make if we were caught. "The Ladies of the Night might not be treated well above the surface, but they see everything. The Lord of Tradesholde likes opium, and this is one of the ways he sneaks it into the city."

Lord Byron had done the opposite, allowing his companions to enter through the front door and pass by his wife in the sitting room as they went to service him. I was his only dirty secret; the only one he bothered to hide.

It made sense, as he couldn't have married me if the High Priest thought he'd already played with me.

Caelum wrapped his arm around my back supportively, ducking low to keep from hitting his head on the roof of the low tunnel carved into the very foundation of the city. Water streamed through it, serving as a drain for the streets inside the city, trickling over the rock base as we slowly made our way through. With Melian at the lead and her men taking up the rear behind us, I kept my hand near the dagger strapped to my thigh, ready to draw it at the first sign of a fight.

Melian turned back when she reached the end of the tunnel, her gaze landing on each of us momentarily before she spoke softly. "The tunnel to exit Tradesholde is by the stables on the other side. If we're separated, look for a stone cover carved with poppies on the right edge. It's another way they deliver the Lord his opium supply."

Beck and Duncan squeezed past us and stepped up beside her, shoving their shoulders into the cover in front of the entrance to the city. It slid to the side, slowly opening to reveal the quiet street of a city at night. Cobblestone lined the walkway at his feet as Duncan stepped out, looking around carefully before he waved a hand and summoned Melian and Beck to follow. Jensen followed in a hurry, not wasting any time with us. "Move," he ordered, starting to heave the cover closed as Caelum and I emerged into the darkened city. Melian nodded once before she and the other men darted off, hurrying through the city as if they knew the way well.

"You stay with me," Caelum growled as we tried to follow, his voice dropping low in a commanding reminder.

Melian's concerns nagged at the back of my mind, joining with the questions I'd asked myself the night before, which had driven me to the library for more information. Despite my assurances to Melian, I couldn't help but wonder about the man at my side. How he'd come to find me, why he'd cared enough to follow me that night the Wild Hunt attacked Brann and I, and how he'd come to know about the Resistance.

I looked up at Caelum, finding his gaze heavy on my face as he studied me intently. He took my hand as he pulled me through the streets, navigating as though he expected something to jump out and attack at any moment. Even so, suspicion still lurked in his eyes, as if he could see through my assurances and knew the doubt I'd warred with since he killed the cave beast.

Something had changed in our relationship in that moment, and Caelum damn well knew it.

"Is there something you want to talk about, my star?" Caelum asked, tilting his head to the side as he drew in a breath.

"Just nervous," I lied, feeling the need to protect my thoughts from him. I couldn't say what Caelum would do if he discovered I'd wondered about his intentions and his obsession with me, but whatever it was, I didn't think it would be good, and the walls closed in around me some more.

"You could have stayed in the safety of the Resistance," he remarked, tugging me around a corner as Melian and the others melted into one of the alleyways in the distance. "You'd be warm and comfortable there, waiting for me to wake you up with my cock."

"Is that all you care about now? I am more than just something for you to fuck," I said, my voice dropping low. I loved his innuendos and his desire for me, but in the moments when I had to wonder about the intensity of our relationship, the last thing I wanted was to feel as if I didn't matter beyond the hole between my legs.

He stopped in the middle of the alleyway, looking down to glare at me in warning. "Trust me when I tell you that I know exactly what you're worth, Little One. I know exactly how irreplaceable you are. That is why I would much rather see you waiting back in the tunnels, safe and sound where nothing can take you away from me," he said, leaning forward to touch his lips to my forehead in a tender moment.

I tried to shrug off Melian's concerns and the way they'd melded with mine, creating a symphony of worry inside of me that I couldn't seem to shake. I sensed that I was dancing on the edge of something, missing what was right in front of my face.

"I don't know what I've done to make you mistake me for a woman of leisure, Caelum, but I most certainly am not," I said primly as my lips curved up, watching as his brow smoothed in the face of my sudden sass and the dissipation of the tension from a moment before.

"Not yet, anyway. I'd very much like to see you live a comfortable life one day," he said, stepping up to the corner of an alley. He peeked around it, guiding me out onto the main street as we followed the shadows of Melian and her men in the distance. He walked at my back as I crossed the open space, hugging the shadows outside the circles of torchlight. I drew my dagger from its sheath and clutched it in my hand, taking comfort in the small blade that drew less attention than a sword would have.

Every set of eyes that fell on me from the windows of the homes lining the street felt like they would sound the alarm, like they would turn us in out of fear they might suffer the consequences of our freedom. We ducked into another narrow cross street, leaving me to breathe a sigh of relief at being less exposed.

"Are we going to talk about what you're keeping from me?" Caelum whispered, his voice hushed as he walked at my back. I inhaled raggedly, the chilly air filling my lungs as I didn't dare to look back at him.

"I'm not keeping anything from you," I said, as I glanced toward a darkened corner of the alley and felt the sweet relief of nothing staring back at me.

We came to the mouth of the crossroad, Caelum pressing his spine into the wall at his back as he chanced a glance out into another main road. He raised two fingers, signaling me to hurry across the cobblestone roadway and into the alley on the opposite side. Once there, I waited, watching as Caelum ducked low and hurried to catch up behind me.

"If you aren't keeping anything from me, then why do you sometimes act as if you've seen a ghost when you look at me, my star? Did I somehow become your enemy in the last two days?" he asked, walking at my side as we traveled down the darkened pathway between the main streets.

"Why would you be my enemy, Caelum? We're on the same side."

"Are we?" he asked, staring at me as I searched for any sign of Melian and the others. "The only side I'm on is the one that keeps you safe and mine. Beyond that, I couldn't care less what happens to this world, no matter what you think that says about me."

"You don't care at all about saving the other Marked?" I asked, stopping in my tracks. I understood wanting me to stay safe, but to not care at all was brutal.

"I only care about you," he reiterated. "I only came on this mission because I knew you would want me to. These people matter to you, so I'll do my part. But I only do it out of loyalty to *you*, Little One. Not the Resistance."

"They're like us. How can you not want to help them?" I asked, forcing my feet to keep moving, because staying in one place would be too risky.

"Do you think us being like them would stop them from throwing us to the Mist Guard if it meant saving their own skins? Loyalty isn't worth having if it doesn't extend both ways," he said, raising an eyebrow at me as if he could feel the way my thoughts had wandered since the cave beast. As if he could feel me pulling away from him, questioning him.

"Does that go for honesty as well?" I asked, swallowing past my nerves to act as he grabbed me by the front of the throat. He pressed me into the wall, letting the stone surface catch me.

I reached up, pressing the pointy end of my dagger to his throat as he grinned down at me. "That depends. There are some truths a person may not be ready to hear. Some omissions or lies are told for your protection. That goes for many things, my star," he said, leaning into the sharp point until it broke the skin and a thin trail of blood dripped down his neck. "Like trust, but your tendency to put your knife to my throat would have me believe you do not trust me. Am I to understand I shouldn't trust you in return?"

"How did you kill the cave beast, Caelum?" I asked, clinging to the event that had brought all the questions to my mind.

"Would you have rather I died?" he asked, his voice pained.

"Of course not! I just want to understand *how*. What is your *Viniculum's* power that you could reduce the creature to nothing?"

"I see Melian has been talking again," he sighed, shaking his head and seeming not to care about the way my blade scratched his skin. "I should've known she was the cause of your distance."

"Is it not true?"

"It's true. Our *Viniculum* is the same," he said, touching a hand to the top of the white and black swirling lines on my neck. "That means we have the same magic flowing through us. I am not capable of anything that you aren't, Little One."

"My magic turned a man to snow," I argued, snorting a laugh. "Not into a puddle of flesh and bone."

"White is for the Winter Court." He trailed a finger over the white line on his own neck, drawing my attention to the swirling line as it seemed to glow lightly in response to his touch. "Black is for the Shadow Court. It means our Fae have a parent from each Court, with both types of magic flowing through them. You seem to have a tendency toward the Winter side of your *Viniculum,* but I stray toward the Shadows and they control the most violent kinds of magic. So yes, Little One, I reduced a cave beast to a pile of flesh and bone, *because he threatened you.*"

I hadn't thought the *Viniculum* worked like that, but even with it threatening me, Caelum had also needed to fight for his life.

It made enough sense to push back the worst of my questions, but something still remained, pressing at me though I couldn't name it.

I dropped my forehead to his chest, the press of his hand still at the front of my throat reminding me of how much everything had shifted in such a short time. Pulling my dagger away from his throat, I sighed. "I'm sorry."

"Don't let them turn you against me. They don't do it for your benefit, but theirs. I will always have your best interest at heart, Estrella," he said, releasing my throat in favor of cupping the back of my head.

"Why?"

"Because I love you. Because I will always love you. It is as simple as that."

"As touching as this moment is, I feel the need to point out how inconceivably impossible that will be," a male said, stepping into the mouth of the alleyway.

His face was angular, free from blemish, and his eyes glowed amber in the night. His body was thinner than I'd expected after studying the drawings of the Gods, but there was no question what he was when the pointed tips of his ears showed in the torchlight.

Fae.

34

We'd known the Mist Guard had a presence in Tradesholde, but I'd never guessed the Fae might be lurking in the shadows themselves, undetected by the guards trained to kill them with their iron weapons.

Caelum shoved me behind himself, drawing a sword from the scabbard on his back, but the Fae's attention stayed rooted on me, as if Caelum was inconsequential to him, despite the Mark on his neck that was the exact same as mine.

"The rumors are true, then. He does have a human mate," the Fae said to me, his voice sympathetic as he took the first step toward us. "I don't imagine the Queen of Air and Darkness will be very happy when I deliver you."

I swallowed, trying not to think of the implications of that statement. What did the Queen of Air and Darkness have to do with me? My Mark seemed to tingle with awareness, humming against my skin as if it could feel the threat in the Fae male's words.

"We have the same Mark," I whispered, the words hovering between us. The Fae narrowed his eyes on Caelum's Mark for a moment, cocking his head to the side as he considered him.

"So you do," he said, a menacing smile tipping his lips up.

"Go," Caelum ordered, reaching behind him to push me back down the alley. He might have been able to fight off a cave beast with the power of his *Viniculum*, but they didn't protect against the Fae themselves. I couldn't leave him.

I wouldn't.

I drew the dagger from the sheathe on my thigh, staying behind Caelum as the Fae strolled up to us without a care in the world. Caelum pushed me farther behind him, blocking my view with his broad form.

His body moved forward, meeting the Fae male's strike with one of his own as their swords clashed together. With Caelum taking the steps forward to fight with the Fae, I watched as he moved his body in tandem with the other.

Whoever had taught him to fight, they'd taught him well. He moved with a fluid grace that I'd never seen from the Mist Guard, knifing through air with dangerous beauty. His blade caught the Fae male on the arm, the skin surrounding the wound sizzling as the cut didn't heal immediately. My mouth dropped open in shock, breath frozen at the realization that Caelum's stunning sword with the intricate golden hilt had iron blades.

"Now where did you get a warded iron sword, boy?" the Fae asked, taking a step back as he grimaced at the cut on his arm. He watched Caelum with far more respect, as he studied his stance and the hold he had on the hilt of his weapon.

"My father," Caelum answered, lifting his chin high as he struck for the Fae male's chest. The male sidestepped it, barely avoiding Caelum's sword. I moved in harmony, twirling around Caelum's legs and cutting the Fae through the fleshy part of his thigh, then withdrew. I ducked away before he could shift his attention to me again, retreating behind Caelum as the Fae stumbled back a step and paused to look down at the blood that spurted from his leg.

The bleeding slowed within seconds as I watched, the flesh beneath the fabric of his trousers knitting itself back together because my blade wasn't forged from iron.

Caelum took the opportunity of the Fae male's distraction for what it was, spinning to me and grabbing me under the arms. He hauled me to my feet, running at my side as he urged me in the opposite direction down the alley. We ran at breakneck speed, winding through the streets and trying to keep to the darker ones when we could.

A hand closed around my mouth and someone hauled me into the alleyway beside us. Caelum grumbled at my side, falling into the dark path alongside me. I shoved my elbow into the stomach of the man who'd touched me, spinning to point my blood-stained dagger in Jensen's face as he and Melian stared back at me.

"There's a Fae," I said, my breath wheezing as Caelum wrapped a hand around the back of my neck. It felt like a possession, but one he needed to know that I was safe with him and not at the mercy of the male who...hadn't seemed at all interested in Caelum aside from him being in the way.

"The city is crawling with them," Jensen said through gritted teeth.

"Is that normal? I can't imagine the city isn't heavily guarded," I said.

"I hadn't expected them to be here, no," Melian answered. "We wouldn't be passing through here if I had, no matter how many Marked are trapped in Calfalls. We would have gone the long way." She glanced over her shoulder at Beck.

"We need to get out of here," Jensen said, looking around the mouth of the alley and waiting to see if our Fae friend had followed us.

"Lead the way," she agreed, her face a mask of pain.

"What about Duncan?" I asked, looking around for the other man who was nowhere to be found. He wasn't Marked; wasn't valuable to the Fae searching the city.

"Dead," she said, touching a hand to my shoulder and pushing me to follow Jensen. Caelum moved at my side, and there wasn't enough time for me to stop and ask what had happened.

If Duncan was already gone, it could wait until we were safe, even with the anguish written into the lines of Melian's face. I stumbled over my own feet as I followed Jensen, my ears ringing in my head with the way that Fae had looked at me.

With the way the Mist Guard and the Wild Hunt had looked at me.

"Are our marks unique to the Fae?" I asked, searching through my memory of the others in the tunnels, trying to recall another with the same colors. There had been white marks. There had been black marks, but Caelum and I were the only ones where the white and black intertwined.

Caelum took my arm, guiding me to follow at Jensen's back as Melian and Beck followed behind us. "Not the time. Let's go, Little One," he murmured, using his hand on the small of my back to keep me moving forward.

I hadn't paid close enough attention to the marks on the Fae in the *Book of the Gods,* too concerned with studying the ethereal lines of their face, but one stood out in my mind. Denial coursed through me as my legs felt like they might buckle under me.

We cut through the alleys, navigating down the city streets when we dared. Jensen found the stone slab that covered the tunnel out, beside the stables, heaving it to the side and motioning all of us in while Melian and Beck hurried to catch up. I paused, waiting for Melian and Beck to take the lead inside the narrow passageway. It would have been too small for us to pass one another inside, and the darkness curved around a corner to make me believe it was far longer than the one we'd taken into the city.

I never saw the iron coming; never felt the stir in the air until it was too late.

Fire tore through my arm, cutting through the fleshy part of my bicep, searing my flesh as I jolted to the side and into Caelum's frame. The throwing knife bounced off the stone wall in front of me, landing at my feet with a clatter, and my stomach turned over with nausea. He caught me, wrapping his body around my back and tucking me into the cradle of his arms as he grunted through whatever must have struck him next.

More iron that had been meant for me.

"Get in the fucking tunnel!" he ordered, shoving me forward and away from him as he jolted again. "Go!"

I hurried into the entrance, cradling my arm in my grip and trying to stem the flow of blood as Melian stepped up in front of me and pulled me deeper. I looked over my shoulder, waiting for Caelum to follow. He and Jensen locked eyes for a brief moment, understanding passing between them. As a dozen of the Mist Guard started to round the corner toward the tunnel, Jensen heaved the cover closed, concealing us from the soldiers.

"No!" I screamed, lunging out of Melian's grip and banging on the stone that was too heavy for me to move on my own. "Help me get it open!' I snapped, tearing at the stone with my fingers. My nails broke on the uneven surface, the tips of my fingers tearing open as I tried frantically.

"Estrella, stop," Melian said, coming up behind me. Her hands came down on the tops of my shoulders, tugging me away from the stone blocking me from getting to Caelum. "We have to go."

"I won't leave him!" I protested, tearing away from her as my breath huffed out of me. "You go if you're so willing to leave him behind. I won't."

"Stubborn fool," she said, shaking her head in disappointment. Beck pulled at her arm, taking her further down the tunnels and leaving me behind while I waited. If, somehow, Caelum made it through, I had to believe we could catch up with them, because I didn't know another way to get back to the Resistance in the end, and we'd have nowhere else to go.

I couldn't think of what I would do if he didn't make it.

The sound of fighting came from the other side of the stone barrier, and the odds that were stacked against the two men seemed insurmountable while I waited. Still, the pained grunts and shouts of terror were all-consuming as I waited, thinking at any moment that stone would be shoved aside and the Mist Guard would come for me.

My arm throbbed in response to the threat, the wound caused by the iron knife that had caught me seeming to burn through flesh like acid. I wasn't Fae. Just an echo of a Fae soul trapped in a human body through the mate bond that linked our souls. If iron hurt me this badly, I couldn't imagine what it did to a Fae himself.

Malice flowed through the air, raising the hair on my arms. My hands trembled as one last shout rang through the night. "Estre—"

The start of my name echoed in the air, making my heart leap into my throat. It hadn't been Caelum's voice that called out to me.

But Jensen's.

I swallowed, taking a step backward as someone hit the stone on the other side. It slid to the side suddenly, the shadow of a man stepping into the entrance of the tunnel as he pulled it closed behind him.

"Caelum?" I asked, the shadows hanging about his face concealing him from me. He stepped toward me, the shadows release him as he emerged into the light. Blood splattered his clothes and face, his eyes seeming lighter than normal as he raised his sword and dragged it through a scrap of fabric he clutched in his hand, cleaning the blood from the blade which he shoved back into his scabbard. "Where's Jensen?" I asked, my bottom lip trembling as fear consumed me.

This wasn't the man I'd fallen in love with. This was the man tainted by Faerie magic, who had destroyed a cave beast.

"Dead," he said, tilting his head to the side. "Do you care, my star?"

I paused, trying to decide if I did in fact care. Not for Jensen as a person, but for another Marked life gone to waste. "Did you kill him?" I asked, regretting the words as soon as they left my mouth.

Caelum grinned, something malignant flashing over his face.

"No, but I didn't save him either."

35

We caught up to Melian and Beck at the end of the tunnel, finding them waiting in the tree line just beyond the secret entrance to the city. "Jensen?" she asked, but from the dejected look on her face, she already knew what had happened to the other man.

Though I suspected Caelum would be dead if she knew he'd allowed it willingly. My head swam with the implications that he might have allowed another man to die, simply because he'd crossed a boundary with me. Still, I couldn't begin to confront my relief at having Caelum at my side, even if he was stained by the blood of those he'd killed. But the comprehension of what he'd done lingered just out of reach, as if I was in shock, waiting for reality to sink in and swallow me whole.

We walked for an hour after leaving the escape tunnel, going further into the woods and leaving the city behind us as we searched for a safe place to sleep. There were no caves to keep us warm here, only the barren fields and wooded lands of the Isle of Ruin to harbor us.

"We need to rest," Melian said, kicking the snow away from a clear spot tucked beneath one of the larger trees. Beck sat against the trunk, leaving Melian to lower herself to the ground between his spread legs and lean her back into his chest. I went silent for a moment as I curiously watched the practiced, intimate moment between the two of them.

"We should go back," Beck said, disrupting the silence as Caelum cleared another spot of snow and sat down the same way Beck had. He grabbed me around the waist, pulling me down so that I nestled into the cradle of his embrace. The warmth of his body sank into me, heating the parts of me that I wasn't certain would ever get warm again.

I wished I'd let him convince me to go back to the caverns, to turn a blind eye to those hiding in Calfalls and suffering.

"We've made it this far. We have to get to the people in Calfalls," Melian said, glancing in the opposite direction of home. "Perhaps Beck should return the long way around the city and warn the others to go on guard, so no one leaves the tunnels except for an emergency. If the Fae have already infiltrated the cities this far North, nowhere is safe."

"I won't leave you out here unguarded," Beck said, curling his arm tighter around her waist. There was something between them that went beyond a casual liaison, but I'd also seen hints of a similar relationship between Melian and Duncan.

Everything was different in the Resistance.

Melian sighed but nodded, accepting that he wouldn't willingly leave her side; not when the Fae were everywhere.

"Have you ever seen the Ruined City, Estrella?" Melian asked.

"No" Shaking my head, I felt certain she already knew the answer. I didn't think there were many people alive who'd seen Calfalls for themselves. It wasn't often that people went to the city that was abandoned and destroyed.

"All of us should see it once in our lifetime. We should bear witness to the destruction the Fae wrought during the last war, so that we can truly understand what is at stake now. You both need to understand that there are greater concerns than whatever it is that's between you," she said, turning to Beck and nodding at him in confirmation.

"Why are they in the Ruined City?" I asked. The place that was devoid of all life seemed like an odd choice for a colony of living, breathing people.

"Nobody thinks to look there," she said, dropping her head. "But if the Fae are willing to infiltrate cities filled with the Mist Guard, nowhere is safe."

I rested my head on Caelum's shoulder as dread crept through me. We'd reached another catalyst, our safety torn from our grasp. There was only so much instability I could stomach. Only so much I could tolerate as my eyes drifted closed.

I breathed in Caelum's scent of winter, the hum of his Fae Mark floating between us on a breath of wintergreen. The knowledge that he belonged to another—he'd never truly be mine if the Fae came for us—writhed between us as I clung to him more tightly while the others fell asleep.

Caelum took the first watch, cradling my head gently as he coaxed me to sleep with gentle fingers and murmured promises. My eyes fluttered open for a brief moment, finding his dark eyes staring down at me as if nothing else in his world mattered.

"If you keep searching for answers, my star, it's likely you'll find them," he murmured as my eyes closed for the final time.

Sleep claimed me, those ominous words and the warning held in them carrying me into the depths of dreams better left untouched. I dreamt of the monsters of Faerie, of the beasts beyond the Veil crossing over the mist and making their new homes in the human realm. I dreamt of ruin, of Brann's ashes in the wind, and the hulking form of a Fae male making his way toward me as he laid waste to the world.

I thrashed in my sleep, rolling from side to side until the cold press of dirt against my cheek jolted me awake. Caelum was gone from beneath me, the warmth of his body missing from my sleeping place. I pushed myself upright, peering into the darkness around me and counting the sleeping bodies of my companions surrounding the fire.

Melian. Beck. But no Caelum.

Rising to my feet, I looked around the wooded area where we'd made our camp for the night. The cold air kissed my cheek as I stepped out of the alcove of trees and onto the snow-covered grass beside them.

Careful not to wake the others, I ventured farther into the woods in search of the man who'd left my side in the middle of the night.

"Caelum?" I called, my voice as loud as I dared in the quiet of the forest. Fear that something might have happened to him consumed me, and my hands trembled where I shoved them into the pockets sewn into my cloak. I spun, looking around the path for any signs of the man I so desperately needed to find. I'd never forgive myself if something had happened to him while I slept.

We were supposed to go together, despite my hesitation in trusting him. I couldn't give myself to him wholeheartedly, not with whatever he didn't want me to know looming between us, but I couldn't let him go, either.

A figure stepped out from between the trees, shadows clinging to him like a second skin. He emerged into the clearing in front of me, the moon above chasing away the darkness until only Caelum remained.

He stared down at me, his chin tucked into his chest slightly and his eyes lighter than normal for a moment. "There you are," I said, a semi-relieved sigh escaping me. He was alive. He was safe.

Even if he was fucking terrifying.

"Is everything alright?" I asked, tipping my head to the side as I smiled up at him innocently, as though I couldn't sense the monster lurking beneath his skin's surface: the beast the mate bond wanted to turn him into.

But I knew the man he really was. I knew how gentle he could be when he rocked himself into me, and how sweetly he caressed my skin when he thought I was sleeping, as if he couldn't quite convince himself I was real.

And I was his.

"You should be sleeping," he said, his deep voice rolling between us as he took a step toward me.

"So should you," I remarked. I suspected we'd passed the time when it was supposed to be Beck's turn to take watch, and yet the other man slept while Caelum stalked through the woods alone. "What are you doing?"

"Always so inquisitive," he answered, tucking his fingers beneath my chin. "Are you ready for the answers to those questions yet, my star?"

"I don't know," I murmured, the words coming out far more hushed than I'd intended. I didn't know how to cope with the man in front of me; the monster staring down at me like I'd hung the moon in his sky of shadows and he intended to devour me whole.

He grabbed my hand from my side, lifting it to rest against his chest, just over his heart. He hummed, the sound rumbling against my hand as he regarded me. "Why don't I make you forget all about those questions dancing in your pretty little head, then?" he asked, laying out his cloak and drawing me down to the snow-covered ground with him. I followed, knowing I would follow him anywhere when he looked at me in that way.

He laid me down on top of his cloak, then unknotted the laces of my trousers, tugging them over my hips so that the cold air made me wince. He smiled, stripping them off my legs and depositing my boots along with them. Spreading my legs wide while I stared up at him in shock, he settled himself between my hips.

"Have you healed yet, Little One? Because I'm going to break you again," he murmured, reaching down to unknot his own laces. The head of his cock dragged against me, bumping against my clit repeatedly and sending a jolt of pleasure through me.

Caelum terrified me, but I wanted him all the same.

Pushing inside of me slowly and spreading me open to his assault, he groaned the moment he filled me, his balls resting against my ass and his body leaning over mine. Cradling me in his grip, he slid an arm beneath my shoulders as he set a slow, hard pace.

Each drag of his cock through me echoed in my soul, drawing a pleasured whimper from my chest. "What will it take, Little One?" he asked, his glittering stare intent on mine. He held me captive, the intensity of the expression on his face making my lungs cease to function.

"What will what take?" I asked, wrapping my hands around to his back. My nails dug into his shirt, pleasure spreading through me with his possession.

"What will it take for you to admit that you are just as fucking in love with me as I am with you? For you to admit that your heart beats in tandem with mine?" he asked, touching his hand to the spot where my heart pounded in my chest.

He held me still, sinking his fingers into my skin until I knew they would bruise.

"Caelum," I gasped, squeezing my eyes shut against his words. I didn't want to give them, didn't want to concede this last part of me.

What would happen when he owned it, too?

"Say it, my star," he ordered, touching a finger to my clit. He circled it carefully, never giving me enough to send me spiraling into an orgasm, but driving me mad as he made deep, slow thrusts with his hips to work himself in and out of me.

Every ridge of his cock dragged through my flesh, every press of him against that elusive spot inside drove me wild. He lifted his other hand off my chest, pressing down on my lower stomach and sending the ache inside of me running rampant. "Gods," I groaned.

"I'm your God," he said with a smirk, mischief dancing across his face. "Now tell me you fucking love me."

"I love you," I sobbed, the words torn from a place inside me I hadn't known existed. Like they'd always been meant to hang between us, out in the open for the world to know.

"I know you do, Little One," he said gently, sympathy filling his gaze as he worked my clit harder and drove into me faster. "Now you come for your God."

I saw stars, my vision filling with the blackness of night as my body followed his command. He owned it in that moment. My body. My heart.

Me.

He warmed me from the inside as he followed after me, murmuring sweet nothings in my ear as his chest dropped to mine and he covered me with his weight.

Horror filled me immediately, a reminder of everything I hadn't meant to voice. He was gentle as he pulled free from my battered pussy, staring at the space between my legs where cum slid free and coated my thighs.

He dropped his hand to it, gathering it with two fingers and pressing it back inside of me with a victorious look on his face. I swallowed with a shudder, the monster in his gaze so close to the surface that I thought I might be facing my end.

But he helped me into my pants and boots, guiding me back to where Melian and Beck continued to sleep, as though he hadn't turned my entire world upside down yet again.

He lay with his back against the tree, nestling me against him so that his breath tickled my neck.

I never fell back asleep, too busy staring into the shadows around us, waiting for the evil I could feel circling to find me.

36

I walked at Caelum's side with Beck and Melian ahead of us as we approached the river at the top of Calfalls. A quick glance over the edge of the cliff showed the remnants of a prosperous city, with nothing but a pile of rubble in place of what had once been gleaming towers of white and silver. The metal and stone of the buildings were twisted or shattered, giving us a perfect, panoramic view of the destruction below. It was covered in a thin dusting of snow, masking the horrors from centuries ago as the sun reflected off of it.

"What could have done this?" I asked, even though deep down I already knew the answer. I'd heard the legends.

Heard his name whispered as a cautionary tale of the monsters beyond the Veil.

He was the worst of the Fae. The worst of the creatures who could kill without thought and bring entire cities to their knees. Just as he'd done with what had once been a shining city.

"Caldris. The *God* of the Dead," Melian answered mockingly. She spat on the ground at her feet as she approached the river feeding the enormous waterfall that flowed through the Ruined City. "God, my ass. There's nothing holy about a monster who could do something like this."

"But...how? *Why*?" I asked, thinking of the rage it must have taken to do something so horrific. Caelum was silent at my side as he stared down at the evidence of the carnage from centuries prior, something like hatred burning in his eyes.

I understood that emotion well.

"This was his city," Melian explained, approaching a pathway laid out across the river. Boulders jutted up from the current, leaving Beck to take the lead as he jumped to the first one while Melian turned back to face me. "He lived here, letting the people who lived here worship him like the God he claimed to be. When King Bellham revealed the truth about what they were, most of the Fae fled back to Alfheimr until tensions settled down. According to the texts written by our ancestors, Caldris chose to remain in the human realm, in his precious city where the humans cared for him," she explained, jumping to the first stone as Beck moved forward across the river. "But Calfalls turned on him, and the people who'd once worshiped him attacked him. They stabbed him with iron, hanging him from the gallows above the city to wave their triumph."

"But how did he survive if they stabbed him with iron?" I asked, jumping to the first stone as she moved forward. I focused on my balance, trying to deny my interest in her words as Caelum hovered behind me, making sure I didn't fall and get lost to the deadly drop of the falls.

"The knowledge that iron could be used against them was new, and it wasn't clearly known that he needed to be stabbed in the heart. they weakened him with the blades they left in his body, so that he lost consciousness for hours while they mutilated what they believed to be his corpse. But he awoke again that night and managed to get free, crawling to a dark corner to heal the worst of his injuries and knit his flesh back together. They discovered him missing the next morning, and he sought his revenge for what they'd done by laying waste to the entire city and everyone in it."

I ignored the sympathy that thrummed through my chest, shoving down the moment of wondering what I would have done in that situation. It was impossible to know if he was a cruel God before they'd turned their backs on him, but to wake to a mutilated body...

I shuddered as I jumped to the next stone. "But why did they turn on him in the first place? Was he cruel to them?"

"He allowed them to worship him, even knowing that he was not worthy of such a thing. The Fae allowing us to lay sacrifices at their feet? To prostate ourselves before them; it was a deception. They may be the children of the Primordials, but we were created by a Primordial just the same. Why should they be above us?" Melian said.

I ignored the clear imbalance of power that must have led to centuries of building tension. "What did they do to him?" I asked, swallowing past the nausea swirling in my gut.

"Perhaps some things are better left in the past, my star," Caelum said gently, jumping onto the stone behind me as I navigated the dozen that created the path across the river.

"Aside from hanging him up like a piece of meat?" Melian asked with a bitter chuckle as she gladly continued on with the story she clearly believed all of humanity should take pride in.

The time they'd bested the God of the Dead, but at what cost?

"They pulled his legs from his body and sawed through the cock he loved so much and fed it to the pigs. They disemboweled him, letting his guts hang down to the ground from where he hung, and tore his piercing blue eyes from his skull before they let the birds peck at his eye sockets."

"That's horrible," I said, holding steady against the glare that she aimed at me.

"How could you think that a man capable of this deserved anything less?" she asked, jumping from the last stone to the shore on the other side of the river. I followed after her, wondering if Melian and I had as much in common as I'd initially hoped. No matter that the Fae were my enemy, no matter what they had in store for me, I was not and would never be capable of cruelty like that. "He is the reason we now burn our dead. He raised them from their graves and ordered them to attack the living. His army only grew more and more with every death, and when there was no one living left, he had them destroy entire buildings. They buried themselves in rubble, one by one, and made the city a tomb."

"If we were capable of doing something like that to a male we thought was dead, were we ever really any better?" I asked, sighing when Caelum lent me the warmth of his hand on top of my shoulder in silent support.

I wanted to wither when Melian pierced me with one of the fiercest glares she usually saved for Caelum, but she rolled her eyes and turned on her heel. "I would think someone like you would understand what it is to be beaten down by someone more powerful than you," she said, in reference to my scars she'd seen in confidence. "What would you do to get retribution against the man who wronged you?"

I paused, considering all that I'd suffered at Lord Byron's hand, and his command as an extension, mulling over the need for revenge I'd felt once. There'd been a time when I wanted nothing more than to watch him suffer for everything he'd done to me.

Now the idea of it just made me tired.

"Nothing," I answered, shocked at the revelation. "I'm free. That's all the revenge I need." The words hung between us as she and Beck angled toward the pathway at the edge of the cliff, where the waterfall disappeared to pour into the plunge pool below. The pathway zigzagged down the rocky cliff face, the steepness of it taking my breath away.

The trail was narrow, forcing us to walk in single file as we descended from the top and picked our way down into the valley of the city. I trailed my hand over the rocks at my side, hugging them as tightly as I dared and staying away from the sheer drop on the other side. Melian walked in front of me as she followed Beck with quick, assured steps. Her body was a testament to the training she'd endured through her life, fine-tuned muscle that gave her the confident stance I wished I had.

"If you so much as twitch toward that edge, I swear to Gods I will tie you up and drag you behind me, Estrella," Caelum ordered, following closely behind me.

"I don't have a death wish today," I said, glancing over my shoulder to smile at his unamused face.

"Tell that to every cliff or hill you've ever met," he grumbled, his hand remaining only a few inches away from mine, as if he could catch me and save me from falling if I really did decide to try to fly.

"Being around you two is absolutely maddening," Melian groaned. "Not every word you speak to one another needs to be flirtatious."

"I don't flirt," Caelum said, his voice dropping disingenuously. "That's too juvenile for what happens between Estrella and I," he added smugly.

"Just stop it and hurry up. We need to get back to the tunnels before Imelda's warding wears off, and we'll have to take the long way if we want to avoid Tradesholde." Melian glanced around the city as we approached the bottom of the cliff. The ruins of the town were everywhere, buildings leveled into piles of rubble. The ones that remained standing were stone behemoths with entire sides missing, rising into the sky as if they had reached for freedom from what had destroyed them.

She continued into the ruined city, disappearing around the corner of a building as Caelum helped me down from the ledge of the walkway. "She's going to get us killed," he growled, keeping pace with me as I hurried to keep up with Melian. It wasn't safe for us to get separated here, not when we'd already encountered the Fae once on this venture.

"She's grieving and trying to make sure the Fae don't take any more of us. Can you blame her for being a little reckless?" I asked, turning to stare up at the side of his face as he looked all around the ruined city.

"I can blame her for just about anything if her behavior puts you at risk," he said, turning that square jaw until his dark eyes pinned me in place.

"I'm not that fragile," I said, hurrying along the side of the building.

Caelum grabbed me by the arm, spinning me until my back pressed to the tarnished silver of the building behind me. He leaned over me, tucking a strand of hair behind my ear as I squirmed away from the touch. "You don't have the first idea just how fragile you are."

His hand touched the side of my neck and the Mark there before trailing over the front of my throat. He grasped it gently, squeezing his fingers into the skin ever-so-slightly, as if considering the fact that he could snap it with a twist of his hand.

I stared into his eyes as a deep chill took over his features. Something ancient peered out from behind the dark eyes I'd gotten so familiar with over our weeks together. "Stop looking for answers you aren't yet ready for, my star," he warned, leaning forward until his lips touched the side of my neck.

Everything in me froze at his murmured words, a jolt of panic spreading to my limbs. He erased all of it by trailing his tongue over my mark, finding the top of the writhing tendrils that seemed to dance beneath his touch.

He sank his teeth into my flesh, using them to grip me hard enough that they bruised me all over again, but he didn't break the skin. My resistance fled, my body sagging beneath the hold, against my will. He pulled back and stared into my face with singular focus that drew a whimper from me, all my fears about him rushing to the surface all over again.

"What are you keeping from me?" I asked, flinching when he took my hand tightly in his and drew me around the corner suddenly. His face was crazed, as if he could sense something that I couldn't. Up ahead, Melian's head of blond hair gleamed from the shadows of the ruined city as I tugged my hand out of Caelum's grip and hurried to follow after her.

Something was wrong. I felt it in my bones, and from the tension in Caelum's body, he did too.

I didn't care about the ruckus I made in my urgency to escape Caelum, while I felt him following at my back, his presence heavy with the weight of an unfinished confession.

But a confession of what?

He hurried to my side while the something Other retreated from his face, all traces of anything but worry gone as he glanced from side to side. Grabbing my arm, he pulled me to a halt and touched a finger to his lips in warning.

"What?" I whispered, staring at him in surprise. His expression was ominous as he turned his focus up to Melian. I followed his stare, watching as she spun back around and looked at the ruined city with her brow furrowed.

Beck was gone.

Melian continued to spin, searching for the man who had been ahead of her only a few moments before. There wasn't any sign of him, and I watched her hand slowly reach toward the sword secured at her waist.

"Did you hear that?" she asked, turning to face us directly. With the rubble of one of the buildings at her side, she glanced across the broken cobblestone street. I listened, trying not to breathe as Caelum kept his grip tight on me.

There was nothing, not even the rustle of trees in the distance, or birds or other wildlife scurrying through the ashes of what had once been a prosperous tribute the God of the Dead.

"Melian…" I hated the distance between us, and Caclum's grip that kept me from going to her. His body was as rigid as a statue in the moments before he took swift strides toward the courageous woman who led the Resistance.

I moved at his side, hurrying to close the distance to Melian so we could stand together against what would come. I had to hope it was the Fae Marked and whatever security they'd implemented, but the concern on her face made me think otherwise.

She took a few steps away from us, shaking her head to deter us from following and holding out a hand in a signal to wait. I stopped at Caelum's side when he followed the order.

She looked at her feet, watching the debris blow across the street with a sudden burst of wind. Then her eyes rose to mine, her brow furrowing in confusion. "I must be hearing thin—" her words cut off abruptly.

Melian gurgled, blood trickling at the corner of her mouth and dripping down her chin as she glanced down to her chest.

To the tip of the sword that slowly skewered her alive, puncturing through her ribcage and gleaming in the sunlight with the stain of her blood as it dripped onto the ground at her feet.

It pulled back as slowly as it had appeared, leaving her to crumple to the stone and debris beneath her. A woman's scream erupted through the air, accentuating the death with the sound of a banshee wailing.

But there was no banshee to be found.

There was only me.

37

"Estrella!" Caelum shouted, his voice breaking through the haze as a member of the Mist Guard slowly stepped over Melian's body and prowled toward us. Caelum's hand came down on my forearm again, slapping against me as he gripped me tightly and yanked me to the side.

The streets of Calfalls we ran through weren't nearly as abandoned as we'd thought, with other men wearing the uniform of the Mist Guard stepping out from the very streets we'd already walked. Caelum urged me around a corner, our feet moving more quickly than was natural over the uneven terrain. He tossed me his sword, which I fumbled to catch as I raced through the streets.

A man stepped into of our path, causing Caelum to release me suddenly in favor of drawing his second sword. The clang of their weapons clashing rang through the air as I ducked low and swiped through his knees with my sword, taking out the fleshy part of his thigh until he dropped to the ground.

Caelum's mantra repeated in my head. My sword was just an extension of me to be used to my advantage.

I'd always thought I would hesitate when the time came to intentionally take a life, and my desire not to see anyone hurt would be enough to keep me from acting toward self-serving interests. But I'd stopped caring the moment I saw Melian hit the ground, and I felt the loss the Resistance had suffered with her death. Caelum and I wouldn't join her in the Void.

Not if I had a say in it.

Caelum moved on to the next Mist Guard, slicing through him quickly while urging me on. "Run, Estrella!" he shouted, his voice filled with panic when I paused to wait for him. Something in that command sank inside me, compelling me forward, even though I wanted to stay and fight at his side.

We were supposed to live together. To die together.

So why were my feet carrying me down the street, leaving him behind, as if I was willing to sacrifice him when I wasn't?

Still I didn't stop, racing over the jagged rock road and vaulting over the debris. I ran over the top of one of the stones, leaping off of it and launching myself through the air as my legs continued to run, bracing for the moment that I struck the ground.

The blow came from my left, hitting me in the side of the neck so hard that it propelled me to the right. It wrapped around my neck, the iron searing into my skin and stealing the breath from my lungs.

I fumbled for my footing as I dropped onto my side, struggling to my feet with my hand clutching at the iron chain wrapped around my throat. The hum of magic that usually ran through my Mark was lost, as lost to me as Melian was now.

In the absence of the magic I hadn't thought I wanted, there was nothing. My body was weighted down by the humanity that I'd had all my life. But I'd grown used to that note of something *other* inside me, and my breath heaved in my chest as I tried to raise my sword.

A boot connected with it, kicking it from my hand as a man stepped in front of me. I dropped to my knees as my lungs ceased to work and I couldn't draw in another breath.

The man's boot struck me in the chest, kicking me backward until my body planted on the ground, then I stared up at him as he stood over me and tilted his head to the side.

He looked like so many of the boys from my village, so painfully human as he studied me. "What a waste. They always choose the pretty ones," he said, pursing his lips as acknowledged how great a loss it would be to kill me.

Because of my fucking face.

I snarled at him, then he raised his sword over his head, preparing to swing it down onto me as I stared death in the face. I couldn't take my eyes off the blade of his iron sword and the maniacal expression on his youthful face, which hinted at everything he thought he was doing right.

He thought my death would matter. That it could make a difference.

I waited for the pain, braced myself for it, and accepted the end that had come for me. My only regret was the knowledge that Caelum would probably follow, lost to his rage and unable to fight.

"NO!" Caelum roared, the sound causing the hair on my arms to stand on end. The Mist Guard swung his blade downward.

But it stopped a foot above my chest, halted in place by the pulse of absolute power that washed over the Ruined City. It exploded out from the epicenter at my right, distracting the man standing over me.

I followed his horrified stare over to where the power had come from, to where Caelum had been fighting with the other Mist Guard.

They all lay dead at his feet as Caelum stepped over them without a second glance. He walked forward, striding down the street as quickly as he could but never running, unconcerned with the soldiers racing his way, their attention focused solely on him.

Magic rolled off of him. Shadow hands left his body and touched the corpses at his feet. I stared at his face, horror consuming me as the power poured off of him, forming into shadows that fell to his feet.

The horror started at the top of his head, a gleaming silver crown appearing as the air itself shifted, parting to reveal something new. Or something very old. The silver crown bled darkness, the black ink of it dripping down the metal and into the top of his hair. What had once been an ashy blond brightened to ashen silver as it grew to a slightly longer, shaggier style where it ended above his shoulders.

His features shifted, becoming sharper and even more stunning, as his ears elongated and his eyes gleamed a bright, frosty blue. He grew taller, his features more brutal, and his beautiful face twisted with cruelty as his tunic and cloak transformed into a mix of pale-blue fabric and black armor and leather coverings. He was enormous, a formidable figure who made the Caelum I'd known look like a weakling as he cut through the Mist Guard that tried to stand in his way.

The swirling black ink of the Mark on his neck writhed with power as he pushed his sword back into the sheath across his back and raised his hands. A dark compulsion flowed from them, black tendrils of inky magic coiling as the corpses of the men he'd killed rose once again.

The ground beneath me shook, a skeletal hand emerging from the dirt next to my head. I screamed, watching as the skeleton pulled itself out of the ground, but I couldn't move, pinned to the spot as it reassembled its broken pieces into the shape of the man it had been and turned on the Mist Guard standing over me. It attacked, launching its entire body at the man and tackling him to the ground.

Finally freed from my paralysis, I scrambled backward on my hands and feet until my back touched the wall of the building behind me. Curling my knees into my chest, I watched on in horror as Caelum and his army of the dead made their way toward me.

He thrust his hand into the chest of a man who tried to fight him, wrapping his fingers around his heart and yanking it out while the organ still pumped blood between his fingers. He dropped it to the ground, stepping over the corpse that rose again behind him to fight off the remaining Mist Guard, who had been stupid enough to think they could ever stand a chance against the monster who strode straight for me.

The man I'd fallen in love with had never really existed; Caelum wasn't real—nothing but a deception. I'd seen the likeness of his true form before. Seen drawings and statues of that beautiful, terrifying face and the horror of his power over the dead.

Caldris.

More skeletons rose all around me as I forced myself to my feet, using my hands on the stone wall at my back to pull myself up, even when everything in me felt like giving up.

Beyond the skeletons that surrounded me, I was vaguely aware of more fighting, and of people emerging from the rubble to run from Caldris's army of the dead as he stalked toward me.

The skeletal corpses formed a circle of protection around me, cutting off any chance I had of escape. They parted slowly as he emerged in front of me, letting him enter the bubble they'd formed.

This close, he seemed larger than humanly possible. His form was taller than any of the skeleton's remains, towering over all of them as he stopped in front of me. The Mark on my neck burned, sensing the power of the Fae so near.

I shook my head when he reached out one of those perfect, strong hands to touch me. With his glamour gone, every line of his body was feral; the sharp lines of his face were as animalistic as the way he moved.

I backed into the wall, my hand brushing against the finger bone of one of the skeletons guarding me and drawing a terrified squeal from my lungs.

My God was nothing but pure, brutal beauty, and I wanted absolutely nothing to do with him; not ever again.

"They won't hurt you, Little One," he said, tilting his head to the side as he stared down at me. Even his voice was deeper, something ancient resting within it as those blue eyes gleamed.

I looked away from him, staring between the skeletons to where the corpses of the dead Mist Guard fought with the Marked who'd emerged from the rubble to escape. We'd found the people we'd come to save, and in doing so, I had led the Fae right to them.

The army of the dead disarmed them, forcing them to their knees and restraining them in groups as I watched in horror.

"Stop this," I pleaded, turning my attention back to Caldris where he waited for me, that hand of his still outstretched, as if he couldn't quite believe I wouldn't sink into his embrace again.

I wouldn't allow him to touch me, ever, after what he'd done, and the way he'd lied to me at every turn.

I hadn't even known his name. He wasn't even fucking human.

"You know I can't do that," he said, something probably not regret shadowing his face as he stared down at me intently. His attention never even so much as twitched off of me, completely unconcerned with the battle waging around us.

"Let them go, and I'll go with you. That's what you want, right? That's what the purpose of all of this was? Just let them go." I begged, swallowing down my terror at the thought of being brought to Alfheimr, and of what might wait for me there.

"Oh, my star," he said sadly, sympathy filling his gaze as his hand dropped to the iron chain wrapped around my neck. He unraveled it slowly, the flesh of his fingertips burning against the touch of the warded metal until he flung it to the side. "You'll come with me anyway."

38

My knees almost collapsed with the rush of power returning to my body. My Mark glowed as white as freshly fallen snow, the inky shadows twirling within it in tandem with the moving Mark on his neck.

I slapped his hands away, wanting nothing to do with them on my skin, knowing that it must have all been a lie. His claim of love. His desire for me. I'd been stupid enough to fall for all of it, while he'd played me like a fool and used me to get to the Resistance.

He grabbed me by the chin with unyielding fingers, tilting my head to the side as he inspected the burn marks on my throat from where the iron had scorched my skin. His brow furrowed momentarily, and then he released me as suddenly as he'd caught me.

Lifting his dagger to his wrist, he slid the sharp edge of the blade against his skin. Blood welled from the wound, flowing over his skin and dripping on the ground as he raised it toward me. He placed his wrist at my mouth, wincing as I drew back from the pressure of his arm against my lips. "Drink," he ordered, his lips twisting into a snarl when I shook my head and pressed back farther into the wall.

He shoved his wrist against my lips, applying so much pressure that I had no choice but to part them or they'd tear open against my teeth.

The taste of him sank inside me, coating my tongue and dripping down my throat with molten heat. With lava flooding through my veins and yet deadly cold, all at once.

He warmed me from the inside, his blood sinking into my belly and making me feel complete for the first time. I squeezed my thighs together, desire building in me even though I knew, logically, that I wanted to murder him for what he'd done to me.

I swayed toward him when he pulled his wrist away from my mouth finally, craving more of the substance that had filled me with euphoria like I'd never known. My body awakened, my skin buzzing with awareness as the sun above us seemed to gleam a little brighter. He drew back and stared down at the wounds covering my hand from when I'd fallen to the rubble after being hit with the iron chain. I watched in fascination as the cuts stitched themselves back together, new skin growing to fill in the bloodied slashes, until there was nothing but a slight pink tinge left.

When I turned my stare back up to him from the healing of my injuries, his eyes were transfixed on my lips. I licked them, finding the slightest taste of blood coating them and drawing it inside me against my better judgment.

"Fuck," Caelum groaned, grabbing me around the side of my neck. The moment his palm came down on the Mark itself, power flooded my veins. The cold breath of winter. The shadows that chased the sun.

The dominance of the God in front of me as he tilted my face up and his mouth conquered mine. His tongue swept inside, tasting his blood as he devoured me, obliterating any delusion I might have had that he'd ever kissed me before. He'd been nothing but a gentleman, civilized as could be compared to the way that he now tried to meld our bodies, pinning me to the wall.

I melted into him, feeling the familiar edge to his embrace that meshed with the reality of who he was, and what he was, hanging between us. With the truth in the open, he was finally free to be himself.

With that thought, I placed a hand at each of his shoulders and pushed him back. He separated from me the moment I demanded it, pulling his mouth off of mine as he turned a frustrated stare down at me in question.

I shook my head, turning my eyes away as they burned with the threat of tears. I couldn't let him see me cry. I couldn't let him see how thoroughly he'd destroyed me.

I'd loved him. Loved every one of his lies.

"How could you?" I asked finally, swallowing past the burn in my nose to pin him with a glare. "You encouraged me to be more independent. For what? After all your talk of having a choice with you? What kind of a choice is it, if I don't know the truth?"

"I'm better because you love me," he said, raising his chin in challenge and daring me to defy the words we both knew were true. "I will do this for us. For the future we will have, even though you are far too young to see past your kind's blind hatred for us."

"I've read the books. I know the atrocities your kind committed and what you do with your mates! I know what you did *here*. The number of people you slaughtered," I snarled, trying to twist away from his grip on my neck.

"The books lied. The Veil didn't save the humans from monsters who wanted to own them; it cut off half your fucking soul, you foolish girl. We never wanted the war, but you can bet everything you know it was the Fae who finally ended it," he said, shocking me into a moment of silence.

"The witches–"

"Wouldn't have been able to form the Veil without the help of a Fae who gave his life to it. And it was me who tore it down after centuries," he said, leaning into my space. His face came over mine, hovering only inches above me. "If I didn't allow *that* to come between us, do you really think there is anything that can keep me from you?"

I scoffed. "You didn't even know me."

Caelum, *Caldris*, smirked. Menace danced over his features, twisted and cruel. "You're still in denial, I see. So let me spell it out for you, my star." He touched his lips to my cheek with a mocking gentleness that seemed so at odds with the brutal expression on his face. "I didn't have to know you, because I could *feel* you." He grasped my hand in his, lifting it to press against the spot where his heart beat inside his chest.

It echoed the beat of mine, pumping in tandem with the one that pounded in my chest.

Oh fuck.

No.

"I waited for you for centuries," he said, his fingers pressing my hand into his chest more firmly when I shook my head and tried to pull back.

"No," I said, the protest loud in my desperation to not hear what he had to say.

"I felt you live and die for countless lives, felt every one of your life cycles end and grieved the woman I never got to meet. I know you, because you are the other half of me." Those foreign blue eyes bled to black as he stared at me, and his magic hummed between us. "You are my mate, Estrella, and *nothing* will come between us now that I have you at my side."

The end...for now.

What Hunts Inside the Shadows: Of Flesh & Bone Book two is releasing August 30, 2022.
Pre-Order now.

Can't get enough of Caelum? Download the exclusive alternate POV scene of the moments leading up to the fall of the Veil, as told from his point of view.
Download now.

ACKNOWLEDGMENTS

To Kelly, Arin, and Renae, who went above and beyond to help me bring this story to its full potential and listened to me ramble when it didn't want to cooperate.

To Sheri, for always being there when I need a shoulder to lean on and for polishing my words until they shine.

To Carla, for being the best friend I could never live without and for believing in me even when I don't.

To the readers who took a chance and followed me to another world.

Thank you, from the bottom of my heart, for coming on this journey with me.

Love always,
Adelaide

ALSO BY ADELAIDE FORREST

Adelaide Forrest writing fantasy romance as

Harper L. Woods:

What Lies Beyond the Veil

What Hunts Inside the Shadows - coming August 30th

Adelaide Forrest writing dark romance:

Please heed the trigger warnings for each book.

BELLANDI WORLD SYNDICATE UNIVERSE

Bellandi Crime Syndicate Series

Bloodied Hands

Forgivable Sins

Grieved Loss

Shielded Wrongs

Scarred Regrets

Settled Scores - Coming Soon

Massacred Dreams Series

Dreams of the Vengeful

Dreams of the Deadly -coming soon

Beauty in Lies Series

Until Tomorrow Comes

Until Forever Ends

Until Retribution Burns

Until Death Do Us Part

Other Dark Romance

Black Heart Romance Presents Heaven & Hell

Wrong

Romantic Suspense Novellas

The Men of Mount Awe Series

Deliver Me from Evil

Kings of Conquest - Cowritten with Lyric Cox

Claiming His Princess

Stealing His Princess

Printed in Poland
by Amazon Fulfillment
Poland Sp. z o.o., Wrocław
20 October 2023

f8735deb-ff4d-4a5a-a176-bd88fd5cbd1dR01